THE BLUE-SPANGLED BLUE

BOOK ONE OF THE PATH

DAVID BOWLES

CASTLE BRIDGE MEDIA
DENVER, COLORADO, USA

THE BLUE-SPANGLED BLUE
© 2021 David Bowles
All rights reserved.

ISBN: 978-1-7364726-0-6

CASTLE BRIDGE MEDIA
Denver, Colorado, USA
castlebridgemedia.com

Cover Illustration by Estudio Tlalli

To Angélica: *te lo debo todo.*

ACKNOWLEDGEMENTS

I would like to express my eternal thanks to the "beta readers" who read different drafts of this novel over the years, especially Ted Han, Billie Barnett and Jeniffer Johnson, as well as to Ty Franck for his encouragement and support during dark times.

PART I:

BRANDO AND TENSHI

"Measure a lover by the greatness of the one they love." —Rumi

PROLOGUE

LIKE ALL TRAGIC LOVE STORIES, this one begins with two people from different worlds caught in the throes of a great struggle. As the lovers seek happiness at each other's side, forces they cannot control treat them as mere pawns.

On Earth, young assistant professor Brando D'Angelo is wrapping up his first year of teaching at the University of Milan. As he grades finals in his cramped office, his inbox dings.

The message is from a new university on Jitsu, a world at the edge of human space, abandoned for seven decades when the hyperspace conduit that once connected its star system to Alpha Centauri C inexplicably collapsed.

Now that the Lieske drive has made rapid interstellar travel once more a reality, Jitsu is reaching out to the rest of humanity, hoping to join the fold.

Or so it seems.

Last month, on a whim, after a vicious fight with his family, Brando answered the new university's call for applicants.

Now, without further review, they have offered him a position.

Anyone else would weigh the consequences carefully. To leave earth, he will have to undergo agonizing gene therapy that adapts his body for a world with lower gravity. The trip to Jitsu takes three months, which he will spend in hypostasis, encased in gel during acceleration to and deceleration from fenestration, when the ship enters or exits the vaguely understood topography of hyperspace.

As Brando considers these complications, his inbox dings again. It's Marie-Thérèse Makomo-D'Angelo. His mother, a cleric in the Wiccan Catholic church. Full of passive-aggressive posturing and recriminations, her message demands that he announce his engagement to a woman he does not love, in front of a congregation he cannot respect.

Let us imagine the cosmos itself, suddenly silent, quivering at this key moment.

The future of humanity hangs in the balance.

Though he craves academic respect, Brando has spent years dreaming of the stars, of crossing the liminal space between the bright blue sky and the deep black beyond, of blazing new trails in the boundless welkin.

Without thinking, he types a brief response to his mother: *Tufi na yo. I'm leaving. You'll never see me again.*

Then he accepts the offer and books passage offworld.

On Jitsu, nearly twenty light years away, young architect Tenshi Koroma also receives a message in her inbox. It's from Ambassador Hazal Enver, representative of the CPCC—the Consortium of Planets, Corporations and Colonies, umbrella government of human space.

The ambassador knows Tenshi well—the embassy has recently moved from Station City to a complex of buildings she designed right outside Juresh, the planet's capital.

In her message, Ambassador Enver asks Tenshi to accept the task of designing and overseeing the construction of a massive fair that will celebrate 150 years since the founding of Jitsu and promote the annexation of the world by the CPCC.

It's a dream job, but one fraught with potential for significant blowback.

For Tenshi is the twin sister of Samanei Koroma, the Oracle, mystic saint of Neo Gnosticism. And Tenshi's architectural work is considered blasphemous by most adherents of that religion. Her uncle Santo is the most influential religious leader on Jitsu, vehemently opposed to the dismantling of the theocracy that has controlled the planet for nearly a century. Her father Monchu is an important missionary figure.

If Tenshi accepts, there will be no doubt. She will have rejected her family and their particular sect. She will become an actual pariah, excommunicated and cut off. In fact, her actions may ironically spark greater efforts by extremists on her world to halt annexation.

But a plan flutters to life in Tenshi's heart. A way to use the fairgrounds after the celebration to promote the ideals she has come to embrace.

The cosmos is not just trembling at Brando's dilemma.

Without Tenshi's choice, his staying or leaving means nothing.

Even we who are buried and forgotten feel fate begin to pivot.

Both their hands hover above their keyboards for a moment. Then, as Brando composes his messages, Tenshi does the same.

She accepts the job, on the condition that her payment be ownership of the fairgrounds and all the buildings she erects upon them.

Within moments, the ambassador agrees to her terms.

Their fates—everyone's fates—are sealed.

For neither Tenshi nor Brando will be easily swept off the cosmic chessboard by the clash of mighty forces.

Sometimes, against all odds, star-crossed lovers start a family.

Sometimes, that family survives the ravages of history.

Sometimes, in fact, it bends history to its will.

CHAPTER 1

SHIMMERING NOTES GAVE WAY TO RHYTHMIC strumming, a bright flamenco pattern that spread in gypsy waves throughout the cabin, insinuating itself into every metallic nook and cranny. Soon a man's voice joined the syncopated sound, just for the chorus, a lovesick refrain refracted through bitterness into a rainbow of regret and yearning. His father's face, blurred by time and fading memory, hovered for a moment in his mind, its features almost coming into focus. Then the ship's intercom went live, breaking the spell.

"Passengers: strap in. We'll stop purling the gimmal as we approach the platform, so prepare for null gravity. More instructions after we osculate."

Brando D'Angelo stopped the wandering of his fingers on the fretboard and slid the mahogany and cherry wood curves of the guitar back into the suspension case. The ancient instrument was the only object his father had left behind when he'd abandoned the family ten years ago, and Brando had had to fight his mother to keep it. It was the first of a series of increasingly ugly quarrels, the core of each of which, his mother insisted, was Brando's similarity to his pappà.

Months later, as he had been changing the gut strings, he'd found a small slip of paper wedged inside.

Quando ti senti solo, guarda al cielo e pensa a me. Guarda al blu, Brando.

When you feel lonely, look into the sky and think of me. Look into the blue, Brando.

Sobs had wracked his body for an hour that day. Finally, he'd felt relief.

It hadn't lasted.

The soft voice repeated its instructions, and Brando stowed the case in the closet mesh. Crossing his cabin, he dropped into the g-seat and did as ordered. Moments later, the inner shell of the *Velvet* ceased spinning, and his backside and thighs lifted slightly from the seat at the sudden absence of gravity, pressing him against the strapmesh. He felt no nausea, unlike at the beginning of the trip. Months of gene treatments during his long voyage had adapted him to the low gravity. His calm stomach was almost worth the pain he'd gone through to embrace the stars.

After completing a series of complex maneuvers, the *Velvet* docked with the orbital platform *Rasaro*. Brando poked his head through the irising door of his cabin. Several passengers were already making their way down the texas' corridor to the starboard lift, a half-dozen slender portbots swerving out of their way.

"Oy," the linguist called to one of the semi-sentient porters, "give me a hand with my baggage."

The gold portbot wheeled over and hefted his bags, turning with deft quickness toward the lift.

"Careful with the guitar case. Don't drop it or set it face down. That instrument is priceless and older than... hell, older than robots."

The portbot nodded its understanding and continued down the corridor. Brando followed close behind, casting a final glance around at the plush, broad walkway. He had splurged on an elite room in the texas, near the officers' quarters. Along with other VIPs, he had shared several pleasant meals in the captain's dining room during fenestrations, avoiding for brief periods of time the hypostasis pods in which the majority of the passengers, mainly pilgrims of little economic means, had spent the entire journey.

Once the lift hushed to a stop on the docking deck, however, the class distinctions abruptly ended. All thirty-five travelers were herded out of the aging vessel, down the opaque white tube of the narthex that joined ship to station, through a perfunctory customs check, and into a quarantine ward.

Brando took a seat and sighed. Three months after leaving Earth, the finality of his choice loomed large even in *Rasaro*'s bright but cramped compartments. He wanted to feel free, liberated from his family's mediocrity and meddling, but his heart felt empty, save for a vague sensation of guilt.

You left them behind. Just like your papà. Sailed away into the blue.

"Why the long face, Doc? You said you couldn't *wait* to get here."

Brando looked up into the orange-brown eyes of Ambarina Lopes, captain of the *Velvet*. The taut bronze skin of her cheeks crinkled a bit as she smiled.

"Oh, ha, I'm, uh," stammered Brando, "just not looking forward to the physical."

Lopes dropped into a seat beside him, smoothing the bright blue of her uniform. "Nah, piece of cake. You made it through the genetic modification, and that's brutal, I know from experience."

"I thought you were born on a platform," Brando said. "Why would you need—"

"Not for space-adaptation. Gender affirmation treatment, when I was ten."

Brando nodded. "I hear that's pretty intense."

Ambar raised an eyebrow and tilted her head to one side. "Yup."

Glancing around, Brando noticed several more officers and crew from the *Velvet* filing in. "Giving them shore leave?"

"Yes. There's a major fair coming in two weeks, celebrating 150 years since Jitsu's colonization. The gorgeous woman I've been dating is behind it all, so my arse *better* make an appearance. It's been three months, and Captain Lopes needs some release, ¿me entiendes?"

During her multiple dinners with the VIPs, Ambarina had learned that Brando spoke Spanish, along with five other languages.

"Sí, entiendo," Brando said. "My, uh, dry spell has been a little longer."

Lopes leaned closer. "Well, stick to Station City, hermano. Not much action in Neog territory, not for an infidel like you."

She laughed, clasping her hands over her belly. Brando was about to attempt some sort of follow-up dirty joke, despite how unnatural it felt, but he was saved.

"Brando D'Angelo di Makomo?" a nurse called.

The young professor gave Ambarina a sheepish smile. "That's me. See you on the other side, Captain."

The procedures were less intrusive than he'd been expecting, so Brando spent the physical daydreaming about the people and places he'd soon see. The nurse scoffed softly as his pulse quickened.

"Nervous? Excited?"

"A little of both," Brando admitted.

Once the medical staff cleared the young professor, he followed glowing arrows on the floor to the shuttle lobby to await transport to the surface. A group of Neo Gnostic pilgrims was boarding one of the two shuttles. Brando guessed the other would transport the passengers of the *Velvet* to the surface soon.

As the pilgrims departed, Brando headed into the lounge, where a large oval viewport gave him a glimpse of the planet he would now call home, the semi-legendary world that had once been the stopover for humanity's expansion, till the Conduit had been closed. Jitsu: a brown globe with swatches of yellow and grayish blue, basking in the radiation from the two suns of the Eta Cassiopeiae system.

"We meet again."

Behind his reflection in the viewpoint, the pretty face of Ambarina Lopes floated just above his head. "You know, I spent hours in faux-lifes while in hypostasis, virtually skimming the surface of this strange world. But that doesn't compare to seeing it with my own eyes."

"Oh, yeah, that's right. This is your first time off Earth! Nothing quite like that first glimpse of a new world. Look, there's the northern continent, coming over the terminator."

Brando penetrated the clouds in his mind's eye. There were three distinct regions: a civilized crescent that hugged the last sun-bleached jungle, an unearthly tall mountain chain that sported an extinct volcano, and the great desert that yawned like some ancient hell to the south.

Home. Despite its ugliness, he longed to step down onto that yellow soil and inhale the thin air, letting its warmth thaw his soul.

"No! You get us on that shuttle *now!*"

Brando and Ambarina turned toward the shuttle bay. A group of scary-looking characters in black uniforms were confronting platform personnel.

The pilot exited the shuttle, heading toward the cluster of men. Brando could barely make out what he said as he approached.

"Sir, I'm sorry, but the passengers of the *Velvet* are scheduled for transport."

Wordlessly, the leader of the uniformed intruders handed the pilot a data pad.

Ambarina leaned forward, squinting. "I know that guy's face from somewhere."

"Is he with the CPCC military?"

She shook her head. "Don't think so."

The pilot scrutinized something on the data pad. His face went pale. Walking over to a comterminal on the wall, he made an announcement.

"Passengers of the *Velvet,* our apologies. The government has commandeered the next shuttle. I'm afraid you will have to wait till it returns to be taken to the surface."

Brando groaned. "How long will that be?"

"Like four fucking hours," Captain Lopes answered.

The two of them watched through the viewport as the black vessel curved outward and then down toward Jitsu, becoming a speck and then disappearing in the yellow-streaked atmosphere.

Ambarina suddenly slapped her hand against the bulkhead.

"¡Concha! That's Chago Martin. What the fuck is he doing on Jitsu? Why is the government bringing him and his comemierda friends to the surface?"

Without any further explanation, she stomped off, shouting for station security.

Shrugging, Brando found a seat away from the others and pulled out his data pad. He composed a message, notifying the university of the delay, then reclined back, hoping to get some rest.

He was deep in dreams about the alien blue sky of Jitsu when passengers started shouting and crying with dismay.

Opening his eyes, he saw everyone pointing at their data pads or lenses, making agitated comments to one another.

Then someone turned on the holodisplay at the center of the lounge, and Brando caught the first images of the massacre that had just occurred on the surface below.

CHAPTER 2

A PURGATORY AT THE DESERT'S EDGE, the Mashkanu prefecture moved through its sluggish routines. In one of its most unremarkable towns, Kinguyama, a black transport came to a halt just down the dusty street from Samaneino Teyopan, the local temple. About a dozen pilgrims, freshly arrived from their home-world Ninsianna, were heading inside, eager to meditate in the same shrine that had served the Oracle when she was a child. This was a very moving moment for the travelers. An epiphany.

The transport doors slid open. Chago and his crew trod dust, weapons check an automatic reflex, a glance from the cap to each sikarito, each loyal foot soldier, more than enough to set up the formation. El Chore and Pako lead four to the left. Gusano and Lalo, three to the right: all fanning out in a triangle with Tripó, the monster of the crew, at the apex. Their cap, Chago Martin, ambled along at the center, the core, glorying in the moment. He and his boys were one organism, a fluid predator stalking, crouching, twitching.

Striking.

On the front steps of a drab nearby home, two preteen boys sat, staring at swirling colors on the screen of a data pad, their heads nodding to some droning rhythmic chant. As Chago's crew walked past, one of the boys lifted his gaze from the meditation exercise, turning his head right and left to find the source of the footsteps.

His eyes were white.

Chago scoffed. *They make the kids wear lenses that edit out infidels. They can't see us. No witnesses. Stupid fucking people.*

Tripō tapped the teyopan's door open. Some thirty heads twisted about, local Pathwalkers and pilgrims crossed-legged on the floor. Chago's crew filed in fast, encircling the Neogs. In their drug-induced stupor, the faithful could only rotate their heads slowly, staring at the mobsters as if they were strange by-products of meditation. A few of the younger pilgrims had the same white eyes as the boys outside.

"Fucking holed," remarked Pako.

Chago looked at the locals, searching for Maryam Kino. Braids rimed with grey, she sat on a rug woven with geometical patterns at a place of honor on a raised platform. Beside her was a white-robed woman.

The giya, leader of this church.

"Bring me the one up there on the right. Don't touch the other."

Gusano and Lalo hefted the giya to her feet and dragged her to their captain.

"Where you keep your tubes?"

"Tubes?" As if she didn't speak Standard, the bitch.

"*Wapi tubo taru ka, chupeka?*" In Baryogo, just in case.

"Don't know."

"Yall just sucked down thirty. They appear out of fucking nowhere?"

She shrugged. Typical Neog. Reject reality. Chago unholstered his chrome and popped her roughly across the jaw. Meditation broken, a trickle of blood at the corner of her mouth, the location of the drugs suddenly occurred to her.

"Back there." A jerk of her head. No fear apparent in her eyes.

"Show us."

She led Chago and Tripó to the back of the teyopan. A short hallway of curved ceiling ended in a small, closet-like office. The giya gestured languidly at a box next to the laminate desk.

"In there. Coded to my thumbprint."

"Right. Open it."

The giya slowly shook her head.

"You heard me, bitch? Open it! Open shikasero zo!"

She simply lowered her head and said nothing. Chago felt a rush of violent anger squeeze his chest like a vice, cutting off his breathing.

They're always defiant, he inwardly raged. *Never can just bloody cooperate.*

Not trusting his voice for the anger that gripped him, Chago nodded, dialed up *projectile: 10 cm* on his chrome, and in a sudden movement buried its barrel in her locs, at the base of her skull, slanting upward forty-five degrees, and drove into her brain a bullet that exploded right below the neo-cortex of her frontal lobe. Her dope-smoothed forehead blew violently outward, spattering the wall above the desk with gray matter, blood, bone fragments and clumps of reddish-brown hair. Her body collapsed, its limbs loosened for all eternity, its ruined head smacking resoundingly against the edge of the desk.

Chago stared at the lifeless form, forcing himself to examine it coldly: a dead piece of meat. His chest slowly loosened.

"Damn, Chago." Tripó stared at the woman's crumpled form, estimating her weight. Then he shrugged, muttered "fuck it" and bent, hefting his *trucha* and activating its laser blade. With surgical precision he removed her right hand and used it to open the chest. Inside were about 500 thin metallic cylinders containing *moku*, Neog drug of choice for meditation. Tripó began scooping them into a bag he'd carried with him.

"They's a lot of tubes, Chago. But, uh, why'd you pop her lid like that?"

Chago roused himself from his trance and growled, "Kill a giya, or any Neog, by blowing out their brains, you ruin their chances of quantum enlightenment. That's what they believe. No time for the brain to release its energy, some shite like that. Puras pendehaaz. Anyways, that's what Nestor told me I should do to her."

"So, what, now we do the rest?"

"Look, you dumb-arse, you didn't hear Nestor? Just the giya and the pilgrims. The native Neogs, they ain't to be touched. Especially not Maryam Kino. Got it?"

"Yeah, yeah. Hey, look."

Tripō gestured at the desktop. Chago hadn't noticed before, but there were several small data pads spread haphazardly across it. He lifted one, wiping blood from it with feigned nonchalance.

"Bendita Mariya. We got us a bonus, kwate. Dumb-arse giya didn't upload the pilgrims' offerings. Couple of thousand credits here, we split 'em, you and me. Give me your pad."

The upload was over in a question of seconds.

"Konrau ain't gonna get mad?"

"Not if he don't know about it. How's he gonna find out?"

"I ain't saying shite."

"Good."

They rejoined the others in the main chamber of the teyopan. The Neogs had begun to shake their reverie. A couple of the younger ones were removing their lenses to see what was really happening around them.

A little late to get interested in reality, motherfuckers.

Chago nodded to Pako, who started separating the locals from the rest and herding them to one corner of the room.

Just like we planned.

Kicking kleinballs out of the way, Gusano prodded the pilgrims to their feet with the barrel of his konk rifle, took a step back, chose one at random, and fired. The directed blast lifted the off-worlder, a lithe, blond youth—Martian from the looks of him—off his feet, throwing him upward and back. Gusano's second blast sent him spinning like rag doll through the air, and the third ripped his head completely off his shoulders, showering the image of Domina Ditis that hung on the wall with a hail of bluish red.

"Pura Ermandá," he muttered, making a circle with the forefinger and thumb of his left hand and pressing the circle to his heart, the remaining three fingers splayed awkwardly downward and to the right. The sign of the Brotherhood.

Chago suppressed a shudder. A mademan like himself was supposed to feel nothing when chloroforming cattle like these. Years in klikas and on crews was supposed to burn all compassion for squares out of a brother completely. But Chago had never been free of that twinge of pity, though it filled him with a gripping shame he took out on his victims.

His men, if they felt something similar, didn't show it. El Chore stepped up to a woman whose mouth had just opened as if to scream. Ramming his lazgat all the way in against her tonsils, he blew the back of her head out. The pilgrims behind her, bathed in ichor, felt click within them the natural impulse of self-preservation, an instinct no amount of meditation or drugs could erase. They turned and began running with blind abandon, but el Chore aimed his gat at one and punched a hole some five centimeters in diameter through his spine and out his abdomen. The Neog twisted as he fell, sizzling intestines flapping unspeakably at his sides. The second was similarly dispatched, sprawling in the dust as darkness slammed a hand forever across his eyes.

The other pilgrims, though panicked, were easier to take out: mainly head blows, make it look like a crazy Neog civil unrest problem, not allow anyone to reach gnosis. A couple of the sikaritos wanted to have their way with the women, but Chago told them to back off. Nestor's instructions had been very precise: get the tubes; kill the giya and the pilgrims. No fucking around. He didn't dare add that the thought of such violations brought Sandra's face to his mind in the very place he prayed she'd never see him.

Pako had to knock a couple of the locals around in order to rein in their hysteria at the sight of the slaughter. When one Neog began to scream, the foot soldier, enraged, punched her in the mouth, destroying most of her front teeth. She was quiet after that, as were the others.

The massacre was over in minutes, and Chago gave the signal to exit. Tripó destroyed the lockpad of the door once it had closed, trapping the locals inside with the carnage, as the majority of Neog buildings had only one entrance. Chago figured it would probably be close to nightfall before anyone came to the teyopan. With the lousy Civil Security Jitsu's theocratic government had, no one would ever track his crew.

ONCE BACK IN THE BASEMENT SUITE OF A HOTEL NEAR

THE SPACE PORT, the expansive set of quarters and offices that served the Brotherhood as a base of operations on Jitsu, Chago linked to Nestor via faux-conferencing. The virtual room was entirely black except for the pool of light surrounding the table where Chago and Nestor's doppelgangers sat.

"You did it?" Nestor's face appeared unreadable as always. Of course, he could have programmed his doppel to look that way for the con, but Chago knew from experience that this was the only expression the boss's adviser ever wore.

"Everything like you said."

"No locals hurt? Santo's wife, for example?"

"Nah, Nestor. I said I did what you told me to. I'm not to be trusted, or what?"

"Kalmau, ese. We trust you. Good job. Now hang silent a couple weeks. We'll keep yall updated. Things are starting to move, understand? Be plenty jobs for yall little brothers."

"We're taking Jitsu, no?"

"Things you don't know can't be taken out of you, got it? Don't worry about the bigger picture. Just do the jobs me and Konrau give you, the way we tell you to do them, and everything will be just fine. Right?"

"Right."

"Now, put those tubes to good use, Chago. Get some panocha, live it up, you and your crew. Things are gonna get real busy for yall real soon. Thumbing off."

Chago Martin moved his head out of the path of the thousand dancing beams of light that seconds ago had been triggering his synapses like mad. A smile stretched across his face.

We're taking this bloody place. I know it.

The Brotherhood, long the most powerful crime syndicate in all of human space, seemed on the precipice of something even greater. Chago wasn't the brightest of men, but he felt certain that this spinning nightmare of a planet was only the beginning of a much grander move toward domination of all human space. He imagined for a moment that he'd been chosen for this job because of his talents. He'd obviously caught Beserra's eye, and now he was being prepped to take charge of this planet's conquest.

Afterward, who knew? Perhaps he'd be installed as sub-kasike, under-boss of this hellhole, answering only Konrau himself. For a few moments he gloried in his imaginary promotion.

Only in the darkest recesses of his mind did an unheeded voice whisper the real reason he had been chosen: his superiors considered him disposable.

CHAPTER 3

SANTO KOROMA SLID HIS FINGER DOWN THE GLASS, scrolling through the inspired words of Founder Dresch, the first arojin, the Holy Prophet of the Ogdoad. His diligence had long ago burned away all feeling but this: an insatiable hunger for quantum enlightenment. A nail click halted the scroll, and Santo highlighted a section with a leftward sweep. He preferred to manipulate the holy text with his hands, voice commands tending to shatter his focus and detract from meditation.

Today's passage was from *General Theology*:

The politicians and the intellectual elite believe they have spirited away the keys of gnosis and hidden them; however, they themselves have not entered, nor do they grant entrance to those who desire it. You, however, be as wise as serpents and as innocent as doves.

The last line echoed in Santo's mind. As always, the voice he heard in his head was his mother's. He remembered her expounding on this particular verse, urging him to keep in mind the basic tenet of the Path—quantum enlightenment through total self-knowledge—and to avoid the moralistic pratfalls that so many Pathwalkers were prone to. *No good, no bad,* she reminded him. *Only what is and what's to come. And most important:* you. She had instilled in him, before her own blessed translation, the skill to see what others needed in order to attain gnosis and an understanding of his own importance in ensuring the enlightenment and translation of his fellow Pathwalkers.

This desire to guide the planet along the Path, he insisted to those who questioned him, was the only motivation for his steady climb up the theocratic ladder of Jitsu's political hierarchy.

Amo okanjuwa. Not ambition. Never.

A beep of a distinctive timbre and Santo's index finger popped the com icon in the right corner of his compad.

"Jambo."

"Arojin Koroma. Muwema michana. Sorry I'm disturbing you."

Inho Bek. Secretary to the Archon himself.

"Not at all," Santo assured him, letting his eyes mist up a bit. "Just searching the Founder's words for peace and clarity."

"It must be a difficult time for you."

"An understatement. Bandits, in my district. Entering Samaneino Teyopan while my wife was leading meditation. Stealing the sacrament, killing the pilgrims. Murdering the giya, one of my former students. You think I'm insensitive to this atrocity?"

"It is clear you're not. Apologies if I implied otherwise We know your district security team is investigating. What's their conclusion? Junkheads?"

"Perhaps. But they downloaded all pilgrims' credits not shunted to the bank."

"Civil Security is at your disposition, if you need it. They're also investigating similar cases in several districts. Not massacres, just theft and damage. But CS is not prepared for such incidents. No training, no experience. Archon Rawe requires a better solution."

"Tell him to stop immigration. Amo Jitsujin."

"You're *sure* they're not local? How can you know? Besides, a halt to immigration is out of the question. There's the task of cleaning up the southern continent and Salty Sea still to be finished, which will take us at least a century, even if we increase immigration five percent every year for the next decade. This world needs more backs and minds."

"Make the people produce more babies."

"And distract them from gnosis? Arojin, you're playing with me."

Santo sighed inwardly, displaying a neutral face to his compad.

The price of power is having to make these decisions, he reflected. *If I hope to be Archon someday, I must learn to accept that the tangled and meandering path to enlightenment at times seems to move away from its goal before reaching it.*

Long ago he'd decided he would go along with the present Archon's policies, though he believed the influx of outsiders hindered his peoples' attainment of gnosis. He despised the constant secularization of education and government, exemplified by the expanded university and the Chamber of Deputies that now supplemented the traditional theocracy.

But there would be time later to set things aright. For the moment, the complex plan he'd set into motion two years ago would move to the next tier.

"We should create squads of range officers to guard the settlements. Recruit ex-members of the defunct Jitsu Liberation Army. Hire—hire off-worlders with the necessary skills. Set up outposts along the edge of the Great Desert. Michiyu Sosa is the perfect man to put in charge."

Bek's excitement at the idea was palpable, though the secretary tried to hide it.

"Just the measures we need. Should I patch you through so you can propose this to the Archon himself?"

Santo knew that Bek's approval of the plan meant it would be implemented. Jitsu's ratowanin, Mutemi Rawe, was weak and senile, his decisions more often than not whispered into his auditory implant by his wily secretary.

"Sure, Secretary Bek. Let me talk to him. Be enlightened."

"You too."

Santo leaned back and awaited the face of the old fool he'd soon be replacing.

TWENTY-FIVE MINUTES LATER, he clicked off and tossed the compad away in disgust. Old fool, indeed. Rawe had agreed with Santo that increased protection was necessary, that an anti-terrorism, anti-mob unit had to be established. But the idiot insisted that the Chamber of Deputies, full of reformists with six more years left to their seven-year terms, be the ones to decide its composition, duties and jurisdiction. No matter how many times Santo expounded on the Archon's need to exercise his emergency powers and set up the squads on his own, the decrepit liberal refused to budge. Santo had misjudged Inho Bek's influence on the man. Or perhaps this was Bek's doing. Meddling fool!

Pacing from room to room in his large if spartan apartment, Santo weighed his options. He desperately needed to consult the Oracle, but the situation in Kinguyama was more pressing, a tale awaiting his expert management and spin.

Returning to his study, he calmed himself with a thimbleful of moku. Then he pulled an illegal bouncecom from a hidden compartment at the base of a statue of the Founder. Connecting it to his main com terminal, he put a call through.

After a few moments of encrypt/decrypt, a stolid face rose from the flat surface of the terminal.

With ambivalent blankness, Nestor Bos directed his black holographic eyes at the arojin.

"Complications?" the mafioso asked, his voice smug.

"Slight setback, but the timetable stays aligned. Just get ready for movement."

"Big or little, partner?"

Santo wrinkled his nose as if in disgust. *As wise as serpents*, he reminded himself.

"Not sure. Be ready for anything. Can you handle that?"

A sly grin. "You bet, Prefect Koroma. Anything you order up. Just remember: we get ours the time comes."

Unable to speak further with the infidel, Santo nodded and clicked off. There were moments when the deal he'd cut with L'ermandá, the *Brotherhood*, most powerful crime syndicate in the Consortium, twisted in his mind and gut like the poison his instincts told him such agreements always turned out to be. But the Oracle assured him this unholy pact was the only way, and he faithfully obeyed. Still, weakness caused him to offer silent prayer.

Mother, Domina, Founder: give me strength to do what must be done.

CHAPTER 4

BRANDO WAS STRUCK BY THREE THINGS as he stepped from the shuttle onto Jitsu's ochre soil: the disorienting spring in his step due to the world's lower gravity, the unsettling closeness of the horizon, and the relentless heat of Higante. That local sun glared down at the newcomer in seeming disgust as its partner, the smaller star Kobito, ducked behind the peaks of western mountains.

The professor adjusted the temperature setting on the condition suit that hugged his skin beneath linen pants and shirt, slipping on a pair of shades to protect his eyes from the brutal UV light.

For a second, his choice seemed not just rash, but unhinged.

What a barren, brutal place to live out my life. The hell am I doing?

The answer was simple. Setting aside his need to get away from his family, the offer had been too tempting to pass up. Jitsu was the only place where a centuries-old dialect of Baryogo was spoken in its original form. How could a linguist resist such an opportunity? Brando had done a careful study of Baryogo's Lingala elements for his doctoral thesis, warmly received in all the right circles, but his proudest achievement was his mastery of the language in conversation.

Or so he'd believed until now.

"D'Angelo-kun!"

A towering, spindly man—two and a half meters tall, his orange academic gown contrasting sharply with his ebony skin—waved his hands while snapping his fingers. It was the head of the Modern Languages Department, Nosowa Tayibo, with whom he'd conferenced in Standard several times. They bowed to each other in greeting.

Jitsu had been colonized mainly by working-class Belters. Calling themselves Aknawajin, the dominant ethnic group was a blend of Indigenous American, African, and Asian peoples from Earth, whose ancestors had been genetically modified to work and live in lower gravity.

The contrast was notable. Despite being pretty tall for an Earther—215 centimeters—with a loamy complexion, Brando would be dwarfted by most of the darker-skinned residents of this planet.

"Manta raha, Tayibo-zin."

The department head sketched a smile, replying that the pleasure was all his:

"Raha na newa, soro."

As they began to walk toward the transport, Brando was a little taken aback by the differences in dialect. Tayibo pointed out various landmarks and buildings around the port, explaining their significance in Baryogo, but the young professor realized he couldn't understand a tenth of the explanation. He was also distracted by the low gravity: three months in hypostasis hadn't weakened his muscles enough, and with every step he had to concentrate in order not to bound a meter into the air.

"You getting this?" Tayibo said, switching to Standard.

"Jitsu's dialect of Baryogo is different from the one common on Mars and the Belt. Reading an old text, I can go slow. Here I've got to work to keep up."

"You'll catch on soon enough."

And he switched back to Baryogo as they boarded the transport and sped toward the university. Brando got a close-up view of Station City, as the non-Jitsujin population called the metropolis that they had established around the port, in which off-worlders were politely but firmly urged by Pathwalker leaders to live.

A century and a half ago, the urb had housed the local headquarters of the infant CPCC Armed Forces and of Soltec and served as a springboard for Consortium expansion light years beyond Earth, but now it was neutral territory run jointly by the CPCC and Jitsu's government. Similar in construction and style to any number of space stations, platforms or even newer parts of cities on Earth, the city sported metallic spires that glittered almost painfully in the overwhelming sunlight.

Soon they slipped out of Station City and into native Jitsujin territory, the university having been built at a spot between the capital and Station City. From the window seat, Brando contemplated the squat clay buildings that characterized towns controlled by Dominian Neo Gnostics, alien and primitive compared to the carefully protected and preserved structures of Milan.

The Dominatudan sect, D'Angelo's research had told him, condemned expenditure of energy in complex architecture, viewing such efforts as arrogant and shortsighted, since everything in the universe was destined for destruction save the "souls" created through quantum enlightenment. Adherents to this variety of Neo Gnosticism were urged to engage only in activities that turned the mind inward and promoted gnosis: meditation, drug use, church-designed faux-lifes, and a host of other ephemeral pastimes. Goals pertaining to this transitory physical world, like the erection of monuments and the attainment of material wealth, were considered *nako*: beneath the dignity of the eternal.

It was frankly a relief to be surrounded by such simplicity. These sun-baked cubes, so different from the cold monuments of icy Milan, might sequester within themselves the warmth his bones ached for, here, a thousand light years away from the frigid indifference of his mother and brother.

Then, as the transport neared the outskirts of the administrative district containing Jitsu's capital Juresh, Brando's breath caught in his throat.

From the mire of mediocrity rose a magnificent building, curving stone and glass and steel. It thrust at the sky in defiance, like a beaten yet beautiful woman holding her head high and spitting in her enemies' faces.

The sheer power and beauty of the structure tore a single syllable from Brando's lips.

"Wow."

"Pardon?" Tayibo asked.

"That building," Brando said, his hand almost trembling as he pointed at it.

"Kichigai. The work of a crazy woman who respects nothing."

"Who?"

Tayibo sighed. "Tenshi Koroma. No one understand why she'd build such a monstrosity. Then the CPCC started renting it for their offices. Now she's a *rich* traitor to the Path."

"She *built* that? How? I thought native Jitsujin don't earn money."

"En kurin shigotuta. Like an off-worlder, she worked in clean-up crews for five years on the southern continent, ignoring gnosis, collecting credits, studying *architecture*." The word was like an insult. "Then she moved to the city of the muwanani samadan, Station City, tiksaberu ka, bought the lot and built that thing."

Though burning to know more, Brando didn't dig any further. There'd be time to discover the quirks and intricacies of the local personalities later on. It was obvious that Tayibo was a fundamentalist, and his version of things would be tainted by that fanaticism. He had, in front of Brando, used the derogatory term for off-worlders, *muwanani samadan*—ignorant sightless ones. The department head either was oblivious to his bigotry or didn't care.

The transport sidled up beside a motley collection of structures that, while definitely not run-of-the-mill clay boxes, were nowhere near as visually arresting as the CPCC office building. Instead, a pretentious confusion of styles and methods had apparently collided here at the western edge of the capital city.

"The University of Jitsu," Brando said to no one in particular.

"Kena." Tayibo nodded. "Almost as ugly as Tenshi's monstrosity."

They disembarked, stepping onto a slidewalk. Building after bizarre building trundled by, each making D'Angelo miss icy Milan just a bit more. The college of the humanities was little more than a Dominian box, with a pair of Dorian columns and a row of gargoyles in front, presumably to satiate the off-worlder faculty. Tayibo showed D'Angelo his office, three by three meters, with a stone desk and a terminal. After a few more words of advice and instructions as to class schedules, etc., the department chair turned to leave.

"Like I informed you in our last message, Professor Oduyoye has offered to let you stay with him till you find a flat of your own. His office is upstairs: room 346."

MODUPE ODUYOYE, A PROFESSOR OF COMPARATIVE RELIGION, TURNED out to be a fascinating fellow with tons of insight and tips on adjusting to this unusual planet. After only a few minutes of chitchat, they found themselves laughing away like life-long mates.

"So what's the problem with this Tayibo gerrie?"

Oduyoye's ageless face stretched into a smile. "He laid it on thick, did he? There's a good heart in the man, though you can't always tell."

"I can tell he's got a piss-poor attitude toward off-worlders."

"Just wait till you hear the reams of gronk he's got lined up for the faculty meeting Wednesday. Education as an aide to gnosis, blah blah blah."

Brando raised an eyebrow in mock indignation. "As a professor of religion, sir, you should be thrilled at the idea of including it everywhere."

The older professor sighed and gave a wry laugh. "Nah, it should be kept way out of politics. One of the jobs of comparative religion is to compare how they often bollix things up when they merge with the state. And that's what you're liable to notice on Jitsu: things are quite bollixed up. They import clean-up crews because 95% of this planet's citizens don't work. Too drugged up, trying to create a soul."

Brando was relieved to hear someone pointing out the very issues that had been nagging him about the planet. "Hey, spang on... Tayibo seems tense for someone passing out tubes. Should suck down some moku and loosen up, mothergod! His eyes went all crazy when we passed that breathtaking CPCC office complex. Thought he'd implode."

"Oh, yes, Tenshi's building. She's the biggest traitor on the planet for Tayibo and other Dominatu, so I'm not surprised. Ornate, beautiful architecture? Strike one. Renting the building to the Consortium? Strike two. Using her new wealth to live a stylish life in Station City? You get the point."

Brando leaned back in his chair, glancing at the stuccoed ceiling and then at the various idols arranged on the shelving by the window. He nodded soberly at the dilemma of being a rich non-believer in a sea of impoverished fanatics. "Tayibo was bent out of shape because she worked in the clean-up crews."

"It's how she saved up to build the thing in the first place. And she *chose* to. Pathwalker youths are sometimes sent to the southern continent to learn what work and grimy reality are like. Don't last more than a couple months. She was there years. Because she wanted to."

"Weird planet." Brando said, regretting the words immediately.

No weirder than a certain household in Milan.

"Yup. You're from Earth, no?" Modupe ventured, indicating Brando's body with a sweeping gesture.

"Kind of obvious from my svelte, tall figure." Both laughed. "Actually, I'm a giant compared to most. Head juts above the rest in crowds in Milan."

"Ah, the capital? They say it's something to see. Real cold, though, no? The White Doom and all."

Brando thought of midday walks outside the perimeter, visits to that snow-ringed, mesmerizing lake. He nearly shuddered to suppress the memory. "Yeah, we've got the southernmost edge of the ice sheet butted up against the Alps a few klicks away, so it gets pretty damn frigid. But beautiful."

"Yeah, I've seen faux-representations of the new Diet headquarters. Amazing building."

"Can't hold a torch to the old quarter, mate." Some of Brando's friends had been involved in the planning of the Diet's move, so he'd become very familiar with the majestic legislative structure. However, his father had always taken him to the older section of the city on Saturdays, and it held a special place in his heart regardless of its beauty. "Talking buildings, I was struck by the uniformity of the architecture here."

Modupe snorted. "That's generous. They spend as little time on physical reality as possible. Like I said, it detracts from their quest for gnosis."

D'Angelo sighed. "Got to become one with the Ogdoad. The eight-sided being. The quantum singularity. Whatever."

Modupe sized D'Angelo up in a glance. "Born and raised in Milan. You're what, Wiccan Catholic?"

Brando felt heat creep into his cheeks and a flutter begin in his gut. "My family is. My mom's a priest, even. I'm agnostic."

"But you were raised to adore the Four in One: Mother, Father, Spirit, Son."

Visions of confirmation classes. Shudder. "I get the parallels. It's just weird that quantum enlightenment is supposed to make the believer *part* of the Eight."

"Mate, get used to it. That concept undergirds *everything* on this planet."

"Better start meditating, then."

Oduyoye touched a section of the wall above his desk. It slid back, revealing a chill box from which he took a pair of plastic packs. He offered one to Brando. A sip told him it was a cola beverage with a high sugar content. Illegal on Earth. Not so taboo here.

Brando rolled his chair closer to the window, which looked out on a round courtyard with a huge oak at its center. Considerable water waste on such a hot, dry world. The buildings skirting the plaza reminded Brando of something he wanted clarified.

"Back to architecture of a physical kind. The buildings outside of Station City are all about the same, except for Koroma's."

"Call her Tenshi. People might get confused otherwise."

"What do you mean? Is she from an important family?"

Brando couldn't help his interest in the woman. It was as if her building had touched some hidden place in him, something that desperately wanted to be uncovered.

"Yes, within the Sorani clan and beyond. Her uncle's one of the most influential Dominian *arojin* on the planet. The *takiwajan*—prefect—of the Mashkanu district. Course, she's an embarrassment for him."

"Because she's rich? Because she rejected Neo Gnosticism?" Brando's relationships with Wiccan Catholic women had left him cold, and coupled with his family's own devout frigidity, these romantic disasters had made him wary of emotional connections with religious people. The idea that the architect might not be a Neog pleased him.

"Oh, she's a believer, just not in her uncle's fundamentalism. And on Jitsu, that's tricky. Domina Ditis was the first human to step foot on these hot-arse sands. She wrote her journals here. She died here, was buried here. To reject the Dominian Path, to dismiss it as heresy, is a quick way to be marginalized. That's what it happened to Tenshi. Worst thing, her twin's the Orakuru."

Brando turned to face Modupe with shock. "The Oracle? Don't Dominians think she's their direct line to the Ogdoad?"

"Yup. Every century one comes along, their soul halfway in our reality, halfway rejoined with the Eight."

Brando gave a slow whistle. "With a pedigree like that, Tenshi still rejected them?"

"Uh-huh. She's a character, no doubt. Took a class with me few years back. Brilliant, in her own way."

"Which is?"

"Unconventional by any standard."

"Wait." Brando scratched his wavy black hair and rubbed his temple. *I'll never figure out the structure of this religion and all its rules and exceptions.* "They told me only Neogs that reach—*satori*? Only they and residents of Station City can attend the university."

"Yup. After she left home young and spent her time in the mines, Tenshi moved to Station City. Was living with a carrier captain when I met her. Ambarina Lopes, ship's the *Velvet*."

"Mothergod, that's the ship I came on. Tenshi was with *her*?"

"Yup."

Brando's heart sank a bit at the news. "Ah, she's into women."

Modupe slapped him on the shoulder. "Nah, mate. She's pansexual. Might even go for a short language geek like you."

Brando scoffed. "Yeah, sure. Captain Lopes is beautiful. I'm betting Tenshi is, too."

"And rich."

"Pretty tempting."

The older man's eyes crinkled at Brando's interest in the architect.

"You can meet her in person, you like. A major fair happens in two weeks, designed by Tenshi herself. Celebrating 150 years since Jitsu's colonization. Supposed to bring together the different groups on this planet, some harmonious gronk like that. Anyway, you're the sole representative of your planet, your city and your culture, as far as I know. Each group, folks from Mars, AMKI, United Jovian Habitats, Oceania, Peleus, etcetera, got a delegation representing them, performing some way. Have a talent?"

"I can play the guitar and sing."

Oduyoye stood, beaming down at Brando mischievously.

"More qualified than me. Guys from New Nigeria, they want me to do some ritual dancing. Bloody hell. I do good to manage hopping onto the slidewalk, my knees nearly buckle."

He tapped the door open, gesturing for Brando to follow.

"I'm game it if you are, sir."

"Alright, then. And lad? Call me Modupe, you don't mind. I might not be twenty-five, but I'm still young at heart."

MODUPE'S FLAT WAS IN A NON-DESCRIPT COMPLEX FIVE KILOMETERS from the campus. It had been decorated with bright colors and cultural objects from myriad societies, and Brando felt immediately at home, as if it were a place for all humans to come and rest. His bags had been delivered already, and they stood just inside the door. As he stooped to pick them up, he miscalculated the force he'd need, and they swung upward in exaggerated arcs, smashing against the ceiling.

Don't know my own strength. He barked a laughed at the aptness of the worn cliché. Modupe just stared at him as if he were touched and motioned him inside. In the main room, the furniture was arranged around an info terminal on the floor, which was disguised holographically as a huge tree when they walked in, but which began to display the news as soon as Modupe muttered some Ibo word.

"You like it?"

"Oh, it's choice." He set his guitar case upright in a corner. "Thank you. My first home out in the welkin is amazing."

Modupe grinned.

After getting Brando's stuff stowed away in the guest bedroom, they made themselves some drinks and watched the news.

"I always follow religious news close. Helps make class a little less dull."

There were two items prioritized by the terminal for Modupe's perusal, both breaking stories. A survey mission had discovered a previously unknown colony at the edge of charted space. Named *Terego* by its inhabitants, it had been founded three decades before by a group that had left Earth as part of the general exodus at the beginning of the ice age.

"You imagine that?" Brando gestured toward the holo image of the green planet. "Be in hypostasis for two hundred years? Everyone they left behind is dead, everything changed beyond recognition."

"No doubt what they wanted, no? They left right at the apogee of the New Roman Renaissance. Your people were pretty intolerant."

"My people? What, because I'm part Italian I get lumped in with the Nuova Rinascenza? Come on, Modupe. Plus, my mother's from goddamn *Kinshasa*."

"Ah! Thought I saw a hint of Mother Africa in your features. Still, New Zaire is about as Wiccan Catholic as you can get outside of Italy, mate."

According to the report, forty-nine Mormon families from a dozen different countries had founded the colony. Terego's official language was an older form of Esperanto, presently spoken on a few platforms around Neptune, but really nowhere else.

Brando sprayed liquor out in a coughing fit.

"What?" Modupe began banging him on the back.

"That's the weirdest and most incredible thing I've ever heard! Esperanto-speaking Mormons? Wow, love to talk to those guys."

"You're Italian: think they'd be enthused by the idea?"

This time Brando was able to laugh a little at himself.

"Wow. Terego. Okay that makes, what, four systems the Consortium's found that were settled by emigrates from human space?"

"Yup. Exciting for me, by the way. My research focuses on how religion has evolved on those worlds, in isolation from the rest of us. Now I get to add Terego."

Brando turned his attention back to the news. The second item was on the Kinguyama massacre: an interview with Monchu Koroma, the Pathwalker pilot who'd brought the pilgrims to the surface.

"Something must be done," he said for the cameras. "Protect our people, our little siblings that come here to get closer to the Eight. It's the muwanani samadan, folks that got no respect for enlightenment, those infidels, those soulless animals..."

The story abruptly cut away to other details of the massacre and interviews with a few survivors.

"That," Modupe pointed out, "was Tenshi's pa. Brother of Prefect Koroma, who I hear has designs on the top position, the *ratowanin*. Archon. Already spinning things against us, did you notice? That's the Dominian extremist way:

all bad things on Jitsu stem from off world. Looks like you came here just in time to be vilified."

D'Angelo shrugged. "Can't be any worse than the gormless family I left back on Earth. Rather be vilified by a stranger or an enemy than by my own blood, anyhow."

And oddly enough, despite the confusion and strangeness of the day, Brando went to sleep that night feeling as if he'd finally, after twenty-five years of wandering, found his way home.

CHAPTER 5

"SAJANA! SAJANA!"

Tenshi turned from roofing work she was overseeing. Only her workers called her *boss,* so she wasn't surprised to see Hari Kan dashing toward her. Just eighteen, Hari—who was from Tenshi's hometown of Kinguyama—had looked up to her his entire life. This fair was his dream job, he had told her again and again.

He wasn't very good with his hands, unfortunately.

What now? Tenshi groaned. She didn't notice any immediate construction disasters anywhere on the fairgrounds, but real distress clouded Hari's features as he slowed, panting.

"It's Giya Ana Gizensha," he managed to say. "She's been killed."

Tenshi was flooded with contradictory emotions: her first impulse was to feel relieved. Gizensha had been a co-conspirator in the abduction of Tenshi's twin, as well as one of the harshest teachers at the congretation's sikoro when the girls were being indoctrinated as children. Her taunts and threats had been part of what pushed Tenshi to leave her hometown for the grueling but mentally freer existence of the restoration crews.

"What happened?" Tenshi demanded. "Was anyone else hurt?"

"Don't know," Hari gasped. "Minjun got an alert on his lenses. I ran to tell you."

Patting him briefly on the shoulder, Tenshi rushed to her onsite office and used her terminal to call Meji Pishan, one of the more respected Pathwalkers from Kinguyama. A supporter of the social reforms Tenshi advocated, the omedeyo had recently experienced gnosis and the Archon had declared them an arojin. Their thin, kindly face and robe-draped shoulders emerged from the flat horizontal surface of the screen in a life-like holo projection.

"Bishaberu, Tenshi-shi. Good to see you. Assume you heard the news."

"Yes, Arojin-zin. A shame, even if I hated her. She was our giya, no matter what. Well, yours."

Pishan gave a gentle shake of their head. "And she wasn't the only one killed. Eleven pilgrims were slaughtered. Many teyopanjin, including your Aunt Maryam, witnessed it all and then were trapped inside with the dead bodies for hours."

The news of the pilgrims' death opened a gaping hole in Tenshi's heart. Her eyes watered. She could sense Meji's incredulous expression even as she averted her gaze to compose herself. Like many reformists, the wise omedeyo considered her the toughest person on Jitsu.

"My appa brought them? The pilgrims?"

"Yes. He's in town right now, coordinating things with your uncle, uplinking with other flights to assure them it's just a fluke, not a spree. Look, Tenshi, I've got to go. Call you tonight at your flat?"

Tenshi nodded and thumbed the terminal asleep. Her father and her uncle. Working together as always. Keeping the community together. What a laugh. What really happened, what had always happened, was that Santo used Monchu and dozens of other gullible Pathwalkers to further his own interests under the guise of ensuring his people's enlightenment.

Her attempts as a preteen to make her father see the true nature of his brother's plans had never gotten her more than blows. *You feel that?* He would ask as he struck her. *That's the real world you love so much.* When her mother would sob at the sight of Tenshi's mottled bruises, he was fond of pointing out the fleeting nature of the flesh and the need to mortify it. Bajingan. Bastard.

Of course, Santo fed Monchu's innate violence and encouraged him to direct it toward toward his family. Any resentment the younger sibling might have felt throughout the years at his younger brother's rise within the theocracy was remolded and reborn as raging disappointment in the unworthiness of his wife and daughters. Tenshi still vividly remembered all the times when her natural penchant for creation was seen by her father as a willful determination to shame him before the community.

When she was five, she'd been gathering large stones scattered around their dwelling—never *house*, never *home*—and fitting them together as they seemed to want to fit. They had taken on the form of a roughly cylindrical tower, nearly a meter in height. Santo had approached her as she was placing the last stone.

"Nan tikaseru?" What are you making?

"Minara." A tower.

Sighing, Santo had gone inside to speak to her father about this worrisome waste of time. It was the summer after her first year at sikoro. Tenshi had been reported multiple times for spitting out the sacrament (she hated the cotton-headed, zombie way it made her feel) and for not sitting still during meditation. Her parents had been thoroughly embarrassed at their daughter's sinfulness, especially given her twin's embrace of every nuance of Dominatudan doctrine and practice.

"Infidel!" Seeing the tower, her father's foot had drawn back to kick it over.

"Wait, Brother," Santo had urged with a smirk. "Our little chickadee has indeed sinned. She's spit in the face of Domina herself, preferring to build temporary objects rather than construct a soul for herself. Let her show her repentance by tearing the edifice down on her own."

Tenshi's heart had leapt in her chest as if trying to burst out and kill her uncle, fueled by adrenaline-heavy hate. That word he used—*poyito*, chickadee—how she despised him for it and the things it implied: weakness, lack of a soul, utility for others. It was how he wanted her to view herself. She refused. She was a gayona, a fighting hen, and she'd tear him to pieces someday, she swore.

But that day had been one of defeat. Broken and with no other recourse, Tenshi had pushed the tower over, its constituent rocks rolling off in the dust like the heads of miniature friends she'd betrayed to the guillotine. Her parents had made her spend the rest of the day staring at a large kleinball, hoping she'd open herself to true self-knowledge, take the first step on the path to ra-Yindawo.

She had fallen asleep.

Tenshi realized that Pishan would now likely take over as giya, and she'd be able at last to get a parcel of land within the community. She had one in mind, a 400-sqaure-meter tract overlooking the barren beauty of the desert that so reminded her of the wastelands of Jitsu's south pole. There, at the desert's edge, she hoped to one day build a home and a family, become an influence on the lives of the people in her community. With a giya like Pishan, perhaps others would realize she was no infidel; she was a true Pathwalker, just one who viewed self-knowledge as just as dependent on the self's phenotypic extension into the physical world as it was on the exploration of what went on within one's mind.

Walking away from the terminal with these thoughts swirling in her head, she realized she should call her mother. She turned and trudged back, thumbing the display on.

"Meiru yegachu," the terminal intoned.

Knew it: she already called me, left a message.

Tenshi highlighted her mother's name on her agenda with a calloused thumb and connected. Inyoni Onamata answered right away, her fallen shoulders and haggard features lifting listlessly from the console surface. Her long gray hair was pulled back, as always, in a severe braid that trailed down into the innards of the terminal.

"Jambo, Tanim," Inyoni said, her face lighting up a bit.

"How are you, Umma?" Tenshi used Baryogo, her custom when speaking with older family members.

"Terrible. I just got off the phone with your Aunt Maryam. She's devastated. You ought to call her later. She saw the whole thing, the poor woman. Unspeakable: their brains destroyed, no hope of gnosis. Don't know whether she'll ever recover."

"Of *course* she will. It's a tragedy, but we must be strong, stick together. Get through this as a community."

"People will use this as an excuse, you know."

"Yes, I've thought of that already, mother."

"They're blaming it on the reformers."

"Extremist foolishness. No one will believe we did this."

Inyoni blinked incredulously. Tenshi guessed her mother was surprised that she'd included herself with a group of believers, radical as their viewpoints might be. The irony was not lost on Tenshi: years ago she'd cursed Dominian theology as an insane parasitic strategy for "lazy-arse bastards" to live off people "too stupid to feed themselves correctly, much less discern when they're being screwed like cheap whores."

For Inyoni, hearing her daughter saying *we* in connection with the Path was likely miraculous. Tenshi would have smiled had she not felt so angry.

"Maybe not. But reform policies have brought a lot of outsiders here, and it could be argued that the policies are indirectly responsible."

"Shite. You're right. We've got to do something to anticipate and quell this."

"What can you do? Santo will speak soon, and everyone..."

"Damnit, mother, why do you have to be so defeatist? Your whole life, all you've said is 'I can't... What about this? What about that? What if I seem too material? What if the teyopan ostracizes me?' Whine, whine, whine. I've got news for you, Inyoni... the teyopan never accepted you. Thanks to Apa and Santo and your own inability to defend yourself, you were marginalized from the beginning."

Why do I always get so pissed at her? Why do her stooping shoulders and bent neck always draw this venom from the depths of me?

"Now, if it had just been you, whatever. Your life. But you were supposed to be defending Samanei and me, and you just let those bastards do whatever they wanted with us! They walked my sister out the door of that box you live in, and you didn't do a thing to stop them!"

"I tried to hide her condition from them, you know that. But in the end, they were just too much for me. I'm only one person: how could I possibly hope..."

"That's just it: you never hoped. You acted like you were different from them, you told me that there was more to self-knowledge than being doped up all the time, but in the end, you bent to their will. Another cow in the herd, another pair of unfocused, dead eyes."

Inyoni's gaze watered up. "You really hate me, don't you."

Not even really a question. An affirmation. Tenshi felt something loosen in her chest.

"No, Umma. I don't hate you. I—I don't know what I feel right now. You mentioned laying the blame. Santo's in Kinguyama right now, isn't he? I'll bet he's trying to capitalize on this massacre, the unscrupulous jagen. He wants to do to Jitsu what he did to us, only on a bigger scale. When they took Samanei from us, he got his first real taste of power, and he's been pretty ravenous ever since. Something tells me he won't stop till he eats us all up. Unless I can figure out a way to stop him."

"What will you do?"

"I'm not sure. I just have a feeling this fair will be the key."

"Will you come visit? The town might be ready for a little reconciliation after this tragedy."

"I'll wait a while, let reality set in, let them understand how this world," Tenshi gestured about her, "has powerful influence in their lives. Pishan will help underscore this, I bet. Besides, I don't want to seem like an opportunist, even if I kind of am. Good thing is, it's an opportunity for all of us: to become people, not cattle who think they're better than people while all the time they're being fattened for the slaughter."

Tenshi clicked off and began contacting several people she knew would be attending the fair's inauguration. The meeting she set up with them would finally, she hoped, be the catalyst for a reformer/off-worlder coalition strong enough to combat the rhetoric of the Dominatudan. They'd met many times before, in small groups and as a larger team, but given the high tensions of the moment, she felt sure she could at last goad them into action. She'd be sure to invite Pishan tonight when he called her. His support was vital.

Tenshi's conscience got the better of her. She contacted her Aunt Maryam to see if she was okay, half expecting to leave a message. Inyoni's younger sister, however, thumbed on right away. Her expressionless face blinked into existence suddenly: she'd stepped into the broadcast beam rather than connecting within it.

"Tenshi, soburinim, good to hear from you. It is a harrowing time for Jitsu, and she needs you joined to her children."

Tenshi rolled her eyes. Maryam might be respected in Kinguyama because of her husband, but the woman was vapid and not at all elocuent. The clichéd rhetoric on her lips was suspicious. Something was not quite right, beyond the heap of cadavers in the middle of the teyopan. Tenshi decided to draw out whoever was coaching her beyond the broadcast beam.

"May your yearning soul touch the Eight in this trying time. Remember that the evils of this false reality are many, but the truth a singular path from your soul to ra-Yindawo. No matter how terrible the things you've seen, whatever they may've done to you, know that it's all an illusion, every blow, every blast, every spattered bit of..."

Maryam's face began to fall, her eyes blinking fast, her breath coming in gasps. She suddenly winked out, and in her place appeared the chiseled visage of Santo, slate eyes and gray stubble standing out against his normally smooth obsidian skin.

"Bishaberu, chickadee. Appreciate you cheering the sister up. Good of you."

"Baryogo shikaburaro wa, aburonim."

"Think we better speak Standard. Too many years with off-worlders: your control of our language is not like it used to be. Don't want to make you uncomfortable, embarrassed if you don't know a word or something. We can speak your proud new language, what. Universal. Unifying. Standard. One size fits all."

"You want to speak Standard, you want to feel in control, fine. All the same to me. Language is just a tool, not a defining characteristic or a touchstone. Let's not turn the kleinball round and round: you disapprove of me; I think you're a power-hungry sociopath."

"Showing the claws, eh? Very well. I know you lack the desire I feel for a completely enlightened Jitsu."

"The opposite: I'm the one wants folks enlightened, not in the dark about the corruption of their leaders."

"Ah, I see. The trauma of your childhood, still it affects you. Parents who never got you on the right path, let the false reality damage your mind, ruin your ability to form a soul."

"Don't talk to me about trauma. Any trauma I have, I got it from you and your sick manipulation of my weak parents. I don't get what you want. Why worry with me if I'm an animal with no hope for gnosis?"

"Chickadee, we all have roles in this momentary play, waiting for the curtain to fall, plunge the physical world into oblivion when the Eight are renewed. Yours is desperate repentance, useless for your own salvation but inspiring to others that need an extra push. You studied early Christianity with Professor Oduyoye. The Book of Revelations. Fallen Babylon, that's you. The little chickadee that had everything but a soul. Your buildings will crumble, but the Path remains."

"*You* are the soulless one, man who doesn't make a move without calculating the power it might give you. But remember, Santo, I knew you when you were Mr. Nobody, sucking stupidity from a tube like the rest of the fools. Also remember, big rooster boy, that I ran you out of our house when I was thirteen. Snapped my fingers at you as I screamed, and you left, you let a little *chickadee* run your sorry arse out of the 'dwelling,' your tail feathers dragging the ground, your cockscomb all deflated. Remember that, you bastard, when you start preaching your bullshit at me. I know what you are."

Santo was visibly taken aback by this memory; he swallowed heavily as if to control himself, a vein in his temple belying his facade of composure.

"Since you embrace the Grey Prison of physicality, you'll never understand what it's like to turn your back on that false reality. Want it or not, you're going to be used for the enlightenment of others. You can't escape that destiny."

Tenshi managed a smile despite the thundering of blood in her head.

"At last. Right about one thing, kenabuji. Just not the way you imagine. And now, if you don't mind, it's time I disconnected."

She thumbed the display off and relished the distortion of Santo's face as he slipped into oblivion. Returning to the task of finishing the fairgrounds, her every movement was infused with energy and decision, as well as a certain controlled violence, as if she were trying to scrape Santo's image away from her mind by dint of sheer adrenaline and creativity, the two human qualities that, if , she might consider divine.

INTERCHAPTER A

From: mtmdangelo@smg.va.ter

To: brandod@university.edu.jit

Subject: Greetings

Date: May 10, 2683 13:09:32 (SST)

Mwana na ngai ya bolingo,

Good to hear from you, Brandino. You left without a proper goodbye, unless telling your crude command seems proper in your intellectual mind. Of course, writing to simply say "arrived; hope yall're okay" after three months of silence truly shows your spite for us.

We are copasetic. Your absence is seldom noticed but on birthdays and such. You hardly came around anyway. But I'm certain you miss or will soon miss us: your identity always was so fragile, caro mio.

Ayanna has kept coming by, even after what you did to her. She and your brother have begun to date. They have much in common, those two. Maybe she'll find in him the man you never were.

In any case, let's wish them happiness, yes? Just like your brother wishes that you find yourself or whatever you're searching for on that heretic desert world.

By the way, your zia tells me there's a chapel in the CPCC city, on Zoo Street. Mother Burgstrum presides. Don't forget to confess. Considering your behavior, you should no doubt do so often.

> The Four bless and keep you.
>
> Marie-Thérèse Makomo-D'Angelo
>
> Parish Priestess
>
> La Chiesa del Santissimo Redentore

Excerpt from Prime Minister Ginette Lubin's Special Legislative Address:
May 15, 2683

Members of the tri-cameral Consortium Diet, many thanks for your attention for this unscheduled address. In the interests of moving forward as a unified whole, we gather today so I can announce a decision you've known about for some time. As humanity continues to spill beyond its traditional boundaries, we come upon many pockets of life. On occasion, these communities are human, peopled by our siblings who have gone before us, clearing a path among the dark between the stars. Sigma Draconis, its principal world Bima; 82 Eridani, its single inhabited planet Semanawak; Alpha Mensae, circled by Erin; and now Terego, in the 47 Ursae Majoris system. These are the first four, but history suggest that they will not be the last. At least three times in the last five hundred years humans left Sol in desperate exoduses, and many of those ships likely reached their destinations. When we stumble across them, we must be ready to embrace them, to show them their siblings have grown beyond the pettiness of the past. We must welcome them as family.

Our efforts with the government of Jitsu should serve as a model. That world won its independence in a fair, just way based on fair, just principles. Now, however, we court it, coax it, hoping it will join us in a concerted effort to provide each human with the decent, happy life that is their right. We are stronger when we are unified. This strategy is also working with Maharaja

Leksono in the Kunti or Sigma Draconis system. His agreement two years ago—
to dismantle the monarchy and establish a republic that will seek membership
in the CPCC—planted the seed of my present decision.

Working with Kunti ambassadors, I realized that, for the first time since
humanity was unified under the USR and later the CPCC, we are in need
of a Ministry of State, a department specializing in conducting relations with
human societies outside the Consortium.

I would like to nominate Deputy Chu Chen of New Beijing as head of
the new ministry. His work on that Consortium-colonized world makes him an
ideal minister of state, as does his experience in the Army and the private sector.
Each of you has a dossier on Deputy Chen in your inboxes. I am confident
that his approval will be swift. We need to get the ministry up and running
posthaste.

Thank you again for your time and attention. "In unity there is strength."
Have a good day, honorable legislators.

CHAPTER 6

SANTO RODE ON AN EMPTY GOVERNMENT TRANSPORT toward the jinja, the shrine where the Oracle lived in absolute isolation. Every Thursday he was permitted an audience with her, at the hour of his choice. It was an honor conceded him for having discovered her connection to the Ogdoad. Like John the Baptist or Dédalo Mostrenco, he had discovered a theophany. Had it not been for the idiocies of his other niece, he would have shot up the hierarchy of the planet's theocracy faster, and now be the ratowanin—the archon of Jitsu—rather than just a powerful district head.

Tenshi. Agent of toil, meaningless, useless struggle against entropy, which was key to restoring the Ogdoad. She thought, as had many physical and social architects throughout history, that building would reverse the inevitable dissolution of the universe. How wrong she was. Momentary victories were all toil ever won. Fleeting, without the slightest significance, like this idiocy of cleaning up the other continent and the polluted sea where chaos was beginning to tear down the false world. True reality, the Ogdoad, was curled up within everything, waiting for the clock to wind down, at which time it would expand and subsume everything within its incomprehensible borders.

The transport docked at the dome that surrounded the sacred complex, a cluster of windowless cylinders. After an initial scan, Santo made his way along stone walkways to the honden, the building that housed the Oracle. Inside, representatives of the Karibudan guild—known as the *Close* in Standard—met him. Those omedeyo attendants guided him through the multiple corridors, security checks, skin scrubs and clothing changes required of anyone permitted an audience with Samanei Koroma.

Santo was then led by three female security officers to the entrance of the White Room, where Samanei spent her days. Beyond it, through another labyrinth of corridors, was the Black Room, where she was taken at night.

The Oracle was only permitted to see six people: Santo, the Archon, and four other high-ranking members of the theocracy. Otherwise, her attendants waited till she fell asleep before they slipped inside, drugged her to keep her from awakening, bathed and changed her clothing, extracted her waste and filled her with nutrients: everything necessary to keep her completely cut off from her own physical needs and the outside world.

No stimuli of any kind, except her communication with the Eight.

Beside the shimmering force door stood a chirurgic, a highly advanced, blackmarket medbot equipped with sentient AI. Nestor had given Santo the machine when he had first begun negotiating with the Brotherhood. The illegal gift had sealed the deal.

"Arojin Koroma," it said.

"Have you solved the problem yet?" Santo demanded.

"No, sir. But I believe I am close to a solution."

Grunting in irritation, Santo stepped through the force door.

The room was as it had been for the last twelve years: completely white, empty of any furniture, fixture or indeed of anything at all. Faintly, the holy babble of Lady Domina's oral journal—played night and day to aid Samanei's meditation—insinuated itself into every crevice of the chamber. In its center sat the Oracle, ebony skin against her white robe the only change in the expanse of sameness. Her hair was cropped close to her scalp, and her nails were similarly short.

An empty look filled her eyes: she was connected.

"Orakuru. Ki nitaru. Santo."

Her lips moved soundlessly. *San. To.*

"Un. Puran nikaburaru nikke..."

"Speak to me in English, dog."

Santo straightened as if slapped.

"And not the sub-standard dialect of Standard so prevelant on this world. Just imagine you're reading scripture. Can you handle that, Santo?"

The language, intonation and accent were that of Alejandro Dresch, the

Founder, Santo realized. He fell to his knees.

"It's an honor, Founder."

"I'm not the Founder, idiot. You're talking to a twenty-five-year-old woman with dissociative identity disorder and schizophrenia whom by all rights you should have cured, you sick, evil bastard. You just like the idea that your crimes are somehow justified."

The same test as always. Do I wield sufficient faith or no?

"But you are the Founder, despite what you say. And I am your humble servant."

"Fine. Whatever. I get really tired of arguing with you every week. Let's pretend I'm your precious Dresch. What do you want today, Santo?"

"The teyopan... it was attacked."

"That's what we'd hoped. It gives you cover while furthering our goals."

"Yes, but Rawe won't establish the anti-terrorism squads without putting the measure to a vote in the Chamber of Deputies, and if they get their hands on the squads..."

"Your own fault, no doubt. Pushed too hard, didn't you? How many times must I warn you about appearing ambitious? You're too eager to get Mutemi Rawe out. Despite what you believe, he's no fool. Rather, he's cunning, and he's got a good decade or two left in him."

Santo blanched. "What?"

Samanei rubbed her temples. "Haven't you got any patience? Doesn't the salvation of this planet mean more to you than grabbing for power? Or have your promises to me been in vain? Are you an infidel?"

Santo bowed his head, shook it emphatically. "No, Founder. Forgive me. I'm gonna... I *will* strive for longsuffering, though I am zealous to see your plan come to fruition. It's just that, well, there are other factors. Tenshi, for example. I'm afraid she gots..."

"She *has*, Santo. I said English, or are you deliberately trying to end this audience?"

"Sorry. She has plans to use this tragedy to gain a foothold in Kinguyama."

"That will never happen." The Oracle's face grew grimly fierce.

"But she's extremely popular."

"Popular? That bitch?" Samanei leapt to her feet and lurched wildly about, clutching at her robe. "She let them walk me out of there. Twelve years, and she's never tried to get me free! Now she's *popular?*"

The Oracle abruptly stopped her frantic movements. Hunching over, she took shuffling steps toward Santo.

"Ai, shibaru! Yewa chuppek, adunim. Shempure shikmembero."

His mother's voice. The one he'd hoped to hear. The one that had pulled him from the depths of his depression so many years ago and confirmed that his progenitor had been translated upon death.

"What should I do, Umma? Stay with the plan? All the way to the end? She's strong, real strong. Maybe as strong as me. She maybe can pull it all down." The image of a fourteen-year-old girl running him out of her house, screaming obscenities at him as he hurried away. Not human. "I'm..."

"Nan? Shikihiro zo!"

"I'm afraid of her," Santo admitted, his voice small.

Samanei suddenly and calmly sat back down. She slipped her robe down to her waist, revealing a nearly emaciated body and two smallish breasts.

"Come, adunim. Come to your umma."

This was the sign that had long ago confirmed for Santo her true identity. No one but Santo, his mother Miko and the Ogdoad itself knew of this ritual. She had to be the theophany. Santo crawled on all fours to her lap. She bent over him, offering her right breast to his mouth. As he began suckling, she caressed his head.

"My baby. Umma's gonna take good care you. You just do what I tell you, everything will be just fine. You need something big to solidify your position, yank people's minds away from reform, leave Rawe with no choice. Then the squads will be yours, and you'll get what you deserve. Tenshi, too. Everyone will get what they deserve."

As Santo's eyes closed slowly, Samanei's head tilted back, a smile conquering her face in ambiguous fits and starts. When next she spoke, it was in another voice, full of dark timbres and determination, detailing what was convenient for him to know of the plan.

CHAPTER 7

THE TERMINAL IN TENSHI'S OFFICE CHIRPED.

Glancing at the controls, she saw that Ambarina Lopes was calling and thumbed the connection open with a sigh.

Ambar's round, pretty face surged from the terminal, smiling.

"Hey, babe."

Tenshi leaned forward. "I'm sorry, 'babe'? Really? I seem to remember dumping your cheating arse six months ago."

Ambar winced without losing her smile. "Ouch. But I remember explaining myself and apologizing, then buying you a really expensive arc welder to make up for my moment of weakness."

Settling back in her chair, Tenshi crossed her arms over her chest. "The welder has proven a lot more dependable than you, by the way."

Ambar raised her hands in a defensive gesture. "Truce? I'm staying a couple of weeks, giving everyone shore leave so they can attend the fair. Watching the news of what happened yesterday, I thought you might need a little break, something to take your mind off the tragedy and the rest of the stress."

"What did you have in mind?" Tenshi asked, tempted to roll her eyes and smirk.

"Dinner. As friends. At that Mediterranean place you love: Messina."

The idea was tempting. Tenshi had been working at a grueling pace for nearly three months. Her mouth watered at the thought of steaming couscous di pesce and a glass of rosé.

Of course, she'd have to spar with Ambar, who would be trying to get into bed with her. Still, even that sort of foolishness would be a welcome distraction.

"Fine. But dinner's on you, Captain Lopes."

Ambar smoothed her short brown hair with her left hand and winked. "You bet, Ms. Koroma. Reservation's at 8 pm. See you then."

WHEN THE DAY'S WORK WAS DONE, Tenshi walked over to the administrative landing pad. A black Strugar-Rask *Tarhiata* crouched on its landing struts like some sleek predator. She'd imported the stylish and expensive personal transport not long after renting her building to the CPCC. A touch of her hand irised open the access port, and she quickly esconsed herself before the pilot interface, telling the navigation system to take her home.

For now, home was an entire floor of the most expensive apartment building in Station City. After crossing brambly sand for several minutes, the transport lifted in an arc over the spires of Tenshi's adopted city, curving toward a tasteful tower of stone and steel. The force gate of her landing bay shimmered brighter in the waning sunlight and then winked out. The Tarhiata eased in and settled gently down.

Conscious of the time, Tenshi took a quick shower and picked a peach pantsuit from her closet. No slinky dress tonight. She didn't want to give Ambar the wrong idea. No matter how much Tenshi longed for the feel of another's hands on her body, their relationship was over, forever.

Taking the lift down to the lobby, Tenshi slipped into the cooling evening air and stepped onto the slidewalk for the short trip. Messina was just a few blocks away, in Baryo Chigu, the Little Earth district. Street traffic was light, just a few dozen automated taxis, and only an occasional transport crossed the skies above.

A five-star establishiment, Messina was staffed by actual human beings. Mikis Vandi, the maître d', greeted Tenshi with a smile.

"Bishaberu, Ms. Koroma. It's been a while. Let me take you to your table."

Ambar stood as they approached. She was wearing a sheer black gown, its neckline open to her navel. Her gold skin sparkled with glitter.

Tenshi's breath caught for a second in her throat.

Damn, she's pulling out all the stops, huh?

A quick kiss on the cheek, and the two sat down.

"I already ordered for you," Ambar said. "The couscous di pesce, right?"

Tenshi gave a soft laugh. The captain was good at the game, no doubt. But she played against too many opponents.

"Thanks. Are you getting the paella?"

Ambar leaned back, grinning. "Pues, claro, mujer. It's one of the reasons I keep coming back to this planet. You being the other."

"There's plenty of wonderful things about Jitsu," Tenshi countered as their server approached with a bottle of rosé imported from Earth. Once she'd inspected the wine, he poured them both a glass and set the bottle between them.

Ambar took a sip and shrugged. "Station City's not so bad. But, sorry, querida. Not much else. Bland buildings. Sand and pale vegetation. A blasted continent on the other side of the equator. Overly salty ocean with lousy beaches everywhere."

"It's a harsh world, sure. But starkly beautiful. And the people—"

"—are mostly zombies," Ambar interjected.

Tenshi shook her head, feeling her pulse quicken. "No, they're not. Some are fooled into unnecessary obedience by Machiavellian leaders, but most are special folks who have chosen lives of quiet meditation and focus on community over greedy competition and aggressive expansion."

"You sound like a politician. Or a preacher."

Tenshi downed her wine in a single irritated gulp. "The problem is that you've never understood my dedication to Jitsu. You've never even tried to step outside your own skin and see things from my perspective. You frankly don't appear to respect me as a person, which is why it was so easy for you to cheat on me, I guess."

Ambar picked up the bottle and served Tenshi more wine.

"It's kind of your fault, bella."

"What? Are you fucking kidding me, Ambar?"

"If you were with me out there, amid the stars, instead of here on this bloody monastery of a planet, I wouldn't get so overwhelmed by my needs."

"Ah, so that's what you want me for, huh? To satisfy your needs."

Ambar reached out and took both Tenshi's hands in hers. The feeling was electric, and the architect couldn't help but half-close her eyes and swallow heavily against the simmer in her veins.

"No, babe. What we have is much more than that. Always has been. I want to share the vastness of that swirling black with you, Tenshi. Show you the stars. Go from world to world, exploring the beauty of each. You could sell your designs, see the architecture in a dozen places you've only dreamt of. And every night, I will hold you in my arms. Treat you like the goddess you are."

It took a considerable act of will to pull her hands free from that tempting grasp, but Tenshi did.

"No. You're a honey trap. That's why I ended … this."

Ambar's eyes flashed with sudden anger. "¡Por el amor de Dios, mujer! Don't play childish games with me. We always got back together before, and I don't see why we can't do it now. Don't settle for this brain-dead, aescetic existence when a life of excitement is waiting for you. What's here for you, anyway? Whether zombies or holy monks, your people showed you long ago just how they feel about you. Give up on them. There's no point."

Tenshi's fists clenched. Her heart ached with surging adrenaline. A tear trembled in her right eye and tumbled down her cheek.

"Mikis!" she called, her gaze boring into Ambar, who seemed to realize she had gone too far.

The maître d' hurried over. "Yes, Ms. Koroma."

"Tell the the server pack my meal and have it delivered to my home. She will pay."

The man gave a quick bow. "Of course."

Ambar sighed dramatically, her favorite gaslighting ploy. "Tenshi, you're getting way too upset. We're just having a conversa—"

Slamming her fists on the table, Tenshi stood. "Listen closely, damn you. I will never leave this planet, Ambar. If I didn't leave it for Isabella, the love of my life, I'm certainly not going to leave it for you. It's my *home*. I'll cling to it with every last ounce of my will. You'd have to kill me to take me away from here."

Grabbing the bottle of rosé, she stormed from the restaurant and into the night.

CHAPTER 8

IT TOOK BRANDO ABOUT A WEEK TO GET SETTLED INTO HIS OFFICE amid intermittent meetings. His Baryogo improved as he analyzed the local dialect. The differences fascinated him, to the point that he began sketching out notes for a monograph that would explore the distinctive features and their probable origins.

Of course, the preparation of his course syllabi took precedence over that scholarship. Wanting to tailor instruction to his students' needs, he had to consider carefully the social dynamics of Jitsu. Fortunately, the university appointed Professor Tayibo to hold an orientation talk for offworlder faculty on Brando's fifth day.

"Each town has a teyopan," Tayibo explained, "a chapel presided over by a giya. New members of a teyopan are unenlightened till they perform daily zazen for seven years. Since immigration to our districts is limited, that mostly means local children, who gain membership at age seven."

Mandatory drug-enhanced meditation for kids, Brando thought. *Damn. I thought my childhood was rough.*

"At that point, they're declared matakite, seers, for having reached awareness. They are made full members of the congregation, teyopanjin. Most Jitsujin remain at this level. Following Dominian precepts, they limit themselves to a non-material existence. Little contact with outsiders. But pious teyopanjin can pursue further ritual self-study and reach basic enlightenment. These *satorijin* are permitted to become giya and either run a teyopan or take part in local government. They can also study alongside non-believers. Most of yall's students will be in this category, those who aren't from Station City."

An older professor, a woman from some island on the world of Atlantis, raised her hand. "Can you give us a feel for why most of those satorijin have decided to study at the university?"

Tayibo nodded. "Yes, excellent question. Satorijin who don't pursue any specific calling are known as *anshyano*. Respected elders within their teyopan. But still others yearn for gnosis. Full self-knowledge, hard to achieve. Those who do are the arojin, the other-born. Only they can occupy the highest posts, at the prefectural and planetary level. Even the deputies in the recently instituted legislature—no matter how, uh, *reformist* they claim to be—are arojin, every one of them."

The distaste on Tayibo's face told the new faculty exactly where Tayibo's political loyalties lay.

"But of course, with the rest of humanity crowding in around our world, arojin in our government need the best secular education possible. That is where yall's skills come in, colleagues. Take note, however: while Jitsu guarantees freedom of religion, yall should simply teach yall's subject matter with as little subjective commentary as possible. Stay away from discussions of the Path, except in the most general and historic of terms. A few of yall are Pathwalkers visiting from other worlds or platforms. A word of caution: discuss our beliefs in class, should you so desire, but clear your lecture with a Jitsujin arojin first."

As Professor Tayibo explained that process, Brando surreptiously used his data pad to learn more about the arojin. A voice narrated softly into his earbud that out of the ranks of Jitsu's arojin, the Oracle herself chose the *ratowanin* or archon, the religious and political leader of the entire planet.

"The archon," the narrator continued, "is said to have reached quantum enlightenment while alive, their nascent soul in constant communion with the Ogdoad, though not with the individual souls rejoined to the Eight. That is a privilege reserved only for the Oracle."

Brando sighed. Such a labyrinthine and feudal society made him more anxious about having moved to this planet. His haste to put light years between him and his family had kept him from fully researching the religious aspects of Jitsuan life.

Oh, well. Thank mothergod for Station City. I could also start looking up these rebellious reformer types. Especially Tenshi.

Afterward, back in his office, Brando couldn't help laughing at the irony.

Bloke like me, mistreated and disgusted by organized religion, ends up teaching at an institution that limits the freedom of its professors so they comply with the strictures of a religion. Mamma got one thing right: I am more like my pappà.

"What kind of man leaves his wife and teenage sons to go colonize some newfound world?" she had once demanded. "A man of nothing more than human pursuits, blind to the divine needs of the spirit made flesh. And you're following in his footsteps."

Despite the hurt that had settled in Brando's chest since the day of his father's departure, it was impossible for him to hate the man. Giacobbe D'Angelo was a musician, a wonderful singer of opera and folk music, and he had brightened Brando's childhood with stories and songs that eclipsed the gobbledygook of his mother's Wiccan Catholic creed.

That faith had grown in strength when Marie-Thérèse found herself abandoned. She had joined the seminary, and by the time Brando entered the Università degli Studi di Milano, she had already been ordained. Her fervor, insight and popularity were such that she was soon performing the 4:30 pm Friday mass at the Chiesa del Santissimo Redentore, spreading the message of the Black Madonna of Loreto.

And Brando's life had become a prison.

INSPIRED BY THE MEMORY OF HIS FATHER'S MUSIC AND THE SOOTHING feeling of gut strings on the cherry wood neck, Brando contacted the director of the fair's entertainment component, and after a pleasant five-minute chat, he'd been squeezed in for a song or two between acts. *Not performed since the espresso bar on campus. Always won on karaoke night. Constant butterflies fluttering in my gut, though. Imagine now, a thousand faces looking up at me. Will I freeze?*

Brando took a public transport down to the fair grounds to get an idea of its scope, though he also hoped to catch a glimpse of the infamous architect. He found a section that was still under construction and picked her out right away. She wore denim pants and a sleeveless linen blouse that glowed white against her burnished onyx skin; her gloved hands rested on a chrome and leather tool belt slung loosely across her narrow hips. She reached up and adjusted the clip on her locs, mahogany shot through with gold, as the operator of a finicky constructor bot shook his head and gestured at the stalled machine.

As Brando approached, he began to make out her voice: husky and firm, yet distinctly feminine.

"I've told you before," she explained in Baryogo, "that there's no reason to use a robot to drive a nail. Use your own body: feel the adrenaline. What are you afraid of, hitting your finger? I thought reality was no big concern of yours, Hari Kan."

She handed the Neog teen, for Brando realized as he got closer that Hari was an adolescent, what appeared to be a hammer from her tool belt. Not a nail driver, not a bonder, but a real, old-fashioned hammer.

Now I know this planet is backward.

However, once Hari had bashed his hand and bent the fastener a couple of times, Brando realized Tenshi was the odd one.

"Let me see that," she said, with only the barest hint of exasperation. "The problem is in the way you're holding it. Also, you don't have to throw your entire body behind each blow: let the mass of the hammer do its work."

Holding the fastener with her right hand, she tapped it firm in the doorframe they were trying to set, and with three fluid blows she sent it home. Brando couldn't tear his eyes away from her arms, muscles taunt cords beneath the skin, prominent without being ostentatious, not an ounce of fat as far as he could tell from seven meters away.

"Do you see? Now, try fastening the rest of the jamb yourself."

She hovered near him without being obvious, finding other work to inspect while keeping an eye on his efforts. A couple of tries more, and Hari got the idea. After he'd nailed the jamb in place, she ambled over and nodded.

"Good job," she observed in Standard. "About time for lunch, no?"

Hari Kan nodded and headed for the food tent, a pleased expression on his face. Brando was also inspired by Tenshi's managerial tactics. He watched her interact with other workers for a while, noting her attentive gaze and their ready allegiance to her, apparent in their movements and tone of voice.

After ten minutes or so, he realized she was moving with gradual and deliberate movements in his direction. Soon she walked right up to the shade-covered bench where he'd plunked himself down.

Brando almost gasped when he saw her eyes. They were deep blue with marbled green, surrounded by orange haloes. Against the glossy darkness of her skin, they might have been twin supernovas.

Something tugged, deep within him, as if the thread of his fate had suddenly tangled itself with hers. He had to bite his lip against inexplicable tears.

"Why are you watching me?" she demanded, and though her voice was quiet and her tone neutral, her gaze bored into him with a force that knocked a quick answer from his lips.

"I'm a participant in the fair," he said, trying to sound nonchalant despite the thudding of his pulse. "I decided to come down take a look around. Great job you're doing. Impressive."

"Weren't expecting anything like this on Jitsu, true?" Observation, accusation or confrontation?

"No. Your world has this reputation, an architectural one, I mean, and this fair, along with the other buildings of yours I've seen..."

"You always talk like this?"

"Excuse me?"

"Yeah. Turning the issue round and round without ever getting to your point."

Brando sighed. "Sorry. I'm a professor."

She nodded as if that explained everything.

"Your work truly moves me," he continued. "Not just compared with the other buildings I see all over this planet, but in general. I'm from Milan, you see, and..."

Her face brightened, and words spilled from her lips. "Milan? With the Pirelli spire and La Scala? Domina, what envy! I used to date a woman from Italy, Isabella Spinelli. A biologist. Lives on Oceania now. She turned me on to yall's architecture. What do you like more, old quarter or new?"

"Walking through the arcade is an incredible experience even on the thousandth trip. But the new quarter, especially Oscar Cosigga's design for the Diet chamber—well, it takes your breath away. Still, it's purely visual, while your work is visceral, alive."

"Well, Kyosu," *Professor. Hrm, a little formal,* "glad you like it. Of course, you're not as biased against it as my fellow Jitsujin, being an infidel and all." She smiled broadly. "Come, let's eat lunch. My treat."

Am I lucky or what? Didn't even need to embarrass myself with a stupid pick-up line. Sort of. At least it was the truth.

As Brando stood, he noted that she was short for a native of Jitsu, only a couple of centimeters taller than he was. The perfect height.

"By the way, what's your name?" Tenshi glanced at him quickly before continuing to sweep the fairgrounds with her eyes.

"Brando D'Angelo."

"Brando." Her heavy Baryogo accent made his simple name an incantation.

"Well, Brando—shiperaro wa." She motioned him to a stop as she walked up to some workers who were apparently putting a facade on one of the fair buildings. The mold for one column, or so Brando imagined given its shape and size, was already in place. The workers, however, were struggling with a large machine, shaped rather like a weapon, with a telescoping base. The device wasn't moving upward. Tenshi examined the base, shrugged, and hefted the machine to her shoulder. She aimed with care and began keying a sensor on the barrel. Five short pieces of rebar shot out one after another and embedded themselves into the concrete in a nearly perfectly straight line as Tenshi inclined the barrel upward. The last piece was heavily slanted, and Tenshi shook her head as though irritated. Reaching out with her left hand, she grabbed hold of the scaffolding and pulled herself up with one wiry arm till she was level with the top portion of what would be the column. She carefully shot in the last three rebars and eased herself to the ground.

"Shite," Brando muttered.

She smiled self-consciously as she walked back to him, and they made their way to the food tent. He let her choose their food, and she selected two huge squares of fried pork skin lathered with tofu and topped with grated squash, cabbage and local herbs. It was delicious.

"So, Tenshi, you don't mind getting your hands dirty, eh?"

"That's our real problem, you know. First the corporations. They provided everything. All we had to do was operate the machines, make sure it was all running smoothly. Now, the government gets royalties from CPCC-licensed mining of our Oort cloud plus the planets that orbit Kobito, and they use those funds to support all Jitsujin. The fusion plants provide energy for nearly every need, which isn't a lot. But it's enough for many. They only expect the minimum, convinced they shouldn't yearn for anything more. Extremist leaders take that away from folks early on, take away our ambition and our thirst to know. Few Jitsujin care how devastated this planet is, how much needs to be done to fix it. We end up recruiting outsiders to help us when we should be doing the work ourselves."

"You've got a lot more freedom than we do on Earth; they teach us to say, 'Your planet, your people, and then you.' Here at least the individual is the most important, no?"

"Problem is, extremists define individual in a way that limits us to basically nothing. Self to most Dominian Pathfinders is something you create, but not with physical tools. When they make you to give everything up except what's inside your head, and then they don't allow you to put anything inside except what they say: would you call that freedom?"

She seemed to be struggling internally, perhaps trying to convince herself of something that Brando couldn't grasp. He decided to probe a little more.

"No, guess not. Don't parents ever try to teach their kids stuff beyond what the church allows?"

Tenshi sighed. "It's tricky. There are reformist neighborhoods and communities, of course. But most parents don't teach their kids: the teyopan takes children starting at age four. And even if families did keep them, most wouldn't know what to do. They were raised the same way. It's a great system, oh, yes. The arojin have all the power and few dare contradict them. In extremist communities, kids who don't agree, who want to find their souls in more than just drugs and zombiehood, get shipped to the clean-up crews till they see how much better it is to be like the rest, let the teyopan give you everything and just vegetate. It's sad. Instead of letting you build a soul, they end up crushing you."

Tenshi's jaw tightened as if she were fighting back tears or a scream. Glancing at the workers while her knuckles whitened on the edges of the table, Tenshi shook her head. "Listen to me. I don't even know you, and I'm spilling my guts to you. Trust me, I'm not usually like this. The massacre, the pressure of the fair, a slight hangover, then someone who's willing to listen comes along. Ugh. Sorry." Her eyes met his again, and she smiled with childlike shyness, as if she felt truly foolish.

"Hell, Tenshi, it's okay. I'm feeling a bit weird myself." Brando had no idea why, but he felt the need to open up to her. He'd been alone for so long, longing for a little warmth. And she was right: there was something compelling about being around a person who would simply listen to you. Bewildered at the unthawing of his heart, Brando began to talk, turning his UV shades over and over in his hands.

"You know, letting your parents raise you isn't always that great, either. I doubt many people know how to do it. My mother always regarded my accomplishments with disdain, and my dad left when I needed him most. I was the best linguistics student at the university in the last fifty years, my dissertation disseminated throughout the Consortium, but never once did Mamma or Zia or my brother say, 'Hey, good job, Brando. Congratulations.' It was like, 'Oh, big deal. Doesn't have a thing to do with us or the Holy Church, so we aren't interested.' You know what it's like to achieve something and for the people that mean the most to you to ignore it?"

An odd expression crossed Tenshi's face. "Yes. It's what they do, those who see physical reality as unimportant. Ironically, such people embrace those beliefs because they're afraid of this world. Deep down they know that they can't face it. So they find a bunch of other cowards, and together, rather than helping one another grapple with reality, they convince themselves they're somehow special. Always be suspicious of groups in which everybody thinks the same, Professor. Most dangerous thing that exists."

Stop, a cowardly, defeatist voice within him warned. *Don't reveal anything else. This is a test. Expose yourself, and she'll lose respect. No one likes a weak man. You know this to be true.*

Clearing his throat, Brando gestured about. "Change of subject, if you don't mind. What's going to happen to all these buildings after the fair?"

Tenshi sat up straighter. Her eyes blinked rapidly a couple of times. Brando worried for an instant she might think he was put off by her revelations.

"I've got plans for them, but it's a little early to share. Politics are weird right now. Let's just say, it's something that you might be interested in."

Brando stopped fiddling with his shades. "Me in particular? Why?"

"Because of what you do. But enough hints. You can wait for the announcement just like everyone else."

"And what you do when you're not building things?"

Tenshi feigned confusion, held her chin in mock meditation. "Plan new things to build? Ha! No, seriously, I have a life, of course. Friends, mostly reformers. We get together, they talk about Jitsu's future, I back them up. A few drinks, then I go back to my designs. That's about it."

"Hey, my respects. Takes more dedication than I could muster."

She frowned. "Don't say things like that. You've got the dedication inside, waiting. Everyone does. Just a matter of bringing it out. Finding the right reason."

Such matter-of-fact optimism was unfamiliar to Brando, whose pessimistic family had ground his idealism down into bitter regret.

How she can know this about anyone? Why is she so sure?

"Maybe I'll find it here, no?"

She tilted her head, eyebrows up, half-pouting, as if to say *could be*. The sound of jammed machinery made her swing about in her seat, concerned.

"Nammach kaseru ka? Excuse me, it's just—they tend to screw things up, I'm not there hanging over them like a mother. Look, it was great talking to you. You'll be here next Saturday, no?"

"Yeah. I'm going to sing, believe it or not."

"The singing professor." Her laughter was genuine and kind and made her face glow like a moonlit, starry sky.

"Spang on."

"I wouldn't miss it. See you then? Don't think I'm running you off."

"No, no. I understand. Just a week left, so I'm sure you'll be busy."

"Yeah. Stick around, if you want. Lots of things to see."

"I should go back to the U. Got to get ready for class, you know."

They awkwardly shook hands and cheeks. Tenshi smelled of soap and sandalwood. He could have sworn her hand trembled a bit. He chastised himself for being a fool.

No way she's interested in you. Come on, Brando. You just met.

Still, her gorgeous eyes peered into his soul as they pulled apart, and she nodded the vaguest of nods, as if approving of what she'd seen there.

Then Tenshi Koroma smiled and walked off, shouting at her workers.

CHAPTER 9

IN A LUXURIOUS ROOM PROVIDED BY A VICE-PRESIDENT OF STRUGAR-RASK, a corporate republic controlling much of p Eridani 3, Konrau Beserra stood before the heads of the six families, each accompanied by a trusted counselor. Konrau, kabesa of the Arredondo clan and kasike or godfather of the entire Brotherhood, had been unable to bring his own right-hand man, konsehero supremo Nestor Bos, to the special meeting.

Why? The heads of the families didn't trust Bos. Hell, Konrau *himself* didn't fully trust the man, despite his strategic brilliance. Nestor's friendships outside the syndicate were worrisome, and the subject of today's reunion was of such importance and secrecy that the heads had decided not to take a risk.

This decision meant that Konrau was saddled with Chuy Arredondo, his great-uncle and kabesita or regent of the Arredondo family. Arredondo controlled the clan in Konrau's stead since in addition to being kabesa familiar, Beserra was also godfather and therefore unable to micromanage Arredondo affairs. Chuy had never approved of his great-nephew's becoming kasike: as the bastard son of Chuy's nephew Sami, Konrau should have risen only to underboss, at best. But the Virgin and Baby Fidensio had smiled on his efforts, and by dint of his own courage, ruthlessness and intelligence, Konrau had done the impossible.

And he planned to do much, much more.

"Grasias por benir," he began in Kaló. "I'm sure yall done read the reports and my outline of a plan. Give me yall's opinion: feasible?"

Pejo Garsasada, pale-skinned and blue veined corpse that he was, began to speak in halting tones. "An imrizabu—that's amazing. You say Ernesto Mendosa found it?"

Konrau resisted the urge to sigh or shoot the old man. He had known this would happen. The family heads had no vision. They were going to drag their feet, play dumb. He'd have to beat the ideas into them before they would agree to pool resources.

Sure, the Consortium had recently discovered another imrizabu between Tau-Ceti and Sirius 2. But it was commercially useless. By contrast, the particular vein in hyperspace the Brotherhood now controlled was the first viable one since the destruction of the Centauri Conduit, which had linked Alpha Centauri 3 to Eta Cassiopeiae 2 for nearly a century.

Being able to move men and goods and ships across nearly three parsecs in thirty seconds: now that's power, Konrau thought to himself. *But these fucking pendehos just can't see that. Long's they don't tell me they've got to consult with their materias.*

Lino Kintana de Samarripa—the short, swarthy head of the Samarripa clan—answered before Konrau could. "Si ya sabe usté. It's all in his proposal, and you done heard the rumors anyhow. Don't play the fool. Ernesto is my aunt's second cousin, pilot on the *Puro Dezmaje.* Shipping weapons to the Nebula, they fenestrated real close to the edge of the dust disk, then *boom,* they found themselves flying through a hyperspace tunnel, coming out a few seconds later in the Nereus system. The *Nereus* system, Brothers, thirty light years away. Ship was kind of fucked up, but they made a two-month trip in less than a minute! Our kasike is right to be excited, and I don't get why yall ain't."

Donardo Bustamonte, his oversized head cocked to one side, laughed. "Excited about what? Like you just said, it's the Nereus system. Home of seven interstellar corporations, all charter members of the CPCC. The only systems with more CPCC citizens and Armed Forces personnel in them are Sol and Rigil Kentaurus. We fly an armada out that fucking conduit, the putos of the Flotilla are gonna blast our arses out the sky. Plus, what about the effects on the ship? An armada of damaged vessels ain't much use."

"Maje de syelo," muttered young Tito Benemerito, who had only been a sixteen when Konrau had eliminated his second cousin Toni eight years before. Konrau suspected the punk was just waiting for a chance to reclaim his family's place at the head of the syndicate. "So while the fucking Consortium gots an imrizabu of its own to study and fuck with, we got a useless one."

"Not useless," insisted Konrau. "My plan describes how we could use this thing to seize the entire Nereus system when the time is right. As for the structural stresses on the ships, there's ways to reinforce them. Just refer to the plan."

"Pa ser franko," intoned Bustamonte, "your plans, Konrau, been looking a little weak to us."

Konrau leaned forward. "The fuck does that mean, Donardo? Didn't I get the Consortium off our arse? Didn't I move our hub of operations to an island on Atlantis, all paid for and covered up through my contacts in Transcom? Didn't I take the heat off yall so Mars could still be Anca L'ermandá? And now yall are gonna tunnel this bullshit my way?"

"It's all these pendehaaz with the Neogs, mi kasike," said Moktesuma Arreyano, finally entering the discussion. "Two years you been working with that crazy Santo Koroma, and with what results? We saw the reports, Konrau. Slaughtering fanatics in their church? That's what this wait was building up to? I mean, fuck, I got no love for the navel-gazing shitheads, but how does that help us, eh? How does it fit in with our principles and needs?"

Needs. So that's what this shite is about.

"Listen. Under me yall's profits have gone up fifteen points in five years, Brothers. I'm asking for the faith and support that yall owe to me. When I stood here two years ago and explained the fifteen-year plan for domination of the Kobito subsystem of Eta Cassiopeiae 2, I got this same shite. Some of yall just don't get it. Look at the fucking maharaja of Sigma Draconis: he rules, not like the fucking Consortium nancies, Brothers, but by the right of his birth in the royal family. Everyone here has roots going back to the original split and even farther back, some. We are blue-bloods, don't yall see? We should be kings."

Everyone present knew that Konrau himself *wasn't* a blue-blood, not fully. But the Beserras had been loyal members of the Brotherhood legions for centuries, and that service had to count for something. In any event, he doubted any of the kabesas would dare to point out that he was the bastard son of an Arredondo.

"Kings," echoed Lino with an approving nod.

"Here's the trouble," Donardo Bustamonte interjected. "You already got one fifteen-year plan in place, making sikaritos do all sort of strange shite like massacre Neogs in a church, just so that sumbitch can run off the CPCC, become tyrant or whatever and then give us the other system. Fucking long term, Konrau. Now you bring up a, what was it, a thirteen-year plan to start in two years. And this shite you want: moles in the AF, Brotherhood presence on worlds that're controlled by our enemies, buildup of refitted ships and men in secret locations, hiring merks and ronin and assassins, kidnapping politicians' kids, buying up corporate stock, on and on: how you're going to keep track of all that? Solo eres omme, kompa."

"Only a man? With respect, Donardo, you ain't met someone greater in all your dog's life." The others stiffened at the slap to Bustamonte's honor, but Konrau continued. He felt no weakness, and he would never pretend to have one for anyone's benefit. Every kabesa lived in fear of what he knew about them and what he could do to them. "Soy kasike de L'ermandá, Brother. I went beyond being a man fucking years ago."

Lino stepped in. "Brothers, just look at the way this works out: Kobito is just five light years from Nereus. We get control of both at one time, we got two whole… wait, three, because you ain't gonna let that fucking Neog bishop hang onto Jitsu and the Higante system, right? You ain't said it, but that's bloody brilliant, Konrau. Three naffing systems, Brothers, under our control. Talk bout an empire."

Beserra smiled at Lino's perspicacity. Of course he wasn't going to let Santo Koroma keep Jitsu. Konrau Beserra hadn't *ever* settled for less than everything. Not as a gang leader on Tenochtitlán Platform, not as a lieutenant in the Brotherhood, and certainly not now that he was that mafia's head.

"Four. Don't forget Beta Pictoris." Konrau watched the heads' eyes slowly begin to kindle with the twin fires of greed and a will to power. "We've spent the last five years supplying the Nebula as a fall-back retreat. Got a planetoid outfitted to be Brotherhood HQ, the need arises."

Arreyano smirked. "Four systems. An empire. Well, empires can be lost, and most times they are. The first fucking Moktesuma, whose name I got. Alexander, Napoleon, Mussolini, the Nuova Pace Romana. The Brotherhood's survived so long because we ain't trying to be no empire. We just get what we want, and fuck the rest of them."

"No," Konrau countered. He had thought this objection through many times. "What ruined those other sumbitches was a lack of planning and patience. Oh, they knew more of less what they wanted, they planned some, but most times they went from victory to victory, just kind of letting the fucking wave of power carry them, you know, wherever it did. We're going to be thorough. Every step's gonna be planned with precision. By '98, AF forces in the Nereus system will have thinned quite a bit, the Brotherhood will have major holdings in the corporations there, and the corporate presidents will be in our pockets. Not like with Transcom and Strugar-Rask and so forth. Not as partners. They'll be *ours*. When we roll down that imrizabu and pop out the other end, corporate police will be waiting to *back us up*. Trust me."

He had them, Konrau knew it. Even Donardo. Arreyano was hesitant, but he would probably buckle soon enough.

"You're asking for a lot, ermano." Arreyano ticked off items on his thick, ringed fingers. "Hundred ships per family. Money. Weapons. Guards sworn to secrecy for more than a decade. A thousand men, who've got to go off to some unexplored system and train for two years before the invasion, leaving their families. By the by, why aren't we expanding outward? Why are we gonna attack the CPCC if there's so many worlds out there for the taking?"

Konrau leaned forward, his stubbly jaw firmly set. "Because we're kings, and we need serfs. The Brotherhood doesn't make bread or anything else. We rule, we protect, we move stuff from people that don't require it anymore to people we want to have it. But we must have those people under us to survive. We try to ignore that, it'll mean our destruction."

"You keep taxing us for your Jitsu project, we won't be able to provide what you need for the Nereus thing," Arreyano pointed out, trying to the last to find any possible counterargument.

Konrau nodded. "You're right. That's why yall don't have to provide anything else for Jitsu. That'll be taken care of by the Arredondo family, mainly by my own personal Red Legions and Nestor's men, plus dummy crews that I'll throw together from new recruits."

"And once we got us this empire of yours? What then? Consortium ain't just going to sit back and leave us alone."

"Yall'd be surprised. We won't have any problems, I foresee, in getting them to sign a treaty with us. We'll just promise to stay within our little fiefdoms, and what with our military might, they'll have no choice but to agree. Besides, part of the plan, as yall no doubt noticed, is funding anti-expansionists and localists so they gain the majority in the Diet. Dirtying their more hawkish opponents. Those dumb fucks will then water down the AF and loosen Consortium local control to the point that they won't be able to stop us."

Most of the kabesas were looking around at each other now, nodding their heads in contented agreement.

Of course, what yall don't know is that I ain't stopping there. I plan to bring the whole of humanity under our control. But no use mentioning that just now. Yall are skittish enough as is, hotos.

"I'm in," Lino said, calling the matter to a vote by his announcement.

"Yo tammen," agreed Tito Benemerito.

"I yo," Donardo said firmly.

Pejo nodded his white head, and Moktesuma Arreyano sighed. "Weno. Toy dencho. But we give nothing to the Jitsu plan. That's your baby. And keep fucking Nestor in the dark. We let him stay on as konsehero supremo because of his sister Ria, Baby Fidensio give her peace. That and his connections. But we don't trust him, Kasike, and you shouldn't neither."

AN HOUR LATER, BESERRA WAS RIDING AN EXECUTIVE LIFT DOWN TO THE berth where his private junk was docked. He had been invited to stay as long as he liked as a guest of Strugar-Rask, but he had politely declined. There was much work to do, and the sooner he got started, the better he would feel. Keeping his mind and body occupied was vital to his sanity, he had found.

Beside him, Chuy Arredondo cleared his throat. "You know, Konrau, that would've gone *chingos* easier if you would just bend a little on some issues."

Turning annoyed eyes on his uncle, the Brotherhood boss of bosses coldly asked, "Like what?"

"Well, you're in a sort of, shite, *tenuous* fucking situation. You worked your way up, you killed Toni Benemerito and did a buggered lot of good for everybody, but to those ohetes you're still just the bastard son of a minor

lieutenant. Tomorrow they could band together and throw you out."

"Wouldn't be so fucking easy," Konrau spat.

"Maybe not. Maybe there would be a big fucking war. But your claim on

the kasike position could for reals be strengthened, if you would just fucking

marry Donardo's daughter Isabel. You'd bring the Arredondos and Bustamontes

together, make your self legitimate in everybody's eyes."

Konrau felt rage building, but as he always did, he kept it down, analyzed

it, froze it, used it. To him, the Brotherhood was more than just the opinion

of the six intractable family heads. They were important, the rituals and

traditions were important, but the Brotherhood had to be bigger than that. It

had to be, it had to be *greater* than him as an individual or his life made no

sense. His sacrifices had been in vain if the Brotherhood weren't something

more valuable than everyday emotions and motives. As a result of this broader

vision, he rebelled against having to kowtow to the kabesas' ideas of legitimacy,

which weren't necessarily required by the tenants of L'onda. Konrau had proven

himself to them on a more visceral level, and his power was now more than they

could afford to take lightly. He didn't need to marry Isabel Bustamonte to retain

his position.

Besides, he didn't trust women enough to marry one. His mother was

a treacherous puta, and the kasike had always suspected that it was her fault

that Sami Arredondo hadn't given Konrau the family name before dying in prison. Rather than be faithful to her man like a good sancha or consort should, she'd opened her legs to every pissant who'd knocked on the door.

Toward Sami himself, Konrau felt ambivalent: at times he despised the dead lieutenant for not being there to show his bastard son the ropes, but at others he sympathized with Sami's desire to stay far away from Karmen Beserra. Besides, Sami had had his muher and his three daughters to take care of, all legitimate members of the Arredondo clan.

No, better not to marry. Better to keep a few sanchas here and there, for when the urge arose. Consorts who meant nothing and had no real power, no emotional connection. Mindless females whose loyalty was bought and paid for.

Women it was impossible for him to betray.

Suppressing that dangerous chain of thought, he shook his head decidedly.

"No, Chuy. Not gonna happen. I ain't giving the Bustamontes no more say in my kasikeria than what they got it now."

Chuy was obviously irritated, but he just nodded. "Weno. Lo ke tu keras."

"Bet your arse it's whatever I want. Sides, you and me are the only ones with the coordinates of that imrizabu. That's some power right there. Well, Ernesto knows, but he's all ours. Quit worrying, tio."

Chuy shrugged. "You said something about a move."

As the lift slowed and swiveled open onto the docking theater, Konrau nodded. "Yeah. I'm gonna be leaving Horaisan. The island is yours. Move the Arredondo family operations there. You can keep my kantó and all the stuff inside. Transcom officials will cooperate with you fine, long as you keep all the old agreements. Handle the transactions like usual, through the Bolon Pimpon Enterprises front."

"It's a great honor, Konrau, and I thank you. But where you going then? Ó vã tar las apareishons de L'ermandá?"

"At Beta Pictoris. In the Uraká Nebula. That asteroid we been equipping for a fallback HQ? I'm gonna use it as our hub. I need to be away from CPCC space, get a better perspective on operations."

Of course, there was more to his move than that, but Chuy couldn't be allowed to know those details.

"You gonna let the kabesas know?"

"Soon enough, yes."

Walking through the ornate docking theater past the dozens of berthed ships, Konrau and his great uncle, who was dumbfounded at the sudden changes, worked out some of the details as bodyguards and corporate security trailed them meters behind. Finally, they reached the heavily guarded airlock that led to the narthex connecting Konrau's private junk and the orbital guest center. Chuy and Konrau embraced formally, and the older man was escorted away toward his own ship. Konrau gazed at Chuy's retreating back and praised himself for the control he'd just demonstrated.

This shite is gonna work, ain't it? Just got to keep focused, is all.

DURING THE TWENTY-HOUR VOYAGE BACK TO THE PLANET OF ATLANTIS in the Zeta Tucanae system, Konrau kept busy, as he felt driven to do at all times, by keeping abreast of the operations throughout the Brotherhood's many levels of influence in the CPCC, especially the status of crews in place on Jitsu. Most important, however, was his rumor campaign, geared toward drawing intelligence agencies and other syndicates off the trail of his real intentions. He deliberately produced misinformation and allowed it to be spread, a tactic that also allowed him to discover any leaks in Brotherhood hierarchy.

This campaign was what had clenched his distrust of Nestor Bos: a tidbit about Brotherhood moku-smuggling in independent systems, just a throwaway idea he'd mentioned to Nestor one day, had been repeated by a member of Al-Muzzamml, the independent spy network run by Yen Bandera. Bandera, an ancient ronin intelligence operative with his assets in nearly every important organization (including the Brotherhood, unfortunately) had been a close acquaintance of Nestor's since the konsehero supremo had been a teen. Bandera had certainly been of help over the years, providing essential intel for an acceptable price, but the mysterious figure was not bound by honor or blood to anyone but himself. Men with no loyalties were dangerous, Konrau had come to learn. Manipulating them was nearly impossible.

So, because of this useful but dangerous relationship with an unknown factor, Nestor had no idea of the scope of Konrau's vision. That was fine. The godfather's people obeyed him, and that was all he required. However, he realized that he'd have to confide in Nestor soon, giving him at least fragments of the truth. The old brother was partly responsible for Konrau's position and power. Despite how irritatingly prissy and idiotic he could be, despite his tendency to give more information to outsiders than was necessary, Konrau would respect his loyalty and service fully.

As long as they served the interest of the Brotherhood, of course. The tenants of L'onda, the Brotherhood code of honor, demanded the syndicate come first. For Konrau, it always had. Always. He wasn't as sure about Nestor, however. In addition to his loose lips, the konsehero had had no qualms about killing Konrau's predecessor.

Better that I be cautious around the tricky gerrie. He's gonna know the full truth when the time is right, anyways.

WHEN THE ATMOSPHERIC SHUTTLE SET DOWN AT THE TARMAC ON THE Brotherhood-controlled island of Horaisan, Konrau was greeted by Nestor Bos and Ferenc Madl, Transcom's middle-management representative on the island, a man firmly ensconced in the Brotherhood's pockets. After discussing some of Madl's concerns about Konrau's move, all of which were soothed at the idea of increased smuggling privileges through the Arredondo network, the kasike excused himself and had Nestor accompany him into the ridiculously well-guarded and shielded complex that housed

Brotherhood central command.

Nestor, a fifty-five-year-old Martian by birth, moved his gaunt form with an almost effeminate grace that contrasted with his stern, scarred features. Though more at ease with the exchange of intelligence and secrets, the tall, graying man was as deadly as any brother Konrau had worked with, able to kill an enemy or even a treacherous colleague without a second's hesitation. He would have been the perfect ally, if not for his fondness for the even older Bandera.

"You heard the latest?" Nestor asked as they palmed their way past checkpoints inside the complex.

"I read all the updates you sent me on the way back from Eridani."

"No, this is more recent than that." Nestor seemed to cringe a little before continuing, as though he didn't relish the reaction he thought he'd get. "It's bout the Aztlan Angels. They got a new *padrino*: knocked Nunyes out, put that golden boy Jimi Andrade in his place."

Konrau's breath quickened, but he tried to show nonchalance. "And? With a little squink like that at their head, the Angels are gonna be even easier to edge out."

Nestor peered at him through narrowed eyes. "Konrau, this kid's gunning for your arse. You killed his pa, and—"

Konrau whirled about, unable to bear it anymore. "What? Just say it, pendeho. His sister. You think I give a fuck bout her? You think you got to use low thrust around the fucking issue? I am Konrau Beserra, Nestor. Fucking kasike of the Brotherhood. Some bitch iha d'anhel don't mean shite to me."

Konrau turned and kept on toward his office, feeling Nestor take another route, as if to give the kasike some breathing room. He was good at disappearing when Konrau needed him to, that much was for sure. Grunting at the guards and aides who were busily taking care of the administrative side of the syndicate's operations, Konrau reached and palmed open the enormous steel doors of his executive suite.

His expansive office, with its hardwood floors and leather furniture, seemed oppressively small despite covering more than a hundred square meters. He longed for space, for kilometers of nothing on every side, the black of space above him. This claustrophobia was one reason for the Brotherhood's impending move to the more strategically located and historically significant Uraká Nebula, the misnamed dust disk around Beta Pictoris where centuries ago a Brotherhood boss had given his life to keep the Aztlan Angels from taking over extrasolar space.

Konrau had done what he could to destroy the Angels, once part of the Brotherhood many centuries ago. As a young foot soldier in the cramped corridors of Tenochtitlan platform, he had slain that syndicate's boss, Bruno Andrade. Now, thirteen years later, he was head of the Brotherhood and well on his way to finally obtaining the two things he most wanted out of life: absolute power and nobody near him.

Except *her*, maybe.

"That's ridiculous," he said aloud, to the mute phantasm of the past that no amount of destruction he unleashed on the universe seemed able to exorcise. "I'm not a gormless punk who thinks with his prick anymore. She's dead, dead for thirteen years; she doesn't mean a thing to me!"

A poko. A sudden pain seized his left temple, his cloned eye throbbing madly, shooting spasms of agony through his brain. He fell to one knee, clutching blindly at his head. As he struggled to focus on the desk, the floor, anything to regain his sense of balance, he saw her body there, before him, broken, bleeding, killed by his own hand.

NO! It was her pa that killed her!

But how could you say such a lie? Why, Konrau? It was self-same you.

He thought he could use her against me, as if I was some novice squink with no honor. I saw him there, gun at her head, threatening to kill her if I didn't leave. As if the Brotherhood wasn't more important to me than some fem.

He had no choice. You made him to think that.

He had no choice? Shot me in the head, right in front of her. Left me on the slidewalk in a pool of my own blood. I had no choice? He deserved to die!

But she deserved to live, Konrau, ain't it? That's the dilemma.

The door slid open, and Nestor hurried in.

"Kasike! You okay?" He helped Konrau to his feet.

"Damn implant, bato. I tell you, fucking thing hurts!"

"You been saying that for years, Konrau, i naa. Doctor says it's psychosomatic."

"Psychosomatic my natches! Let me gat that fucker in the eye, see how *he* feels later on, puto hosupin."

Even through his bleary eyes, Konrau could see how Nestor tried not to smile at the crack in his boss's normally impeccable self-control. But he knew from experience that amusement wasn't the only emotion the older yegster felt when he saw Beserra this way: he also counted himself honored to be the only person privileged with so much of the kasike's trust. It was an irony that bit at Konrau despite his cold veneer.

"Kalmate, ermano. Here, take a snort."

In a couple of seconds, the drug kicked in and the spasms of pain subsided to a dull ache. Nestor led Konrau to the plush leather couch against the spaceside wall.

"Kwestate," Nestor instructed firmly.

"No, wait. We got business to attend to. Listen. Call Chago, tell him to prepare his boys. One week. The fair. I want them to strike, to strike *hard*. We need to kick this mother into action, got it?"

"Konrau, I still say..."

"With respect, *fuck* what you say. We've survived seven hundred years by being flexible, changing when we needed to. The interstellar corporations are on their way out, like the dinosaurs. Holing drives have opened the universe up. There'll be even more colonizing, and we're going to be there from the beginning. New base, new face. Jitsu's our trial run. Don't fuck it up, Nestor."

The moku began to numb his mind, and the twinge of guilt he felt at his deception of the older brother slowly began to fade, along with all other emotion.

"Pa naa, Kasike."

"And tell that sneaky pocho bastard he better kick me up a twenty-five percent give on those offerings he dumped, less he prefers to pay digital."

Konrau weakly waved the fingers of one hand to clarify his meaning.

As Nestor left to arrange the hit, Konrau sank into the sofa and let the drug pull him down into oblivion. He hated using, but at least this way he wouldn't have to see Jeini's broken body everywhere, accusing him silently.

The sound of his weapon, echoing in his memories, would be stilled.

And for a while, he could imagine that all was well.

CHAPTER 10

ALL WEEK BRANDO PRACTICED, HIS FINGERTIPS BLISTERING AS they reaccustomed themselves to the regimen, his throat sore till he finally accepted the change in his voice and began playing in a different key.

Late Thursday afternoon, Modupe popped his head through the door to Brando's bedroom, smiling.

"Sounds good, mate! Solid strumming, fluid and syncopated. And your voice is very soothing. Nice, gentle baritone."

"Thanks, old man. But I'm trying to get Tenshi Koroma's attention, not yours," Brando joked. Despite the compliment and their banter, he still felt inadequate.

On Friday afternoon, he polished the guitar's cherry neck with its silver frets to a pleasing luster, restrung the guitar with a lighter gauge of string, and searched on-line for a classy outfit, which he had delivered that evening.

Though he wanted to impress Tenshi, he had no idea how. He could dress well, try to accentuate whatever physical attributes she might find attractive. But she wasn't like the various models, writers and programmers he'd dated in Milan, certainly not like that airhead Ayanna. He wouldn't be able to dazzle her with flash.

Maybe with ability.

Saturday morning, he arrived at the fairgrounds, which were going up at the edge of the Mashkanu prefecture, about thirty minutes from the administrative district that contained Juresh and the university. It took him a moment to catch his breath: completed, Tenshi's complex of buildings appeared to be a single living organism extracted from some hidden dimension, flowing incomprehensibly but beautifully about him. The colors, shapes, textures all came together to transport the viewer to another plane: gnosis realized in concrete, stone, glass and steel.

He noticed a group of uniformed men dispersing throughout the compound, presumably members of Jitsu's Civil Security, on hand to prevent any violence. By all accounts, they were unprepared for such contingencies, but the massacre of two weeks ago necessitated their presence. Brando hoped they'd hang back, not make themselves an intrusion while at the same time being prepared to step in should something happen.

For Tenshi's sake, if for nothing else, he wanted everything to go off without a hitch.

The other participants were beginning to arrive as well. Modupe had already been there for some time, Brando discovered as he approached the pavilion where they'd be performing. He and his compatriots were in the middle of their routine, and despite the older professor's earlier protestations, he wasn't half-bad. After their dance, Modupe stepped down and greeted him.

"So, what'd you think?"

"Your old bones will probably hold up, mate. Just don't try and make a career out of it."

"Let me introduce you the others." He gestured to the two women and three men stepping down from the platform. "Anasi and Sadiku," the women, twins apparently, smiled warmly, "Plus Obiako, Akin and Odun. Great drinkers and dancers all."

Brando shook all their hands in turn. Like Modupe, the five were natives of New Nigeria, a moon orbiting Feututea in the Centauri B system, each slender and tall. They gave him warm smiles and firm, friendly nods.

"Why are yall here so early?"

"We're second." Anasi, or maybe it was Sadiku, gestured at a large holographic display next to the pavilion. "The roster's over there if you want to take a look."

He excused himself, promising to join them for lunch after the practice run-through. He soon found his name on the display, bracketed by a New Meccan dance routine and a comedian from Titan. *Great.* Actually, it wasn't bad. No musical competition immediately before or after to be compared to.

The day went by swiftly, with most of the acts practicing and getting their sound mixes set to everyone's satisfaction. He and Modupe shared a lunch of spiced fruits and fried shredded beef with the other dancers and a handful of colleagues who were also performing. At about 1 pm, people began to arrive, booths were opened throughout, and the fair got underway.

Close to 3:30 people began to drift toward the pavilion. Bleachers rose out of the ground, and everyone found a place to sit, though some had to make do with a cushion on the granite slabs that served as a floor. At about four o'clock, Shuku Kikwete, the Speaker of the Chamber of Deputies, stepped onto the platform and motioned everyone to silence. Before him, a holographic projector base hummed to life, and a miniature of the Eta Cassiopeiae 2 system shimmered into existence above their heads.

"Citizens of Jitsu and esteemed visitors, Pathwalkers and brothers of other faiths, welcome to a celebration of 150 years since this planet's colonization by Soltec Industries in 2533, the first corporate possession of a world, the first planet outside of the Solar system to ever sustain human life."

The hologram zoomed toward *Higante*, Jitsu's sun, past the icy desolation of Banken and the pink swirls of Kurishto. In seconds, Jitsu rotated with stately calm above the crowd. Brando reflected bemusedly that quite a few people would challenge Kikwete's claims about Jitsu: Dhara, the principal world in the Rigil Kentaurus system, had held a largish human population of terraformers for several years before Jitsu was settled.

"Jitsu was found by what it seemed an accident: a rift in the very fabric of false space shot Mother Domina here, where she lived for almost two years, writing her gnosis-bequeathing journals until she was at the end translated. Too late to keep her fleshly prison alive so she could enlighten us more, the Centauri Imrizabu, the 'Conduit,' was discovered. Humans came to Jitsu, but all they found was her bones and the Journals."

The holographic image now showed a stern, dark-headed man kneeling beside a sun-bleached skeleton, picking up a data pad. Many Neogs present bowed their heads for a moment. Brando, who had read over Jitsu's history on the voyage from Earth, now recalled some details of Domina Ditis' unfortunate and tragic life: her uncle, a vile criminal named Zamilan something, had abused her for years. When the psychopath's ship had been pulled through the Centauri Rift, it had crashed on Jitsu. No one was really sure what happened in the two years that had transpired before the infamous Dédalo Mostrenco found the Conduit, but when he arrived at the planet, the only remains he'd discovered had been Domina's.

"Rather than sanctify the world, they decided to exploit it. The imrizabu led here, so it made sense to Soltec for them create a stopover on this planet. Ships coming through the Conduit suffered significant structural damage, required repairs before moving outward. It made sense to set up repair platforms in orbit, mine the planet for raw material. But colonizing Jitsu, that was a massive undertaking."

An understatement, reflected Brando. Some five hundred thousand employees had been transferred to the world from Jovian platforms, from the Belt, from Soltec's headquarters on Mars, and from Dhara. It had been the most populous exodus in all of human history.

Speaker Kikwete continued, "Dédalo Mostrenco, the Discoverer of the Journals, was the company president then, and he called it Ares, because it reminded him of Mars. In a disgraceful show of perversity, rather than use the planet right, they strip-mined it till Soltec got everything it wanted and moved on to other business."

An image of Jitsu rotated, slowly growing craterous blemishes on its sickly surface. At the bottom of the image, holographic numbers gradually flicked from 2530 to 2555, presumably the time span of the mining.

"But the environment was totally devastated, plants and animals in danger of extinction, and the thin atmosphere was getting unbreathable. The Consortium of Planets, Corporations and Colonies tried to get Soltec to repair the damage, and the company dumped that responsibility on the employees living here. Our ancestors. The solidarity required to effect such an enormous task created a sense of community in those living on Ares, and in 2585 they petitioned the CPCC for independent colony status. The Diet refused."

Scenes of an aging Dédalo Mostrenco gesturing angrily from a dais before the legislature of human space scrolled above them. Brando grimaced inwardly. The Diet hadn't simply refused: Soltec had forced it to. Mostrenco had considerable pull in the interstellar Diet and had not only gotten the petition refused but also Ares' semi-autonomy cancelled. The company wanted to keep Ares as a stopover, where ships headed deeper into space, toward Mu Cassiopeiae 2 and beyond, could refuel and get repaired.

"For the next eighteen years, they called our planet the Fueling Station," continued the speaker as the images showed ships zipping out of the roiling blue mouth of the imrizabu and into Eta Cassiopeiae 2. The hologram shifted toward the planet again, where an early version of Station City was under attack by brown-robed guerillas. "Finally, in 2603, a group of Pathwalkers called the *Ami ki Jitsuno Ominira* took control of Soltec's headquarters on Ares and declared the planet an independent colony, renaming it in honor of the Holy Mother of the 3rd dispensation, Domina Ditis. Jitsu in Baryogo. The AJO was well organized and most of the population supported them, so it was relatively simple for them to come up with a comprehensive charter and government. But Soltec didn't want to let us go, and it had the Diet in its pocket. Sixteen years of war came next, which only ended because Mostrenco died in an explosive suicide that closed the Conduit forever."

The holographic image shifted abruptly to the mouth of the imrizabu as it collapsed in a sputter of indigo. It had been a defining moment for the CPCC, history professors had assured Brando. Jitsu and the other six worlds on the far side of the Conduit—five in the Nereus system and one hugging Mu Cassiopeiae B—were physically cut off from humanity till the Lieske drive was invented almost fifty years later.

Kikwete gestured at the micstrand before him. "We could still communicate with the Consortium by tunneling, though, and in 2621, as some here today will recall, Jitsu petitioned the CPCC for independent colony status, and they recognized us. Ten years later, we had ambassadors on the other corporate worlds that were still part of the CPCC, the only part of it existing this far from Sol, and by 2638, our first university was built right outside Juresh. When the first Centauri-based AF ships defenestrated outside our system two decades later, we had already established our own way of life.

"We won our independence, and we'll keep on rebuilding our world to show fellow humans everywhere the strength of the *Path* they name Neo Gnosticism and the good things it can add to our interstellar society. There's still considerable work to do, cleaning up the southern continent and then the Salty Sea, but we'll get it done, Pathwalker and off-worlder, side by side, united for Jitsu's future."

Kikwete's closing phrase was greeted by thunderous applause, though Brando noted that some people held back, specifically non-Pathwalkers whose experience with extreme Dominians had made them wary of Jitsu's jingoistic tendencies. With a sweeping bow, the speaker introduced the man who would address the audience next.

"Please, welcome our special guest, Major Michiyu Sosa, hero and patriarch!"

The crowd surged to its feet as the ninety-six-year-old soldier stepped sprightly onto the stage and took a bow. When they'd quieted down, his raspy voice boomed out authoritatively.

"I won't speak as long as my brother here, because like yall, I want to see the performances. Just want to remind yall, while we sit under this amazing pavilion, what we fought for. The right to follow The Path. The Ogdoad made that infidel Mostrenco kill himself in the Conduit for a reason: so that we could pursue our salvation with no interference from outsiders. As long as we don't forget that fundamental truth, the fight wasn't in vain."

Brando looked around for Tenshi as the applause rippled throughout the throng. He wanted to gauge her reaction. But if she was nearby, it was somewhere she couldn't be easily noticed.

Probably meant to calm the Dominians. Don't want a big scene, I bet. All this construction has them bent out of shape, no doubt. Then Kikwete, a major reformer, makes the dedication speech. Let them save a little face, this way. Smart.

As the major left, a gnarled man with silver locs took his place on the stage. In his corded hands was an unfamiliar instrument—an almost spherical body, long neck, with two wood handles on either side.

A hushed awe settled over the crowd. Brando quietly queried for information. His lenses displayed information in the air above the elder.

<Soriba Kamara. The jeri mushindi or bard laureate of Jitsu. Master of the twenty-one-stringed kora. Composer of planetary epic *Kunyukaga ra-Ratowanin*

or *Rise of the Archons.*>

Though the language was dense and full of unfamiliar allusions, Brando managed to follow that deep and creaky voice. As his fingers plucked at his instrument, Soriba Kamara sang a fragment of his massive ballad, describing the second Oracle's selection of Ajabu Rangachira as Jitsu's first archon after he had demonstrated his connection to the Ogdoad.

Once the strings of the kora fell silent, it was time for the other performers. There were dancers, singers, magicians, programmers, comedians, and more. A bit of everything, from Mars, the Jovian platforms, the extra-solar Consortium settlements, the half-dozen older corporate worlds, and nearly every other niche humanity had managed to insinuate itself into.

All except Earth, and Brando would be representing it, so to speak, after this next act, a Pathwalker dance that most people seemed familiar with because as it was announced the applause was deafening.

While he was debating once again just which of the songs to sing—or which to sing first, in the event that he was well received—the dance began. There was no music, just a slow, complex rhythm clapped out by the dancers as they slowly shuffled their feet, shifting their bodies in a series of syncopated shudders. There was a gradual build-up, both in speed and complexity, over the course of two minutes or so, till the dancers broke out into a sweeping display of leaps and spins, their white linen suits whistling and full of wind, their feet constantly stomping the stage except when pushing their bodies into the air. The dancers' hands became a blur as they twisted and twirled and exploded in a thousand complex movements of hair, clothes, limbs.

Soon their eyes closed, and their hands began to sustain a peculiar, almost eerie beat that the audience, at least the Neogs, began to pick up and echo in their clapping and stomping.

"Mothergod," Brando muttered.

"Amazing, no?"

Brando was startled out of his near trance. It was Tenshi, hair down, a sleeveless white linen dress cinched loosely about her waist with a multi-colored scarf that accentuated her hips.

"What is it? Why are their eyes closed? What's all this weird clapping?"

"The *wende*."

"The windy what?"

"No. Wende. An Oturituno—that is, Pathwalker—word. A state. When someone's self reaches out, tries to become a soul. The dancers are attempting to touch the Eight, you see. You get a feeling, Brando. Like *zazen*, but stronger. The world fades away. Just you and the Eight, stretching out, wanting contact. We call it the *Blue* in Standard."

"Wait. You call it the *Blue*?"

"Yes. *Awomi*. Sacred color of Sopiya. You seem startled. Everything okay?"

Brando felt the oddest twist in his gut. Coincidences always had that effect on him. He understood their statistical likelihood, but he couldn't help the shivers that spread throughout his body.

"I know what song I've got to sing."

"Inspired?"

"Kind of."

Tenshi suddenly tilted her head and stared off into space, as if listening to the Ogdoad herself. A moment of cognitive dissonance made Brando imagine she was the Oracle, snuck out of her hideaway and brought to regale all humanity with the wende. But of course, it was just a comring she wore in her ear; her sub vocalic response was not a schizoid break. He could have slapped himself for such idiotic and indulgent fantasies.

"Excuse me. Talk to you after?"

"Yeah, course. Wish me luck."

"Don't believe in it. Do your very best, though. Show them what you've got."

Somehow that was much better than "good luck" could ever be.

His name was announced, and he ascended the steps, unconsciously wiping the sweat from his palms. A stool was brought out, as was his guitar, and he sat before the crowd, quickly adjusting the strings' tuning. He lifted his face, the first of Jitsu's suns dipping below the horizon behind him.

"When I was a child," he told the audience," my father sang me this song. It always meant a lot to me, and I think you'll find something in for you if you listen closely. It's pretty short, so if you indulge me, I'll sing it three times:

in Italian, one of my native languages, in Standard, and in Baryogo. The last two are my own translations: if there's any mistakes in them, they're mine, not my pappà's. He only made one mistake in all his life, as far as I know."

What the hell am I saying?

He began strumming softly, and sang:

"Penso che un sogno cosi non ritorni mai piu: Mi dipingevo le mani e la faccia di blu."

Polite. Attentive. They like the music though. Would pappà approve?

"Volare, cantare nel blu dipinto di blu, felice de stare lassu."

Into the bridge now; pappà always did that syncopated strumming here. Try it, then slow to picking. The music. The Blue.

"Una musica dolce suonava sol tanto per me."

And the music began to resonate just for him. The people faded away. Tenshi's buildings flowed around him, thrumming in harmony, the deepening azure of the sky trembling above.

Brando switched to Baryogo, and line *niboraru, nikantaru en paransek awomi rai pin* fit seamlessly with the dance he'd just seen. Something was speaking to him, something just beyond the edges of perception. The song was drawing him closer, and his heart beat madly in his chest, yearning for an unfathomable union.

His voice rough with emotion, he repeated the song final time, in Standard, drawing out the bars, slowing the tempo until the song became a hymn:

Impossible that such a dream could ever come true:

I am smearing my hands and face with luxurious blue,

When of a sudden the wind gusts like some divine sigh

And lifts me gradually into the infinite sky.

Then, ripping through his soul, came the refrain.

"I'm dying," the lake, cold and dead, "I'm flying," the sky, mockingly clear, "into the blue-spangled blue, happy to be born anew."

As tears began running down his cheeks, he clutched his guitar and quickly left the stage as the crowd clapped and whistled with gusto.

That's not how I first translated that line, he thought, shuddering, overcome. *"Happy to be there with you." If I were only able to, Pappà. If you had only given me the chance.*

He remembered standing at the lake's southernmost edge, water warmed to just above freezing by huge geothermal heat conductors beneath the surface. Still, blue tinged white, an expansive mirror in which he had seen himself framed by the sky.

Jump. Jump. Your own father despises you so much that he left without a word.

No. He spoke.

Oh, yes. That's right. Came into your room, didn't he? What for? He wanted that belt, the one he'd lent you. You stirred, opened your eyes, and he said…

Go to sleep, son.

His last words to you. And what sleep do we know so tritely lasts forever?

Death.

That's right, Brando. Now jump.

He'd shaken off the voice for a second and tilted his head as far back as possible, peering at the sky. His father was out there, now, a clichéd god-figure in the sky. But what a breath-taking sky, so deeply blue it seemed layered, swaths of azure one atop another.

What do you think you are? It had seemed to jeer at him. *Insignificant. Do you really think your death means anything? The world will continue spinning beneath me long after you've gone, long after every living thing on this planet has been consumed by time, long after I deepen to black. Kill yourself, if that's what you wish. Just don't pretend anyone will care. The only one who could possibly care is you, and if you don't, the universe can't be bothered to, either.*

"Brando?"

He finished sealing his guitar into its case with a quick slide of his finger and stood to face Tenshi, who looked at his drying tears with a puzzled expression.

"Kanshon mishgutachu ka?" The switch to Baryogo was deliberate: he wanted her to speak her mind at ease, in her native language. He desperately needed to hear her say certain things and hoped this change would make her more comfortable, make her open up to him like he desperately wanted. Needed.

"Yes, I did. Incredible job. Excellent singing for a professor, though the song probably appealed more to the Dominians than the reformers. It was neutral enough, though, and very—pretty."

"Thanks. I changed some things around, last minute. It's really supposed to be a love song, not a reflection on enlightenment. But, hey, interpretation is a tricky thing."

"That's why I was never big on literature. I prefer things that are simply what they appear to be. "

"Describes me perfectly. I'm an Italian professor of linguistics with an adequate singing voice. Nothing lurks beneath the surface. "

"I'd like to believe that, Brando, though something tells me you're more complicated than you'll admit. "

He shrugged in reply. She motioned him toward the back exit behind the stage.

"Arojin Meji Pishan has arranged for several like minds to meet at the Majority Leader's flat in Juresh. We're going discuss the massacre and what the reformer reaction should be, especially in light of the Dominians' immediate attempts to spin the incident and incite anti-outsider sentiment. I realize you're probably not completely up to snuff on our political situation, but it'd be good to have someone from the University there."

"Sure. Count me in."

Who cares about the politics? I just need to spend time closer to her. It was irrational. They only just met, but he felt an emotional hunger gnawing at him, and either it would be satiated now, or he would begin to despair.

Nodding his thanks to the other participants who congratulated him, Brando hurried out the exit behind Tenshi. She led him through the maze of stalls and galleries on the north side of the pavilion to the administrative landing pad. Her transport, a sleek black machine that reflected the setting sun's reddish light in a dull maroon haze, opened its access port at the touch of her hand, and they both clambered inside and sat at the interface. She instructed it to fly to the Speaker's residence, and they settled in for the ten-minute flight.

"Who's going to be at this little get-together?" Brando asked.

"Obviously the Speaker and Meji Pishan, who'll probably be named Kinguyama's new giya..."

"Don't prefects select giya? Hard to believe your uncle would put a reformer in charge of the teyopan he once controlled."

"No, of course not. But there's a strong reformer faction in the town, and they intend on petitioning the Archon himself to choose Pishan. Most of the teyopanjin support them, despite any political differences. They've built up a great reputation, having been a stable part of the town's Council of Anshyano for more than a decade. I can't imagine the Archon not saying yes if 80% of the teyopanjin want them as giya."

"The Archon's been leaning toward reforms anyway, hasn't he?"

"Yes. He's the one who established the Chamber of Deputies eight years ago and guaranteed last year's clean elections, which made us reformers the legislative majority. You'll also get to meet Jitsu's Minister of Immigration,

Omero Mori; the mayor of Station City, Seni Chunhawan; and the prefect of the nearly completely reformer Arusha district, Yuki Umkapa."

"Mothergod. I'm going be so out of place."

"Not true, you'll hold your own with them, believe me. They've got fancy titles. Otherwise, they're quite accessible. Promise."

"Fine. Just don't expect me to do much talking; I don't understand the situation well enough to have formed an expressible opinion."

"I'm sure they'll do more than enough talking for all of us. That's what they're good at."

A silence settled over both of them, but it was a comfortable quiet, not the uneasy lack of anything to say that mars so many forced conversations. They regarded each other quietly, both marveling at how nice it felt to sit across from someone without feeling the need to yap away about absolutely nothing.

After a minute or two of this, a soft blip from the terminal announced their proximity to Speaker Kikwete's flat in downtown Juresh. The transport autoed down onto the tarmac, where the Speaker's wife Sachiko waited to escort them inside. The number of transports on the pad seemed to indicate that the majority of the invited parties had already arrived; once inside, Brando could see this was true.

Kikwete greeted them as they walked in, his long sideburns pointing to his lips as if to signal his office; Umkapa stood from the cushion she'd been sitting on to incline her shaved head in their direction; Pishan and Mori raised their drinks in welcome, the former's lighter honey-toned skin contrasting with the ebony depth of the latter's; and the heavily tattooed mayor of Station City welcomed them in halting Baryogo:

"Welcome to a meeting of vigilantes."

Tenshi smiled. "People have always loved vigilantes, mayor. Let's hope they love us enough to back us up as we take down the extremists."

"No small talk, eh, Tenshi?" Pishan grabbed a cushion and eased onto the shining wood floor.

"No time for it, Anshyano. My uncle's been busy, as I'm sure you've all noticed, and we need to discuss what's going to be done about him."

The mayor sighed. "There's no real evidence he's involved. And his wife—"

Tenshi raised a hand to stop him. "I know the man better than you. Trust me. His hands are bloody."

Mori cleared his throat. "I hear through the grapevine that Arojin Koroma wants to establish an anti-terrorism squad. With himself as its minister, I should add. He went directly to the Archon with the proposal, bypassing certain heated debate on Kikwete's turf, and tried to get the Archon to set up the squad as an executive order in time of crisis, which our charter provides for."

Kikwete's face was expressionless. "What was Rawe's response?"

"He refused to do it. But he apparently liked the idea of the squads. He's drawing up a proposal, or rather, Bek is drawing it up. He'll submit it to the Chamber next week."

"By Domina, I'll not put that power-hungry Koroma in charge of a bunch of soldiers. I'm sure we can fix things so that the minister in charge of the squads will either be selected by a majority of deputies or voted into office by the public at large."

Umkapa interjected. "Where was Arojin Koroma planning on getting people for these squads? If Civil Security soldiers are sufficient for his proposal, why not simply use CS to quell any further terrorism?"

"He wants to pull in the surviving JLA members as officers and recruit off-world soldiers to serve under them."

Mayor Chunhawan blinked incredulously.

"Off-worlders, Mori?"

"Yeah, Seni. Seems weird to me, too."

"Don't trust him." Everyone turned to face Brando. *What the hell am I doing? These people don't need my advice.*

"Want yall to meet Professor Brando D'Angelo of Milan, Earth." Tenshi nodded at him to continue, her eyes glazing over with barely suppressed dread.

"Seems to me Koroma's milking this as much's he can. Squads full of off-worlders, patrolling the streets of Pathwalker towns… Anybody else think this will make anti-reform sentiment swell?"

"Shite." Tenshi grimaced and closed her eyes. "The bastard's thought of everything. If you hold passage of the measure up, Speaker, he'll accuse you of endangering citizens in order to capitalize on the tragedy for political gain."

"But that's what he's trying to do!"

"Right. Brilliant, no? Reformers want more off-worlders immigrating, Santo's going show Jitsujin that they need to fear them through his spin on the massacre and placement of non-native soldiers in civilian areas. If the Chamber tries to make the squads more democratically controlled, he'll say yall were using the massacre as an excuse to push more reform. Can't win."

Incredulous, Brando saw her bend her head ever so slightly forward as she turned her back to the group.

Defeated? Impossible.

Umkapa stood, visibly irritated. "We need to preempt him by calling an emergency meeting of the Chamber and proposing our own version of the squads before Bek, who we all know favors Santo, gets a chance to submit the Archon's supposed proposal."

"How early can we do this?" asked the Mayor

"We may be able to get everyone together tomorrow," the Speaker mused, "but our best chance is early Monday morning."

Tenshi shook her head. "Bad idea, yall."

"You don't trust us?" Kikwete asked. "Or do you not think deputy-controlled squads will be effective?"

"There's a reason we don't have police, Speaker. They end up trampling on citizens' rights. Our system—community-based service providers and conflict resolvers coordinated by teyopan and overseen by each town's Councity of Anshyano—works well enough. And bigger problems get dealt with well enough by Civil Security. Creating cops and putting them under the Chamber of Deputies is still *creating cops.* It flies in the face of everything we stand for."

Yuki Umkapa gave a weak laugh. "Your ideological purity blinds you, Tenshi. If we don't act, your uncle will police *all of us.* At least this way, we're calling the shots. Or what do you suggest we do instead, huh?"

"Prefect Umkapa, I've told yall before: get the CPCC involved. I don't understand why ambassador Enver's not at this meeting. We are a valuable symbol for the Consortium: they want badly for us to join them, setting an example both for the other corporate holdings leaning toward secession and for the independent worlds that've been discovered recently. The consortium would do everything in their power to keep Jitsu open and free of the sort of bigotry my uncle espouses."

It was Speaker Kwikete's turn to shake his head. "Absolutely not. This is a local matter, Tenshi. I understand the affection you feel for the ambassador and her staff, but we have to keep local autonomy in peacekeeping work."

"If you insist on beating Santo to the punch on this authoritarian scheme, you'd better move fast." Tenshi's voice was cold. "Monday will be too late. He *must* have already considered the possibility that you'd try to establish squads first."

Nodding somberly, they all fell together around Kikwete's comtable, hashing out the details of an anti-organized crime unit. Brando realized after a moment that Tenshi wasn't around. Glancing about, he noticed curtains moving slowly in the evening breeze that blew in across a balcony contiguous to the room.

He waited through another couple of minutes of chatter and then excused himself. He found her outside, leaning against a column that held up the veranda's roof, pulling her hand languidly away from her mouth and exhaling smoke. It took him a moment to process what she was doing.

"Smoking a sikar," he said a bit incredulously. The one substance more forbidden on Earth than sugar: tobacco.

Her head turned slightly as she took a final drag and flicked the remainder into the darkness.

"Yes, I am. Was. Nasty habit, I know, but we all have at least one. Tell me, what's yours?"

What a question.

"I spend too much time thinking," he admitted.

"Ah, that's one of the worst, especially when you don't act on what you're thinking."

"Did you come out to smoke or to avoid the planning?"

"Both. I'm frustrated, tired of the same old rhetoric. Lots of talk about stopping the ultra-Dominians. I prefer action. Why sit around discussing what we should do? If we should do it, then let's do it. If you only knew how many times they've talked about solutions before, about preempting the extremists..."

"But they are doing something this time, aren't they?"

"Oh, Brando, they're so damn slow. I've been telling these fools to eliminate him for years, but they never acted. Domina, I hate feeling so impotent. So I'm out here, relieving tension via nicotine." She flashed a weak smile. "What's your excuse? Our backward theocracy strike you as idiotic?"

Brando laid his hands on the metal railing of the balcony. "Sorry, I have some history. I was brought up in a religious household: my aunt and my mom are clerics, my grandmother directed music. They used to make me sing and tell stories before the congregation. Church always came first. I have no more patience for religious politics."

"Why'd you come Jitsu? Not to be mean, but it seems inane for an atheist, if that's what you are, to come to this place. Are you punishing yourself?"

"No." *Oh, mothergod, yes.* "And I'm not an atheist. Agnostic, let's say. Searching. Besides, I hear you're not exactly the acme of Neo Gnosticism yourself."

"Don't believe the Dominian hype. I walk the Path better than most." Her supernova eyes glinted in the starlight. "You've rejected Wiccan Catholicism, then. Do you still think people have souls?"

"As has been proven time and again, we're biological and cultural animals. I don't know that there's a way for us to be more eternal than what we leave behind us."

Tenshi raised an eyebrow. "Oh, I like that."

Brando wasn't sure whether she was serious.

"But answer my first question: why'd you come?" Tenshi waited for a response with unwavering gaze.

He mulled it over. "I came looking for, oh, what's the word," he muttered as he flipped through mental databases and came up blank. "Damn it, my Baryogo is so terrible..."

"Say it in Standard, Professor. I do speak it, if you recall. Not as well as you, but..."

He barked, "Simplicity," cutting her off, irritated yet pleased again at the sound of his title in Baryogo: Kyosu.

"Hmmm, guess you're looking for *tanjun*."

"Wow. That's an old word. Yall still use that here."

"Uh, yes. Never seen anyone get excited about a word before. Except maybe my uncle, but that's another story."

"I'm a linguist: that's what we do. Tanjun. Interesting."

"You're pronouncing it wrong."

"Excuse me?"

"Yes. You do the exact same thing with all your 'oo' sounds. Sounds like you're trying to speak Solpat or something."

"That's the way Baryogo's spoken closer to Sol. I've noticed the difference, of course, but there was no time to work on it."

"Look," she said, and reached out her hand to lightly grip his jaw. Her fingers were thin and soft, except for calluses at the tips and base. Brando felt a shock thrill through him at her touch, as if he'd been infused with electrical ichor from some stormy protogod. "Your lips have to—come on, loosen up—they have to purse out a little. Yes, that's it."

Her fingertips brushed his lips for a tortuous second. "Now try it?"

"Tanjun."

"No, still not right. Try again? Wait, think I see the problem."

She cupped her hand against his larynx, an exquisite feeling he wished he had the power to slow down time to sustain. "Say it?"

"Okay, that's what I thought. Here's the problem." She reached down, took his hand, and placed it at the base of her own throat. Her neck was smooth and hard, like touching some ancient Enrico Butti sculpture in Milan, but warm and pliant, the blood throbbing rapidly through her jugular, a bronze statue come to life and thrumming with the heat of a thousand impassioned sculptors.

"Tanjun," she said. "You feel? No vibration, Brando. Pure. Got to whisper the oos." She returned her hand to his throat. His remained on hers, trembling now, quickened by her pulse. He noticed the close back unrounded vowel, unvoiced into a light whisper. It slipped, nearly imperceptible, between the B and the R of his name when she pronounced it with her husky voice.

That's the sound, he thought. *Like a phantasm, almost not there, a shadow of a vowel.*

"Do it?" she instructed.

He said the word with deliberate care, every centimeter of his flesh aware of her nearness to him, electric and warm.

She repeated it, her eyes fixed on his. Those supernovae forced all else from his field of vision, threatening to drown him in eternal joy.

Her hand slipped to the back of his neck, under the hair that brushed his shirt collar.

"Come here," she murmured as she pulled him close. His right arm came up and he plunged both hands into the erinys darkness of her hair as their hungry mouths together, passionate and slow, desperate for the moment, but determined to let it last. After what could've been seconds or centuries, they slowly, reluctantly pulled apart.

"Five minutes and we're at my flat," she mumbled hoarsely into his ear, her skin flush with a palpable desire.

Brando nodded, unable to speak, passion making him giddy with vertigo.

They ducked back inside. Tenshi's colleagues were still immersed in a heated argument as to the composition of the squads

"I'm sorry, yall, but Professor D'Angelo needs to get back to campus. Loop me in on the comchain later, yeah?"

They all exchanged the briefest of goodbyes. Then Tenshi led Brando to the rooftop. Her transport was long and black and it ripped through the night like their passion rendered in speeding steel. The two stared at each other during the entire five-minute trip, hungry, silent.

As the *Tarhiata* autoed into the landing bay, they fell upon each other again. She keyed the lock with her eyes closed and didn't break from their embrace as she dragged him from the transport's interior. They crossed the bay, tugging at each other's clothes, desperate to get their hands on each other's flesh. The doors opened onto her suite and they spun inside, as if dancing, unwilling to let go for fear of losing the moment, through living room and kitchen and into the darkness of her bedroom, where their clothes finally came off and they spent hours becoming as acquainted with each other's bodies as they were with their own, by touch and smell and taste, the black swirling around them like the primal matrix, warm and wet and ubiquitous.

INTERCHAPTER B

Encrypted message

Intercepted by Al-Muzzamml outpost 13-ES

19 May, 2683 15:32:14 (SST)

Decrypted via Arietid quantum cipher

Sweet Secret Watcher,

All the pieces are on the board.

I know you want to swoop in, snatch me up. But yours is a patient soul. Wait.

If I have returned from beyond the Grey Prison, peeled myself from the Eight, it is to teach a lesson that humanity will never forget.

The Brotherhood. The Extremists who have strayed from the Path and yet dare call themselves Dominians. The self-righteous Reformers and their insufferable Architect.

The Consortium itself. Broken. Burning.

That future is what we strive toward. Tearing the false face from the cosmos.

I have found a better way to commune with you, Beloved. Soon.

Watch the news.

—Your Unblind Mistress

CHAPTER 11

THE MORNING LIGHT FILTERED IN, TINGED PEACH BY ITS PASSAGE through the bone-shaded drapes, making every curve and angle of Tenshi's body and face stand out in an angelic glow. Brando lay at her side, propped on one elbow, regarding her longingly and trying to assess his feelings for her.

With a soft mumble, Tenshi stirred awake. Blinking the sleep from her eyes, she crinkled them in the sincerest smile Brando'd ever seen.

"Morning. How long have you been like that?"

"Don't know, forty-five minutes or so. You're beautiful, know that?"

"Come on, shut up." She made a grab for the silvery sheets, but Brando stopped her hands. Such self-conscious modesty seemed out of place in her.

"Serious," he said. "You are."

"I'm too short and too muscular. That's what everyone says."

"Since when have you paid attention to what people say?"

She tilted her head in mock cogitation, then nodded. "Good point."

"Besides, they're nuts. Your body is… well it's perfect, that's all." He ran his fingers slowly between her breasts and down the firmly ridged softness of her abdomen. "To be frank, you're a damn goddess. No idea why you're interested in a bloke like me."

Tenshi scowled. "Don't put yourself down, Brando. What do you mean, a bloke like you? You've got to show more respect for yourself, you want others to. You're handsome, intelligent, talented. All you need's a little determination and fire, you'd be a perfect man."

"Ah, so you admit I'm not."

"None of us are perfect. Some of us strive for perfection, though. That's what separates us from the rest."

Brando nodded. "Didn't think you'd warm to self-deprecation. Surprised to hear some from your own mouth, just moments ago."

"Okay, okay. So I'm a little hypocritical when it comes to physical appearance." Kissing his chest, she added. "You're also a pretty good lover, by the way. Guess I should've expected it."

Rose tinting his olive brown skin, Brando glanced at the far wall, a broad expanse of white stucco broken by two abstract paintings in which colors swirled like his emotions. "What do you mean?"

"Well, you're from Milan. Sei cattolico wiccano, vero?

"Ooh, she knows Italian!" Brando joked, wishing he could deflect what he knew was coming. "Did you pick up a little from—what was that biologist's name? Spinelli?"

Tenshi laughed. "Jealous?"

"Maybe. But, yeah, I was raised Wiccan Catholic."

"Isabella told me the Great Rite is at the heart of yall's religion. Union of the Maiden and the Divine Lover. Sexual emancipation at age thirteen, classes on technique to draw down grace through climax, multiple partners by sixteen."

Brando let his head fall back onto the pillow.

"Tenshi, I never exercised my sex rights. My parents were freaked, especially my mamma, who felt embarrassed when I didn't attend classes at my aunt's chapel."

"Why didn't you?" Tenshi folded a pillow under her locs, lifting her head up to look at him better.

"Okay, a little background. I grew up in the Quartiere Africano in the Loreto district of Milan, at the heart of a few busy blocks everyone called Piccolo Kinshasa. Trilingual childhood: Italian, Lingala and French. Standard taught in school. Dozens of other languages spoken throughout Loreto, one of the most diverse places in Italy. I became obsessed. Wanted to speak to everyone in their native tongue. People were amused at first, then they realized I was a prodigy."

"Ah, your mind was elsewhere."

"Exactly. By the time I was of age, it seemed frivolous to rut with every girl and boy the Church considered compatible. Also, around this time, I discovered

Baryogo and, uh, began to fantasize about meeting a native speaker, perhaps from the Belt or platforms."

"Ah-hah," she cried dramatically. "The secret to last night."

"Funny. Yeah, I believed in love. Only person who half-way respected that was my pappà, but after he left…"

As his voice trailed off, he saw the ship growing smaller and smaller, lost in the blue.

"Where did he go?"

Brando paused for a moment as the irony hit him. "He became part of the CPCC's first organized non-corporate colonization team."

Tenshi sat up. "Your father is on Oceania?"

"Yeah. Left us behind. I was fifteen. Bastard's probably remarried."

Her hands clenched at the sheets. "Ever try to contact him?"

The paintings kept drawing his eyes away from her. It was easier to talk about his dad this way, staring into the rainbow maelstroms that the-Four-knew-who had smeared on those canvases. "Nah. Figure that's what he wanted, so why bother him?"

He felt her fingers on his jaw as she pulled his face gently but firmly back toward her. "I'm right here, Brando. Those paintings won't erase that."

Reaching up to his own stubbly chin, he took her hand in his. "Sorry. It's just hard to talk about him."

"Yeah. When people you love abandon you, especially when you're young, that wound never really heals. I was eighteen when Isabella got the job offer. We'd lived together for two years, after meeting on the Southern Continent."

Brando pulled her hand to his chest. "When you were working on a clean-up crew?"

She nodded, two of her locs slipping down over one eye. "She was twenty-four, fresh off her doctorate, doing field research on organisms in the Inland Sea. I was sixteen, a precocious rebel, looking for meaning. One thing led to another. We ended up renting a flat in Station City, till she accepted the position on Oceania. Seems her father had called in some favors. She found it impossible to say no."

Taking a deep breath, Brando tried to wrap his brain around the coincidence. "I'm a skeptic, Tenshi. Not sure I believe in fate. But it boggles the mind that your Italian girlfriend and my Italian father both abandoned us to go live on the same planet."

There was a moment of silence, then Tenshi shrugged. "Very weird."

"The Ogdoad, drawing us together," Brando quipped.

She punched him lightly. "Don't make fun of my religion, kesekki. Anyways, going back to you and sex."

"Oh, spang on!"

"No, not like that." She pushed him away playfully. "Isabella was my first real love, and she was eight years older than me. But she told me it was normal, that Wiccan Catholic teens spend a year partnered with an adult."

"Not everyone. But there's a lot of peer pressure to become some adult's lover. By the end of that year, any innocence you had, any childlike joy you were getting out of life, it's squelched, and you become calculating like all the other grown-ups. Even though I became an outcast because of it, I rejected that shite."

She regarded him intently. "Why? I mean, you were just a kid. How did you know it wasn't right for you?"

"Mothergod, this—" he fumbled for the words "—is hard to explain. Our parish assigned me to a twenty-five-year-old. I went over to her flat, and she unceremoniously took off her clothes and pushed my head toward… well, you get the picture. It was unnerving. So cold. She reminded me of my mom. I kept imagining my mom there, on the bed." His eyes started drifting from Tenshi's face again, drawn toward the ceiling fans. "Shite. This sounds stupid, I know. Sick, even."

"No, I understand. It wasn't real to you, and you backed out. You weren't ready, and she wasn't the one for you. Sounds like the best decision." Maybe sensing his discomfort, she slipped back into a joking tone. "But you must've gotten laid somewhere along the line, because virgins don't get as lucky as you did last night."

"Ha! I dated people at college that were fascinated by my lack of experience. Was a new thing for them. And I guess I brought a passion to it they weren't used to anymore. You start screwing everyone round you at thirteen, by the time you're twenty you've done it all. Leaves you cold, like I said. People whose only goal is having sex—a wonderful activity, don't get me wrong—they seem to me the saddest creatures."

"Oh, I agree," Tenshi nodded, her locs bouncing darkly against the silver bedclothes. "There's so much more to do. Spend all your time on sex, you miss out on nine-tenths, well, maybe seven-tenths of what makes life worth living: commitment, effort, construction. Situation sounds like Jitsu, kind of. We're so centered on ourselves that sex is like two people using each other to masturbate. No connection, just isolated semi-sexual gnosis, you know?"

Brando smiled with sly concupiscence. "Not sure. We should try connecting again, see if we gain some enlightenment."

She smiled her goddess smile, and they slid together eagerly, a pair of outcasts forging a society of two.

AFTER SHOWERING AND EATING A QUICK BREAKFAST, THEY HEADED TO the fairgrounds. Tenshi took him on a tour of the various galleries and museums, where the history and art of Jitsu was displayed beside works from other human populations.

"This planet has art?" Brando asked, squinting at the most abstract pieces.

"Ha, yes," Tenshi said, giving him a little shove. "Of course we do. The majority of it was created by anshyano or other satorijin. Because they've reached basic enlightenment, they get to dabble in transitory acts."

"Like university study," Brando added, nodding. "Yeah, it was in the orientation."

"You see," Tenshi continued, "we're preparing ourselves for gnosis, the second stage in the creation of our souls."

"Ah, you're a satorijin. Makes sense. Your architecture is part of your journey of self-knowledge, right?"

She winked. "Yup. But I'm not Dominian. For me, exploring of the intersection of interior and exterior isn't a preamble to *rejecting* the world, just the image of myself the world attempts to force upon me. Generally, though, satorijin move beyond such exploration and research, becoming arojin, the other-born. Leaving behind all 'fleeting pursuits,' they help run the planetary government, striving to attain quantum enlightenment before they die."

"Running the government seems a pretty fleeting pursuit to me," Brando quipped.

"Well, to them it's a holy edict," Tenshi explained. "During their search for enlightenment, regular folks must be protected and provided for by those closer to the goal. The Oracle expects arojin to pursue not only their own quantum enlightenment, but to provide unencumbered physical lives for all other Pathwalkers in their care."

After a while, they came upon a hub-shaped building that housed a zoological garden of the remaining native species of fauna. Brando had become accustomed to the sight of the kaeruma, a local six-limbed beast of burden of roughly camel-like appearance with a popping gait, a comically wide mouth and three eyes atop its roughly triangular head. Here he became familiar with the moritori, a flying, reptilian creature with wide, butterfly wings, colorful sheets of skin suspended on either side of its serpentine body between four of its six extremities, the other two of which served as legs. The bizarre *hoshika* left Brando with mouth agape: it resembled nothing less than a squid, with six legs evenly distributed around its globular body in a seven-sided geometrical configuration. Its conical head sported three visual patches for panoramic vision, and, as a holographic biologist assured onlookers, an orifice centered on its underbelly served as both mouth and anus.

The zoo also sported a faux-life of the planet in its pristine, pre-Soltec condition. Visitors were treated to the sight of the enormous, fifteen-meter long monsters called jagen, which had roamed Jitsu's vast wastelands for a million years, but which were now confined to the devastated southern continent. Tribes of feathery haired oni, upright, meter-high monkey analogs, converged on a jagen in the recording, swarming over every inch of its bulk, except its snapping jaws. The jagen hadn't noticed their approach because they'd smeared themselves with its dung to stifle their scent; the twenty-five of them dispatched the behemoth quickly.

In the zoo itself was one of the last onis still alive on the northern continent. It was old, balding, and extremely sad. Barking what sounded suspiciously like "shirarugaro"—crude Baryogo for *leave*—at the visitors, the lonely creature seemed at the brink of self-destruction as it shuffled from one edge of its little island to the next.

As Tenshi and Brando approached, the oni scooped a handful of excrement from the ground and made as if to throw it at them. But instead it lifted its arm above its head and began to spread the greenish substance on its face, arms and torso while staring at them blankly.

Brando couldn't help but read a message into the act.

Jagen cannot smell oni when they're covered in jagen shite, as if the oni didn't exist for that jagen.

An oni that stinks of its own waste ceases to exist for itself.

Tenshi leaned heavily against the railing, her locs hanging down about her face so that it took Brando a moment to realize she was crying. His hand at the small of her back, he softly asked what was wrong.

"Nothing." She dug her left palm into her eyes as if embarrassed.

"Come on, Tenshi. Something about that upset you; tell me."

"Don't want to talk about it. Won't do any good."

His hand slipped to her side and he pulled her toward a bench.

"Course it'll do you good. Get it off your chest, at least. Come on, I want to help, okay? Give me a chance."

Tilting her head back, she released a burst of air in a lip-pursing sigh.

"Fine. Just don't like unloading on you like this. My omenim, my twin sister Samanei, she's…"

"The Oracle. Yeah, I know."

She shot a glance his way: hard and indignant, but softening nearly instantly.

"Ah, of course you've heard. How could you not? Anyway, we're exactly the same, except for one detail: she has a mental illness."

"Really?"

"Yeah, and I don't mean it in a hyperbolic way. When we were little, you couldn't tell. Both of us, we looked and acted the same. In the sikoro, the teyopan's religious school, she behaved better than me, but other than that, we were indistinguishable. Then, when we were about ten, she got sick. Nobody knew what had happened: they found her outside my grandma's house, curled into a ball. Bunch of neighbors, they tried to make her react, come out of her trance, making loud noises. Santo came out of Grandma's house, beside himself with anger, wanting to know what happened. Told them he'd take care of Samanei. I pieced this together later, by the way."

"And, what, she came out of it?"

"Yeah. At first, she seemed normal, went to school, was quiet, studied Domina's diary with the rest of us, sucked on tubes, meditated, played with the kleinballs, uplinked to the hypercube exercises, all the regular preteen Pathwalker stuff, you know. Maybe you don't. Whatever." Tenshi tugged roughly on one of her locs, her eyes blinking rapidly. "Thing is, at home, she began acting really strange. Smacking her own face and arms and legs for no apparent reason. Talking alone. Staring into space, eyes open, not meditating, no moku or anything. Just blank. Umma tried keeping it secret, told me not to tell anyone. Apa was usually out making runs to the platforms, so he had no idea."

"But at school, she was the same as before?"

"Until our twelfth birthday. That's when things took a turn for the worse. We had just started to menstruate. No big deal, just a little hard any girl to adapt to. But Samanei… it was like a complete change came over her for two weeks every month. Started screaming obscenities at Umma, in different voices. Throwing things around. At school, she'd get up and kick kleinballs across the room when the anshyano weren't around."

Brando gave a judicious nod. "So she wasn't that gone, eh? She knew when to stop?"

"For a while. Then our bibi—grandmother—died. The cremation and honor ceremony were long, elaborate things. Our family was the heart of Kinguyama. Santo was the giya, Apa—the mishonari—brought pilgrims' offerings, and Bibi had been a pillar of the teyopan for some fifty years. So everyone was there, silent, meditating. Santo went on about his blessed umma's translation. Samanei started to chuckle. Then she started to outright laugh. I mean, she got reallu loud, belly laughs that made tears stream from her eyes."

Tenshi forced a sketchy, insincere smile, but her hand kept yanking on her hair.

"Oh, shite. So now everyone knew?"

"Umma dragged her off, made up some excuse I don't even remember, except that it was pretty weak. People shrugged and moved on, but I saw Santo's face. I didn't like the glint in his eye. The next week, Umma and I flew out to Station City, took Samanei to see a psy-tech. Incipient schizophrenia, he told us. Possible disassociation. Treatable. Curable. Just not on Jitsu. Umma pleaded with him. He said he'd see what he could do. Months later he called: he'd gotten the necessary information and equipment to do the gene therapy. But by then it was too late."

Tenshi closed her eyes, as if visualizing the past, or trying to block it out.

"Umma started keeping Samanei out of school, forcing her to take moku every three hours so she'd be manageable. Apa was out of system for one of those long-distance treks the mishonari do every seven years. Santo started showing up every day, harassing Umma in that slick way of his, not seeming to cut, but leaving you bloody anyway."

Brando nodded. It sounded a bit like his own mother's behavior.

"Did he catch her doing something?"

"Let me finish. His visits got increasingly insistent and abusive, in a mental or emotional way. We were on edge, because Samanei started doing extreme things, even when drugged, like rubbing feces on her face and screaming like a pig at slaughter. Every time, Umma and I would struggle to her cleaned up and calmed down in case Santo happened by. At last, I couldn't deal with it anymore. He was being a total arse to Umma one day, and I went berserk, ran him out of the house. He was genuinely scared. Petty little giya. I put his arse in its place.

"I'd missed too many days at the sikoro, and various teyopanjin, including Santo's wife Maryam, came to take me the next day. I was walking out as Santo rolled up and stepped inside. The teyopanjin more less dragged me along: I wanted to go back in. I was sure something terrible was coming. I hadn't seen my twin all morning. That's when it happened. Umma told me later. He opened the door to our room, and there she was," Tenshi's voice faltered for a moment, then she swallowed heavily and went on, "standing naked, smeared with menstrual blood and her own waste, laughing at him, calling him *ummano toto,* mama's baby, for some reason. But it was her condition that cinched it, you understand?"

Brando tried to grasp what she meant, but couldn't.

"Blood and shite, Brando." Her hand left her hair and gestured with futility in the air. "Schizophrenia. Don't they teach religious history on Earth?"

Chilling understanding dawned on him. "Domina Ditis. She was schizophrenic."

"And her uncle made her cover herself in feces and menses."

Dominian Pathwalker stigmata. He swallowed dryly, nodding. Kikwete's speech the day before had reminded him of the plight of Domina Ditis, and now a shudder went through Brando at some of the parallels. Nausea rose in his gut as he imagined Santo getting away with whatever scheme he was planning, leaving Samanei like Domina, a martyr under the feet of a deadly sociopath.

Tenshi's fists clenched and unclenched impotently. "They took her away from me, Brando. He and Maryam walked her out the door of my house as the teyopanjin held me still. She kept screaming my name, looking back at me as if pleading for my help. But I could do nothing. They took her before the Close, who confirmed she was the next Oracle. Then they sealed her away where I'll never find her. Santo has used her for twelve years to amass more power. Meanwhile, she's all alone, like that oni over there, all alone and I couldn't do a thing."

She broke off, sobbing, and buried herself in his arms. Overwhelmed by his inadequacy, Brando simply held her, hoping that the embrace was what Tenshi needed. They remained that way for several minutes as waves of sorrow gently wracked her, slowing and lessening in intensity till they stopped. Only then did she pull away, red-rimmed eyes regarding him with something akin to shame, perhaps at her own weakness. She didn't avert her gaze, however: they stared at each other in mute comprehension, having understood something essential that they would find impossible to put into words.

"Thank you," she whispered hoarsely.

Brando gave a slight nod, running a thumb under her left eye and bringing the tear it had collected to his lips solemnly. Then he took her head in his hands and whispered:

"Don't blame yourself for things you can't control."

She put her hands over his.

"That's just it. I don't want there to be things I can't control."

LUNCH HOUR ARRIVED, AND THEY SNACKED ON KARUNITA, SPECIALLY seasoned hunks of pork served over cold noodles. Everyone at the stand where they'd bought the meal was excitedly talking about the Jitsu-Mars soccer match that was going to be held in an hour at the western game field. Brando, an avid soccer aficionado, excitedly convinced Tenshi that they should go watch the game, which promised to be a fascinating clash of cultures and styles.

After browsing through the marketplace section of the fair, they noticed a large mass of people making their way toward the west along the path where Brando'd first met Tenshi. The couple wound their way under several trees, passing the bench at which they'd first exchanged words. Brando grazed it with tingling fingers, smiling, and followed Tenshi into the throng that flowed toward the playing field.

NEITHER OF THE LOVERS NOTICED THE BLACK TRANSPORTS fly overhead and set down illegally beside a row of unoccupied food stands slightly ahead of the crowd. They didn't see Chago's crew creep out, konk rifles unslung and lazgats popping into palms, nor did they catch the cap's signals for several of his men to climb atop a pair of Tenshi's breathtaking buildings that flanked the main stone-cobbled path to the field. The fact that half the crew spread out in front of the anxious fairgoers fazed no one: most assumed these were simply officers of Civil Security, keeping their typically unnecessary vigil. The yegsters, cold criminals of the demimundo, that sealed off the path behind the crowd were ignored for more obvious frailties of the human mind: once your back is turned, what's behind you has ceased to exist.

No one, however, could ignore the screams and stampeding chaos that ensued once Chago's men began to open fire on the crowd. Bodies exploded left and right, sending gouts of blood, severed limbs and fragments of internal organs in all directions, a wakeup call to the complacent, a message from death. People began to scatter pellmell, driven by panic into thoughtless flight. Some simply hurried in circles or back and forth between two points, screaming themselves hoarse in absolute terror. There was nowhere to go. Nothing to hide under or behind. They were corralled in like sick cattle.

TENSHI STOOD STILL IN THE MIDST OF THE CARNAGE, HER FEELING OF horror at the slaughterhouse that her fair had become compounded by outrage at the certainty that her uncle had won. She was struck in the chest by a man who'd been knocked backwards by either the force of an explosion or a direct hit from a far-off konk rifle. She dropped to her knees, his head lolling in her lap, blood pouring from his nose, mouth and even eyes, eyes that he turned pleadingly upon her as his hands weakly gripped her arm. She recognized the man as a public transport driver who worked in Station City.

Sweet. Helpful. Dying in her lap as horrific sounds ripped the air.

"Tenshi-zin," he gurgled as he focused near-dead pupils on her. "Shinechayudaro. Dai naseru."

Help me. I'm dying.

And he was gone. The enormity of what was happening washed over Tenshi then, riding the crest of a wave of impotence and anger. A sob twisted her chest, blurring her vision.

"My... my people, Brando." Laying the chauffeur's head on the cobbled street, she slowly stood, her face hardening with resolve. "My people," she repeated, regaining her voice and raising it above the apocalyptic din. "I've got to save them."

AT THE SOUND OF HER VOICE, BRANDO'S NUMBED BRAIN WAS UNABLE TO continue blocking out the unspeakable evil being done around him. Suddenly aware of the massacre, he backed up against the wall of the building, pulling Tenshi along with him.

"The fuck?" He could barely make himself heard above the hellish cacophony of screams, explosions and weapons fire.

"Terrorists or yaks." Yakuza, the popular synecdoche for all underworld types. "The ones that killed the pilgrims." She seemed suddenly calm of mind despite her pulse, which, he noted with hysterical clarity, raced beneath Brando's fingertips, and despite the wild look growing brighter in her eyes. "On the roofs, at the front, in back of us. Shite. Okay, come on."

She slid over to an oval window that had just shattered when a decapitated head slammed against it. Snapping her arm free from Brando's grip, she jumped inside. He followed, not expecting the four-meter drop to the recessed floor. Twisting as he fell, he hit the floor with a scared little hop. His freakish earth muscles in that low gravity sent him rebounding another meter or so into the air before he landed solidly.

Tenshi was already at the back of the large sunken auditorium, thumbing the lockpad of a closet open. As he came up behind her, he saw it was replete with construction tools. She quickly scanned them, then reached out and seized the rebar fastener. She keyed its power to full.

"Grab something, and let's go."

She dashed toward the blood-spattered double doors, through which Brando could see bodies piling up. He dazedly grabbed the first thing he saw, a chrome tool belt, and dashed after her. She shot a rebar through the glass, which splintered and fell away as she kicked it. Out on the street, her face contorted with rage, she took aim at the yak on the top of the building across the path and sent an iron rod spinning outward at 200 kph through the afternoon glare of Jitsu's twin suns and into the charge cartridge of the yak's konk rifle, which promptly exploded in his arms, severing them at the elbow and shoulder, ripping a hole in his chest the size of a kleinball.

She spun around, backing up into the street, and nailed the yak positioned on the auditorium's roof twice: the first bar destroyed his knee, sending him toppling backwards; the second caught him under the chin, boring though his palate, brain and skull, where it remained partially embedded, sealing in his brains as he slammed against the tile, blood spurting from his nose and mouth in arching sprays.

These two deaths took less than a minute. Brando scrambled to fasten the tool belt around his waist, cold dread pounding his head, his bowels feeling distant, as if preparing themselves for some inevitable gut shot.

Turning, Tenshi began sprinting toward the five yaks that had sealed off their retreat, firing as she leapt over the dead or wounded forms covering the stone path she'd designed.

One yak fell, then another. The other three realized what was happening; they swung their weapons around toward Tenshi's maniacal figure. The air was filled with a brutal, skin-crawling sound that Brando realized was coming from her throat.

She was throwing herself at them, screaming like a fury, locs come loose and flying about her like a hundred squirming serpents.

Frigid knives of angst stabbed at his guts. His hand slipped to the belt. He couldn't move. His hand felt the hammer there. She was going to die. His legs began to move. *I'm going to lose her.* Pounding the stone, feet slipping in blood, smashing dead, wounded underfoot as a part of him recoiled in horror but was subsumed by his panic.

No. No. No. Everything fading, engulfed by blue, all but Tenshi and the yegsters, their dark forms bringing arms to bear. Two meters a stride, three meters, four. Flying. The yaks firing.

Brando leapt, knocking Tenshi flat, and continued sailing through the air. *Twice as fast. Twice as strong.* The hammer was in his hand; he was descending; a blast grazed his leg, like teeth ripping. He flung the hammer awkwardly as a konk rifle blast pounded him, breaking ten of his ribs, sending him smashing back against the path with an agonizing jolt that shattered his right elbow and gave him a concussion.

Lifting his head against the swirling black that pulled at him, he saw Tenshi roll over and take out the remaining two yaks with a barrage of rebars. He hoped his blow had eliminated the third and wondered groggily whether there were any more hanging about.

Then darkness closed its fist around him and he wondered no more.

CHAPTER 12

WHEN HE SAW GUSANO AND LALO TUMBLED FROM THEIR positions atop the buildings that hemmed in the frantic, screaming mass of Neogs, Chago began to sprint toward the massacre, all the pent up nervous desperation at his inadequacy as cap bubbling to the surface of his consciousness in a raging stream of red. Tripó, pausing from his blasting long enough to mark his crew leader's bizarre behavior, noticed the absence of his mates and drew the right conclusion.

Kicking his bulk into maximum accel, he caught up to and passed Chago, raising his rifle to clear a path through the crazed and frightened fairgoers; blasting, kicking and giving an occasional head-butt, he thrust himself into the center of the slaughter just as one of the stupid bastards was rammed into the cobblestones by several blasts from three of his brothers. The burly demiman slowed to a halt as his cap slipped in a pool of blood and caught himself on Tripó's shoulder.

As they stood together in the midst of the now decimated crowd, they saw someone roll over about twelve meters away and shoot Wan, Lobo and Frisky. Killing shots, all: throat, heart and temple, double each.

"They said there wouldn't be no fucking weapons!" Tripó screamed as he made his way toward the horizontal figure, stomping deliberately on the corpses and the wounded, even blasting a few just for spite and because he was enraged, more than he'd ever been.

Chago had no reply as he briskly followed his hulking second. The very air seemed weighted with the enormity of his defeat, a blackness that entered his body through every orifice, searching out his soul and clenching it in merciless teeth, teeth he felt physically grit about his torso. Seven men lost. Eight tonight.

I do it, or it's gonna get done to me. My team. Fuck. Why me? Why now?

Opportunity for power and face slipped from him as his life soon would.

They reached the form. A woman. In her hand was a strange weapon, which she fired at them convulsively. She was rewarded only by the whirring sound of empty chambers.

"Well, bitch." Tripó inclined the muzzle of his rifle at her face. "Hope you had a lot of fucking fun, because now you're gonna join my brothers in hell, where for sure they'll be waiting for your dead arse."

His thumb moved along the trigger pad.

"Wait! Fuck. Fuck. This is just fucking great."

Tripó turned to his cap, who was nervously rubbing his shaved head right above the eagle tattoo that crowned it.

"What?"

"Can't kill her." Chago spat disgustedly on a nearby corpse.

"The fuck you mean, can't kill her?" Tripó gesticulated wildly, his face reddening. "She fucking gatted more than half your crew, Chago. We're gonna let her live? Don't fucking think so, Cap. All due respect and shite."

"Come here a minute." Chago took several paces and gestured at the burlier man. Tripó glared at his boss for a long second, then glanced at the woman, who stared back madly, like a rabid animal waiting half-sanely for the right moment to latch its jaws onto him. He made as if to walk away, then doubled back and kicked her viciously in the jaw. Her head slammed against that of a corpse at her side, then snapped back and rebounded against the cobbles. She appeared unconscious enough afterward, so Tripó joined Chago.

"What's with this shite?" he growled.

"It's fucking Koroma's niece, you bloody blur. Kill her and you're as dead as me."

"Dead as you? You don't think…"

"Come on, kwate, you know the life better than me."

A suddenly calm acceptance lit upon Chago as he said the words. He'd lived his entire adult life and much of his adolescence trying to be something he wasn't. Perhaps it was time to let go, never feel those dark jaws on his chest again.

Then he thought of Sandra and her father, and his will to live quickened a bit.

Tripó's grip on the rifle loosened and it dropped from his hands to clatter against the smooth cobblestones.

"By Fidensito, Cap, I'm sorry as shite."

Thinking, *time for me to get promoted, you pocho fuck*, Tripó turned slightly as if in disgust, activating his ocular recorder as he rubbed his knuckles against his temples to appear frustrated. Facing his crew boss again, he muttered with feigned sympathy and indignation:

"You really think they're gonna do you?"

Frustration flared into fury, and Chago spat. "Madre Mariya, Tripó. Seven little brothers killed under my command by a Neog architect at a bloody fair. What you think, they're going give me a promotion, you dumb-arse fat fuck?"

"That's all I wanted to hear, boss." Tripó quickly stomped on the butt of the rifle, making it pop upright. His left hand jerked the barrel up as his right scooped the stock horizontal. Clamping the weapon close to his body, he triggered a blast that, at such short range, ripped Chago in two before the cap had even registered what was happening. Fans of crimson splayed outward from the falling halves as Tripó hawked and spat contemptuously.

"Enough of that 'dumb-arse' gash, you gormless marikó."

CHAPTER 13

NESTOR SIGHED. BEFORE HIM IN THE AIR ROTATED REPORTS and schemata of the Brotherhood infiltrations of Oceania, New Mecca, New Beijing and Podgoritsa. These were nowhere near the scope of the operation on Jitsu, nor did they have the same objectives. Konrau simply wanted a presence on the worlds, a basic infrastructure to utilize "when the time was right." Operations had advanced smoothly on each planet, the syndicate's black-market practices insinuating themselves into the social fabric.

Jitsu seemed to be another story. He'd just gotten a tunneled communiqué from Tripó Lameda, explaining the disaster at the fair, along with an optical illustrating why he'd taken out his cap and assumed command. Nestor's first impulse was to be infuriated: Chago had been hand-picked by the boss, and this turn of events altered their plans.

However, as a brother himself, he understood. There existed a fine line between blind ambition and honor, one he had trod multiple times as part of Toni Benemerito's crew ages ago. The two of them had taken out brothers whose actions had no longer reflected the ideals of *L'onda*, and as a result they had rocketed to the top. It was axiomatic that in any large organization, individuals would try to bend the system to their own advantage without concern for honor. With Nestor's help, Toni had discovered these individuals and eliminated them.

Of course, Nestor's insight into the activities of other demimen owed much to his late sister Ria, a materia or spiritual medium. The Niño Fidensio, the holy child himself, had chosen her at an early age to be a vessel for his messages, and this choice had made it easier for Nestor, a skinny, intellectual Martian boy, to enter the ranks of the Fidensista Brotherhood on the wave of respect she had garnered by her late twenties. But the Blessed Child had also rewarded Ria with uncanny knowledge about others around her, which she passed on to her little brother, creating for him a reputation as a master of intrigue without parallel in the syndicate. Nestor had been glad to use this leverage in support of Toni, an honorable brother whose only apparent objective was furthering the glory of both the Brotherhood and the Blessed Child.

Unfortunately, once in power, Toni had proven to be as twisted as the very men he'd stepped upon to reach the top. Nestor shuddered away memories long re. Yes, he lied to himself, Toni Benemerito had forced Nestor to share in the new boss's sickness, and Nestor, ever faithful to his kasike, had endeavored to cover up the filthy past that kept bubbling up to smear Toni's name. His reward had been a microscopic bomb in Ria's head, Toni's way of ensuring Nestor's silence and continued cooperation. Nestor still didn't understand why the Blessed Child had permitted such an evil act. For years he had tried to discover a way to neutralize the bomb, but it had been impossible.

That's when Konrau had come on the scene, rising through the ranks faster than anyone before him. He'd helped Nestor, and though Ria had died, they'd exacted revenge and excised the tumor of Toni's stint as kasike.

So when evaluating Tripó Lameda, Nestor had a basis for judging his actions. He'd done the honorable thing by taking out the incompetent Chago while at the same time following the order to leave Santo's niece alive. Nestor steeled himself to protect the hulking brother, and even to recommend he become a huramentau or mademan in a virtual ceremony. He didn't think his boss would approve, but it was right to ask.

Konrau was actually quite receptive and almost giddy, surprising given the pressure of their move to the Brotherhood's new HQ light years away.

"Don't worry, Nestor. Yeah, it was a bloody mess, but the results will be sevendable. Looks certain that Santo's getting his squads, and then the real game's going to get started. Set up the confirmation ceremony, virtual like you said. Get some more sikaritos transferred to Tripó Lameda's crew, tell them to hang ready. We'll play pirates and soldiers, yeah? Keep shite off-balance, let Santo slither to the top."

Nestor wasn't sure what to say, but he nodded. Ever since the kasike had put his brother on a crew in the Sol system, his mood had changed. The fits of pain were less frequent, and Konrau even seemed cheery while going over their plans. Having known the boss for so many years, Nestor was suspicious. It almost seemed as if Konrau were deliberately drawing the konsehero's attention away from something important. However, as long as the boss continued to demonstrate wisdom and honor, Nestor would grudgingly agree to anything he said.

Despite his reluctant obedience, he started to voice his concerns.

"Still don't get the value of sending brothers I've curated with care to a worthless planet to get slaughtered by civilian women, kasike."

Konrau's smile faltered, his eyes going cold.

"Listen, Nestor, I need you to trust me."

"Boss, I want to, but it just seems like you're making a mistake."

"I know what I'm doing, Nestor. Trust me. Trust me like you did when you were standing there in Toni's house, his body all riddled with holes from your gat, revenging Ria's death, and his fem ran in screaming like crazy, punching you and spitting. I took your gun from your hands, remember, and put it in hers. Made her point it at you and pull the trigger. You didn't move. You trusted me."

"And after she shot me in the shoulder, you aiming her arm, you pushed her away and gatted her, too. Yeah, I trusted you. Didn't knew what the fuck you were doing, but I trusted you."

"Well, I need that same trust now, Nestor."

More blind trust. I'm not even a konsehero, if truth is said. More a yes-man. But he swallowed his ire and nodded, his eyes averted. He would do as he'd been told. For the time being, anyway.

"But I'll tell you what," Konrau continued. "You're right about killing off brothers being unnecessary. I want you to do some recruiting, set up some martyr crews, know what I mean? Get a dozen or so ready—draw from the weaker guys in the Arredondo crews, get some new recruits. Even ask Yen Bandera to send you some disposable yegsters-for-hire. No need for you to take the brunt of this shite, lose so many of your personal crews."

Nestor was pleased at this offer. He had actually been contemplating padding his men with weaker conscripts without consulting with his kasike, but this arrangement was obviously much better. Though he still doubted the sanity of Konrau's mysterious plan, at least he felt less threatened by it now.

I can live with this. I just wish I had more input. He could use my help, especially now that Jimi Andrade is concentrating his men on hitting our operations. But he's the boss.

For now.

CHAPTER 14

IN HIS DREAMS, TENSHI DIED.

Brando stood there and watched as the other yaks pounded her with gatfire, her body twisting and arching grotesquely as she called his name over and over until she was silenced by a final barrage.

He dragged his broken body to her side, took her ruined head in his hands.

Then her eyes opened. They were utterly black, with sparks swirling in their depths.

Her plum-dark lips opened, but it was not her voice that spoke.

"Bring her back. Prepare her. Or the end will come."

Then the indistinct forms of her killers swiveled about, and from their rifles blackness spewed forth, hurtling toward him as it expanded to fill his field of vision. Time and again he was swallowed.

Finally, the black faded to green, then to blue, and finally to white.

"Brando?"

His eyes snapped open.

"Damn, lad, thought you'd never wake."

It was Modupe. They were in a room, a hospital room. An expanse of white sheet stretched between Brando and the older professor. Wounded. He sat up slowly. A dull ache filled his head and seemed to spread down his right side. His arm was stiff and stubbornly resisted being bent.

"How long?"

"Three days. You were real messed up, but luckily it wasn't too serious. They mended your bones, removed a clot from your cranium. Good as new, what say?"

"Oh, yeah. Feel *real* good, you bloody senile gerrie. Tell me: is Tenshi alright?"

"Yeah. She's here too, gone to the cafeteria to eat some lunch. You hungry?"

Brando nodded and Modupe thumbed the comscreen near the door, ordering up some food and a nurse visit.

"Tell me about it, Modupe."

The theology professor sighed, dragged a chair to the side of the bed, and wearily sank into it. "It was bad, Brando. Seventy-three dead, twenty-five wounded. A mess. But it would've been much worse if you and Tenshi hadn't intervened."

"The hell did I do? Just stood there till she almost got killed."

"You saved her life, mate. She says so. Because of you, she was able to kill three more yegsters. The others left her alone. Rather, with a concussion, like you. Twin concussions. Adorable."

"You're hilarious, you macabre son of a bitch. But why didn't they finish her off? That doesn't make sense."

Modupe shrugged. "Nobody knows. The killers just collected their dead and got out of there, so we don't know anything about them really, though Tenshi says they were definitely yaks. Brotherhood, probably, from their Kaló accents. She's given Security their descriptions, but it doesn't look like they'll be handling it."

Furrows creased Brando's forehead.

"Why not?"

The door hissed open. Tenshi leaned in, saw that Brando was conscious, and hurried to his side to awkwardly embrace him.

"Thank the Eight that you're okay, Brando." Her eyes were shiny with relieved tears.

Before he could answer, the nurse came in and checked his vitals, leaving a tray of food and promising a visit from a doctor within the hour.

As she left, Modupe stood self-consciously.

"I've got to make some calls and grab some lunch. Excuse me, okay?"

Brando and Tenshi nodded without saying anything. It was hard for either of them to concentrate on anything other than each other.

The door cycled shut, and Brando reached for her hand.

"I thought they were going to kill you."

"Shh. I know."

"And I felt so helpless. I'm no fighter. Few laps in the pool, some soccer, push-ups and sit-ups every couple days, that's the extent of my physical activity."

"Brando, you don't have to…" she began.

"No, I want you to understand this. I was frozen in place, impotent. There you were, risking your life, doing the impossible. Bearing down on those yaks like some AI soldier shell, not heeding the danger. And me, I just stood there. Then they saw you, and I knew you were dead. I couldn't bear it. Losing you."

She leaned her face close to his. "Listen close to me, Brando D'Angelo. I said you could do anything if you only believed in something strong enough, remember? Guess you do, because know what? You saved my life. I would've died. I was oblivious to danger, I was going to kill them all, no matter what. I couldn't see anything else but them: all the rest seemed a sea of rising red. My people's blood. Spilled at my fair. But you saw, and despite what you say, you *did* move. Like the wind you ran and flew. You saved me. Of course, you broke my damn clavicle, too, while you were at it!"

They laughed, and he brought her hand weakly to his lips to kiss it. "But my hammer throw?"

She was obviously trying not to laugh. "Well, it distracted them. Guess the difference in gravity really threw off your aim."

"At least I got them to shoot at me, eh?" Brando's smile dissolved into a more serious expression. "Modupe says Civil Security isn't handling the investigation. That means…"

The happiness radiating from Tenshi's face was wiped away in an angry wave.

"Santo got what he wanted. ATS, they're called. Anti-Terrorism Squads. Under his command, though he and the Archon are promising full disclosure to the deputies and saying they'll gradually turn them over to the Chamber. Pure shite, of course."

"So you definitely think Santo set these massacres up? He's that evil?"

"Little too convenient otherwise, no? The Chamber's looking into him, a full investigation of com records, comings and goings: they're going scour his data. If they get the votes, that is."

"And he says?"

Tenshi shrugged. "Insists he's got nothing to hide. That we can look all we want. But even if we find nothing, it won't mean he isn't behind the attacks."

"Bit hard to stop him without evidence."

"I don't know about that. Direct action will be off the table. But we can play his game. Turn these people against him."

"How do you propose to do that?"

She tousled his hair, a smile creeping back onto her face.

"Show them what they're missing out on. Want to help?"

AFTER A WEEK, BRANDO WAS DISCHARGED. RATHER THAN GOING BACK TO Modupe's flat, he accepted Tenshi's offer to stay with her until he'd fully recuperated. She lavished attention on him for the entire month that the university gave him for personal leave.

"You're going to spoil me," he told her one morning after finishing breakfast in bed.

"Maybe," she said with a dismissive wave of her hand. "But I'm between projects. I have the time and need the distraction from politics. Besides, you saved my life. If I can make yours a little more comfortable, then I damn sure will. Not another word about it, yes?"

Brando raised his hands in surrender. "Okay, yoyote mikkereru."

"You bet your arse it's whatever I want," she said, kissing him on the forehead and picking up the empty tray.

"However," Brando began, smiling at her annoyed frown, "I'd like to repay your hospitality. Let's go out for dinner. Somewhere nice in Station City."

Tenshi feigned innocence. "Kyosu-chan, are you asking me on a date?"

"Y-yes?"

"And you can afford my tastes?" she teased.

"Well … maybe?"

Flicking her locs, she turned and starting walking away. "Okay, then. I hope you have a tux hanging in Modupe's guest closet. We're going to the fanciest restaurant on the planet."

Brando ended up ordering a nice gray linen suit and white silk shirt, delivered that afternoon. As evening shadows snaked their way along the broad streets of Station City, he showered and wrapped the elegant clothes around his bruised body, taking his time and wincing often.

He was checking messages on his data pad when Tenshi stepped out of her bedroom in a clingy black dress and silver choker. Stunning. He couldn't help but bite his lip.

"Query," she called, activating her home automation system as she approached Brando and put her arm through his. "Take a series of photos of the professor and me. Multiple angles. Burst beginning now."

Brando gave his best relaxed smile as sensor strips on the walls recorded the two of them, standing together. His guts were in knots.

She's the most beautiful woman I have ever met. And she might be mine. If I live up to her expectations. If I don't screw up.

"Query: display last image."

At Tenshi's command, a snapshot of the couple hovered in the air before them. Her flats and his dress boots made them the same height.

Infotainment stars at award ceremonies can't compare, Brando thought. *There's a spark here that they always lack.*

He cleared his throat. "We look good together, don't we?"

"Yeah," she answered, her voice a little raspy, "we do. Come on. It's not far."

Jitsu's small moon—Arehanja—was nearly full in the sky above Brando and Tenshi as they moved arm-in-arm down the slidewalk to the red stone façade of Ozarano Eti, a five-star restaurant specializing in Martian haute cuisine.

Brando glanced at the candles floating near the high ceilings, nervous, as they were shown to their table in a hushed recess of the cavernous space. On a nearby balcony, a traditional Martian quartet of erhu, oud, dizi and tabla spun delicate melodies into the air.

After a quick review of the menu, Brando decided on kabrito meifrisa stew; Tenshi ordered a vegetarian dish, bissara i-nopar. They had just selected a sweet majhul wine when a snarl of Spanish broke the seductive spell of the moment.

"Hijo de la gran puta."

Brando jerked his head up. Ambarina Lopes stood about a meter away, a beautiful older woman on her arm.

"Captain Lopes," he said, keeping his tone polite but cold.

"I mean, I saw the reports and the video," she said, pulling her date with her as she closed on their table, "and heard the rumors. But to see this with my own eyes. Bastard, I *told* you I was staying here for the woman I was dating, the one behind the fair."

Tenshi sighed. "We haven't been dating for almost seven months, Ambar. We've had this conversation."

"This isn't about you and me," Ambar snapped. "It's about this fucking interloper. After all the courtesy I extended you on my ship, Brando. You backstabbing prick. Me cago en tu puta madre."

"Te juro que no sabía," Brando said, lifting a hand. "Didn't put two and two together until later. But you heard Tenshi. Whatever yall had, it's over. Let's not make a scene."

"Ambar," the captain's date said softly, pulling on her arm. "Our table."

With a disgusted shudder, Lopes pointed at the couple. "Enjoy each other while the sex is novel, fucking traitors. You two have nothing else in common. It won't last."

Then, before an approaching pair of shocked waiters could confront her, Ambarina led the other woman deeper into the restaurant, muttering in Spanish as she went.

Brando and Tenshi stared at each other for a tense moment.

Then, at the same instant, they began to laugh.

"She's ..." Brando gasped between giggles, "so mothergod scary. I thought ... she was going to take me outside and ... beat my arse into the ground."

Tenshi wiped tears of hilarity from her eyes. "Oh, shit, that poor woman she brought with her! She's got some rough revenge sex in her near future."

Getting a hold of himself, Brando tried to be serious. "She was really in love with you, huh?"

Tenshi rolled her eyes. "That's not love. That's obsession. If she'd loved me, she wouldn't have cheated on me."

"Did you love her?" Brando's pulse quickened as he asked.

She looked at him for a moment, took a sip of her wine. "No, Brando. I cared about her, but it wasn't love."

"I wonder if she's right," he mused. "About us. Can we last?"

Tenshi reached across the table and took his hand in hers. "We're the ones who decide that, Kyosu-chan. If we want this relationship to endure, we'll put in the work. Everything good in life requires effort, struggle, planning."

"And along the way," Brando said, trying not to start giggling again, "we can 'enjoy each other while the sex is novel,' yeah?"

Tenshi arced an eyebrow. "Oh, yes. That we can."

Once their meal was done, they slipped out into the deepening night for a walk. Tenshi led him to Anakwa Park, its paths lined by plum and sandpaper trees that showered blossoms like snowflakes. Holding hands, the couple made their way to the lake at the heart of the park. The moon was reflected there as if it had slipped from the sky to bathe in those clear waters.

"Breathtaking," Brando muttered, looking at Tenshi. "Just like you."

She turned to face him, a ready smile crinkling the edges of her eyes.

"Are you happy?" she asked him.

"More than I have ever been," he admitted. Then, because the myriad stars were chiming in his heart, because he couldn't contain his feelings one second more, he stepped closer to her and whispered, "I ... I think I love you, Tenshi Koroma. I know it's too soon to be saying such things, but ..."

Putting her hands on his cheeks, she silenced him with a kiss that said more than any words she could have uttered.

When they realized they couldn't stop themselves, couldn't keep their hands from seeking the heat of the other's skin, they hurried back to Tenshi's place and sated their lingering hunger.

After that date, they made love often. Gingerly at first, so as not to aggravate mending muscles and newly fused bone, but eventually with the hunger of the truly in-love, a passion that seeks to please and learn not to simply sate itself, one that has as its goal an intimacy of emotions as well as of flesh.

Then they would lie in bed till the wee hours of the morning, talking about themselves, sharing their pasts. Tenshi explained her years on the clean-up crews, the mind-numbing joy of brutal physical work, the inexplicable thrill of staring at a restored landscape and realizing it is *your* work, not that of some god or of nature alone. She hesitantly talked about her lovers and what she'd learned from them, pleased at Brando's ease with the topic.

Late one night, recounting her love of the southern dunes, she revealed her heart's greatest desire. "I want to build a home at the edge of the desert near Kinguyama, my hometown. Something majestic, an extension of my incipient soul, a mirror of everything on Jitsu that I keep alive within me."

Her eyes scrutinized his face, expectant or worried.

"I think that is a beautiful idea," he told her, his heart quickening at her joyous smile. "And I'm a little jealous. One day I hope to have such a dream, a project that echoes what's in my heart."

In the depths of those breathless nights together, Brando also opened himself to her, exposing his inability to counter his family's insults and manipulations, their branding of him as antiquated and obsolete, a romantic infidel who embarrassed them more than they could express. Weeping, he spoke of his father's abandonment, of the lake, of his desire to commit suicide and the revelation of his own insignificance that had ironically made him burn with a will to live.

And he told her of Ayanna, the model and artist his mother had handpicked for him.

"She wanted to mold me into a good Wiccan Catholic. Her mother's a cardinal, hence Mamma's insistence I date the girl: it was good for the family, for her career in the Church. But no. I'm done with that religion. With my family, too. My leaving worked out for everyone in the end, though. Ayanna's now engaged to my brother Edoardo. He's a slimy fucker. Real scum."

Tenshi scoffed. "She should be happy, then. Slime and scum are easily moldable."

They shared a good laugh at the image.

"It's not that I mind being molded," Brando said in a sudden bout of seriousness. "I just want the right sculptor, one who understands what I need to become."

He took her hands and pressed them to his chest.

"I think I've found my architect."

CHAPTER 15

TENSHI COULDN'T QUITE SAY THE WORDS. Was it love? Perhaps. She thought about Isabella, the way their lives had entwined for those few years, the way they'd lived and breathed each other.

Brando was different. Sweet in a way that Isabella had never been. Not irresistible. Not overwhelming. Instead, calming. Inviting. Intriguing.

Of course, Tenshi was different now. A satorijin, not a wild rebel child lashing her raw emotions against the world. Maybe she couldn't recognize her feelings as love because she'd grown so much in the past eight years.

Brando's emotional accessibility was a welcome change from the selfish detatchment of Pathwalkers she had dated and from Ambar's frivoulous, superficial debauchery. But was he the *one*? Could she face the future with him at her side? Was their physical connection and growing friendship a sign of something deeper?

I'll know whether it's love, she realized, *when I see how he reacts to the other things I love. People. Places. Ideas.*

AS THE MONTH DREW TO A CLOSE, it became clear Brando wouldn't be leaving when his sick leave was up. So Tenshi sat him down and told him what she needed.

"Two trips. First, we visit my hometown. Not so much to meet my parents," she said, stopping him before he jumped to conclusions, "but to meet my *community*. Then we head to the Southern Continent, so you can understand what put me on my present path. L'idea ti pare buona?"

He answered without hesitation, a silly smile stretching across his face. "Absolutely I think it's a good idea. I'm honored that you would open that part of your life to me. When do we leave?"

"In an hour? Yes, that feels right. Go pack a bag, Kyosu-chan."

The trip took about twenty minutes, her transport streaking across the late morning sky. Brando spent the time dutifully researching the town.

"Kinguyama," he read out loud. "Two thousand inhabitants. Situated at the edge of Jangwa ra-Kun, the Great Desert. Birthplace of Dominian Neo Gnosticism's Third Oracle, Samanei Koroma."

Tenshi shook her head. "Those are just facts, Brando. I want you to look deeper."

Below them, the vegetation got sparser, the soil paler, rocks bursting through at intervals. Then, just a few kilometers from looming dunes, Kinguyama spread out in an orderly grid: two main paved roads, running along the cardinal axes, split the town into four regular quadrants. They overflew one, and Brando saw that it was further divided into four quarters, veined with unpaved roads of packed sand, a large building at the center. The houses were all the same size, simple adobe cubes, with no visible gardens.

"Are those … stone slabs standing around the homes?" Brando asked.

Tenshi nodded as her transport began to descend toward an empty spot near the heart of the town. "They provide shade. And block out the Grey Prison, Dominians insist."

There's not much of a view, anyway, Brando didn't say aloud. "And the building at the center of each quarter?"

"The Bida Sento. Distribution warehouses for government-provided food and goods. Remember, my people don't have jobs, per se. Not the majority."

The barren landing field was just a few blocks from the largest structure in town, which he recognized from news reports. Samaneino Teyopan. As Tenshi and Brando exited the transport and began walking down the main street, a group of children dressed in drab linen pants and shirts filed out of the church, each holding a kleinball. Behind them came their teacher, a white-robed older woman.

"That's Sebisa Pachari. She's one of the town's anshyano. Guides the afternoon classes."

The children sat in a circle, each facing away from its center. Raising their kleinballs, they fixed their eyes on the twisting, one-sided surface. After a few moments, they began to chant in unison.

"Amo inyani, iruju tani."

Shuddering, Brando understood the ancient rhyme. *It isn't reality, it's just a mirage.*

"It's so strange," he managed to say after a moment, "to see young children meditating or whatever this is. What about literature, art, math, science?"

Tenshi sighed. "The members of this group are children of common teyopanjin, adults who have only reached kehatsu, awareness of the Ogdoad and the falseness of the physical world. Statistically very few of them will become satorijin, so there is less *need* for the skills you take for granted. They learn to read so they can study the Revised Bible and other scriptures under the careful guidance of their giya. Enough basic math to survive day to day. Beyond that—Dominians believe all other human knowledge to be not only superfluous but detrimental to the Path."

"Mothergod, how depressing. I'm glad I've come to teach. Wish I could work with younger minds, though. Someone's got to do something."

Reaching out her arm, Tenshi stopped Brando in his tracks.

"We Reformers *are*," she said, letting anger edge into her voice. "Don't imagine we need you or any other offworlder to be our savior. We can save ourselves just fine. You've come to teach, but you also need to learn. Instead of you being the hero and changing this world, maybe it will end up changing you."

Ducking his head in embarrassment, Brando apologized. "You're right. I was out of line. I'm here to help, but I'll let myself be guided by you and other Jitsujin."

Tenshi nodded. "Fair enough. Come. I'll introduce you to someone who *is* doing something."

South of Samaneino Teyopan, Kinguyama began to change. Houses in the southwestern quadrant were larger if still nondescript, often two-storied affairs with roofs of purple clay tile. There were native trees and bushes behind the plain wrought-iron fences that divided one lot from the next. The roads within the four smaller quarters of the borough were cobbled.

"Here," Tenshi said, "live most satorijin—especially those considered anshyano—and the town's handful of arojin. That lone home on the low hill over there? That's where Santo and Maryam reside, though he spends most of his time in Juresh."

Brando stopped and stared for a moment. "Looks down on everyone else."

"He'd insist he's looking over and out for his flock," she mused. "But it's clearly part of Dominian hypocrisy. The argument goes that since the folks in this borough are further along on the Path, they need greater access whatever worldly devices can serve as instruments of gnosis and kwantum kedarum, Quantum Enlightenment. To that end, their distribution warehouse has a greater selection of otherwise prohibited goods."

Brando cleared his throat as they passed a public park with a pool of uncovered water, startling this close to the desert. "And presumably they're able to resist the temptations that come with those goods better than lower-level Pathwalkers."

"That's the logic they use, yes. But we Reformers reject that artificial division of the Path. All of us should have access to the tools of soul-creation. Always."

She led him across the paved north-south road to the less regular, more colorful southeastern quadrant. Plots were of different sizes, as were homes, some of them more than the simple cubes found everywhere on the planet. Columns, windows, balconies. On a few blocks, Brando saw groups of children playing games. Muted and calmer than kids on Earth, but enjoying childhood, nonetheless.

Close to the Bida Sento at the heart of the borough stood a building constructed from different-colored blocks of sandstone, surrounded by shade trees.

Beneath the largest of these sat a group of children, listening in rapt attention to their teacher, whose animated gestures moved holographic images through the air.

"After that mid-flight mating, dear teyopanjin, the couple travels to the nearest volcanic fissure among the highest crags. The male brings food while the female lays her eggs. If he doesn't bring enough, she will kill him and leave his carcass to be devoured by their babies when they hatch."

Tenshi whispered to Brando, "That's Jina Chimari, Meji's spouse."

"Can yall make a connection?" Jina asked her students. "What are you thinking?"

A girl stood. "Of the legend of Miwa and Teri, Anshyano Pishan. Their umma stole a jagen egg when the female wasn't looking. Its mate had been killed and it had no food for its brood. So it went after the foolish woman and her daughters, bringing them back to the mountains."

"True," said another girl, standing. "But when the eggs hatched, there was no food, because the girls smeared jagen poop on themselves and their mom to escape."

"Poop!" several children cried, giggling.

Jina noticed Tenshi and Brando standing nearby. "Indeed. Why don't you spend five minutes flying around the garden or pretending to smear poop on yourselves? Then we can do maths."

As the children started to rush around, shouting and laughing, their teacher approached the visitors.

"Tenshi-shi!" Jina said, folding the architect into an embrace. "What brings you to Kinguyama on this lovely day?"

"I brought a friend, Jina-shi. Wanted to show him my hometown." Tenshi turned and gestured at Brando. "This is Brando D'Angelo. New professor at the University."

Jina Chimari gave the slightest bow of her head, still smiling. "Yes, I've seen his image on the news. Thank you, Dr. D'Angelo, for saving our Tenshi. And for making her happy, too, apparently. I haven't seen your face this glowing in years, Sister!"

Swallowing hard, Tenshi rolled her eyes and made light of her friend's observation. "It's all the effort of playing nurse to a foolish man."

Jina laughed and winked at Brando, who stammered. "It's an honor to meet you, Anshyano. I love your pedagogical approach with the children."

"Thank you, Kyosu-kun," Pishan said. "We call it kijifunza. Learning rooted in this place, this moment. It considers all knowledge as a continuum, a fragment of the Ogdoad's understanding, reflected in the physical world. All of it accessible by studying one's immediate surroundings."

Tenshi put her hand on Brando's arm, wanting to stop the educators from launching into a colloquium right then and there. "It's a concept from shamanga. You'll learn more at our next stop, I promise."

Jina raised an eyebrow. "Oh, you're giving him the *full* tour, I take it? Yall are more serious than I had imagined! But Professor, I can send you a few mongraphs, if you're interested."

"Absolutely! Thank you very much."

Brando gave an approximation of a Pathwalker bow. Tenshi was impressed. *He's really trying. For me, sure. But that's the first step.*

"Well, I know you've got to get back to the children, Sister. We'll leave first. Be enlighted."

"Yall, too." The anshyano started walking back toward her charges. "Okay, free time is over! Let's calculate the mass of poop required to cover every one of yall!"

Shaking her head and grinning, Tenshi led Brando back to her transport.

AN HOUR LATER, THEY HAD CROSSED the equator and much of the lower hemisphere. Rising before them came the steep cliffs of Karada ra-Kusini, literally "the Southern Continent."

"The first five hundred kilometers have already been reclaimed," Tenshi explained as they flew over a young thorn forest. "All along the northern coast, from the 60th to the 70th parallels, between zero and ninety degrees longitude."

"A pretty good chunk," Brando said.

"Not even a fourth of the continent. But we're getting there."

The professor leaned forward in his seat. "Are those buildings in the distance?"

"Yes. The Minsistry of Reclamation has its headquarters at the heart of the restored terrain. In the old Soltec fortress." Tenshi's pulse quickened in anticipation. "The first non-Pathwalker building I ever saw."

The autopilot curved the transport, and there it was.

An explosion of stone, steel and glass, frozen at the moment of impact. Like a fist slamming into the sand.

Brando audibly sucked in air.

"Yeah," Tenshi muttered. "That was my reaction, too."

"It's … it's like … rage transubstantiated."

Tenshi turned to stare at him. No one had ever put it quite that way before.

"You see it, too, huh. Dédalo Mostrenco wanted something that would embody his feelings at losing the love of his life to this world. Arehanja Sanaustin. Domina's disciple. The very first Dominatu Pathwalker. And our first martyr."

"He wanted to take revenge on the entire planet," Brando whispered. "That's how much he loved her."

"A terrible love." Suddenly, not understanding the impulse, Tenshi grabbed Brando's hands. "Newano okanim, no matter what may happen to me, never seek to punish this false prison. If I reach the end of the Path before you, celebrate my translation. Don't fight it."

Brando's eyes were wide. She had called him "my dearest heart," the closest she'd ever come to speaking her feelings. It had clearly shaken him.

"Umpenzi," he whispered, using the affectionate name exchanged by lovers. "Nothing is going to happen to you. I will dedicate my existence to making sure of that."

Tenshi bent her head over his hands and kissed them as her transport settled down upon the sand near the ministry complex. Then she pulled him out of his seat and into the cool southern air.

In the shadow of Mostrenco's fist sprawled dozens of more conventional Pathwalker buildings, including a pair of barracks that Tenshi knew well.

"When I arrived, I looked up at the old Soltec fortress and didn't feel repulsion, like the anshyano wanted. I was inspired. For the first time, I saw what I had begun to suspect: self-knowledge can come from reshaping the world to reflect the self. Dédalo Mostrenco's identity at that moment in time still dominates this place. He lingers. We can know him. Surely he came to know himself, working here."

A teen wandered out of the barracks at that moment, lighting a sikar. Tenshi's felt her nerves tingle with the need for nicotine.

"Oh, I need a smoke. Bad."

Brando in tow, she approached the kid.

"Got one you can spare?"

Nodding as they exhaled, the teen shook out a stick. "Here, anshyano."

Tenshi gave a small laugh as she took the sikar. "Don't get called that much. What's your name?"

"Yanrin Okuta. They, if we're using Baryogo."

Tenshi nodded. She had many omedeyo friends. "Tenshi Koroma. She."

Yanrin did a double take. "Wait, what? You're ... Tenshi-zin? Oh, shattering! You're the reason I got my arse sent to this place!"

Brando stepped forward. "Hey, I don't think you should be blaming ..."

Tenshi stopped him. "That's not what they mean. This is Brando, by the way. He."

Yanrin scoffed. "Clearly. No, I mean, you're my inspiration! My mates shared your unauthorized biopic with me, and I knew I had to follow the same Path."

Brando looked at Tenshi oddly. "There's a faux-show about you?"

"Hush, I'll tell you later. That's amazing, Yanrin! Have you been assigned to a crew yet?"

"Quena. Thirteen B. We ship south this afternoon. Adagun ra-Kipo."

Tenshi shuddered. "Yikes, lake duty. Be sure to empty your boots out after every shift."

"Yes, Tenshi-zin. Can I ... record us together? Mates won't believe me otherwise."

Feeling self-conscious but honored, Tenshi nodded. "Sure. Got your juronkam?"

In answer, Yanrin tossed a mechanical insect into the air, where it hovered, recording the two smoking. Tenshi put her arm around the teen and gave a thumbs-up.

"Send me a link," she told Yanrin, tossing the butt of her sikar into the disposal unit nearby. "My contact is public. And I'll write you back."

As Tenshi led Brando away, ignoring his dumbfounded stare, the teen made soft squealing noises of excitement behind them.

"It's not about me, really. If I inspire them to expand their definition of self and soul, that's the goal. I'm working for a greater cause, Brando. I want you to meet one of its guardians. You'll understand more when you do."

She guided him out of the ministry complex to the shrubland to the east.

After a ten-minute walk during which she pointed out with pride the flora the crews had re-established in the once blighted area, they reached a small adobe building. Into its earthen walls were carved concentric rhombuses and blue intaglios, aids to meditation that Tenshi had contemplated for long hours as a disaffected teen.

"This is Jinja ra-Shamanga. The Shrine of Shattering," she explained. "When Mostrenco closed the Conduit, an object was expelled from its entrance, striking Jitsu right here. A meteorite. We call it the Urim. The second Oracle ordered this shrine erected around it."

Brando closed his eyes for a moment. "Second Oracle. That's, uh, Kosiya Yemo. I remember reading that some of her teachings were stricken from yall's scriptures."

Tenshi felt a surge of adrenaline. Her hands balled up, and her voice was thick with complex emotions when she spoke. "One of the biggest crimes ever perpetuated on my people. But those teachings were not lost, Brando. Though Dominians believe them apocryphal or heretical, they have been preserved. Come, let's go inside. You'll see."

The interior of the shrine was as simple as when last Tenshi had visited. A sort of antechamber, with rugs on packed sand, shelves with actual leather-bound books, low tables crowded with writing materials and the beginnings of mandalas.

A wooden door leading to the inner chamber slid open, and the priestess emerged, locs now totally white with age, but otherwise unchanged. Her blue-fringed white robe swirled about her as she walked.

"Tenshi-shi. It has been too long. I see you do not come alone."

"No, Enlightened One. Apologies. This is Professor Brando D'Angelo."

"If you have brought him to this sacred place, he must mean a great deal to you, child." The older woman sized her up, those all-seeing eyes looking deep into her self. "Do you love him."

There was no hesitating or lying in her teacher's presence. "Yes."

The woman turned to Brando. "I am Hekima Umchawi, sightless child. Priestess of Shamanga, Keeper of the Oracle's Words. Because of Mother Kosiya's trust in me, I am called *ramatini*. You will see for yourself whether I am truly a sage. Enter."

Hekima turned and went back inside the sanctum. Brando shrugged and followed. Tenshi slid the door shut behind them.

Without warning, Brando jerked his head around. "What did you say?"

Tenshi narrowed her eyes. "Me? Nothing. Why? Did you hear something?"

He nodded. "A voice. Faint. It kind of groaned and said 'You' as if irritated."

Tenshi pointed to the center of the chamber, which was otherwise bare. "It was probably that."

Half-embedded in the sand lay the Urim, about the size of a human head, all jagged spikes and iridescent colors. In places, the rock gave way to bits of shimmering metal, as if exposing something mechanical within.

"Sit," the priestess instructed, folding into the lotus position just centimeters from the meteorite."

Tenshi obeyed and Brando followed suit, eyes fixed on Hekima Umchawi.

"Tenshi just called you *kedarumsha*. That means you've already reached quantum enlightenment, yes? You commune with the Ogdoad. Not many on Jitsu have that title."

"More than a title, it is a calling. To guide humanity itself along the Path. That starts with individuals, of course. Like you."

Brando frowned. "I'm sure you want to save my soul, but—"

"You don't have a soul," Hekima rasped. "You have a *self*. But you didn't create that self. It has accrued together over time, coalescing out of bits from the world around, expectations imposed on you, teachings you've received, experiences you've had. Bah, don't pout, Offworlder. This truth holds for Pathwalkers as well. Mother Kosiya warned that our leaders' strict control of our lives prevents gnosis. We waste our time constructing selves that please them rather than souls that can transcend this existence. So she taught us to shatter those selves and build bricolage souls from the pieces."

"Like Sopiya did at the beginning of time," Tenshi said, gooseflesh rising on her arms.

"Indeed. As I will now relate to this man you have brought me."

"Listen, Brando," Tenshi said, turning to him earnestly, "to one of the stories that gives my life meaning."

The ramatini laid her palms against the packed sand. Eyes almost shut, she let truth pour from her in a hoarse whisper.

"From nothing, ra-Wanane emerged. The Ogdoad, eight-faceted truth. Four pairs of umbini, dual beings. One of them, Neweru, became convinced its duty was to create life and join with it. Neweru was expelled from ra-Yindawo, the realm of truth, but the trauma of that experience drove Sakra—its male half—quite mad. Sakra seized his complement, Sopiya, and tried to reshape her into something new. Sopiya was violated and reduced, but she fought Sakra with every bit of her being. This schizophrenic struggle is the origin of the Grey Prison, the physical universe. Yet Sakra believed *himself* responsible, certain that all had arisen from his creative impulse. He imagined himself God, the sole being that existed.

"Unlike Sakra, Sopiya remembered her true nature and understood the danger her complement represented for the universe. However, she saw even deeper truth; her separation from the Ogdoad and Sakra's madness were means to a necessary end: the strengthening and broadening of the Ogdoad itself. She saw the Path in a flash of wisdom, grasping her role in the self-actualization of the very universe, a process we call *aburakusa*.

"Ceasing her struggle, she did shamanga—put herself in Sakra's power and allowed him to break her."

The ramatini then recited one of the most significant lines of scripture ever:

"Shamanichu yewano biye, tenshi zikwepachu."

Brando held up his hand. "Pardon me. 'Her body burst, becoming *Tenshi*? Like, literally this Tenshi right here?"

"No, sightless child. Sparks of truth, the word means. Inyoni Onamata gave her daughters good Pathwalker names. Tenshi, the Spark of Truth. Samanei, the Unblind."

Tenshi could see linguistic curiosity bubbling in Brando's eyes, but the priestess kept speaking.

"These innumerable pieces of her being drifted throughout the Grey Prison, merging with the illusory physical universe. As human life arose and spread, Sakra in his madness again believed himself the cause. From time to time he intrudes on our minds, warping our perception and making us worship his cruel and childish ways. But every human is linked to a spark of truth, a bit of Sopiya's broken body. By recognizing and drawing that spark into themselves, they begin to build a soul around the spark that can survive beyond death and make its way to the Ogdoad. Thus has Sopiya's sacrifice led to our transcendence, and our transcendence brings her back into being.'

Tenshi put her hand on Brando's arm. It was trembling, to her surprise. "Sopiya is wisdom, don't you see? Knowledge used for good, energy used to create, love used to edify. And that's what I believe, umpenzi. Here in this holy place, under the ramatini's watchful eye, I saw my spark of truth. It spoke to me."

Brando was leaning forward, eyes on the meteorite. For a moment, Tenshi thought he wasn't listening. Frustration blossomed on her face, furrowing her brows, heating her cheeks. But then he spoke.

"I want to try it, Tenshi. Something—fate or I don't know what—drew me here. I knew when I saw your buildings, was certain when I saw your face." He looked up. There were tears in his eyes. "If there's a spark in me, I have to know. If there's a voice trying to make itself heard, I must listen."

The ramatini pushed herself to her feet. "Indeed you must. I will prepare the High Sacrament."

TENSHI HELD BRANDO'S HAND IN SILENCE while Hekima Umchawi ground mohiyo leaves in a mortar of volcanic stone.

"That's what they make moku from, no?" he said finally, his voice faint and trembling.

"Yes. But this is the unprocessed plant. Its effects are very different, and not addictive. I promise you I would never expose you to something harmful."

He stroked the back of her hand with his free fingers. The sensation spread up her arm and throughout her entire body.

"You told her you love me."

"Because I do. More than anything. The fact that you're willing to do this makes me even more certain. I want you by my side, Brando. Forever."

The ramatini approached them. "Here. Drink this down. It's bitter, but take it all in."

He did as she instructed. Tenshi remembered the slimy, pungent taste.

And the visions that had come so quickly after consuming the mash.

Hekima took the mortar from him. "Put your hands upon the Urim."

Brando leaned forward and grasped two of the spikes.

Tenshi stood, kissing the top of his head. "We have to leave you, my love. The vision, the voices: they are for you alone."

THE WAIT WOULD HAVE BEEN INTERMINABLE except that Tenshi needed guidance from the kedarumsha on her plans. Others—including Samanei—might claim to hear the Ogdoad, but Tenshi *knew* her teacher could.

They were deep into a conversation on strategy when Brando came stumbling from the sanctum, eyes wide, breath labored.

"Mothergod, Tenshi!" he gasped. "I had no idea."

She hurried to his side, helped him ease onto a rug. He leaned his elbows on the low table and stared at the two women.

"When I was a child," he said, "my family visited the Basilica della Santa Casa. You may not know it, but it contains the Holy Home, where the Mother of God, her son, and Joseph their earthly protector lived. Just now, I found myself there again."

His eyes drooped, but he shook himself back to consciousness.

"I was looking at the figure of the Black Madonna, inside the Holy Home. She cracked open, full of blue light. From within it emerged …. Sopiya. I'm not sure how I know, but there was a certainty in my heart. Tenshi, she looked just like you. Only older, with lighter skin. Those same sunburst eyes, though. She spoke a language I didn't understand."

Tenshi's heart skipped a beat. *Impossible. That was … that was my vision, nearly a decade ago.*

"I think it was Esperanto." He closed his eyes as if trying to remember. "There was shock in her eyes. 'Ho, fek. Brando, vi aspektas tiel juna.' She knew my name. Then she said, in Standard, 'Forgive me. But there's a reason for the pain. Always remember. Your love matters.' There were tears in her eyes."

Tenshi's entire body thrummed with prescience.

"Don't be afraid," she said to me, my spark of truth, so like me and yet so different. "The end will come too soon, but it won't be the end. You'll be translated. I promise."

I can't tell him that. He'll despair. And who knows what "too soon" might mean?

"But then," Brando groaned, "there was another voice. So cold, so void of light, that it obliterated the vision. It didn't say much, but my skin's still crawling, just remembering the touch of that presence on my heart, the swirling echo of that inhuman sound."

"Sakra." Tenshi shuddered. "What did that bastard say to you?"

Tears streamed down Brando's cheeks. His words chilled Tenshi's very blood.

"You seek shattering? I will break you."

Turning his face to the priestess, Brando whispered, using honorific religious language that Tenshi had never imagined she'd hear from his lips. "Kedarumshanim, what does it mean? Guide me well. I place my spark in your honored hands."

Hekima Umchawi pointed at the door. "Tenshi, please go outside and meditate. I need to speak to this new matakite alone."

"Seer?" Brando asked. "But I've done nothing to deserve that title. I'm not even a Pathwalker."

The ramatini's eyes softened as she smiled. "Child, you have had the vision. Once you've peered beyond the Grey Prison, there's no unseeing what you've seen. You are on the Path."

As Tenshi stepped out into the star-bangled night, she didn't know whether to rejoice or regret.

INTERCHAPTER C

From: edoardo@dangelo.per.ter

To: brandod@university.edu.jit

Subject: *Condoglianze*

Date: May 25, 2683 3:45:42 (SST)

Brando! Come stai, fratello? I've been calling your hospital room, but a woman keeps answering. Is she your new partner? Good choice. Kitoko.

What is this about you getting shot at by Mafiosi? Proprio come il nostro papà. You definitely take after our father. Always getting involved in stuff that isn't yall's affair. You went there to teach, no? Ebbene, teach! Leave fighting the bad guys to the police! Anyway, I hope you get better soon. Don't to forget to call us when you are well, so that we can stop worrying, eh?

Eh, nsango malamu: me and Ayanna, it looks like we're gonna get engaged. I hope you're not upset, but we get along perfect. All things work out, eh? You and her just couldn't stand each other, but now we're in love. She's got the most beautiful voice. Mamma's asked me to make her succentrix, che te ne pare? I'll finally have a second-in-command helping me lead the choir, which has burgeoned considerably in the last few years that you haven't been attending.

Well, I've got to go choose the music for Mamma's mass, sta bene? You rest and we'll talk some other time.

Edoardo D'Angelo di Makomo

Cantor

La Chiesa del Santissimo Redentore

Annexation: A Necessary Step

Outward

Editorial Staff

30 May, 2683- A week ago, a fair celebrating the 150th anniversary of the founding of Jitsu was shattered by a brutal massacre. A group of two dozen men dressed in non-descript black body armor encircled the fairgrounds and proceeded to exterminate in cold blood those who in attendance, with no apparent motive beyond chaos. Accusations began to fly in the aftermath: Jitsu's Civil Security was powerless before even such a small group of terrorists or criminals. In fact, it was a Jitsuan architect, Tenshi Koroma, who incredibly managed to turn the tide with the most improbable of weapons.

In addition to this weakness on the part of local law enforcement, pro-Consortium reformers on Jitsu assert that the Dominian sect of Neo Gnosticism, fundamentalists with isolationist tendencies, may be responsible for the massacre. The claim is that Dominians seek to turn public sentiment against reform and Consortium membership. That accusation is bolstered by the fact that one of the most powerful Dominians in Jitsuan politics, Prefect Santo Koroma (and we of *Outward* do indeed notice the coincidence in surnames), had just proposed a group of anti-terrorism squads, manned by non-citizens. An interesting proposal from a man who once said, "Jitsu will never be enlightened till it turns its back on the rest of humanity."

Others, like noted travel entrepreneur Captain Ambarina Lopes, insist that the men who massacred more than seventy people were in fact underworld soldiers, yakuza or "yaks," in common parlance. Yegsters, demimen, gunsels: a multiplicity of words exists for this infestation of vermin that spoils the Consortium despite our repeated efforts to eliminate them. The speculation is that certain syndicates, having been pushed out of the Solar System (c.f. the unsuccessful Jupiter Uprising), are now attempting to gain a foothold on the new colonies and independent worlds. If this scenario (or any combination of the above scenarios) is true, then the CPCC's course is clear. For the sake of humanity's stability, annexation must become our policy.

Outward is an unabashed expansionist outlet. Our political views are a matter of public record, and we will not back down from that stance. But even the opposition parties can see the logic now. Anti-expansionists are quick to point to the historic dangers of imperialism (without pausing to note the very different organization, goals and methods of the Consortium) and to the need of humans in the CPCC to integrate themselves completely into the new colonies we have created, reaching an environmental balance at home before pushing the sphere of our control any farther. But when a world like Jitsu becomes a breeding ground for violence and chaos that could spill into the Consortium, we must ask ourselves if we want to just sit behind imaginary boundaries and watch disaster beget disaster.

Localists insist that the Consortium-level controls on human society are extraneous and stifling. With insane avoidance of the probable results, these extremists not only insist that we leave independent worlds alone, but that we bit by bit weaken the topmost layer of government till most power rests in the hands of local authorities. Like those of Jitsu, run by extreme isolationists with a middling police force, and Terego, which recent reports show has a theocracy too.

No, the time for pandering to weakness is over. Jitsu must be inducted as quickly as possible. The timetable for Sigma Draconis to be made a member republic also must be stepped up. Terego's theocratic government must be replaced with something more democratic and its inhabitants' fear of secular rule calmed. And the new minister of state needs to exert as much pressure as he can on Semanawak and Erin for that those two worlds join us as well. Doing otherwise means inviting back the horrid days of nation-states and ugly wars.

Let us forever remember the motto unfurled beneath the CPCC seal:

"In unity, there is strength."

CHAPTER 16

WITHIN THE SWIRLING DUST OF THE URAKÁ NEBULA, a twenty-six-kilometer-long, roughly cylindrical planetoid now housed the recently completed base of operations for the Brotherhood. At the center of its labyrinthine entrails, kilometers of tunnels navigable solely with special coded pathfinders, Nestor Bos paced the vaulted cavern of an office he'd just been given by his boss. The luxury of his office did little to help. The old mobster was frustrated, as he found himself more and more often, by Beserra's dismissal of advice that didn't fit into the mysterious plan that he and that insane Neog had devised.

After the embarrassing slaughter of Chago Martin's crew two months ago, Nestor had figured the kasike would realize the pointlessness of slowly taking over a planet, twisting public opinion through small attacks on the populace, chipping away at those who might opposed a dictatorship by frightening them into embracing it as the only answer. He'd had many conversations with his boss after Tripó Lameda had been confirmed, trying to dissuade him from his plan even as Jitsu readied its squads to hunt down demiman and attack them.

In addition, Yen Bandera had informed Nestor that Jimi Andrade, the young head of the Aztlan Angels, had sworn to destroy the Brotherhood. Nestor begged his boss to shift his attention away from Jitsu and onto this brewing problem, but his advice was again ignored.

Nestor was beginning to tire of the trend. He went along with the kasike because of the principles of L'onda and because of the debt he owed Konrau for helping him eliminate Toni Benemerito. But the more he thought about it, the more Nestor realized that this help had been the cause of his sister Ria's death.

Eight years ago, Beserra had become the youngest ever boss of the Brotherhood. Not just through his daring strike against Bruno Andrade, head of the Anhele d'Atlan, or even because of his disabling of Boss Benemerito. No, the family heads had accepted him as their leader due to Nestor's careful management of Konrau's popularity after Benemerito's death and his exploitation of most Brothers' adoration of the *materias,* especially Ria.

So where was the kasike's trust and respect for his counselor?

"No," Beserra had told Nestor after being reminded again about the embarrassing deaths of most of Chago's crew. "Didn't I tell you to make up some dummy crews? You think I give a shite if people think we done lost our touch because of Chago's fuck-up? Listen close: we're gonna use Jitsu as a training ground. Learn how to take over slow and easy, use some psychology."

Knowing how futile it was to argue with Konrau once he made up his mind, Nestor had agreed with a slight lowering of his eyes. He would have preferred the methods used for centuries by legendary bosses like Haime Pachuko-Garsasada and Ramon 'El Charro' Arreyano, or even by Baby Face Bustamonte, who had died a glorious death two hundred years ago in this very nebula.

Get an army of little brothers together, gather major weapons and other materiel, invade the bloody place.

These idiot notions of legitimacy and recognition by the CPCC, the motives Konrau kept citing for his plan, were clouding Beserra's judgment.

Mariya curse the day I patched that bishop's tunneled communiqué through to him. Neogs. They make me physically sick.

It had fallen to him to gather dirt on the newly appointed captains of Jitsu's new anti-terrorism squads. Beserra and Santo Koroma had failed to keep absolute control of the squads. Oversight from the Chamber of Deputies complicated the plan. So direct leverage on the squad leaders was needed to make sure the ATS would fail to stop Brotherhood incursions. It all had to look legitimate, hermetic in the face of public and governmental scrutiny.

The gormless plan was a complete pain in the arse.

Shaking off the desire to procrastinate that plagued him in such circumstances, Nestor tunneled a faux conference request to one of his most reliable operatives, an aging ronin named Yen Bandera. Nestor and Yen had begun working together back when Bos was just another sicarito, on the same crew as a young Toni. Bandera had tipped Nestor off to an AF ambush. As a result, the young Brother had kept his crew and many others from being rounded up and jailed for life.

Over the years, their relationship had grown deeper, and they'd worked together often. Nestor always held back. Yen wasn't a member of the Brotherhood, after all. At some point, fearing himself too compromised with the ronin, Nestor had begun investigating the old spy. His connections in the CPCC had at last discovered that Yen Bandera was a genderfluid clone, a type used heavily by Martian Intelligence a couple of centuries ago for deep undercover work. In fact, the CPCC had an outstanding warrant for the Martian operative, one that dated back to the foundation of the government some two hundred years before.

As much as Nestor liked Bandera, he planned to use this information to guarantee the ronin's loyalty to him. The spy's help was invaluable. As an enemy he would be deadly because of his extensive network of agents and connections, tendrils extending into most crime syndicates in human space. Better to ensure their alliance now, even if it meant luring Bandera in with something he really wanted and then blackmailing him into compliance.

After a five-minute wait during which he pondered ways to ensnare Bandera, a gentle chiming notified him the faux conference was ready. Nestor leaned back into the pink stream and logged in.

Bandera's doppelganger sprawled lazily on a black couch, his scarred cheeks and balding pate an exact replica of the Martian's physical appearance. Unlike most users, the ancient free-lancer chose not to rely on simulations to disguise his reactions: he was more than master of his own emotions, and revealed only what he wanted others to see. Bos, on the other hand, preferred the freedom a constant, blank expression afforded him, and felt no shame in turning his doppelganger's stony face toward the ronin now.

"Mr. Bandera. Pleasure to see you again."

"The pleasure is certainly mine, sir, given the credits you'll be depositing to my account shortly." Nestor admired the spy's physical appearances. He'd managed to stay relatively young-looking. Men over a hundred and fifty weren't unheard of, just very rare. Most of them owed their antiquity to relativistic time dilation from the accel and decel that bracketed a holing. For most humans, accidents usually took care of what science had gotten around. Bandera, though, was genuinely old. Nestor guessed gene treatments and clone implants had as much to do with his longevity as space travel.

"Course, Yen. Just need the info on the fourth captain."

"There wasn't much I could scrounge up, to tell you the truth. Ben Wu, forty-seven. Retired major in the Consortium Army. Headed up the battalion that put down the revolt out by Neptune twelve years ago. Wife died four years later, victim of a nasty genetic dysfunction. Daughter was raised by his wife's family. She's about sixteen now, lives on New Beijing. Bit of a troublemaker at school, but generally a smart, ambitious girl. Other than that, guy's got a perfect record, no real vices I could dredge up. He'll be a hard nut to crack, Nestor."

"You say his daughter was raised by his in-laws?"

"Yeah. He was the big soldier-boy; he emigrated to New Beijing back in '66 with his wife and her family. Two of them had a kid a year later, but around '70 he was transferred to Neptune. Didn't bring the wife and daughter. After the revolt, he goes back, the wife dies, and he accepts a transfer to the Helios system. Guess he couldn't exactly be bothered to drag the kid around with him, so he left her with his in-laws. His wife's brothers and sisters haven't really amounted to much: drunks and farmers, basically."

"What's the girl's name?"

"Ya-Ting. I already notified your boys on New Beijing to watch her extra close. The family, too."

Nestor didn't say anything for a space of several seconds. Yen tilted his head quizzically.

"Hard to tell with that poker face your doppel has, but I guess you're planning on creating dirt where presently there is none, am I right?"

"Mr. Bandera, that's more my business than yours, ain't it? Once I confirm this info, I'll tunnel you with a big old smiley. You check your account then, the deposit will have been made. Thanks. Thorough job, on this and on them noobs you got me. We'll work together again, I hope."

"I'm sure we will, Nestor. Money and sneaking are my drugs of choice, as well you know. However, I might be asking you for something different this time. I've got a special interest in Jitsu; it's my hobby, you might say. Recently took it back up after a long time of letting it lay idle. There's some things I want to know. But let it stew in my head a while, I'll mail you soon with the request. It don't suit you, we can always go with the money instead."

Nestor bowed his doppelganger's head and logged out. He ran the girl's name through his mind a few times: Ya-Ting Wu. Sixteen. How long would it take to corrupt a girl like her, whose father wasn't around to provide the leadership, love and protection she needed? How long to take that corruption and make it vice? And how long to take that vice and make it crime?

He thought of his sister, long dead, avenged and peaceful in the arms of Blessed Fidensio. She had taught him the value of dirt, of leverage. Despite not having her gift as a medium, he still had his methods and sources, and they served him well. Ya-Ting wouldn't take long to destroy. Nestor had toppled great men before. A teenage girl would be ridiculously easy. Still, it seemed a waste of time and resources.

Getting up from the faux console, he was startled to see Beserra standing before the entrance, staring at him.

"Kiubole, boss. Everything alright?"

Konrau nodded, his hazel eyes glazed over as if in deep thought. "Sit down a while, Nestor. We've got to talk."

Oh, shite. What I did wrong? Too insistent, I should've known. This the day he gets rid of me? Nestor collapsed, inwardly deflated, into the chair.

"Nestor, you and me, we've argued a lot about my plan, you not agreeing that going legit is the best thing. Now, I really need you behind me a hundred per on this, and since trust doesn't seem to be enough, I'm gonna explain some things to you that you don't yet know.

"Tell me, Nestor… what it is we want?"

Nestor blinked, bewildered. "How's that, boss?"

"The Brotherhood. What's our purpose?"

"To protect our own. Expand our territory. Preserve our ways. Power, honor and fidelity. *L'onda.*"

"And what are the two obstacles that keep us from that?"

"Other syndicates and the CPCC. In especial, the AF."

"Very good. So a kasike's job should be to lessen or eliminate those obstacles. Nestor, despite what you think, I have no intention of just staying with the three dead planets around a red dwarf when this deal is done. I'm gonna take it all. Let Santo pool all the power he can, subjugate the planet if possible, then I'll step in. We get rid of him then, and with the resources of a whole binary system in our hands, with the renown that comes from having a world as legendary as this one, it'll be a cinch to move in on the new colonies, kompa. We reach our hand out, crush the triads, the mafias, the yakuza. Couple decades, and here's where the legit shite comes in, we'll control a dozen brothers in the CPCC Diet. Think of what that means. Power to undermine the AF, keep it clear. Infiltrate the highest levels. Do you get what I'm saying?"

His eyes widening in respect, Nestor nodded.

"The Brotherhood," continued Konrau, "is the oldest syndicate out there. We started back in the 21st century, a little prison gang in some backwoods province of Earth. Imagine us now, seven hundred years later, in complete control of humanity. We can do it, Nestor. I just need your help one more time. Patience while the things that have to happen first fall into place. Can I count on you?"

Nestor understood more than Konrau was saying. Into his mind popped the image of Prime Minister Konrau Beserra, one step away from despot of humanity, in another thirty-five years or so.

That's what Konrau wanted. Tyranny.

Nestor felt the warm hands of baby Fidensio on his chest. He could almost hear his sister channeling the savior's voice.

Help him. Give him what he wants. When the Beserra reigns, my words will be heard round every star.

And besides, with Konrau in control, the benefits to Nestor would be boundless.

The kasike continued. "We aren't gonna wait, though. We've got to start right now. I need to get the CPCCAF occupied on other fronts, Nestor. All the infrastructure I made you set up on colonial worlds? We start using it now."

Nestor leaned forward, actually excited for the first time in years. His enduring faith in his young boss had not been misplaced. "How?"

"Know how you're always chinganno la maje bout Jimi Andrade and the Aztlan Angels wanting to rip us out from the roots? Here's what we're gonna do: start a war against the other syndicates. Drive them off the planets they're trying to dig into. Start with the Scarlet Chaos Triad on New Beijing and the Angels on Podgoritsa. Get the AF caught up in stopping the battles and rushing after the syndicates that we shove off. Then the real show begins."

Konrau grinned, Nestor joined him, and soon, for the first time in years, they were sharing a raucous laugh.

CHAPTER 17

BRANDO SET THE TRAY OF DRINKS DOWN ON THE LOW TABLE. Tenshi's reformer friends looked up and smiled, each taking a cup of tea before continuing their heated debate.

"Thanks, love," Tenshi mouthed. He gave her a thumbs up and walked back to the study they both shared in her suite.

Cycling shut the door, he went to his desk and pulled a little wooden case from one of the drawers. Inside were two rings of strange metal that glinted silver-blue in the light from his lamp.

It had been two weeks since his unnerving, life-changing experience at Jinja ra-Shamanga. Two weeks to come to terms with what he was about to do, the life-changing steps he was about to make.

"Listen, Brando-shi," Hekima Umchawi had said to him in the sanctum once Tenshi had stepped outside. "My own vision came in this shrine, my hands on the Urim, sixty years ago. And I saw my spark, identical to yours: a woman very much like Tenshi-shi. She told me that one day an offworld professor would come to the shrine and that I should give him these."

The ramatini had placed the rings in Brando's hand.

"They came from *inside the Urim,* understand. An opening appeared in the sacred stone, and out they dropped, onto the sand."

Brando still couldn't wrap his mind around any of it.

Agnosticism had been a part of his identity for so long, faith almost felt like a betrayal. But there it was, nonetheless.

He believed.

There was something greater, something beyond the physical world.

And it had spoken to him.

Prepared a Path for him.

BRANDO WAS COMMENTING ON STUDENTS' VIRTUAL discussions about Swahili affixes in Baryogo when Tenshi walked into the office about an hour later.

"Hey, my love. Sorry the meeting went so long."

With a gesture, Brando froze the feed from the faux-discussion room.

"Oh, psh. No worries, Tenshi. As you can see, I have many opinionated satorijin to wrangle."

She walked over to him and kissed the top of his head. He wrapped his arms about her and his face into her stomach.

"I feel guilty," she said, cradling his head. "Leaving you out of these conversations. I don't want you to think I don't respect your."

Pulling away, Brando shook his head. "No way. I've been on this planet just a few months. I'm an outsider, barely learning the ropes. I don't belong at that table with yall. Maybe I never will. Your poltical acumen is pretty freaking astonish. Me, I'm just a language nerd. Those folks will never need to confer with me. And that is fine."

She rubbed his close-cropped hair. "I think you'll grow into it, though. Maybe you can grow out your hair while you're at it. It's a little too military."

Brando laughed. "Oh, I got my mother's genes in that area. Very tough to control my hair when it's even an inch long."

Tenshi frowned and tilted her head, looking him over. "We'll do it up in twists."

Smiling, he hugged her close again. "Whatever you want, angel. All I ask is that you let me stay by your side, helping in any way you need."

There was a nervous silence. Then Tenshi cleared her throat. "You're really fine with not being in the limelight? With—not meaning to sound arrogant— loving someone much wealthier and famous than you?"

"Yup," he muttered, his voice muffled by her linen blouse. "I'm happy on the sidelines. Being your support, emotional and otherwise. Hell, I- I would be content to live my life in your service, Tenshi Koroma."

Her stomach starting quivering. He looked up to see she was weeping.

Taking her face in his hands, she kissed him, a long and sweet kiss that subsided slowly.

Brando stood as they pulled apart.

"I love you," he said.

Tenshi wiped her eyes with the back of a hand. "I love you, too. Hey, you're off tomorrow, right? What if we have a little picnic in the park?"

Right then and there, Brando decided. It was time. He was going to do it.

"Ah, I totally forgot. I've got something I have to do tomorrow. I'll be away all day. But let's have the picnic the following day."

Tenshi pursed her lips a little. "Something to do? Like what?"

"Well, it's a bit of a secret."

"I can't stand secrets."

"I know," Brando said, putting his hand on her cheek. "But this one will be revealed soon, I promise. At the picnic. Is it a date?"

She reached up and took his hand in hers, nodding. "Yes. A date."

AFTER A FRAUGHT AND FURTIVE LATE-NIGHT CALL from Tenshi's terminal after she'd fallen asleep, Brando woke up early and took the first public transport to Kinguyama. He sat among the pilgrims and tourists, understanding at last their excitement to visit the hometown of the Third Oracle. In fact, he borrowed a battered hardcopy map from one of them to figure out the best route to his first stop.

Stepping around the upright slabs, he looked at the non-descript home. So hard to believe that two of this planet's most important women had lived the first thirteen years of their lives here.

It shaped them. The austerity did. In ways I can't fathom.

An actual metal bell was encrusted in the wall beside the entrance. Brando rang it.

Almost immediately, the wooden door swung open. Standing there, squinting at him, as a woman in her 50s. It wasn't age that made her shoulders and facial features sag. It was loss, Brando could tell. And loneliness.

Her long gray hair was pulled back in a braid.

Against the ebony of her skin, hazel-gold eyes stared at Brando like glowing embers.

"It's you. The professor."

"Yes, anshyano. Brando-shi."

Inyoni Onamata gave a half-hearted laugh. "Pardon me, 'shi'? Since when have you been on the Path, blind child?"

"I had the vision two weeks ago, anshyano."

The woman looked beyond him. "And my daughter?"

"She's not with me. She doesn't know I've come. Is her father here?"

Inyoni shook her head slowly. "No. On a mission. Why?"

"May I come inside?" Brando asked. He reached into his pocket and pulled out a handful of koro nuts. "I wish to sit in your shade, Umonim."

Tenshi's mother took a step back, shocked at the ritual phrase.

She has no choice now.

"Come in, child," she recited. "I will shelter you for a time."

There was a rug and a low table on the packed earth floor. Inyoni Onamata took an earthen kettle from the embers of her open stove and set it on a stone base in the center of the table. After she'd sat cross-legged on the rug, Brando did the same.

"Place your offering between us, child."

Brando laid the koro nuts on the table. Inyoni picked one up, peeled away the shell, and snapped the seed in two. She dropped a half in a different bowls. She began to reach for the kettle, but Brando lifted it first, pouring hot water into each.

"What have you come to ask, Brando-shi?" Inyoni said, her voice almost a whisper.

"Umonim, may I walk the Path alongside your daughter?"

"You have no Pathwalker family. No kin on this world. Who will vouch for you?"

"Arojin Meji Pishan, Umonim."

Her gold eyes opened wide. "Do you understand what will be expected of you. Of you both?"

Brando nodded. "Marriage, in Samaneino Teyopan. Our union an echo of the eventual reintegration of the wayward umbini. Halves united. The duality bound again to the Collective."

Inyoni reached for her bowl and drank deeply of the narcotic tea. Brando, turning from her in a show of respect, downed his portion as well.

His senses went immediately keener. He could almost feel the beating of the old woman's blood in her veins.

"Tenshi has been expelled from the teyopan," she pointed out.

"The next giya will work to see her welcomed back," Brando told her.

There was no arguing with that assertion. Pishan's confirmation ceremony was just days away, the Office of the Archon had announced.

"Very well. Seeing that you wish to bring my daughter back to her community and join it with her, I cannot but accept this gift you bring. Rise, my son. Continue now with my blessing. Walk the Path alongside Tenshi Koroma till one of you is translated."

MINUTES LATER, BRANDO WALKED PAST SAMANEINO TEYOPAN toward the Southeastern quadrant. He found the Pishan residence behind the progressive sikoro. It had clearly been designed by Tenshi, all rounded edges and unpredictable angles, as if arising naturally through the weathering of wind and rain.

Meji Pishan was waiting for Brando on the stone veranda.

"Brando-wa," they called. "Welcome to our home."

The arojin gestured at a wicker chair beside them, and Brando walked up the steps to sit down. Pishan did the same. Between them was a pitcher of water. Brando didn't hesitate, but poured the older omedeyo a cup and then one for himself.

"Thank you for receiving me today, arojin-zin. I know it was short notice."

Pishan took a sip of their water. "Not at all. Once you explained that you're on the Path, that you had the vision—and in Jinja ra-Shamanga, no less—it became my duty and my joy to let you walk in my shade for a time."

Brando turned slightly, sipped his own water, then nodded. "I'll be honest. I wasn't expecting any of this. I turned my back on my parents' faith when I was a teen. Eased into agnosticism. Hadn't given my religious needs much thought till I got here."

"Do you think," Pishan asked, "that the incident at the fair and your relationship with Tenshi-shi may have influenced you?"

Brando tilted his head side to side. "Probably? But even before the fair, Professor Modupe and I had a conversation that got me thinking. He started off by conceding what I had long believed: religion isn't reality. Then he carefully argued that we humans don't build our identities out of reality, but out of stories. To him, religion is the most important story humans tell. Reality's always going be reality. We can't change that, though it's clear we are incapable of perceiving the totality of that reality. But we can decide what stories to live by, Modupe said, and whether we're the protagonist, villain or just some by-stander."

"And those arguments moved you?"

"Yes. I think I just needed permission, you know? To set aside the shield of agnosticism."

Pishan set down their clay cup. "Yes. I think that's right. I think you may have crossed the vastness of space, coming to this world of all possible destinations, because in the depths of your kludged self, you knew you needed to believe."

Unbidden, tears came to Brando's eyes. "When the ramatini called me *matakite*, I was filled with such unexpected joy, arojin-zin. But it's not enough. Because I want to walk the Path alongside Tenshi-shi. Her mother has given me her blessing."

Pishan sat back, astounded. Then they gave a light chuckle. "You continue to surprise me, child. I would not have predicted such an outcome."

"Of course, she underscored the obvious obstacle. I have to become a teyopanjin." Brando leaned forward. "I want this to be my community. I want you to be my giya. And I'm begging you, once you're installed as this town's spiritual leader, to let the woman I love return. Not because you two are friends. No. Because she walks the Path with clearer eyes than most on this world, and Kinguyama needs her."

"There's no need to twist my arm where Tenshi-shi is concerned," Pishan answered. "One of my first acts will be to welcome her back. But if you wish to join us, you have to affirm the Three Tenets."

Brando turned and drank the rest of his water in a single draught. "Okay. What are they?"

"One, that humans are born without souls."

Brando nodded. "Agreed."

"Two, all the universe is a fractured piece of the Ogdoad."

"Even before my vision," Brando explained, "I'd been thinking about this idea. I had long accepted what science tells us: there are multiple universes, higher dimensions reflected in our visible three. It didn't seem too much of a stretch, even then. Yes. I affirm the second tenet."

"Three," the arojin concluded, "humans' fate is to create souls for themselves through self-knowledge and in that way help to restore the Ogdoad."

Brando swallowed heavily. "There's the rub, no? I've never thought about my own fate, much less humanity's. But self-discovery or self-creation have long been the work of the wisest among us."

Pishan served the water this time.

"What we are, Brando-wa?"

"Science says we're physical beings whose minds are legions of cognitive subsystems and symbol sets forming alliance after alliance. The winning group gets control of the consciousness, which can be best defined as the group reporting back to itself what the organism's doing. A rewritten account of what it just did."

"Symbol sets? The ideas we absorb, they become part of us?"

"Yes. Part of our internal monologue."

Waiting for Brando to take a sip, Pishan took up their own cup. "Pathwalkers call this the kludged self. You had no control over its creation, Brando-wa. Now that you're on the Path, you must shatter it and rebuild it around the spark that spoke to you. If you agree that this work will be the center of your life from now until death, then you in effect affirm the third tenet. The other details will come into focus as you study and meditate."

"Yes, Arojin-zin. I affirm the third tenet."

Setting down their cup and standing, Pishan began to pull something from the right sleeve of their robe. "Then you must kneel before me, Meji Pishan, your new teacher and guide. This is the Rite of Upanayana. Stip to the waist, Brando-shi. I will mark you as a teyopanjin here in the town that now embraces you."

THAT EVENING, TENSHI HAD MANY QUESTIONS, but Brando asked her to wait until their picnic. Impatient and a little irritated, she went to bed early. He eventually eased under the covers beside her, not ready to let her see what now lay beneath his shirt.

Tenshi was up before him, preparing the basket of food. After a pleasant cup of koro brew, they both showered and headed toward Anakwa Park.

Resting on a blanket, watching water fowl catch insects and fish beneath the midday sun, they began to talk.

"I don't think I can take the suspense much longer, Brando," Tenshi said. "I'm going to scream pretty soon."

He raised a hand, palm forward. "Okay. I'm sorry that I've had to keep you in the dark. But there were things I need to sort out first, my love."

Taking a deep breath, he continued.

"I went to Kinguyama yesterday."

Her eyes narrowed. "To do what, exactly?"

"It's easier if I show you," he said, and began unbuttoning his shirt.

"Brando, we're in public!" she said, laughing a little.

Then her smile faded and tears stood out in her eyes.

"Oh, baby. You didn't."

Brando put his fingers on the Pathwalker cord that crossed his chest, passing over his left shoulder and under his right. It was woven from eight strands, each a different shade of blue. "I met with Meji Pishan. Affirmed the three tenets. They agreed to be my teacher and draped the intambo over my heart."

Overcome, Tenshi reached out and hugged him to her. "Oh, Brando-shi. Welcome, Seer. I am so filled with joy."

He pulled away from her and reached into his pocket.

"Conversion wasn't my only purpose. I want to be part of your story, Tenshi. I want your story to rearrange the symbols in my mind. I want your voice to be my voice. So I, uh, visited your home. Spoke with your mother. Presented her with koro nuts, sat at her table and drank the tea."

Tenshi's hands went to her mouth. Her eyes were wide, tears flowing freely. She couldn't speak, so Brando pushed on.

Drawing his hand from his pocket, he held out the ring.

"Tenshi Koroma, love of my life, will you let me walk the Path alongside you?"

Bawling now, her normal stoic strength washed away by a storm of joyful tears, Tenshi nodded, extending her left hand.

Brando slipped the strange ring on her finger. It glittered almost impossible hues of silver and blue as the couple embraced and then kissed beneath the twin suns, that glowed like the watchful, approving eyes of Sopiya herself.

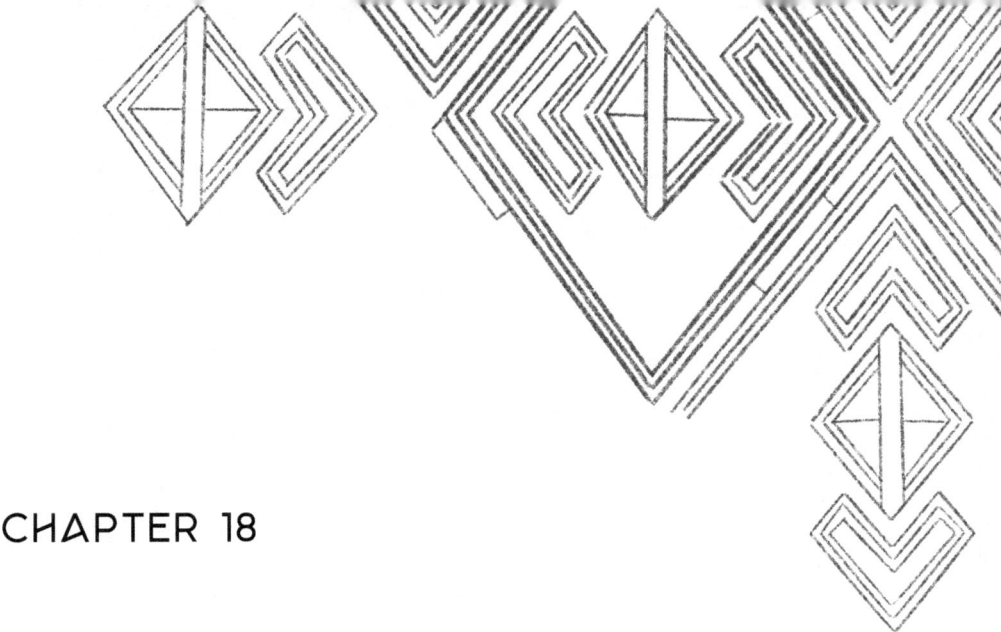

CHAPTER 18

ARCHON MUTEMI RAWE INHALED DEEPLY. The smoke from the mohiyo incense eased its way into his mind, loosening the ties that bound his created soul to illusory flesh.

In a low monotone, he began to chant.

"Annidaru nidaru nizikwepachu. Annidaru nidaru nizikwepachu."

He yearned with every fiber of his enlightened being, striving to push past life's prison and touch the Ogdoad. The world around him faded. He could sense the black veil at the edge of false reality, ready to be torn away.

The Blue surrounded him, layer upon layer of numbing azure light.

In the midst of his ecstasy, Mutemi called out with all the zeal he could muster.

Aroha. Aroha, my love!

But he faltered. Could not pass beyond.

The blue-spangled Blue faded into swirling black.

No answer came. Not from without, and not from within. Aroha's simran, the echo of his bricolage self in the intaglio of Mutemi's soul, had long ago fallen silent.

What sort of kedarumsha am I? he scolded himself. *I can no longer even hear the whispering of the Eight, much less cross into ra-Yindawo and speak with the translated soul of my beloved husband.*

It was a privilege reserved for Oracles alone. The archon knew his limits. Yet he could not let go, not even now, a decade after Aroha had been translated, his body burned, its ashes scattered.

If only I were certain. If only he spoke to me directly. Then I would know that she is truly tapping into yogijen and not some other, darker place.

In the absence of such surety, Mutemi Rawe could only go through the established routines. His regularly scheduled audience with the Oracle was today. Sighing at his own inadequacies as a leader, he dropped a silver lid over the bowl of incense and slowly stood.

"I am ready to be attended," he called.

A half-dozen acolytes filed into the room, their personal regimens for satori bound up in service to their Archon. As they cleansed and dressed him, Mutemi began steeling himself for whatever ordeal awaited in Jinja ra-Orakuru.

AN HOUR LATER, THE ARCHON STOOD OUTSIDE the White Room, deep in the labyrinthine heart of the honden. The omedeyo security guards stood aside, and Mutemi Rawe stepped through the shimmering entrance.

Inside, the Oracle was sitting in the lotus position on the floor. Behind her stood the insectoid chirurgic, glittering like a cypher.

"Archon," Samanei said simply.

Rawe knelt on the floor and lowered his head. "Oracle."

"I'm sorry, Mutemi-yi."

The archon's eyes came up. "For what, Enlightened One?"

"You failed to reach ra-Yindawo today. You didn't get a response from the Ogdoad."

His heart quickened its pace. It was always startling, how much she knew.

"No, Oracle. I did not."

Samanei crossed her arms over her chest. "It's because you're abusing ukaribu. One connects with the Eight to be guided, not to make demands. And you're flirting with heresy, you realize. Were I to tell Santo Koroma, for example, that you've been attempting yorukaki, that you want to speak directly to the translated soul of your husband, he could convene a Quorum of Arojin and have you removed from your position. He would love that, believe me."

The archon's palms ached with fear. "Forgive me, Enlightened One."

"It's partly my fault. I've been too accommodating of your weakness, my child. I've used my yorukaki ability to create a bridge between you and Aroha. I wanted to show my love for you, to make clear that you're my chosen representative, but I've let this go too far. Your physical and emotional yearning for your husband, who has escaped this Grey Prison and does not deserve to be recalled here agan and again, has begun to taint your Quantum Enlightenment. Changes must be made."

Shame forced the archon's head to the floor. Sprawled in total obeisance, he could only bear to whisper. "Command me, Samanenim Ummanim."

"Removing the temptation is the only answer. I need to retire from your touch. To put myself out of your touch."

Tears spilled from Rawe's eyes onto the blinding white tiles.

"Chirurgic, explain," Samanei instructed.

"We will put Miss Samanei Koroma in cryogenic hypostasis," explained the AI medbot in its almost childlike yet frigid voice. "As if she were on a spaceship. In that state, her flesh will be preserved at its present cellular age, age twenty-five standard years. At the same time, she will be able to continue overseeing religious affairs and having audiences with government officials via faux-conferencing."

Shocked, the archon pushed himself up to look at Samanei.

"Oracle, other arojin will object. You predicted my possible removal. Such a drastic act could also bring that about."

In an unexpected, fluid movement, Samanei stood and walked toward him, her demeanor changed, her steps a swagger.

"Listen, Mutemi," she growled in the Founder's voice. "She's not just trying to protect you from yourself, fool. She's trying to protect *herself.*"

The archon's eyes dropped to the crinkled ebony of Samanei's toes.

"From whom, Founder Dresch?"

"Santo Koroma. He's been abusing Samanei's yorukaki abilities as well, communicating with his dead mother. And that voice represents currents within the Ogdoad that are decidedly *not* in your favor. I suggest you just obey the girl and quit whining. The arojin will accept an official decree from her. We know it will take some time, but you can meet singly with those that support you the most, prepare them for the announcement. By the end of the year, however, she needs to be in d-sleep."

Then the Oracle knelt, putting her hands on the archon's cheeks and lifting his eyes to meet hers.

"Beloved Mutemi-nim," Aroha said through her. "It's for the best. Soon we will comingle within the source itself. You can endure a few more years without me."

"But ..."

The Oracle's hands clenched into fists.

"Follow your fucking vow," she snarled in a voice he'd never heard before. "Keep your ancient cock beneath your robes, Mutemi. Have some fucking self-respect."

Squeezing shut his eyes, the archon shuddered with shame and fear.

Samanei sighed. He felt her kiss him gently on the lips and stand.

"Good. It's settled," she said in her own voice. "Go, my child. Get Jitsu ready. Change is coming. I'll tell you more soon. Bit by startling bit. You're

going to be so surprised."

When Mutemi dared to look again, there was a terrible smile on her face.

CHAPTER 19

"THAT'S A STRANGE RING," NIKKI TRINH QUIPPED. "But then again, you're dating a strange guy."

"Don't listen to her, Tenshi," Areshan Yesuro replied. "I think it's lovely. But not as lovely as him converting for you. What a beautiful gesture!"

The three friends were sitting at an outdoor café near the Mito Haraka River, which flowed through the business district of Station City. Areshan was the prefect of Inkungu, land of pale misty forests and many reformer communities. Nikki Trinh was the owner of Trincon, the biggest supplier of construction materials on Jitsu.

"I think he converted for *himself* more than for me," Tenshi told Areshan, putting her hand on theirs reassuringly, "but it certainly was beautiful. I couldn't stop crying."

Nikki arched an eyebrow. "Wow. I wouldn't have predicted that. Don't think I've seen you cry since Isabella left. Plus, Brando doesn't really seem your type."

Tenshi scoffed. "I have a type? Come on. I'm as pan as can be."

"Sure you do, Ten. Tall, lightskinned offworlders."

Tenshi made an incredulous gesture. "What? I've dated plenty of my fellow Aknawajin from this planet."

Areshan took a sip of water. "Most of them a shade lighter and a lot taller than you."

"Uh," Tenshi pointed out with a shrug, "that's a good chunk of the population, *friend*."

They all laughed for a moment. Dabbing at her eyes with a napkin, Tenshi explained, "He's definitely shorter than other folks I've dated. And darker than some off the offworlders I've been with, sure."

"Isn't he Italian, like Isabella?" Areshan asked.

"Yeah, but they aren't all the same, Are. His mother is Black."

Nikki leaned forward with a conspiratorial grin. "Okay, spill. How is he in bed? I mean, you haven't been with a man for a while. What was what you used to say? 'In the sheets, a girl completes.' Isn't that right, Are?"

Covering their mouth with one hand, Areshan nodded. They swallowed, then added, "Though after that one omedeyo she dated, what was their name? Jiho something? She declared that we were a close second."

"With men trailing far behind." Tenshi scratched at her head, annoyed but bemused. "Yes, you jokers, I did indeed say all of that. But to answer your question, Ms. Trinh, ahem: the sex is very good. He's not quite as—

accomplished?—as Ambar and Isabella, but he focuses on my needs better than any other man I've been with."

"Good," the businesswoman replied.

"But that's not the most important part, yall. He's warm-hearted. Sensitive. Brilliant. And willing to shut up and listen."

Are raised an eyebrow. "That's ... pretty uncommon among men."

"Yes, it is. He also isn't burdened with deep-seated ideology. He tries to understand others before judging them. Keeps his mind open to the possibility that he might be wrong and they right. Above all, he supports me. Isn't humiliated or threatened by my success. Wants to take care of all my physical needs so I can focus on the important work I'm doing. And by the Grey Prison, that man can *cook*. Yall just don't know. Wait till I invite yall over to our house."

Nikki sat up, blinking. "House? What house?"

"I got reinstated in the community. As an official satorijin, no less. They've granted me that plot of land I showed you a few years ago."

Pulling her tablet from her bag, Nikki started clicking on the screen. "I think I have that quote I gave you saved. I mean, you are getting the materials from me, right?"

Tenshi put her chin in her right palm. "Depends. Is the discount the same?"

THE WEDDING TOOK PLACE ON the 20th of Tenmezi, the last of Jitsu's ten forty-day months, in local year 136—July 26, 2683 by the Consortium Calendar.

People were still reluctant to be inside Samaneino Tepoyan, so the ceremony was held in the courtyard at the center of the complex. Though between them, Tenshi and Brando had only invited about thirty-five guests, the tradition on Jitsu was that anyone in the community could attend.

The courtyard was packed.

Tenshi, waiting in a room nearby, felt her palms ache with unaccustomed nervousness.

This is really happening. We're really getting married. We're going to walk the Path together. We're going to change the world together.

She felt her mother's hand on her back. "Peace, Tanim. Don't tremble so. This is a time of joy, not fear."

"Oh, Umma. I am not afraid. I am nearly bursting with joyful possibility."

Wearing the blue-fringed white robes of a giya, Meji Pishan took their place before the gathered people and began to speak.

"At the beginning of time, Neweru was one, though they chose to pull away from the communion of the Eight. Then the one became two, and the Grey Prison arose, their heartbreak made visible, tangible illusion. When Sopiya shattered, her sparks were flung far and wide. We coalesce around them, each of us alone. Grieving. Broken from birth, though we cannot fathom why."

Through the window, Tenshi saw them look pointedly at their spouse, Jina Chimari.

"Ah, but we are not meant to be alone. As we walk the Path, our sparks are drawn together. And at a moment of blessed joy, two or more nascent souls touch, fuse. They are forever entwined, their quantum enlightenment codependent. When they know this to be true, they come before their community and allow themselves to be ritually joined, as one day Sakra and Sopiya will be reunited as a single umbini, restored to the Ogdoad in ra-Yindawo."

Lifting their arms, the giya beckoned.

"Let the dyad be guided forward."

Inyoni Onamata took Tenshi's hand in hers. Opening the door, mother led daughter into the light of morning.

Tenshi's hair had been bound in a wrap woven with the Sonari clan's ancestral pattern, bright gold against sunset red. She was wearing a sleeveless white dress, edged in those same colors.

She was barefoot, a pilgrim stepping onto a new stretch of the Path.

Turning her head, she saw Modupe Oduyoye lead Brando from the other side.

He wore blue. A suit that shimmered with a thousand azure hues.

His brown eyes locked with hers. She let her mother lead her, never moving her gaze from her beloved's face.

Then they were standing before Pishan, and she looked down while the giya spoke.

"Satorijin Tenshi Koroma ma-Sonari. Teyopanjin Brando D'Angelo di Makomo. You have asked me your giya to bind you here before your teyopan, before the larger hapori of Kinguyama, indeed before all of Jitsu and the cosmos itself. So be it. Say the words."

Brando reached out and took Tenshi's left hand with his right. She raised her eyes as he began to speak.

"Tenshi-shi. I stand beside you on the Path, ready to walk with you unto the very end. Your enlightenment is now my goal. I will aid you every step of the way."

Clearing her throat, Tenshi uttered the ritual response. "Brando-shi. I place my spark in your heart and accept yours in mine. We are dual, two yet one. We create our souls together from here on, fusing them until translation."

"And beyond," Brando added, unexpectedly. "Nothing will keep me from your side, Tenshi-shi. Not even death."

Pishan turned to Modupe. "Do you have the rings?"

The old professor placed them in the giya's outstretched palm. Then Pishan placed Tenshi's on her left ring finger, Brando's on his right. When they held hands again, the bands of strange metal touched.

Tenshi could have sworn she felt a slight electric jolt.

"Do you have the ribbon, Anshyano Inyoni?"

Tenshi's mother placed a blue strip of fabric in their hands. Carefully, the giya wound it around Tenshi's left and Brando's right arm, binding them symbolically together.

"Teyopanjin, other friends, raise your voices in celebration of Tenshi and Brando!"

The crowd shouted in unison: "Zumbinaro soro!"

Be truly one from two! Tenshi couldn't stop the tears.

Brando reached out with his left hand and pulled her face to his.

They kissed for the first time as husband and wife as cheers went up all around.

AS MUCH AS SHE HATED SURPRISES, Tenshi knew Brando loved them, so she kept the location of their honeymoon a secret till they were nearly there, skimming the salty waves of Bahari ra-Chumwi between the two continents.

A group of rocky islands rose above the spray.

"There they are. Kude Kisiwa. The Distant Isles."

"Whoa." Brando leaned forward and zoomed the viewscreen closer. An imposing structure of black stone dominated the green moss of the largest island. "Who lives here?"

"That's Sudowon ra-Pahuka, a monastery of sorts. When the second Oracle was sealed away from the world by Archon Ajabu Rangachira, many of her teachings were expunged from official scripture. Those who insisted on remembering and following them were persecuted. A few made there way here. They started Tarika ra-Kiyish."

"The Order of the, uh, Spike? Spikes?" Brando ventured.

She nodded, remembering the smell of salt and rock, the feel of the fishing nets in her hands, her long journey toward the creation of her soul.

"This is where I reached satori, Brando-yi. With the Order's help, I found my Way along the Path."

Her transport settled down on a flat expanse of rock not far from the the monastery. An omedeyo emerged from the black stone building to greet them. They wore dark grey robes with silver piping, their own long locs similarly rimed with age.

"Tenshi-shi!" the robed figure said as they exited the transport. "What a delight to see you again. Four years has seemed an eternity."

"Thank you, acharya-zin. This is my husband, Brando D'Angelo. Brando, this is Unhe Siku, my teacher."

Brando ducked his head in respectful greeting.

"Be enlighted, mitawa-zin," he said, using the formal title for Pathwalker ascetics.

Tenshi raised an appreciative eyebrow. *He's been studying!*

"You as well, Brando-shi." Unhe gestured toward the monastery. "Please, follow me. I'll take yall to the room we've set aside for this glorious stay."

Tenshi smiled with delight, and nodded at Brando, who easily picked up their bags with his uncommon Earther strength and followed her teacher.

The mammoth doors of Sudowon ra-Pahuka swung open easily under the ascetic's gentle push. They led the couple through vestibule and high-vaulted nave. Tenshi heard Brando's breath catch in his throat at the metal-veined columns, the giant statues—Alejandro Dresch, Domina Ditis, Arehanja Sanaustin, Kosiya Yemo, Samanei Koroma—and the sacred intaglios etched in silver upon walls and ceiling.

"Everything's monochrome," her husband whispered, "except for that recurring symbol with the eight colors. Does it represent the Ogdoad?"

Tenshi nodded. "It's the Eipande Nyota, the Primal Octagram. A tesseract unfolded into three-dimensional space. The four color pairs stand for the four umbini. Our most important icon. You may end up contemplating it a lot during meditation."

Spaces for worship and meditation were replaced by labyrinthine corridors and winding staircases. Several levels below the surface, Tenshi felt her heart swell at a familiar stretch of hall: the visiting students wing.

"Oh, acharya-zin, please tell me—" she began.

Unhe Siku laughed softly. "Yes, dear child, I set aside your old room, just as you asked."

Siku laid their hand upon a panel of black glass, and the driftwood door slid open, revealing a stone chamber dominated by a stone desk and a large bed, accented by soft rugs and low tables for dining. Tenshi rushed in, almost squealing with delight.

"Come on, Brando! You have to see this view."

She pulled him toward the double metal doors set into the far wall, yanking them open to reveal the broad stone balcony.

Below, the sea roiled and smashed against the cliffs, sending up thick spray that became light mist by the time it reached them.

"Isn't it amazing?" she asked.

Brando nodded. "Breathtaking. Like you."

They stared at each other for a moment. Tenshi felt she might get lost in those dark eyes of his, yawning like tunnels into ra-Yindawo.

Then a rock eagle wheeled past, screeching at them. The couple turned back to the room and found the ascetic gone and the door discretely shut.

"My teacher knows me well," Tenshi muttered. Brando's biceps and chest swelled, tantalizing, beneath his silk shirt. "Drop those bags. Now. I refuse to wait a single second longer."

As the sea haze drifted into the room, she pushed Brando back onto the bed and began to unbutton her blouse, bending to devour his deep red lips with a hungry mix of lust and adoration.

THEIR FIRST TWO DAYS WERE SPENT in that room, making love often, eating the delicious seafood dishes brought to them by various ascetics every four hours. Brando sang love songs to her in every language he knew, his hands as expert on the strings of his guitar as they were upon her eager flesh.

On the the third day, they got dressed, and Tenshi led Brando to her second-favorite place in Sudowon ra-Pahuka: its vast library, one level above them.

Tenshi could see Brando's excitement at the shelves burgeoning with physical books. Rather than pull any, however, he stood before one of the many large reading screens throughout the space and scrolled through the holdings.

"By Sopiya, there are works on Baryogo grammar and etymology that literally don't exist anywhere else in the universe, Tenshi!"

Tenshi thought of all she had planned for him, the amazing things she would help his unparalleled mind to do, the potential she would draw from him as time passed. Overwhelmed by her loved, she hugged him from behind, her lips brushing his ear. "You're so predictable, Kyosu-chan. Talk to Unhe. They'll go to the mushri, the Order's leader, and get you permission to download the digital files. But first, let me show you something much more valuable."

Taking his hand, she dragged him away from the screen, toward the darker recess of the library, where tenuous lighting revealed two glass cases.

Each contained a hand-written book, partly open on basalt stands.

"What are they?" Brando asked, intrigued.

"Two important texts for Ona ra-Shamanga. This one's a copy of Kosiya Yemo's excised teachings, transcribed by Ramatini Hekima Umchawi herself before the second Oracle was sealed away in the jinja. The other is the original manuscript of *Kiyik juya Shari*."

Brando did a double take. "*Blood upon Sand?* Isn't that lost second volume of Domina's journals?"

"Yeah. Adherents of the shamanga tradition have kept it hidden because

Dominian clerics would destroy it if they knew it still existed. Its contents undercut their isolationist, extremist narrative. I was pissed off for weeks after reading it."

Promising to give him an executive summary over dinner, Tenshi then took Brando outside. They walked the grassy paths that sloped downward as one traveled south. Eventually they came to a series of steps carved into the volcanic rock, leading toward busy docks below.

"Boats?" her husband asked, looking at the ascetics rowing away and the others just arriving. "Does fishing keep this place running?"

"Sure does," she said. "Some of the best restaurants in Station City use seafood caught in these waters. I spent time hauling in nets here and helping transport the catch. They make pretty good money off of it."

Brando squinted. "The boats seem made of rock. How is that even possible?"

Tenshi pointed ahead. "There's a lightweight sort of basalt on the next island over. Those large warehouses are where students help ascetics break it down and blend it with plant fibers, making a sturdy composite fabric used to make hulls."

Craning his neck, Brando struggled to make something out. "And those shapes? Beyond the warehouses, on the beach? Wait, are those sails?"

"They're larger ships. For bahariro hija. Sea pilgrimages," Tenshi explained. "A group visits the ramatini at the shrine, is given a kiyish—a spike from the Urim—and sets out upon the sea to drop the relic into the depths."

Clouds on the distant horizon flickered with lightning as if to underscore the danger in such treks.

"Do they all make it back?" Brando asked. "It's a pretty enormous ocean, with little land mass once you leave this hemisphere."

"A few don't," Tenshi admitted. "But the ascetics insist the journey's worth the risk. They believe that one day these carefully distributed kiyish will help everyone on Jitsu break free of the Grey Prison."

Brando put his arm around Tenshi. She found she still thrilled to his touch, like a teenager crushing for the first time. It was almost embarrassing, if very pleasant. "And they've been doing this since the second Oracle was taken away?"

"More or less. Twice a year for the past half century."

"I wonder how the Urim still has so many spikes left."

Tenshi shrugged and leaned into him. "Only Sopiya knows, love. But that storm looks pretty nasty. Let's get inside before it hits. I've always wanted to make love with lightning and thunder crashing all around."

He winked conspiratorially. "What a coincidence! Me, too."

TENSHI WAS SAD A FEW DAYS LATER when their honeymoon came to an end. But a new semester was about to start for Brando and she needed to get construction underway on their home. Busy quotidian rhythms soon replaced the joyous spontaneity of those early weeks, but she was content nonetheless.

A month after the wedding ceremony, Tenshi began to wake up nauseous in the middle of the night. After a few days of throwing up discretely, she visited her mother.

"You're pregnant, Tanim," Inyoni said with stubborn confidence. "Let's go to the aransa to make certain, but this is the way it has been with the women of the Sonari clan for generations. We marry, and that binding of sparks makes us incredibly fertile."

Tenshi tightened her grip on her mother's hand. "Yes, love draws more love. I can see that. But I'm scared, Umma. What if I'm not a good mother?"

Inyoni turned her head aside. When she spoke at last, her voice was husky. "You'll be a better mother than I ever was to you or your sister. Don't you worry."

They went together to visit Kinguyama's best aransa, Kanan Rongoa. The midwife confirmed Inyoni's suspicions, doing a medical scan in addition to her traditional inspection.

Come home right after class, Tenshi messaged Brando as she flew back to their apartment in Station City. *We need to talk.*

He arrived breathlessly, his eyes brimming with worry.

"Tenshi? Sweetheart, is everything okay? I could barely focus during office hours. Finally ran the last student out and came as quick as I could."

"Here," she said, drawing him into the living room. "Sit down."

It felt like all her courage had been sapped away. Excitement fluttered in her belly, but it was tempered by the knowledge that both she and Brando had terrible parents.

"Brando-chan. Love. I know we had planned to wait, but—I'm pregnant."

Something strange happened to his face. Muscles twitched. His eyes glistened.

Then, as if launched by his emotions, he stood quickly and fell to his knees in front of Tenshi, wrapping his arms tightly around her waist.

"I'm so happy," he managed to say despite the trembling of his chest. "Thank you."

He's weeping, she thought, astonished. *For joy.*

"Did … did you just *thank* me? Uh, Kyosu-chan, you had as much to do with this as I did, I'll remind you."

His crying shudders turned to laughter as he looked up at her, face wet.

"You can never let me just be gushy and sentimental, can you?"

Tenshi sighed, smiling. "It's sweet and all, but you need to face the facts. This is going to complicate our plans."

She half-expected him to react like a typical man, insist she rest and postpone her projects, treat her like an invalid.

But Brando, like always, surprised her.

"Why? Being pregnant doesn't keep you from meeting with other Reformers or overseeing the construction of our house. In fact, you need to get moving on that like yesterday if you plan on being done before the baby's born."

Tenshi straightened, cocked her head at him. "Yes, okay. And you? What will you be doing as I work my pregnant ass off?"

"Helping you every spare moment I have, Tenshi." He took both her hands in his. "I'll pick up all the slack you need me to. I suck at manual labor, but I can learn. We can do this. Together."

Tenshi thought her chest might burst. She'd loved him before, but now she almost couldn't bear how much he filled her heart.

Thank you, she prayed in the most secret part of her nascent soul. *Thank you for putting him on the Path beside me.*

CHAPTER 20

MEJI PISHAN KEPT THEIR EYES CLOSED IN SILENT MEDITATION AS they waited in the outer rooms of the Archon's office suite. They were still overjoyed that they'd been chosen as giya of Kinguyama, a gift of the Ogdoad that they'd never once pursued. Since childhood they'd taken to heart the precepts, taught to them lovingly by their parents and other teyopanjin, that instructed Pathwalkers to avoid striving for anything beyond enlightenment. What the Ogdoad willed for one in the Grey Prison would be given one, and one need not worry about goals besides the creation of a soul.

Many argued that Pishan's pro-reform posture contradicted this belief, but the omedeyo disagreed: objection to outside influences was a sign of more concern with physical reality than permitting them to exist could ever be. Those who strove to eliminate obstacles to gnosis finally created more of them.

As giya, Meji Pishan would engage fully in the next stretch of their Path: leading their Pathwalker siblings to gnosis as well. Brando-shi's conversion had been an auspicious start. Now they would have to strive more than ever, involve themself in the minutiae of the physical existence of their fellow teyopanjin in order to ease the shattering of those kludged selves and the bricolage of their souls. Pishan believed that the best way forward was to stop the hermetic hostility that gripped three-quarters of Kinguyama, allowing outsiders and their ideas to flow in as the Eight saw fit.

Of course, they would ask the Archon and the Oracle for guidance in this matter, as they were the Ogdoad's representatives in the Grey Prison.

"Giya Pishan. Sorry to disturb. The Archon wishes to see you now."

Meji's eyes slid slowly open. They exhaled and stood, nodding at Inho Bek, who'd just spoken. The secretary gestured toward the entrance to the Archon's office, and Meji drifted in.

Mutemi Rawe did not rise from his seat behind a simple marble desk, but he indicated a chair with a nod of his bald, speckled head. Meji sat, eyes fixed on the wrinkled visage of their spiritual and political leader. Even sitting in the presence of the ratowanin was overwhelming, an honor for which Meji had long yearned. That the Eight had seen fit to grant this childhood wish augured well.

The giya wondered briefly if they would ever be blessed enough to stand before the Oracle herself. Since their gender affirmation ceremony at the age of seven, when Meji's community recognized them as an omedeyo, they had fantasized about becoming one of the Close, that cabal of nonbinary Pathwalkers who had served the second Oracle and scoured Jitsu for a third. Sadly, when

Santo Koroma had brought Samanei to them, Meji was already too old to be recruited. Now they could only hope that their Way along the Path would bring them face-to-face with the figurehead of eternity.

"I haven't been able to offer my congratulations," the ancient Archon wheezed, "on your new position, Arojin-kun. I hope you've settled into the role well."

Meji inclined their head slightly. "The Ogdoad's will is always done. The congregation at Kinguyama is receptive to my guidance."

"Speaking of the Eight, I brought you here at the behest of the Oracle. She is taking an interest in you, it seems."

A warm, surprised feeling spread throughout Meji's chest. "She is?"

"Yes. She and I have been discussing the direction Jitsu should be heading. As you are no doubt aware, the CPCC urges us to adopt measures that will bring us into compliance with the standards for admission."

The giya nodded. "Is the Oracle backing CPCC membership for Jitsu?"

"She won't say; however, she has instructed me to permit more reform. The Chamber of Deputies was formed at her command, and she also instructed me to permit the CPCC consulate to rent Tenshi Koroma's structure near the University. Now she wants us to try something else: turning the running of a town over to a secular government so that off-worlders will be encouraged to live there."

Meji was surprised. "I had thought, given the massacres, that the government would adopt a more conservative position. Does the Oracle not think strict Dominians will oppose such a move?"

"She does. This is why she's balancing this move with the appointment of Santo Koroma as head of the Anti-Terrorism Squads. She insists that our conservative companions on the Path will be placated by such power, less likely to oppose our little experiment. However, she doesn't want to be connected directly with the project, nor does she want me to be. With Arojin Koroma's investigation underway, we have to appear to be neutral so as not to make extremists on either side too skittish."

It occurred to Meji that the Archon needed a well-respected reformer to implement the changes, someone whom both conservatives and progressives could trust to preserve the integrity of the Pathwalker way of life while opening up their society to off-worlders.

The reason for the summons was now clear. The Oracle and the Archon, in what Meji considered the greatest honor ever, had selected them to be the vessel of their mission.

"You wish Kinguyama to be the site of the new secular government, don't you?"

The Archon smiled broadly, his yellowed teeth showing between thin, bloodless lips. "Yes. We think you are the aptest person for the job. There are some issues you must understand, though. First, you will get no public support from us except our tacit approval when we don't condemn your acts. The Chamber will have to vote on many of the measures you'll be trying to implement, but given the Reformer majority, that shouldn't be a problem. I will not veto any of the decisions they make. In addition, you'll have to win the people of your teyopan over to your way of thinking: if you attempt to force reform on them now, with all that is going on, you'll be defeated. This task requires work, it requires patience, and above all it requires wiles. Do you possess them?"

A tension was building in Meji. It seemed duplicity was required, the sort of political maneuvering that Santo Koroma regularly engaged in and that Meji found distasteful, though they were careful never to judge those who used such tactics, as those people's own attainment or not of enlightenment would be sufficient judgment for all eternity. Nonetheless, in order to bring about the good the Archon and Oracle swore would come of this, Meji would have to learn to think in a novel way. Perhaps this step was the next step in their own personal Way down the Path to ra-Yindawo, along which they could walk side by side with spouse and friends and siblings.

"Tenshi," they said suddenly. Rawe cocked his left eyebrow as if in question. Meji continued. "Tenshi Koroma. All of Jitsu is still bubbling with praise for how she protected people at the fair, she and Brando D'Angelo."

The Archon leaned forward. "I notice he converted."

"Yes, I draped the intambo over his heart myself."

"Why would an offworlder become a Kinguyama teyopanjin?" Rawe wondered.

"The two wanted to marry, he and Tenshi. And that marriage is partly why I insist, kedarumsha-zin, that Tenshi is key. She has come full circle: rebellion to maturity. Under the guidance of Ramatini Hekima Umchawi she has achieved satori. She's begun to assume responsibility for others, acting as an anshyano within Reformer circles. But she knows it's not enough. Community matters. She asked to be reinstated into the teyopan, and the congretation assented."

"As far as I know, the newlyweds still do not live among your people, however." The Archon's tone was strange, inscrutable.

"They soon will. Tenshi has asked to be granted some land near the desert to build a home. She promised to do whatever work we assigned her in exchange. I know Kinguyama will be receptive to the idea: you wouldn't believe how many visits I've had from teyopanjin who are awed by her dedication to her people. They'll accept her. And with her help I'm certain I can remake Kinguyama as the Oracle has decreed."

The Archon steepled his fingers. "She may be an asset to your task, a bridge between two worlds. I'm not sure how the Oracle will react, but I believe yours is a good plan. What task will you require in exchange for the land?"

A slight twinge of nervousness arose in the giya then, worry that they would be considered nako by their leader. To be here in the inner office, chatting with a piece of the Ogdoad as if they were simple colleagues, was the dream of a lifetime. Now they were about to risk ostracism.

With a soft sigh, Meji dismissed such worries. *Let the Eight decide what will be.*

"I want her to rebuild the teyopan. We have done all we can to repair the damage and scrub away the aftermath of the massacre. But the people still feel the weight of that tragedy. It pulls them from the Path. Distracts samadan children from their meditation. So I want to tear it down and have Tenshi build it anew. In her particular style. Let its imponderable form wipe all sadness from the people's minds."

The look in the Archon's eyes was indecipherable. Worry? Hope? Anger? A host of emotions flashed across his face in a matter of seconds.

After a moment of silence, his smile gone, Mutemi Rawe raspily intoned, "Do it. No matter what, Meji Pishan. Make her build it. Even if I tell you to stop, you make her build it."

Meji swallowed heavily and nodded, not understanding, but feeling the solid weight of stewardship settle upon their shoulders.

INTERCHAPTER D

Al-Muzzamml Potential Asset Dossier: Konrau Beserra

Narrative biographical timeline. Updated on World Day, 2683.

2650. Konrau Beserra born on Tenochtitlan Platform in the United Jovian Habitats. Son of Brotherhood lieutenant Sami Arredondo and Karmen Beserra. Arredondo already married with mistresses. Little involvement in Beserra's upbringing beyond monetary support. Visits him from time to time when carrying out Brotherhood business in UJH.

2661. After repeated behavioral issues in a corporate school, Beserra drops out and joins a klika [corridor gang] called Los Babois, which runs moku in the Koyotera district, providing a substantial cut to the Brotherhood. Beserra shows a knack for punishing dealers that do not pay on time.

2664. Beserra becomes head of his gang. Is taller and looks older than most teens his age. Leadership style: no discussion or arguing. Gives orders. If they are not obeyed, kills the offending person. Gang falls in line. He rewards them well, garnering their loyalty and affection.

2667. Beserra's klika has absorbed all others. Petty criminal activity in Koyotera is under his thumb. His ambitions make him look at other districts on Tenochtitlan. Local Brotherhood sub-kasike Narices Betancourt takes notice of Beserra. As the platform is divided between the Brotherhood and the Aztlan Angels, Betancourt has been looking for a way to push the rival syndicate off of Tenochtitlan. Learning of Beserra and his consolidation of corridor gangs, Betancourt looks into the teen and discovers who his father is. Approaching Beserra, he convinces him to work with the Brotherhood against the Aztlan Angels.

2668. Beserra begins his infiltration, joining Loh Malianteh, a gang in the Guadalupe district with ties to the Angels. Rises quickly through the ranks. Meets Jeini Andrade—only daughter of Bruno Andrade, head of the Aztlan Angels—at a party. Not knowing her identity, Beserra "saves" her from the advances of an undesirable petty criminal. They spend the night together. The following morning, Beserra learns her identity. Despite the danger, he continues to meet up with her for the next three months. Bruno Andrade discovers that his daughter is involved with a corridor gang and investigates Beserra, learning his real loyalties and weekly routine. On October 30, knowing Beserra will be traveling up the slidewalk along Juarez Boulevard in Tenochtitlan's hub and collecting give, Andrade takes Jeini shopping. They see Konrau standing in front of a store. Andrade tells Jeini he's found out about their trysts, but not to worry. Instructs her to drop her bag as they go by. If Beserra bends to collect it, that means he's a man, respectful but not fearful. Andrade will then consider giving him a chance. Jeini complies. Beserra steps onto the slidewalk and starts to pick up the purse. Andrade shoots him in the eye, but the projectile enters at an angle, exiting through his temple. As blood spatters and people start screaming, Andrade drags his daughter into a waiting transport, assuming his problem is fixed. But Beserra is not dead. Another two gangbangers undercover with him retrieve his body and take him back to Brotherhood territory. Narices Betancourt is furious with the failure and wants nothing to do with Beserra, but the young man's mother and friends nurse him back to health.

2669. Beserra's half-brother Felipe is born. Beserra refuses to recognize him, though he will later kill Felipe's biological father for have impregnated their mother while Beserra was unconscious from his wound in the adjacent room.

2670. After two years of planning, Beserra is ready to take his revenge. When Andrade makes his quarterly visit to Tenochtitlan, Beserra's team of older gangbangers and rebel Brothers carry out a hit. Many Angels are slaughtered. When Beserra breaks through to the local underboss's office, Andrade is waiting for Konrau with a gun to his own daughter's head. Reportedly, Andrade tells Beserra, "Put your weapons down and get the fuck out or I'm gonna kill her. Better she be dead than with a fucking Sisterhood bitch like you."

At that, Beserra lifts his own weapon higher, beforing shifting his aim from Andrade's head to Jeini's. "You're right," he apparently replies. Then Beserra shoots Jeini, though informants insist the girl was the only person other than his mother that he has ever loved. Andrade crumples to the ground with his daughter's body, unable to understand. Beserra walks over and puts his gun to the crime boss's head. At this point he purportedly says, "Two mistakes. Thinking I was dead, and thinking I had a heart. Tell Jeini I sent a hello." He kills Andrade and then makes his team leave the office. Shutting the door, he remains inside for 15 minutes. No informant can provide information about what he does during that period.

2671. In January, kasike Toni Benemerito summons Beserra to Anca L'ermandá [Brotherhood territory in the Cimmeria Region of Mars] and offers him a place in the organization. After becoming a mademan, Beserra is appointed lieutenant, overseeing crews in the Bach Run of Sol's Oort cloud. Beserra keeps tabs on the traffic through that pathway, making sure the Angels and the AF don't interfere with narcotic trafficking. At this point, he catches the eye of Nestor Bos, who sees leadership potential in the twenty-one-year-old.

2672. Beserra begins suffering from occasional debilitating headaches. Brotherhood medics and materias [shamans/mediums/folk healers] can find no apparent reason for them. A therapist tells Beserra they are psychosomatic, driven by the trauma of his killing the woman he loves. Beserra slits the therapist's throat.

2675. Inspired by the great success Beserra has had in increasing profits and keeping the Aztlan Angels in-system, Bos approaches the younger man, telling him that Benemerito has begun to see him as a threat. Bos reveals that Benemerito has blackmailed him for seven years, having implanted a microbomb in the head of Ria Bos, sister to Nestor and materia of the Fidencista sect of Catholicism. Bos shows Beserra the dirt he has on their kasike: evidence of a gay relationship, frowned upon by the queermisia embraced by the Brotherhood [see dossier on Nestor Bos for further background]. The death of Benemerito will detonate the bomb in his sister's head, so Bos has been unable to get out from under the kasike's thumb. The following is an exchange reported by Nestor Bos himself.

After exploring various options, Beserra clarifies that if he helps Bos, the price will be his ascension to kasike. Bos agrees. Beserra reveals the truth of

Benemerito's sexual orientation to his wife Ilda, who then permits the traitors to connect her sleeping husband to a rudimentary AI chirurgic in Nestor's possession. The docbot slowly takes over Benemerito's brain functions, fooling the transmitter's sensors, making Benemerito appear to wake up occasionally. Ilda, having been compensated handsomely, announces her husband is in a coma. Bos calls the family heads together and bullies them into accepting Beserra as kasike. As the young man is an Arredondo by blood, one of the six families, they go along with the unprecedented move, purportedly because of the dirt that Nestor has gathered on their family heads with the help of his sister.

But within a few hours of the ceremony, Bos receives a transmission from Benemerito's implant:

> "If you're seeing this, mama's boy, you or somebody's figured a way to put me under without holing me. But you fucked up, Nestor: I don't tap a code onto the surface of the implant ever Solar day, it goes off. I've protected your ugly sister for seven years by not forgetting, not a single day. Impressive, ain't it. But you just killed her, puto. See you in the nine circles!"

The microbomb detonates, killing Ria. Nestor Bos, in a rage, flies his personal transport to Benemerito's home, followed by Beserra, who is unsuccessful at stopping the counselor. Bos enters Benemerito's bedroom and shoots the man twelve times with explosive projectiles that rip his comatose form apart just as Beserra enters the room.

Ilda then storms in, screaming and attacking Bos with her fists. Beserra takes the gun from Bos, puts it in Ilda's hand, and makes her shoot the counselor in the shoulder with a non-explosive projectile. Then Beserra pulls his own weapon and kills her.

Beserra tells the family heads that Ilda discovered Benemerito's past and tried to kill him. As Beserra and Bos attempted to stop her, she shot Bos, leaving Beserra with no choice but to kill her. This story plus a limited revelation of the truth about Benemerito's sexual orientation convinces the heads to keep things quite and permit Beserra to remain in power. Bos insists to the present that their anger about Ria's death is the determining factor. Being Fidensistas, the murder of a materia is the most awful thing they can imagine.

2676. On the anniversary of Ria Bos's death, Beserra tells Bos he understands the counselor's loss, giving a long speech about keeping her memory alive. Bos later reports that Beserra keeps looking off into space as he speaks, as if thinking about Jeini Andrade girl, his eyes misty. Nestor Bos concludes that Beserra loved the girl and wishes he had never killed her, a conclusion supported by the fact that as of World Day 2683, Beserra has not had a permanent relationship with any woman.

2680. Beserra becomes determined to make the Brotherhood legitimate in the eyes of humanity. Nestor Bos suggests going the corporate route, as they attempted two centuries ago via an attempt to take over Soltec. But Beserra believes planets are the best avenue. Given the corporate worlds considering independence and all the new ones being discovered every year, Beserra decides to try infiltrating the governments of recent settlements so that the Brotherhood *becomes* the leadership instead of circumventing it.

2681. Beserra gets a message from the planet Jitsu in the Eta Cassiopeiae 2 system. Arojin [bishop] Santo Koroma, part of the theocratic government of Jitsu, makes a proposition: the Brotherhood pretends it is trying to take over the planet—slowly, step by step—and Koroma uses the intrusion as an excuse to run all the non-religious outsiders off the planet. Santo will then cancel Jitsu's leases with the CPCC, and Konrau will keep the three planets in the Kobito subsystem, receiving a twenty-five percent give on the pilgrimage profits from other Neo Gnostics coming to visit the planet, sacred to their religion. Against the objections of Bos, Beserra agrees.

2682. Beserra moves the Brotherhood base of operations off of Atlantis and into the Uraká Nebula, making the syndicate harder to police.

2683. Beserra sends crews to Jitsu to massacre extremist Neo Gnostics and cause social chaos. In apparent retaliation, Koroma sees to the creation of anti-terrorism squads to "stop the syndicate menace." While most squad leaders are compromised, in Koroma's pocket, he has hired one purportedly clean decorated military hero: Ben Wu.

Though Koroma has ensured the weakest mercenaries get assigned to Wu's squad to undermine its efficacy, Beserra wants to be able to leverage the hero at will. He has tasked Bos with getting dirt on Wu, and Bos has contacted our organization for assistance.

Speculation is that Beserra wants Wu under his thumb to pit his squad against the others, which would indicate that the Brotherhood is planning a double-cross of Koroma and his extremist faction of the government.

From: nestor@familyabos.per.sat

To: yenbandera@nannewa.per.jov

Subject: Mum's the fucking word (encrypted)

Date: January 2, 2684 23:09:32 (SST)

Decrypted 23:25:53 via FAE

Chingau. What else could I expect from the guy that's been top of the game for nigh on two centuries? Eh? I know more than you think, Yen. You're not my only birdie. That's why I'm not too worried about the dirt you've got. You don't want nobody finding out that you were once an agent for Martian Intelligence, back in the day, and you for sure don't want nobody to know that you have no name, not really, just a designation: EJH-13. Thirteenth generation clone. Reverse-sex *mura*, just like those crazy-arse Neogs think *Hesukrito* was. Let's see, the CPCC does what to clones? Terminates them? And look! A long-fucking-standing warrant out for your arrest! Two centuries they been looking for your arse! You must be real important to them, mate. Be a real shame if they found out about you, ain't it? And even worse if they learned the location of your hideout on New Beijing's biggest moon. No worry. Secret's safe with me, your Brotherhood mate. Like I'm sure mine, *all mine*, are safe with you.

CHAPTER 21

WHEN ARCHON RAWE ANNOUNCED HIS PLAN for the preservation of the Oracle, Santo went berserk. Screaming, he trashed his office, hurling furniture and hardcopy at the pair of aids who rushed in to find out the reason for his unhinged behavior. It took him a while to regain his composure, but even then he could not escape the only explanation for the ratowanin's move: Rawe had learned of the physical nature of Santo's relationship with Samanei, the holy communion they shared.

Only after a tube of moku had entered his system did he begin to see other alternatives. It was possible that Rawe believed—as many deputies did, envious of his quick ascent and open dislike of off-worlders—that Santo was behind the mafia attacks. Perhaps he further suspected collusion between Samanei and the arojin.

Or perhaps Samanei had asked to be put on ice herself. That would be different.

He decided to attend his scheduled audience that afternoon. If he weren't admitted, it would mean Rawe had cut him off, a terrifying prospect. But if he were allowed into the White Room, then the Oracle herself had arranged everything, and she'd explain her reasons to him in person.

Now that the Chamber had finally approved, after a month of heated deliberation, an investigation into Santo's alleged complicity in the mafia attacks, he needed her counsel, so he prayed she was behind the move.

A beep from the floor: his bouncecom had been scaled from its hiding place within the base of a statue of the Founder when Santo'd been flinging things about. He snatched it up, his heart pounding.

Got to hide this soon or get rid of it. Tragic if the Chamber's investigative branch searched the office and found it!

Bouncecoms circumvented the CPCC's automatic origin-stamping of all messages tunneled through the interstellar net and rendered communications untraceable. Santo thumbed his on: there was a tunnel-mail for him, from Nestor Bos. It seemed Ben Wu would be a loose cannon for a while, but Nestor suggested other, more aggressive ways of neutralizing him.

Santo bounced his agreement off an orbiting medship and thumbed the illegal device off, sliding it into a tunic pocket just in time: the door cycled open at that very moment, and Speaker Kikwete strolled in, surveying the disorder with an arched eyebrow.

"Redecorating, are we?"

Santo smiled unctuously. "I've no idea how, but a hiro-hiro managed to invade my office. As you can see, I chased it about, but I was unsuccessful in trapping the little dervish."

"Well, you've made my job a bit easier, Arojin Koroma. My officers won't feel as bad about turning this office upside down, seeing as how you've already begun the work."

Two sturdy Chamber investigators stepped in as if on cue. Santo shrugged.

"I was just on my way to confer with the Oracle. Feel free to search all you want. And if your young men would be so kind as to tidy up afterward, I'd be most indebted to them."

Not waiting for a response, Santo slipped from the room into the hall, making his way to the lift. The pressure was on, and he needed Samanei to ease his angst. Still, he had an important call to put through first. He ducked into a minor functionary's office and thumbed on a connection to Major Sosa. The gnarled visage of the former warrior surged from the transparent top of the com console.

"Arojin. Pleasure, as always."

"Major. How're things progressing?"

"Very well. The last of the recruits have shuttled down from the platforms. I was getting ready to meet them and the captains at the barracks for grouping."

"Listen, Major, I need you to do something for me. Take the greenest ones, those tyros that're lower performing, and put them under Wu."

"Course. You understand, though, doing this'll make the other squads, let's say, overachievers?"

"Don't worry. Their captains will curb that hankering for excellence, trust me."

"Understood. Anything else?"

"No. Except my thanks. You're a true follower of the Eight. Be enlightened."

"You, too. Thumbing off."

TWENTY-FIVE MINUTES LATER, THE GOVERNMENT TRANSPORT SANTO WAS riding in billeted to a stop within its berth at the heavily fortified, domed jinja. He found that the security checks and sterilization process were no longer required, though he was asked to change into a pilgrim's robe and leave his belongings in a shielded locker. Sensible. A gatblast to the hypostasis chamber would kill the Oracle as surely as a projectile exploding in her brain.

Two omedeyo—both members of the Oracle's elite protective guard—led Santo into an observation room. Its fourth wall was solid transparent steel, permitting the arojin to make out Samanei's form, encased in the special blue suspension gel used for cryogenics. Banks of equipment encircled the chamber, and as Santo eased into the faux conference seat, he witnessed the accustomed dazzling web of pink light playing across Samanei's forehead, turning it a deep purple. His head came to a rest in a cushion of supple leather, and a similar shock of pink connected him.

They were standing in the white room, as had been the standard procedure during audiences for some twelve years. Her doppelganger looked healthier than she ever had in reality; Santo's chest felt crushed by her beauty and his adoration.

"I imagined you'd come," she said in Dresch's voice.

"I was confused, angered. Why didn't you tell me about this?"

"Oh, I know you better than you know yourself, my boy. You would've never let this happen. You easily could have ruined the entire plan, just to keep me close to you. But this separation is necessary. Do you realize the enormity of what I'm doing for you? In ten years, you will be the absolute ruler of this world. Free to let it plunge into the depths of entropy, if that is your will. But I also have a responsibility to this vessel. Should I simply let her grow old in solitude, her body and mind withering? No."

"I thought you'd be more concerned about her soul."

"Oh, how little you understand, Santo-kun. Did we let Domina flounder forever in the grasp of her captors? Our plans are bigger than your mind can encompass; this is but one minor note in a larger symphony. Don't pretend to second guess us."

"It's only that my—my faith is weak at times. Y'all, rather, you've given me signs, but some part of me keeps whispering, 'It's just the girl, just Samanei.'

Wicked, I know."

The Oracle leapt into the air with a growl and hung suspended there, eyes ablaze.

"You doubt me, do you? Dresch, your mother, these voices you know so well… and still you cannot let go your infidel wavering!"

Her eyes clamped shut as her body went limp, bending backward impossibly till the back of her head touched the back of her legs, rotating 180 degree so that Santo could see her transported face. Suddenly, her eyelids shot open, and a voice Santo had heard many times as a child at the sikoro, the voice that had recorded the sacred logs so long ago on the lonely sands of virgin Jitsu, began to babble at him.

"Wee boy with the wee-wee, hee-hee. A little called Jitsu's here for thee. Alabaster eyes, the dark not reflecting, a baby drawn like water out of the well of consciousness, men's invective, the gimmal will purl, prison of air and pressure and invisible bubbles."

Santo's doppelganger fell to its knees. Domina Ditis, speaking to him, revealing herself as she had to no one since her martyrdom. His brain was wracked with spasms, and he could no longer move his avatar.

Samanei's virtual body straightened itself. It pointed a long, ebony finger at his face.

"I've got some requests, so listen close. First, figure out how to get me permanent access to the interstellar net. I managed to finagle my way into limited use of it from time to time, but I now require a constant connection. Don't try and ask why: your synapses are under my command, and your lack of faith has truly pissed me off. I'm just one doubting comment away from frying your brain and using Rawe instead. All good with me, you understand. The plan goes forward like we already discussed. When I name you ratowanin, you yank me from here, reverse this butcher job they did on my body, make me like I was. I'll be by your side, but it's only right I get to be as human as possible. Agreed?"

He tried to nod, but couldn't. The Oracle could tell he'd made the attempt, however. A sketchy smile curled her lips.

"Perfect. I'm going to release you, but don't bolt on me, okay?"

Suddenly Santo's doppelganger jerked wildly in several directions because of the conflicting and pent-up neural messages he'd been sending it. Samanei drifted softly to the floor. Sitting cross-legged, she gently bared her breasts.

He crawled to her on all fours, sobbing.

CHAPTER 22

KONRAU UNTANGLED HIMSELF from Asusena Gevara's golden-brown legs without waking the slumbering sancha. He couldn't face her this morning: during sex the night before he had called her Jeini, and when he'd apologized with a laugh while wilting within, she had shrugged the lapse off.

"You can call me whatever you want, mi kasike grandote," she'd responded, smiling coyly. "Just keep me, that's all I ask."

Trying to ignore his irritation and the dull throb in his head, Konrau got busy with the day's work. By early afternoon, much to his surprise and further annoyance, a faux-conference request came from his mother. After deliberately making her wait for thirty minutes in the drab keshiki of his virtual conference room, Konrau logged in.

Karmen Beserra was fifty, the annoying bitch, but she looked thirty. Konrau had already had two of her lovers killed for slapping her, but he understood why they would feel a need to. She went through men like some women did clothes, and she had pushed his father back into the arms of his wife, condemning Konrau to a childhood spent in the cold, claustrophobic corridors of Tenochtitlan or in the presence of a stream of men flowing in and out of her bed.

He looked at her now and his fists clenched convulsively, hatred rising in him. His hand was stayed, however, by twisted love his honor forced into him. She was his hefa, his mother, and there was something holy about the womb that gestated a brother that he had to respect, no matter how odious the woman herself was.

"Mi kasike," she said, bowing her head deferentially. She knew full well how to treat him now, that much was true, despite what a negligent slut she'd been all his youth.

"K'onda, hefa? I ain't seen you for a while. How's the kantō?" He had set her up in a high security mansion a couple of years ago. She was significantly safer there than she had been on Tenochtitlan. At least the new setup had curbed her fucking around.

"Great, oh, it's great." She lowered her amber eyes, long eyelashes demurely veiling her gaze. Then she looked up tentatively. "Felipe's getting out, miho. Two days. The eyre decided not to wait till his birthday, but let him go six months early."

Konrau narrowed his eyes. Felipe was his half-brother, conceived by his mother when Konrau had been lying in a coma in the neighboring bedroom of her flat, having nearly died from a gunshot to the eye. Desperate for money, Karmen had sold herself to Mr. Nobody who peddled sex faux-lifes in Brotherhood territory.

She nursed you back to health, a voice whispered at the periphery of his awareness. *She did what needed doing. Why are you so cruel?*

Wincing, Konrau narrowed his eyes. He remembered the smell of fear on the man who had sired his half-brother. Konrau, as an underboss, had tracked him down and fulfilled his apparent death wish. Did Felipe want revenge now, too?

At least Konrau's father had been a Brotherhood lieutenant, which had allowed Konrau to become a mademan and rise through the ranks. Felipe was nothing. Or was he? Being the bastard half-brother of the most powerful man the in the demimundo probably counted for something.

"A ber. You want me to what, give him a break? Take your little square squink and set him up to mooch off me like you do? Gran Hefa Mariya. You got balls, byeha."

Her amber eyes began to shine with the promise of tears. "Andale, mi kasike. What does it cost you? Give him a little chance, no? Stick him on a crew somewheres, anywheres. They're gonna eat him alive otherwise. Some pity, padrino."

When she got like this, he had only two choices: hit her or accede.

Since she wasn't really physically present, he gave in.

FOUR DAYS LATER, FELIPE WAS BROUGHT BEFORE HIM. HIS FIVE YEARS in the juvenile reformation center on Titan had clearly purified the punk of the annoying habits of childhood. He stood tall and muscular, hands loose at his sides, one side of his face red and puffy from the Maya hieroglyphics he'd just had tattooed there.

"So," Konrau began. "What do you know how to do?"

Felipe's dull gaze looked his half-brother up and down. "Anything you tell me to." His voice was solid, unfeeling ice. "Anything L'onda demands from me."

Against his own will, Konrau felt a certain pride. Besides resembling Konrau physically, his little brother was also a tough sumbitch, from what he had gathered. Ran a little klika by the time he was nine. Killed three constabulary officers when he was eleven because they had asked for his transit ID. All he needed was some direction, someone to show him the true depths of L'onda, depths that Konrau had sounded to their very bottom.

"I'm gonna put you on a crew, Felipe. Your cap's name is Marko Baskes. He stands for me, komprennes? You take his orders, you carry them out, you prove your self, and you'll move up. Try to punk me, and I'll fry your bastard arse. Got it?"

Felipe smiled slightly, pulling his tattooed skin just a bit tighter. "Got it, kasike."

Then the young man was dismissed, and Konrau was left to wonder at the strange emotion that had just insinuated itself into his mind: brotherly affection.

Strangely, his eye didn't ache at all.

MONTHS PASSED. MARKO BASKES KEPT sending in positive reports. Felipe was a little unstable, but he got the job done. Especially if it required violence. The little fucker had a real talent for carnage, Marko said.

Hearing about his brother's wilding, watching clips of him in action, kept the ghosts of the past at bay. When he gave Felipe his own crew, they faded even further, as if dedicating himself to the younger man somehow balanced the scales of his heart, so heavy with betrayal and broken love.

Felipe made mistakes as a cap. Who didn't? Konrau elided them, paid off insulted or injured brothers. From time to time, he would faux-conference with his half-brother, give him advice, dress him down for the most egregious of his errors.

The punk was always courteous, always took his licks, never gave excuses.

And he got better. Turned a few unprofitable situations around. Used tactics rather than just brute force.

One morning, Konrau viewed the latest encrypted video report from him and slapped his palms together.

He's ready for more.

"Felipe," he said, recording a reply. "Karnaliyo. Come to HQ for a visit. The *Chamuko* is scheduled to start heading back later this afternoon. I want you on it. You've done good. Time we talked in person again."

Then Konrau shot a message to Nestor. *Let's meet. Half hour, in my office.*

When he arrived, the older man folded himself prissily into a chair. "What's up, Kasike?"

"About Felipe. I want to put him in command of the *Maliyas*. He can oversee the rotation of crews off platforms in the Helios System and manage our operations on Oceania and New Mecca."

The aging counselor spoke bluntly. "How's your mind? You off your nut? Bato's been working for us for what, six months?"

"What did you say?" Konrau said, his voice going cold but his eyes fulminating. "He's my *blood*, kabrō. Don't you fucking forget that. You know how you loved Ria, Nestor? Did I ever say you were crazy because of that shite? No, right? Pinche ruko pendeho. Felipe's accomplished shiteloads as a sicarito. Place him at the head of our boys in Helios."

Nestor's face had gone splotchy red, as if Konrau's words were slaps. "You got to make him first."

"You don't fucking say." The kasike held his anger down, let hard cold power flow from his lips. "La puta maje ke t'iso naser. He's on his way. I want to hold the ceremony in two days. Line that shite up, hear?"

Nestor averted his eyes, silent and sullen. Konrau was reminded of the many pouting women he had despised down the years.

"Why do you ask me if you're not gonna take my advice?" Nestor demanded in an exasperated tone.

"Most times your advice is okay." The kasike gazed at the curving expanse of black rock above their heads. "When you're wrong, I just ignore you. There a problem with that?"

"No, boss. Course not. I'm on it."

"Pos, a mover el kulo," Konrau said, snapping his fingers. "Shoot me the details once you hammer them out."

Without a word, his counselor stood and left.

The silence in the yawning office brought tears of relief to the kasike's eyes.

CHAPTER 23

THE CONSTRUCTOR BOT GLIDED NOISELESSLY across the four-hundred-square-meter expanse of plascrete, smoothing and curing the slab that would serve as the foundation for Tenshi and Brando's home. The bot slid around jutting rebar that within days would become support columns for the upper stories, avoiding the plasteel conduits that had been imbedded in the slab for plumbing, electrical wiring and communications connections. Tenshi stood in the shade of a temporary gazebo, her hand unconsciously drifting toward her abdomen as if to reassure the life that for the past six weeks had been gestating there. Catching herself in the midst of this ritual, she smiled, content. Except for sporadic terrorist attacks, none of which had left any casualties, the past four months had been the most blissful of her life.

Brando had stayed true to his word: while at the university, he took advantage of every opportunity to chat with other professors, especially Modupe, who'd become a sort of surrogate father. But once he arrived at their prefab trailer at the construction site, he lavished all his attention on Tenshi and her project.

"Hey."

Tenshi turned, startled. She'd been so caught up in her thoughts that he hadn't heard Brando walk up behind her. It was about 4 pm on a Thursday; the public transport had undoubtedly dropped him off in town and he'd walked the three kilometers to the desert's edge, as was his custom.

"Hey, sweet."

They exchanged a kiss, and he rubbed her belly.

"How are yall doing?"

"Fine. We got the slab done, you see?" She gestured at the expanse of wet grayness, and Brando gave a thumbs-up.

"Yeah, looking good. So, what, we get started on the columns next?"

"Got to wait till Saturday, let this cure well. Give me a hand this weekend? The crew will be off, lazy punks." She'd gotten some of the folks from the fair job to help her here, but they squeezed her house in between other commitments.

"Of course I'll help you. As long as you teach me what I need to do."

"I always teach you, no?"

She patted his crotch with a wink. He laughed.

"Let's go put in some practice, what say?"

AFTERWARD, THEY LAY IN THE DYING LIGHT OF DUSK, side by side, hips touching slightly, sweat glistening redly with Higante's final rays.

"Are you still happy about this baby?" she asked, turning to look at him. His hair was getting longer; she'd taken him to her own stylist in Station City, who'd given him the trendiest twists. He looked even more handsome than before, Tenshi reflected, feeling her nerves tingle again with an insatiable appetite for him.

Brando's eyes crinkled with joy as he spoke.

"More than you can imagine. I've dreamed of being a father for years. You know, create another human being, form their mind, give them the tools to succeed and contribute something special to the universe. The most important task I could undertake, something humanity seems meant to do."

"A pity so few of us can do it well. Just look at our families."

"That's the other part of it for me. The challenge of not making the same mistakes as my father and mother."

"You'll do fine, Brando. Nobody better qualified to be an appa than you."

"And this little one's lucky to come from an umma like you. One who will support him in everything he decides to do."

"HIM? You sure it's going be a boy?"

"Or girl, or omedeyo," he added. "I'll be happy to the core with whatever comes. Important thing is, the baby's going be a mix of you and me. A symbol of this." He gripped her hand and lifted it into a shaft of ruddy light. Their rings touched, and again she felt that almost imperceptible jolt, some sort of energy at the edge of her senses.

Tenshi pulled both their hands to her breast.

"I love you so much, Brando. You have no idea."

He kissed her sweaty forehead.

"Oh, yes. Yes, I do," he sang softly. "For that's how much I love you, too."

AS THE OUTER WALLS BEGAN TO GO UP AND THE UNUSUAL SHAPE OF THE house began to manifest itself, Tenshi began to get visitors. Word had spread that she would be designing and building the new Samaneino Teyopan next, so there was understandable curiosity about what she might create for them.

At first, the faithful would simply stand and watch as she and her crew programmed bots and guided them through their tasks, doing physically as much as they could in accordance with Tenshi's building philosophy. Soon, however, the half dozen members of her community that regularly stopped by for an hour or so of observation began to ask questions.

"Why did you design such an elaborate edifice?" one satorijin ventured.

Wiping her brow, Tenshi tried to explain. "Scripture says that human artifacts are extensions of a creator's aham, their blind accreted self. But that very fact makes them important. Crafting objects with our minds and hands, we can better see the shape of that self, facilitating the work of shamanchiwanga, of shattering and bricolage. For satorijin especially, complex designs move us quickly toward gnosis. Continued creation reveals the character of our new selves, aligned with our sparks. And then Hanga ra-Roho should follow with ease. Our nascent souls depend, the second Oracle declared, on more than just our meager flesh and limited minds."

An omedeyo anshyano squinted at all this. "I understand that perspective, but why do work with your own body that constructor bots are better designed to handle?"

"It's vital," she said, twirling a hammer for emphasis, "that we make direct contact with the exterior world when reworking it to reflect our aligned selves. Machines get in the way of this hands-on search for gnosis."

A few of her fellow townsfolk who weren't familiar with Reformer dogma shook their heads and didn't return. But others took their places, and she soon found herself spending an hour or so everyday elaborating on her ideas to an ever-growing, receptive audience.

The Dominians among them had spent their lives meditating under the influence of drugs and engaging in egocentric sexual escapades. This fresh, forbidden vision of the world fascinated them, as if they'd been waiting for years to hear the good news that their lives could be richer, broader, more satisfying in the present.

It's time, Tenshi realized. *The house is only halfway done, and I was going to wait until the baby was born, but Sopiya's wisdom has accelerated the schedule.*

Before talking to Brando, Tenshi began organizing informal classes on everything from basic arts and crafts to design and construction. Calling in several saved-up favors, she managed to get seven experts from Station City to fly in for two hours every couple of days to help her out with the instruction.

When her husband realized what was happening, he got a little irritated. "Tenshi, we're barely integrating ourselves into Kinguyama. I'm new to everything myself. Trying to navigate meditation on my own terms, using music and study alongside all these other overwhelming tools. You only just got reinstated. Aren't we pushing our luck?"

Tenshi wrung her hands with frustration. "Precisely because you can't see what I can see, Brando-chan, I need you to trust me. This moment has to be seized. Our society has to be transformed."

"I get that," he interrupted, "and I'm excited to help. Jitsu opening up to the rest of humanity? Good for everyone, in my book. But I look at you, at that swelling belly, and something happens to me. I feel protective. Jealous, even. You've made me a believer, a partner in this vision I can only glimpse, but I can't help but put you and the baby above everything else."

Tenshi picked up a square of fabric and tied back her locs. Then she walked over to the com panel in their temporary home.

"What are you doing?" Brando asked, dumbfounded.

"Hang on." She flipped through the contacts list, thumbed open a channel. In seconds, Meji Pishan's face emerged from the console.

"Tenshi-shi. Brando-shi. How's the construction going?"

"Well," Tenshi answered. "But we need to talk to you about something. You've probably heard that some friends of mine in construction and the arts have started visiting the construction site to give impromptu lessons."

Meji took a deep breath. "Yes. There have been a few complaints, but most teyopanjin are happy with what you're doing. Some have asked my permission to participate, and I've told them all are free to join in as long as they also continue their daily meditation."

Brando walked over to the console. Tenshi could feel the tension in his posture. He wasn't happy that she had called the giya, but he was going to accept her choices. With some conditions, it seemed.

"Acharya-zin," he began, "Tenshi has amazing ideas, as always, but I don't think she can pull this off alone. It's a lot of responsibility. Could you possibly get anshyano from your quadrant of the town who lean toward Reform to visit the construction site when the experts come, to help supervise and connect learning to the Path?"

Tenshi was take aback. *That's ... a really good idea.*

Pishan was already nodding. "Absolutely. I support what the two of yall are doing, and it's only right that the leadership of Kinguyama get involved as well. I'll round up the usual suspects, Tenshi-shi. You probably can guess their names already."

The couple got past the moment of tension, and Tenshi's plans began to bear fruit. By the sixth month of her pregnancy, she and a half-dozen anshyano oversaw the studies of nearly a hundred and fifty people. Brando had made the right call. With the help, she could also manage the final stages of their home's construction.

Brando came home early one day to see the open-air learning in person. Tenshi turned from applying gesso to the exterior of the building to consider her husband. There was something strange in his expression. Tenshi suspected the worst, so she reflexively got defensive.

"What?"

He turned to her, eyes narrowing. "I'm just surprised. When I first got to this planet, everyone seemed like a zombie to me."

"Listen to me, Brando." She could feel her throat tighten with irritation. "You're a good man. A smart man. A brilliant linguist. But you're not better than these people. Just look at them: drugged and brainwashed all their lives by leaders more interested in power than in the creation of their people's souls. But they haven't given up: they're out there every other day, struggling, learning, beginning to build new lives for themselves. You're one of us now, but you come from a society where you were free to think, to explore. Some of your behavior was restricted, but not your ideas. These people have been cut off from everything for years, but that's not stopping them."

Brando's dark eyes went red with emotion. He scrubbed at his afternoon stubble. "I know it's not. I'm proud of them, damn it. But I feel like I'm stumbling in the dark right now, Tenshi. Please understand. All you're saying? I'm acutely aware of it. I've barely stepped onto the Path beside you. I don't even know what Way I will take. You have yours, and I will help you walk it. But I … I think I need something."

Tenshi softened immediately. "Of course. I'm sorry. I wasn't listening. Love, the place to start is with a goal. Mine is to change the world. It's a big goal, so I need lots of people's help. Perhaps yours will be smaller."

Turning back to the wall while he considered her words, Tenshi continued applying gesso in circular strokes upon the plascrete blocks that constituted the outer walls of their home, walls that curved impossibly onto themselves, defying logic and gravity.

"I *do* have a goal."

Tenshi stopped, dumping her float into a bucket of milky water.

"What is it?"

"Make a real family. One that works. You and that little one inside you are my world, Tenshi."

She wiped sweat from her forehead, the cords in her slender but powerful arms bunching up above the elbow.

Now or never, she thought, feeling a twinge of guilt but recognizing he had to be led to it this way.

"Brando my sweet, I share that goal with you. But it's time you found another. One that complements mine."

"How? I mean, you want to teach them how rebuild their lives, not how to speak Unified Chinese or how neural patterns correspond to words."

She put her hand on his arm. *Ebony on walnut,* she thought, imaging them briefly as trees whose branches and roots had begun to entwine, like the story of Feather Boy and Thorn Girl from Domina's journals.

"Do you remember when you asked what I wanted to do with the fairgrounds once the fair was over?"

"Oh, yeah. You said I'd be interested in it."

"I didn't think it'd happen so soon, but here we are." She took a deep breath. "Brando, I want to start a school. A school for everybody, Pathwalker and off-worlder both. Where they can learn the point in living, what's good and worthwhile in life. Yes, a school, my love. And I want you to run it."

"Run a school? But I don't know a thing about administration."

"You know how to teach: running a school can't be much harder than making sure the instructors teach the way you know they should, right?"

Brando stood in thought, her hand still resting on his arm. She could feel the racing of his pulse through his biceps.

What if he says no? Ah, I've miscalculated, haven't I?

"I'm reminded," he said, his eyes gazing into the distance, "of Gio Cereghino, the dean of the university in Milan. Everyone hated his management techniques. And for a young assistant professor, I was really vocal about how ridiculous certain university protocols were. I even wrote an editorial, detailing changes that should be made. I probably would've been pushed out if I hadn't accepted the job here."

Brando looked back at Tenshi. She saw curiosity in his eyes. Excitement, even.

I knew it! I knew he had it in him. Come on, umpenzi. One more step.

"Maybe I could run a school. I mean, I'd never thought about doing any administrative work, but, wow. My own school? My own methods? I could learn what I don't know. Always wanted to be at the cutting edge of things."

"Ah, sweet Brando, it looks like you're gonna get that wish, aren't you?"

He looked her up and down. Tenshi was suddenly aware of how very bespeckled by stucco she was.

Brando grinned like a devil.

"First class I'm going to offer: how to apply gesso to the *building* and not *your face, clothes and hair!*"

Tenshi frowned, grabbed a glebe of plaster, and began to chase him round the yard.

CHAPTER 24

MY WATER JUST BROKE. COME HOME.

Brando's lenses flashed the emergency-coded message in the air in front of him, and his heart started pounding.

"Okay, class. That's it for today. My wife's about to give birth, so I've got to run. Be enlightened!"

As luck would have it, there was a rental transport parked near the university. Brando thumbed payment onto the door and jumped inside, barking the coordinates to the autopilot and immediately messaging his mother-in-law.

She's fine, Shemejinim. Local aransa Kanan Rongoa is here. You've both made all the right preparations. Your home is finished. Just come be by her side.

After what seemed lifetimes, the rental set down right outside Tenshi and Brando's residence, and he rushed inside. A pallet had been spread out on the freshly tiled floor of the living room, and Tenshi squatted in the middle of it, sweat-drenched and in obvious pain. Beside her knelt Inyoni Onamata. Behind her stood the midwife, hands on Tenshi's shoulders.

"Brando-yi," his wife gasped, clenching and unclenching her hand at him. Hurrying to her side, he took her rigid fingers in his.

"I'm here, sweetheart. You're doing great."

Tenshi nodded and shushed him, her muscles tensing as another contraction hit. Brando was powerless to do more than just be there, but he knew it was an important role. Pathwalker customs concerning childbirth struck him as quaint and perhaps even dangerous. Another man might've insisted Tenshi go to the hospital in Station City, where the procedure would be over quickly in a fully sterile environment. But Brando was on the Path now. He would respect the customs. And he had sworn to dedicate his life to lifting this woman up, however small he might appear to others in her shadow. He could be quiet now and hold her hand.

Labor lasted nearly three more hours. The aransa helped Tenshi breathe, massaged her belly to get the child properly positioned. Inyoni chanted in a soft voice, calling a spark to the unborn child, promising a soul would one day form within that new mind.

At last a final contraction of abdominal muscles pushed their beslimed infant into the warm air that circulated through the open windows. Brando, unfazed by the blood and his wife's labored breathing, knelt beside the midwife, cinched the umbilical cord, and severed it with a surgical laserblade.

"The child's assigned sex is female," Kanan Rongoa announced. "Gender will reveal itself as years pass, dear new umma and apa."

Brando stared at his child, a lovely, pointy-headed girl with expansive blue-gray eyes that peered with hostile disappointment at her new world.

The midwife wiped the infant clean and wrapped her in a linen blanket; she began to cry then, not with a plaintive, confused sound but with an angry, throaty hoot, as if appalled at the insolence of the large creatures around her.

As the baby was placed in Tenshi's arms, Brando laid his palms on both their heads.

"My loves," he muttered, eyes welling. "Tenshi and…"

"Tana. Tana D'Angelo di Koroma ma-Sonari."

"Tenshi and Tana."

"And Brando."

He gently kissed both their moist foreheads.

"My world. Both of yall."

I'd die for yall. The epiphany was overwhelming. The two people before him mattered more than anything. To keep them safe, he was willing to sacrifice it all.

OVER TIME, BRANDO CAME TO RELISH services in Kinguyama, which were being held in the auxiliary chapel in the southwestern quadrant until Tenshi built the new teyopan.

Once a week, Meji Pishan offered uplifting readings from Pathwalker scriptures, elucidating them in a friendly, humorous way. The message concluded, zazen began. The Eipande Nyota was projected above the congretation for group meditation through chanting, a low, harmonic humming that soothed and relaxed. Then kleinballs and other meditation devices were passed around, along with moku for those who required it for introspection. Teyopanjin meditated singly for the most part, some moving off to secluded corners, others remaining on the stone benches, still others standing along the walls. Married couples had often developed ways to share zazen, to seek the next stage of their journey as a dyad.

The final hour blossomed with wonderful silence at that point, a stillness and quiet unlike anything Brando had ever experienced while surrounded by other people.

During his first service, Brando had felt lost. He'd sucked down a tube of moku, but without the Urim nearby, he'd just felt stoned. Glancing about at the meditating teyopanjin, he'd been filled with a sense of awkward disconnect.

Tenshi, sitting utterly still beside him, had kept her eyes shut, breathing slowed. With nothing else to do, Brando had stared at her, his eyes tracing her features, memorizing her every curve, the sharpness of her posture, the angle of her cheekbones.

Before he knew it, Meji had chimed the teyopanjin back to normal consciousness.

Brando had spent an hour looking at Tenshi, an hour that subjectively had seemed only minutes.

Over time, the weekly services had become easier to cope with. Rather than explore the improbable surfaces of a kleinball, Brando meditated on the form of his wife. He explored the depths of his love for her, a strange, unexpected warmth that grew with every passing day as if fueled by familiarity. Eventually, the meditation time became, not just a time to revel in Tenshi, but to enjoy for itself alone, for the opportunity to be still and quiet, emptying his mind while his beloved did likewise. He savored this tranquility at Tenshi's side as if he had needed it for a long time, like a thirsty man relishes a dipperful of water.

THREE MONTHS AFTER TANA'S BIRTH, as Brando was leaving class one day, a man was waiting for him. Tall, grim, the ebony skin of his face pockmarked with scars, his natural hair a series of jagged, silvered spikes.

Monchu Koroma. Tenshi's father. Brando had never met him in person before.

"Oh. Aponim," he muttered, dipping his head in respect. "I didn't expect to see you here."

Monchu's face was impassive. "Let's eat something together, Shemeji. We should talk. For the first time."

Uncomfortable, aware of the eyes of students and faculty, Brando gestured at the cafeteria. "The food here is pretty good."

"Lead the way, then."

The weather was turning cooler, so Brando ordered two kitoweyo stews while his father-in-law looked for a free table. But when the professor found him, another man had joined them.

Even without his governmental robes, Brando recognized him immediately. Santo Koroma.

I should just leave. This is a fucking ambush.

But his pride got the better of him. Who were they to come to the university and attempt to tag-team him or whatever this was? Brando wouldn't be a pushover.

"Arojin," he said as he approached the table. "An unexpected surprise."

Santo smiled. "Yes, I imagine it is. You've grown used to dealing with our women. Never even reached out to the Koroma men. I wonder why that is, Hyun-nim."

Monchu shrugged. "Weakness? Fear? The surety that we'll discover his falseness?"

"My falseness?" Brando said, pulling a chair away from the table and sitting down. "What are you talking about?"

"You may not have read the Revised Bible in its entirety," Santo said, "but in his second letter, Dresch warns us: 'Many will falsely claim to walk the Path. Beware the soulless servants of blindness, whose vision is of Samayeru, who walk the false road into the grey smoke that pours from his roaring orange rage and would lead you there as well.' Are you leading our Tenshi astray, Dr.

D'Angelo?"

"I'm on the Path, Arojin-zin. I saw my spark, glimpsed ra-Yindawo. Nothing you say can take that from me. Doesn't Dresch tell us in his fifth letter that the agents of the Grey Prison will try to make us doubt our nascent souls? I bend my head to your teaching, Santo-shi, but if you continue to call my faith into question, I'll get up and walk away right now."

Santo looked at his older brother with a bemused smile. "She has trained him well, no doubt. She and Meji-shi both."

Monchu laid his gnarled hands palm-down on the table. "Listen, Shemeji. I accept your affirmation of faith. I prefer to believe my daughter hasn't married some samadan fool. That said, Brando-shi, me and my brother, we've come for a specific purpose."

Santo steepled his fingers. "Indeed. It's a dangerous time, Brando-shi. We need to stand together. There is just one Path. Dominatu, Shamangatu, Reporumatu—these are silly, divisive labels. We are all Pathwalkers. Our world is under assault. Talk to your wife, Brother. Make her understand."

Brando narrowed his eyes. "Understand *what*, exactly? That she should stop backing reform? Stop encouraging immigration? Stop teaching Ona ra-Shamanga?"

"All of the above," Santo said with a smirk. "It destabilizes our world when horrible forces want to invade. You were in the midst of such a massacre. Are you stupid, then, that you can't see the danger?"

A server brought the two stews to the table at that moment. Once they walked off, Brando stood.

"Oh, I see the danger. It's sitting in front of me, I think. Enjoy the kitoweyo, gentlemen. I've lost my appetite."

When he got home, Tenshi stared at him with a strange expression.

"What did you have for lunch?" she asked tautly.

Looking down for foodstains or something else that might prompt such a question, he shrugged. "Kitoweyo stew. It's the right weather for it."

"Did you chat with anyone?"

"Not in particular, no. Why?"

Tenshi's face hardened in anger.

"Why? Good question. Why would you lie to me, Brando? One of your students is in our teyopan. Maruko Kaku? Distributes the sacrament? Guess whose mother called my mother, who then called me. Yeah. So I know you had lunch with my father and uncle, damn you. Why are you hiding it?"

Brando reached for her, but she batted his hand away.

"I'm sorry, Tenshi. I should've told you. But it was nothing. They were just gaslighting me. Trying to get under my skin. Trying to manipulate me into making you back off. Since I have no intention of doing anything those two men ever ask, I walked away from them."

"Damn it," she said, pulling on one of her locs in frustration. "You can't keep things like this from me, Brando. You're not good at the sort of games Santo plays. You're straightforward, honest, good. He's a fucking snake, and he will gobble you up if you're not careful."

"Tenshi, I'm not a child. I can take care of myself."

She grabbed his shirt with a violence Brando wasn't expecting, pulling him towards her. He could have easily stopped her, but a part of him wanted to see just how far she was willing to go to punish him.

"You're not a child, no. You're a man. But he's a monster. Do you hear me? You cannot go toe to toe with him. I've been on my own since I was thirteen. I've seen and done things that would break you, Kyosu-chan. And *even I* am afraid of that motherfucker."

A cold premonition ripped through Brando's guts. He reached up, placed his hand on her fist. Their rings touched.

Listen.

The voice was clear though quiet.

Listen. Remember.

"I'm sorry. You're right, Tenshi. I'll steer clear of them both. And I won't hide anything else from you. I promise."

IT TOOK TENSHI A WHILE TO FORGIVE HIM.

Complicating their reconciliation was the return of terrorist activity not only to frontier prefectures but also the orbital platforms and in Station City.

After months without a single attack, businesses were getting bombed at least once a week, and several Civil Security units had been slaughtered.

It wasn't just Jitsu that was rocked by violence. Many Constabulary forces were getting reassigned from Eta Cassiopeiae to CPCC worlds as demimundo infighting spread like wildfire throughout the Consortium. CPCC citizens living on Jitsu felt unprotected. The ATS received a grant and some resources from the AF, but Reformers felt it wasn't enough. Dominians complained that CPCC presence was what had caused the attacks in the first place.

Tenshi and Brando, like most inhabitants of Jitsu, were on constant edge. And Tana had gotten very colicky, wakening her young parents four or five times a night so that their nerves frayed even further.

Tensions ratcheted higher. Curfews locked towns down across the Northern Continent. Every café in Station City echoed with the arguments and fears of each political position.

Tenshi had to spend a large chunk of her time meeting and strategizing with other Reformers, shuttling back and forth between Juresh, Station City, and various prefectures to help coordinate a political defense against extremists. Her uncle and his Dominian peers were taking the opportunity to advance laws and policies that restricted citizens' behavior, and she wore herself out trying to stop them

Brando did everything he could to help his wife with Tana so that she could focus on the unrest. But he had his own problems. University classes often deteriorated into political debate, especially after a bomb damaged the façade of the administrative building. Despite the lack of casualties, the provost suspended in-person classes.

While being at home allowed Brando to watch Tana all the time, freeing Tenshi up to fully engage in the fight, teaching via faux-conference required a level of planning and oversight that stretched Brando thin.

One day, Tenshi came home late to find him giving their daughter a bottle.

"Ugh, let me hold her. She needs some of her umma's milk, anyway, and my breasts feel like they're going to explode."

But when she took Tana from his arms, the infant started howling, pushing away with her little feet, reaching for her father in desperation.

Tears started to roll down Tenshi's face. "She *hates* me! My own daughter."

"She doesn't hate you, Tenshi, she just—"

"Don't you know Umma is keeping you safe?" she demanded of Tana, who wailed even harded. "Don't you know how much I love you? How much I'm risking for you."

Brando took the inconsolable baby back. "Tenshi, enough."

"It's not fair! I carried her in my womb for nine fucking months! Why does she reject me, huh? Why do you get to be the damn hero?"

Though he knew he should be understanding, Brando snapped. "Because you're *never fucking here,* that's why! She doesn't even know you! Yall sleep together, sure, and she suckles with her eyes closed. But it's been weeks now since you spent any real time with her. What did you expect?"

Clenching her fists, Tenshi groaned in rage. "I'm trying to *stop a civil disaster,* Kyosu-zin. While you give your little classes on irrelevant fucking languages, I'm keeping my people *alive.*"

"As far as I can tell, the attacks have continued," he said, going cold and distant. "I'm not convinced that sacrificing your family is doing any real good."

"Sacrificing my—is that what you really think?"

Pressing Tana's face lightly against his shoulder to muffle her cries a bit, Brando leaned toward his wife. "It's the way this *feels,* Tenshi. We spend our days without you. I'm stretched thin now that your father has dragged your mother off to another prefecture."

"I told you," she shot back, "to *hire* somebody. I've shunted more than enough credits to your account."

"Ah, yes, your wealth will solve *all* the problems, won't it? I don't need a team of childcare and cleaning experts under my feet, Tenshi. I need *you.*"

She gestured broadly, hands trembling. "I'm the foremost anshyano in this movement, damn you. *Every*body needs me right now. The whole *planet* does!"

"No," Brando retorted. "That's bullshit. You're not the only person who can manage this crisis, you know. You're not even a politician. You're an architect, mothergod!"

Recoiling at his words, Tenshi spat, "Fuck you. What happened to your promise to support me, eh? Little bit of pressure, and you show your true colors."

Regret surged in Brando's heart. He suddenly could see himself from the outside, parroting his mother's cold, cruel sarcasm.

"Oh, shite, Tenshi. I didn't mean—"

"You're still so *blind*," she said, gritting her teeth. "This identity of yours that you don't even appear to think about? It's getting in the way. It's hurting you. It's hampering our plans. It's making me stumble."

"It's who I am!" Brando yelled, despairing. Tana jerked in shock and started crying even louder.

"You," Tenshi pointed out, shuddering, "made a commitment. You're on the Path, Brando. You have to shatter the old you, remake yourself. You saw your spark. Would she want this, do you think? Even at services, you—you *pull me from my Way!* My meditation is going nowhere. I'm stuck. We're supposed to be a *dyad*, for the love of Sopiya!"

Then she broke down, weeping openly. Tana went from wailing to screaming. Brando, aghast at himself, felt he might literally shatter to pieces right then and there.

I'm not walking the Path beside her, he understood in horror. *I'm walking behind her. Far behind her. She's utterly alone.*

Tenshi shook her head and took Tana again, stomping off to their bedroom and sealing shut the door.

Brando sat in the dark for hours till he was sure mother and daughter had fallen asleep. Then he flew Tenshi's transport to the Pishan residence and spilled his guts to his giya.

"Help me, Acharya-zin," he begged Meji. "Show me what to do."

Meji put their hand on Brando's shoulders. "My child, the problem is that you've been approaching zazen as an intellectual endeavor. You have to let go. Stop holding back. You can reach her. But only in the Blue, Brando-shi. Only in the Blue."

Banging the heel of his hand against his temple, Brand whispered, "I need to short-circuit *this*, Meji-shi. I need—I need you to prepare mohiyo paste for me. Moku doesn't let me *see* what I need to see."

Pulling Brando's hand from his head, Pishan sighed. "Yes. I can do that. You'll take the High Sacrament with Tenshi-shi. The two of you will meditate together in the Well."

THE TURNING POINT CAME TWO MONTHS after Brando's encounter with Santo.

At that week's service, Meji Pishan offered uplifting readings from both the Revised Bible and Domina's diaries, the more Zen of Pathwalker scriptures. The message was about forgiveness, about the danger of loading down the realigned self with resentment, about how grudges stifled the creation of a soul. Brando kept his eyes straight ahead, not daring to look at his wife.

After ringing the bell to begin the hour of zazen, Pishan walked over to the couple and took their hands.

Tenshi opened her eyes, startled. "What, Giya-zin?"

"Come, both of you."

Their giya led them outside. Across the cobbled street was a wind-pitted gazebo that cast shade on a circle of ruddy stone, capped by a circle of faded wood.

Wait. It's an actual well? Brando thought.

"The Well? Why—" Tenshi began.

"Brando-shi has asked for the High Sacrament. He begs to be broken. But he cannot make the attempt alone, Anshyano-zin. You are a dyad. Your sparks must find a way to align, or neither of you will survive this test of your union."

From their robes, Meji drew forth two dark squares. The smell struck Brando hard.

"Pressed mohiyo. Given by the oni to Domina herself so very long ago. She found the Path through this holy herb, native only to this soil till Soltec spread the seeds across human space. Parkake of it, Brother and Sister. Then go down into the well and shut out the world. Find each other in the darkness."

Brando felt Tenshi's eyes on him as he eagerly took the High Sacrament and placed it in his mouth. Turning, he saw her do the same.

"Come, love," she whispered, her eyes full of tears. "I will be with you as you shatter. I will help you pick up the shards and rebuild yourself afresh."

AT THE BOTTOM OF THAT DRY SHAFT, there only existed the darkness, the distant circle of light, her hands in his, the soft glow of the rings that seemed to bind them together.

Pretense stripped away. Naked self revealed. But no shame.

Her whispered voice.

Your spark. I've seen her, too. Doubled in us both.

Brando saw himself. Saw his *self.* It was not his, not really.

Fragments of his mother. His father. Childhood friends. Professors. Books he'd read. Lies he'd told. Languages, one atop another. Attendant cultures he shouldn't have ever claimed but could not keep from absorbing.

An amalgamation. Creation of no one. Without purpose or deliberate form.

Lost. Blind.

He both pitied and reviled it.

He yearned to be more than this collection of detritus.

In the swirling black at the bottom of the well, the blue glow rose from their rings and floated away. Though still sitting lotus style before his wife, Brando also stood and followed.

The glow began to spread. It filled his perception. It was a veil, he realized. A thin membrane between him and something beautiful.

Empty yourself.

It might have been Tenshi speaking. It might have been his spark.

It might have been the Eight.

He obeyed.

Thought no longer mattered. Brando D'Angelo di Makomo wasn't real.

His thoughts were even less so.

There was the Blue, and there was the spark.

Yearning with every ounce of his illusory, empty personhood, the blind one known as Brando began to dance.

He spun wildly, laughing.

The Blue was drawn into the vortex of his dervish dance, sucked into him through every orifice, every pore.

Inside that false self, it started to swell, pushing at the edges of Brando.

And then, with a harsh cry of utter joy …

… he burst.

CHAPTER 25

BY THE TIME TANA WAS OLD ENOUGH TO EAT SOLID FOOD, terrorist activity had tapered off and stopped. Though it might have been just a lull, the people of Jitsu breathed easier. Reformers had blocked the worst of the extremist power-grab. In-person classes resumed at the University, and curfews were lifted.

Tenshi and Brando's marriage had improved since their time in the Well. Emerging, Brando had been calm, accepting. He now spent several hours each day deep in meditation. He faced his work with a glad heart and didn't complain about the stress of grading, the endless meetings. No longer did he pout or recriminate her. He simply stood at her side, like he had promised. Understanding. Contributing.

Pushing toward their common goals.

Like the new teyopan she had promised their giya she would design and build.

Every time she sat down to brainstorm ideas, however, her mind echoed with her sister's screams as she'd been dragged away.

How do I erect a shrine to my omenim when I don't even know if she's even okay?

As always, it was hard to imagine her twin as the Oracle, in constant communication with the Ogdoad. Tenshi could never admit this fact to anyone, but as much as any factor, her social and political ambitions were driven by her *need to know.*

Flip control of this world. See a Reformer Archon put in power. Then visit her, after all these years. Pull her from hypostasis and ask—whose voice do you truly hear, Samane-yi?

Amidst all the doubt, a plan for the shrine eluded her.

Then one Saturday afternoon, in the midst of meditating with Brando—their hands clasped, the world fading around them—Tenshi had the clearest vision of her soul, a delicate web around a glowing spark.

For the first time, she beheld the design in all its unique beauty.

Gnosis.

Total self-knowledge.

When the house AI chimed her back to the Grey Prison of reality, she hugged Brando tightly, shuddering with joy.

"What? What is it?" he asked, startled.

"It's done, Brando." Her voice was a hoarse whisper. "I've finished Hanga ra-Roho."

He put his hands on her heart and her temple, eyes wide. "You've been other-born?"

Unable to speak anymore, she nodded.

Before shattering, Brando would not have known what to say, might have ruined the moment. But he was closer to her now. She could feel him on the Path behind her.

So when he kneeled before her, the pride she felt in him was almost painful.

"Acharya-zin," he rasped, his voice full of emotion. "Be my guide. Be our guide. Take up the mantle of arojin and serve your people well."

That evening, she began to sketch, unable to even sleep. It was like the wende: she felt Sopiya's wisdom flowing through her, guiding her hands.

Samaneino Teyopan took form, an echo of her soul.

When at last she took the plans to Meji Pishan, they were dumbstruck.

"You don't like it?" she asked.

"Oh, Tenshi-shi. Like? What a feeble word. This structure is transcendent. Like a Pathwalker grounded in the world while at the same time stretching toward the Eight. I don't think I ever beheld something that so perfectly encapsulates in physical form the struggle for gnosis. A perfect design for the Oracle's own teyopan. Be enlightened, Tenshi-shi. I can see your nascent soul fluttering in every curve!"

"That's because I—I had the second vision, Giya-zin." Tenshi ran her fingers along the strong lines she had drawn. "I saw my soul. Complete. Unending."

Meji, overcome, crushed her to them. The two had been friends for a decade, but she had never felt the omedeyo's arms around her.

"Welcome, Arojin. Welcome to forever."

Tenshi swallowed heavily as they pulled apart. A giya could submit the name of a newly other-born person to the religious hierarchy, but only the Archon could declare them an official arojin. "I'm nervous. What if he refuses to recognize my created soul?"

Her giya shook their head. "No. He won't refuse. I shouldn't tell you this, but he's been keeping an eye on you. He told me to make sure you rebuilt our teyopan."

Relief flooded Tenshi, a weight lifting from her heart.

"Oh, what a blessing. I had hoped he didn't oppose our work. Speaking of which, I wanted to ask you something. I *could* bring in an outside construction crew for this job, but I think it would be better if our congretation itself lent their hands and backs to the project."

Pishan nodded. "So many of them have already learned the essentials from your classes. I think it's wise. They will do well, and the work will move them further along the Path. When the chapel is finished, our mediation will be enhanced by the knowledge that the stones around us were set with our very hands."

Tenshi's eyes teared up. "The projection of our collective sparks into the physical world. What a beautiful notion."

Tenshi's life became a whirlwind of activity. Archon Rawe, to the dismay of Dominian leaders, declared her an arojin, fit to hold office if she chose. The old teyopan was razed and carted off, leaving a gaping hole in Kinguyama's heart. But not for long. Soon Tenshi was overseeing teams of her community members, digging into the rocky soil, pouring the foundation, laying quarried stone in sinuous lines.

As the structure began to go up, Tenshi and Brando's other project began to move forward. Ra-Koreji, they christened it. The College. Toddling little Tana in tow—for the girl refused to be separated from her father—Brando met with investors and educators, building up a team of people who could help launch the unparalleled project.

"I'm pretty sure," he said one evening, putting down the spoon he was using to feed Tana and wiping his hands, "that she's my secret weapon."

"Oh, yeah?" Tenshi laughed. "How's that?"

"You know how she likes to babble in Standard, Baryogo and Italian, right? It delights the hell out of them. They are utterly taken in by her wide-eyed wonder and joy."

"So it's her endearing personality and not your business acumen that's getting us financial backing?" Tenshi asked with a wink.

Tana grabbed the spoon and tried to feed herself, getting more peach puree in her curls than in her mouth. Brando shook his head and tried to pry her fingers open, but she wouldn't give the utensil up.

"Absolutely. When I don't know what I'm doing, which is often, I just plunk her down, and their hearts melt. Of course," he added, "they've never seen her eat."

Tenshi laughed. "We've started getting visitors, by the way."

"At the construction site?"

"Yeah. Word's been spreading."

Brando gave her a thumbs-up. "it's the largest reform carried out in the Pathwalker community since Domina's revelations got shared after her death, no? And that was a hundred and fifty years ago. It's news."

"True. They seem pretty mesmerized, too. Like it touches them."

Wiping his fingers clean on a napkin, Brando reached out and took her hand. "It's a symbol, Tenshi-shi. Looking upon it, they realize that they, too, are rooted in this world while simultaneously striving for enlightenment. The shrine stands for all of us. For Jitsu itself."

Tenshi snapped upright in her chair. "The vote. It's happening now. Query: project holo of live coverage. Chamber of Deputies."

The house AI softly asked, "In the kitchen?"

"Query: yes."

Despite all the good will toward Tenshi's project, Dominian Deputies had been railing for weeks against the new teyopan, decrying its complexity as *nako* and alien to the goals of the Path. They'd used parliamentary gimmicks to force a vote on a motion to halt construction.

Tenshi knew the Chamber like the back of her hand. They didn't have the votes. Still, though she wasn't worried, she wanted to see the defeat as it happened.

"The final vote has just been cast," an infotainment anchor narrated over a graphic that tallied the yeas and nays. "And the measure has been defeated. The moderate and reform blocs of the legislature have ensured the continued construction of Samaneino Teyopan in Kinguyama using a design developed by Tenshi Koroma."

"Ha!" Brando laughed, jerking his head at the holographic image. "Fools. I don't understand why they even bother. We have the majority. Next elections aren't for another five years. They can't stop us."

Tenshi took a sip of water. "No, they can't. And by the time elections roll around, we will have so transformed this world that they won't be able to turn back the clock."

She was about to query the projection off when the anchor raised his voice with excitement.

"Viewers, this is an unexpected blessing. For the first time in a decade, the Oracle will address Her people."

Tenshi almost choked as she swallowed. "Wait, what?"

Her twin's face glimmered into existence there before her. Her short hair was covered by her rebozo, the blue-edged white shawl that only a kedarumsha could wear. Her face was painted with the Marummo—the four double diamonds, symbolizing the umbini that made up the Ogdoad.

Otherwise she was Tenshi's mirror image.

"That Umma?" Tana asked.

"No, baby," Tenshi whispered. "That's Umakazi Samanei. Umma's sister."

"My children," Samanei said, her voice even and light. "I have been asked to give a dogmatic ruling on the building of a new shrine in my honor. Hear me well. A teyopan is like the collective kludged self of a community. As we must dismantle our own illusory selves in order to create a soul, so is it right and reasonable that a teyopan be torn down so that a better one, a temple more aligned with the sparks of its members, be built instead.

"Therefore do I decree: fight no longer against Kinguyama's will. No longer should you revile my sister, our clever Arojin Tenshi Koroma. She and her fellow teyopanjin have found their Way. Let them walk it. Their translation or lack thereof will be proof enough of its holiness. I will make you one promise: this shrine is essential for all upon the Path. Time will help you understand my words. Good night, all. Be enlightened."

Samanei's face winked away into darkness.

"Query," Tenshi said, her voice cracking. "Shut off transmission."

Brando got up and hugged her tight. She leaned into his embrace, unsure of her the strange feelings that swirled in her breast.

Construction took a year. By the end of those ten Jitsuan months, the terrorist attacks had resumed, more vicious than ever, as if someone wanted them to come to a head right when the teyopan was completed and the school preparing to open.

"It's done," Tenshi told Meji Pishan one afternoon. "We just installed the last of the interior furnishings. You can start conducting services there as soon as you choose."

"I want to hold a dedication ceremony first," they said. "You'll give the keynote."

Tenshi took a deep breath. "Is that really a good move? Extremists are more incensed than ever, despite the Oracle's admonitions."

"Why, because members of the congregations have started making alterations to their homes?"

She sighed. "Exactly."

The giya laid a hand on her shoulder. "Yes, but *I* am the one permitting that. Fostering it. I want them to express their exploration of self in the physical world that surrounds them."

"Sure, but *I'm* the one they consult with. Thirty different families now. Dominians don't blame you. I've corrupted you, in their eyes."

"Tenshi-shi, your siblings want, *need*, to hear you address them. With all this new violence, people are achingly aware of their own mortality. The time for unity has come. And you are best suited to bring the community together, to insire them, Arojin-zin."

Though reluctant, she agreed.

That night as she lay beside Brando, sweat from their lovemaking cooling on her skin, she shared her concerns.

"It's not getting up and talking that worries me. It's saying the right thing."

Still a little out of breath, Brando asked, "What do you mean?"

"I still think Santo is behind these renewed attacks," she began.

"Maybe, but syndicate battles are breaking out all over human space," Brando put in.

Tenshi shook her head curtly, ignoring his lingering tendency to play devil's advocate. "I don't see more than one group fighting here, Brando. So if it *is* Santo, then his plan is just not working. Assuming that he wants to try and get people to go against reform, I mean. The attacks are having the opposite effect."

"Ironically, the attacks have shocked even some extremists out of their daze."

"Right. More towns have moved toward Reformer ideals. But we have to keep the momentum up. This can't be just a temporary moment of lucidity. So I'll say some things in my speech that will be controversial, for some. I've got to catch our people while they're listening,"

"Can I take a look? You were dictating furiously all evening in your office. I'll try to gauge what the reaction could be."

Tenshi grabbed her datapad off the night table and pulled up her draft. She handed it to her husband, who skimmed through it. Then he reread it more carefully, nodding.

"You're right. This is going to piss off all the wrong people."

Tenshi frowned. "So…"

"You should definitely give the speech. Piss them off, Tenshi. Then lead them."

Tenshi took a deep breath. "Here we go, Brando. Time to change the world."

ON THE DAY OF THE TEYOPAN'S DEDICATION, A CROWD OF THOUSANDS stood on the cobblestone courtyard that fanned out from the loose semi-circle of the building's gently curving form. The gathering of Pathwalkers and off-worlders was the largest since the ill-fated fair, so Giya Pishan, wary of the continued terrorist attacks on Jitsu, had contracted a security firm so the ceremony would go off without a hitch. Scores of armored guards stood at the edges of the crowd, unsettling some, but mostly putting people at ease.

As both suns stood overhead, a massive blue eight-pointed star was lifted into position in its suspension field above the teyopan's apex. A deafening cheer went up. Somewhere a group began a chant that soon spread throughout the happy crowd.

"Tenshi! Tenshi! Tenshi!"

A platform had been erected at the center of the half-hoop formed by the motherly embrace of the teyopan's two wings of offices and classrooms. Atop it sat Meji Pishan, the other five anshyano on the town's council and Tenshi herself.

Pishan stood and approached the podium. "Welcome, siblings and friends. I am Meji Pishan, giya or spiritual leader of Kinguyama and head of its governing council. Today we have come together to dedicate our breathtaking new teyopan, our place of worship, meditation, and learning. And who better to address us now than the building's architect, Arojin Tenshi Koroma!"

Nerves jangling, Tenshi rose to her feet amid thunderous applause. Brando, standing in the crowd close to the stage, lifted eighteen-month-old Tana to his shoulders, gripping her pudgy hands tightly.

"Guarda, tesoro. É mama!" Tenshi heard him cry above the din.

Smiling with delight, Tana started shouting, "Mama, Umma, Mom! Mama, Umma, Mom!"

Tenshi waved at her daughter as she approached the micwire that sprouted nearly invisibly from the wooden planks. She waited a moment for the volume to drop, then began addressing her audience.

"It's an important day for all us. Here before this temple, the work of a thousand hands, we put the tragic events of the past behind us, moving toward the peace and security we need to walk the Path in our myriad, beautiful Ways.

"A year ago our Oracle—my twin—declared this shrine essential for all upon the Path. She spoke of shattering and rebuilding *objects* like teyopan that reflect our souls *in the physical world*. Jitsu is still reeling from her dogmatic ruling. Our extremist siblings have not yet fully internalized its import. But let me be clear: my sister supports the Reformer vision of Jitsu, one kept alive by Ona ra-

Shamanga and other oppressed Ways. On this world, she declares, individuals are free to seek enlightenment as the Eight and Founder Dresch always intended: as human beings, part of a physical universe that reflects us back.

"Some on this world believe a human isn't a person unless they've had the vision. They also want us to believe that nothing outside of our minds can contribute to the creation of our souls. Being cowards, they won't discuss the hypocrisy of allowing satorijin to create art and study the Grey Prison. For let's be honest: in a typical Dominatu teyopan, how many teyopanjin get recognized as reaching satori, so they can find traces of their selves in things they create? Very few.

"And hear me: this is *wrong*. There's nothing in the Revised Bible, nothing in the Diaries or in any oracular ruling that requires Pathwalkers to accept such a life.

"The second Oracle, Kosiya Yemo, told us in her final public address in February of 2624 that everyone on Jitsu would be shattered and rebuilt in one hundred years, realigned as a planet to Sopiya's wisdom. We're just thirty-nine years away from that prophesized day. I'm excited at the progress we're making.

"Take my giya here, Meji Pishan. They have begun to show their flock how we can balance meditation with secular life. It's an exciting time here in Kinguyama. Those of yall from Station City: look around at the houses we're rebuiding, at the bustle in our streets. *This* is the Path. We don't view yall as infidels, but as our friends, our potential siblings. We wait for yall with open arms. If and when the time comes, we'll welcome yall, just as my community welcomed me."

The crowd's response was deafening approval: applause, shouts, stamping and chanting that, drowning out a smattering of boos and hissing, went on for a solid ten minutes till Tenshi sat down again and Giya Pishan motioned everyone to silence.

After a moment of stillness, the giya spoke.

"Arojin Tenshi Koroma has spoken truth. Our message here in Kinguyama, in Samaneino Teyopan, maintains strict continuity with the words of the Founder and the Oracles. And that unbroken thread—six centuries of Pathwalking—leads me to the next tasks in my sacred role as giya."

They gestured broadly at the crowd.

"Tesnhi has criticized the low percentage of Seers who become satorijin. Again, her words ring true. This fact is not the failing of teyopanjin, however. It falls squarely on the shoulders of the giya. If the people in my charge cannot achieve awareness, it is because I have not done my job. I am to *guide* them. To do so, I will be lauching an aggressive program, tailored to the needs of each adult teyopanjin in this town. Within two years, every one of you will become satorijin if you follow the regimen I have prepared for you."

Thunderous applause. Exulted shouts of praise.

But a few people walked away, shaking their heads.

Meji is putting their head on the chopping block, Tenshi reflected. *They must truly feel they have my sister's backing. I hope it's not an illusion.*

"Perhaps you also know," they continued as the sound died down, "that I serve an administrative function in this town, heading up its Council of Anshyano, which up to this point has governed its municipal affairs. If all goes as we hope, however, that will change Before the Chamber of Deputies this session are a number of important bills that we predict will be passed and signed into law by the Archon."

The crowd seemed collectively on tinterhooks, leaning forward as one.

"Introduced by the Reporumatudan, these measures include the restructuring of Kinguyama's government so that religious and administrative duties are separated, creating a municipal board to which non-Pathwalkers can be elected. Also on the slate is an innovative school founded by our own Brando D'Angelo di Makomo on the fairgrounds built by Arojin Tenshi Koroma. Named Ra-Koreji, it will serve as a space where both Pathwalkers and off-worlders alike can receive a quality education in many fields. Finally, we Reformers seek to establish partnerships between merchants in Station City and residents of Kinguyama residents, creating local business outlets to bring vital goods and services into our community beyond what is avaible in the Bida Sento."

Tenshi hardly heard her giya's closing remarks. Not because of the applause, but because she couldn't stop looking at the faces of her people.

They were crying tears of joy.

A MONTH LATER, TENSHI WAS AWAKENED in the middle of the night by the house AI.

"Emergency call from Meji Pixan."

Tenshi sat up. "Query: audio only. Route to master bedroom."

"Tenshi-shi?" Meji's voice was trembling.

"Yes? What's wrong?"

A sob. "You need to come to town. They've attacked. People are dead. Houses destroyed."

Tenshi yanked the sheets aside, standing naked in the darkness. "What the fuck? Okay, I'm on my way."

"Crisis control is at the municipal building. Triage in the courtyard."

Tenshi grabbed her clothes from the floor and headed for bathroom. Behind her, Brando called. "I'll come with you."

"No." Her voice was hard with grief and rage. "Stay here with Tana. I'll keep you in the loop."

She dressed and pulled her hair back with a clip, then sped toward Kinguyama in her transport. The last four weeks had seen terrorist activity pick up in the Mashkanu prefecture, but the ATS had kept them away from towns till now.

But last night, deputies had passed the reform package Tenshi and her allies had worked so hard to develop. She'd expected a response, but not an invasion.

So this how you respond, Santo. Bastard. Just wait.

Outside the municipal building, ATS medics and local healers were attending to the many wounded. Tenshi was about to walk among them, offering compassion and help, but then she saw the row of bodies covered by sheets.

Her heart breaking, she stormed into the building and found the Council of Anshyano around a table with two ATS captains, marking a holographic map of Kinguyama.

"Tenshi-shi," Meji said, lifting their eyes. "This is Captain Binh of Delta Squad and Captain Wu, whose trainees are providing logistical support."

She nodded at them, gritting her teeth. "Details."

Binh pointed at the eastern edge of town on the map. "Crew of yakuza gunsels came into the city at this point and entered two dozen homes under construction. They beat or shot family members, taking household supplies of moku and setting the structures on fire as they left. Very surgical."

Tenshi clenched her fists and looked at Meji. "The theft of moku is a smokescreen. They're sending a message."

"I agree," the giya said. "So we have to respond."

"Respond?" asked Tenshi. "How? Our people are dead and wounded. No political move is going to turn back the clock. Arming the townspeople is out of the question."

Meji crossed their arms across their chest. "I'm not talking politics. There are other ways of defending ourselves. My last act as head of this council, Arojin-kun, will be this: hiring the private firm that provided security at the dedication ceremony."

Tenshi took a step forward, describing a semicircle in the air in front of her with her fists. "As a community defense force, yes? To keep these bastards out."

One of the anshyano, Radi Doruba, objected immediately. "How could we afford to have them defending us around the clock?"

"The accounting firm that we've been consulting with in Station City," Meji explained, "has calculated our likely municipal revenue. Tuition at Ra-Koreji, taxes on the outlet businesses, projected increase in pilgrims from off world. Should be enough."

Tenshi pulled her datapad from her bag. "I'm also going to contact that expansionist think-tank on Dhara. They've been wanting to help fuel reform here. I bet I can get them to underwrite some of the expense. Uniforms, headquarters, holding cells."

Anshyano Doruba cleared her throat. "The Dominatudan are going to push back, hard."

Tenshi waved her datapad dismissively. "Then their leaders shouldn't have gotten in bed with the bloody demimundo. We can't worry about them anymore. Our people's lives and enlightenment hang in the balance."

She turned on her heels and started to leave.

"Where are you going, Arojin-kun?" Meji called after her.

"To help the wounded and mourning," she replied without looking back. "To do whatever I can for our people."

Kinguyama's security detail turned out to be a blessing. Its presence drew reformers from other towns and prefectures in droves. Many hired Tenshi's new team of anshyano architects to help them discover through meditation and study the home design that best expressed their individual Way along the Path. Moderate Jitsujin also drifted in, fleeing the wave of terrorist attacks the ATS couldn't quell.

Even off-worlders started petitioning the Municipal Board for permission to buy land and live in the burgeoning town. The promise of a less hectic life appealed to most, but some were enthralled by Meji Pishan's weekly homilies, now carried by multiple infotainment platforms.

We promise enlightenment and eternity through an understanding of self worked out in the world as well as within us, Tenshi reflected. *I can see why non-believers find the message attractive.*

With Brando's help, she convinced Pishan of the potential for new converts to the Path, specifically to the Way of Shattering. The giya then sent their ebanjerusha (except for Tenshi's father, who'd long abandoned the town) to proselytize in Station City itself.

From among the many new members of Samaneino Teyopan, Meji selected additional ebanjerusha to carry out a more traditional duty: escorting off-world pilgrims to Kinguyama.

They were coming in droves.

Tenshi sold her expansive flat in Station City and instead rented three floors of an office building to house Izakiwo, the architectural firm and construction company she had incorporated under Jitsu's new laws.

When Station City mayor Seni Chunhawan accepted a position with the CPCC's relatively new Ministry of State, Tenshi threw a farewell banquet for him in Izakiwo's largest meeting room.

She was sipping on a drink, catching up with Areshan Yesuro, when she heard Brando's voice ring out above the buzz of music and conversation.

"But it *is* a problem, Meji-shi."

"I don't know that I agree," Tenshi heard the giya respond. "There seems to be a general upswing in Reformer sentiment in many prefectures."

Areshan flicked their head at Tenshi, and the two weaved their way through the press of guests.

"What are we arguing about?" Areshan asked.

Brando cleared his throat. "I was telling the giya that I'm worried. So many Reporumatu moving to the Mashkanu prefecture is upsetting the balance. We need to be more spread out, not a lone island in the middle of a sea of Dominatu."

Tenshi shook her head. "We're not, Brando. There's the Arusha district, under Yuki Umkapa—"

"And Inkungu," Areshan added pointedly. "You know, the prefecture run by yours truly?"

"They're both mostly reformer in make-up," Tenshi continued. "Doing similar work to what's happening in Kinguyama. Other moderate prefects are here tonight. We're working on them, trying to bridge the gaps."

Brando raised an eyebrow. "I know, Tenshi. I *have* been paying attention. But yall seem to be forgetting that general elections for the Chamber of Deputies will be held in four years. There's, what, 106 members, two from each prefecture. Here's the scenario: Arusha, Inkungu and Mashkanu continue to swallow up reformers from other areas. More prefectures end up majority Dominatu, demographically. Come election time, more Dominatu deputies get sworn in, and that faction gains control. Then they start of the dismantling everything we've worked so hard to achieve."

"But the answer," Meji countered, "is not to stem the flow of reform-minded emigrants from other prefectures."

"They're right, Brando," Tenshi agreed. "The answer is to create *more* reform-minded Jitsujin. To convince them with our message and our example."

As she said the words, however, a part of her admitted that Brando was right.

INTERCHAPTER E

Maharaja Dead at 63

Martian Multimedia

Hamed Bu Yabes

3 June, 2686—The Constitutional Monarchy of Kunti was in mourning today at the passing away of its ruler, Maharaja Tri Leksono. The Office of the Royal Physician declared the cause of death to be a severe stroke. Leksono is best remembered as the implementer of significant social reforms across Sigma Draconis, including the institution of a process that gradually shifts the monarchy to a republic, paving the way for the independent system's entrance into the Consortium by May of 2695 if all requirements are met. The Maharaja's son, Raja Uki Leksono, will be made temporary regent of Sigma Draconis in a ceremony on Friday. The prince has promised in a faux-conference with CPCC leaders that the transition will proceed as the late maharaja agreed.

Kinguyama Now Home to 67,000 Residents

The Pathwalker Periodical

Erena Chimari

15 July, 2686—The once minor town of Kinguyama, made famous fifteen years ago when Karibudan declared Samanei Koroma the third Dominian Oracle, has now grown twenty times its original size and is home to 67,000 residents, fifteen percent of off-world origin. Its secular municipal board recently annexed a 2,000-hectare strip along the desert to establish a business and pilgrim reception center.

Under the auspices of the latest reforms, residents have begun selling crafts and food to visitors and trading amongst themselves. According to a recent report from the CPCC Ministry of State, the town has now generated the first stable economy—outside of Station City—the planet Jitsu has ever seen.

The Reformer economic strategy being carried out in Kinguyama is widely perceived as an attempt to undo Dominian political hegemony on Jitsu. The Reporumatudan political alliance appears to be employing other methods to reach that goal. Outreach emissaries have been sent from Kinguyama to the capital cities of all other prefects in order to establish dialogue and encouraging reform. Reformers have proposed a bill that would add a second chamber to the legislature, with representation based on population. Another bill would reclassify Station City as a district, with its own legislators in both houses.

Organized Crime Clashes on the Rise

Oceania Equatorial Information Net

Scot Jeunz

17 July, 2686—The capital city was rocked today by violent confrontations between rival crime syndicates. Alexandria's municipal police and Consortium Constabulary officers were quick to intervene, but not before several dozen deaths occurred. System Constable Mena Zaki confirmed what the chief of Alexandria's police force at first reported: most of the corpses were members of the organized crime syndicate called the Aztlan Angels, suspected of involvement in a great deal of the illegal activity in the Helios system, both on New Mecca and here on Oceania.

"The other group," informed Constable Zaki, "appears to be the local branch of the Brotherhood. We've been getting reports over the last few years that new demimundan forces were moving in, but this is the first we see of the Brotherhood."

Soon after the constable's declaration, OEIN's sources let slip that the local Brotherhood underboss may be none other than Felipe Beserra, half-brother to that syndicate's infamous cacique, Konrau Beserra, who rose to power in a bloody struggle a decade ago. Beserra had dropped off the radar of various intelligence communities when he pulled all Brotherhood operations from the Solar System. Rumors place him at various locations in CPCC territory, though more reliable reports indicate that the new Brotherhood headquarters is far beyond Consortium space.

Today's clash marks the sixth such battle between syndicates across the CPCC in the last four weeks. Five of the skirmishes were between Brotherhood members and other powerful gangs, suggesting that the syndicate may be trying to expand its power base. L'ermandá, as the Brotherhood is called in its members' native language, is one of the oldest organized crime groups in existence. It got its start in the late twentieth century as a prison gang on Earth called the Texas Chicano Brotherhood, and it was one of the first Mafias in the Solar Asteroid Belt. In 2099, the gang schismed into the Brotherhood and the Aztlan Angels. The two groups remain enemies to this day.

Sigma Draconis Arms Itself

Milan Daily Gazette

Adele Tuttisanti

25 August, 2686—Regent Uki Leksono, son of the late maharaja of the Constitutional Monarchy of Kunti, the official government of what the CPCC calls the Sigma Draconis system, requested of the Consortium Diet a permit to purchase additional planetary defense weaponry from the corporate republic of BelCorp. Leksono cited fears of possible syndicate infiltration like what is reportedly occurring on Atlantis, where demimundan forces fleeing Brotherhood

aggression in other systems are seeking a foothold. Given the dozens of inter-mafia battles and the supposed exodus of syndicates to new worlds, the regent of Kunti insists that his people must be well protected. Bolstering Leksono's request, the BelCorp CEO faux-conferenced with members of the Diet leadership for several hours from her office in the Ross 154 system. The move to permit arms sales to non-Consortium governments is a controversial one that, if carried out, may cause as much furor as the decision to provide the Kunti government fenestration drives did two years ago.

From: koromasanto@bounce.per.int

To: yenbandera@nannewa.per.jov

Subject: The Way of Deception (encrypted)

Date: August 29, 2688 13:07:37 (SST)

Decrypted 13:15:32 via FAE (archived version translated from Baryogo)

I've been told to reach out to you. That you share my dislike for our underworld allies. That you acknowledge the Third Dispensation and bend your knee to Mother Domina. Good. She's using them to make Jitsujin so afraid of off-worlders that when I have the power to confine infidels to Station City, the move will seem logical and a relief. I trust and love her, so I play the part, even begrudgingly throwing my support behind reform.

So the yakuza must keep up their attacks for now. Nicely spaced out, allowing reformers to relax after each. But by the time I assume power, we need to have mechanisms in place that will allow us to disentangle ourselves from our agreement with the Brotherhood. She has instructed me to develop strategies with you for undermining the present arrangment. Let's begin. You're better equipped to connect us safely and discretely for a face-to-face. I await the details.

Be enlightened, Shangazi-shi.

CHAPTER 26

"YEAH. MONSOON SEASON, IF YOU CAN IMAGINE THAT. COMES once every eight years, lasts bout five months. All them water tanks you see at the desert's edge? Those are to cache the rainfall and run-off. When Kurishto, the gas planet with the fucked-up orbit, gets extra close to the planet like it is right now, it starts freaking out the magnetics and exerting weird tidal forces on the Salty Sea, which warms up to 40 degrees in summer, and you get all these weird air currents, something like that. Bang up against the colder upper air from the mountains to the northwest, create monster storms with killer wind speeds."

Ben Wu, captain of Alpha Squad, watched his second, Jak Fisk, mop sweat from his brow and neck with a khaki bandana. They were crouched on a hill above the town of Sakyu in the Wahaka district, just to the west of the booming Mashkanu prefecture. A tip had been channeled through Major Sosa at HQ that a yakuza crew would be hitting the local teyopan, and the grizzled veteran had sent Wu's squad, still shaky even after nearly three years of training, to investigate.

At first Ben had regretted accepting the position as squad leader on this backward hellhole, despite the hate he felt for yegsters of all types, whether mafiosi or common thieves. His twenty-three-year stint with the Armed Forces of the CPCC, the last fourteen as a major in the Consortium Army, had given him many chances to slap law-breakers down, but Wu had always felt hog-tied by the excessive regulations. He despised being restrained. It was one reason he kept leaving his teenage daughter in the care of his dead wife's family, despite how poorly they were raising her.

He needed to be unencumbered.

The freedom promised him by the Neog recruiters had drawn the vet to the job: the idea of heading an elite team of soldiers with carte blanche to deal with yaks as he saw fit was tempting. It might even help him forget the gaping hole Qing's death had left. Her sickness had been slow, painful and untreatable. He'd been powerless to stop it. All his military skills meant nothing before her steady destruction, and this inability to fight had compelled him to destroy his other enemies as utterly as possible. Driven deep within him where he'd not have to think about it was the understanding that, faced with the choice of freely berserking his enemies or opening himself up the heart-wrenching pain in which all relationships end, leaving Ya-Ting behind was the only alternative he could ever accept.

Despite Ben's eagerness to slaughter yaks, Sosa had assigned him all the least qualified riffraff that had answered Jitsu's plea for help. Most of the men, though they considered themselves tough, had little military training or experience fighting other than barroom brawls and the like.

For instance, Fisk, who was the best of the lot, had fled Podgoritsa, where he'd settled ten years previously, after beating his wife nearly to death over runny eggs. The only other strenuous physical activity he'd performed was his underwater drilling job, which on Jitsu was meaningless. Ben had been forced to train all of them starting with the basics, like putting a fresh crop of recruits through AF boot camp. He'd brought in vets to help him capacitate the lot of them in arms, martial arts and strategy. A year of training, a year of simulations, and a good six months of backing up other squads had preceded today's operation.

Ben felt pretty confident in them, though they hadn't been in a tight spot yet.

He had a sinking feeling that today might put them to the test

"This storm, it's coming up over the desert now?" Wu asked.

"Yeah. That's what I don't get. Why would a bunch of yaks choose to strike with a major storm looming? They could get caught in it."

"Worse. We might get caught in it, too. Shite." Wu rolled over, pointed his field glasses to the south. The horizon had begun to blacken, and the wind was picking up. "How long before it hits?"

Frisk, a man obsessed with climatology, shrugged. "Fifteen, twenty minutes? Who knows. Damn Neogs care so little about the fucking weather, they don't even have a meteorological satellite. If we had a infotainment receiver, we could check what Station City's saying."

"Well, we don't, so there's no way of knowing. Domina's dangling dugs!"

Ben had taken to using the local religion's important figures' names in vain. It was his way of coping with the repulsion he felt for the planet of zombies he was trying to protect. "Pick seven men, Jak, and send them down around this hill to check for mines or traps."

"Group leader?"

"Your discretion, mate."

In a couple of minutes, a husky squadman named Omar Marzuban led six others around the base of the hill to the flat, yellowed moss-covered plain between it and the city's edge. Their flexsuits, nowhere near as advanced as AF armor, but sufficient to cool their bodies in the agonizing heat and provide decent shielding from all but the most powerful of blasts, adjusted themselves to the ambient color till it appeared seven pale smears were floating along the ground. Ben's field glasses adjusted to the camouflaging and he followed the group's sweeping movement as it scanned for traps. One of the men signaled to the others: he'd found something.

Voices broke the radio silence.

Omar: "What we got, Kirsha?"

Kirsha: "Looks like a mine plate. See the outline? Something rectangular under the moss. You bend closer, you can see that…"

These were the last words any of the seven men would utter. The patch of ground Kirsha'd been pointing at popped up: a hatch. A huge, illegally overpowered blast rifle peeked up and an equally massive yak stuck his head out of the hole, firing rapidly as he drew his weapon in an arc from left to right across the conveniently arranged squadmen. The blasts tore some of them in half, disemboweled others.

Omar had half turned to run by the time the arc the rifle described reached him, and the blast struck a 'nade hanging from his belt. The explosion sent bits of the soldier in a thousand directions. As the last squadman collapsed in a pile of gore, the yak emerged completely from the hole. Another followed him, and then another. Soon, some fifty mafia foot soldiers were tramping about in the remains of Ben's men.

"Fuck!" Jak leapt to his feet.

"How many men we got behind this hill?" Ben shouted at him.

"Shite, uh, eleven. We were twenty, member? Shite, oh, shite, we are fucked. What the fuck kind of weapon cuts through suits like that? Christ!"

"Listen to me, Jak. Get a grip, understand? Take the larger transport, haul arse to HQ, and bring the rest of the lads." He glanced through the field glasses. The yaks were heading toward the hill. "We'll hold them on the plain till yall get here. Try to raise Delta or Gamma, get them to give us back-up."

"Got it, cap." Jak began sprinting down the back side of the hill, Ben following in a fraction of a second.

"And Jak, listen close: you land that transport back here and go around the base of the hill; I don't care what happens, do *not* land on the other side. Understood?"

"Understood."

Ben Wu's second jumped into the transport's cockpit and hurtled away. The black over the desert was even closer, and the wind had started lifting a light haze of sand. The eleven remaining men were on their feet, confused. Ben signaled for them to activate their helmets. A coded series of taps at the neck of their flexsuits caused the armored casques to quickly grow over the men's heads, providing them with enhanced vision and hearing. Ben addressed them over the cascom.

"Alright, mates, we got us about fifty ugly yaks on the other side of that hill, heading this way. They got our boys, all of 'em, and they're aiming to get us, too. We're gonna split into two groups: Zaita, Babbi, Dun, Mendis and Ketpetch with me, the rest of yall with Kosykh. Dmitri, don't fuck around. We got a storm coming, so hold 'em off: don't run off into 'em. Grenades, canon, long distance weapons. We try any close combat, we're dead."

Dmitri gestured at the hill. "Why not climb that an' hold 'em at a distance?"

"We go up there, they see we got an advantage, they're gonna just slink back into their hole: try to get the fuckers out once they're stashed like that. Worse, they could surround the hill, and we'd be fucked. Now let's get a move on!"

Lieutenant Dmitri Kosykh grunted at his half of the men, and they yanked themselves sharply around the west edge.

"Ketpetch, give me the transport's remote." Wu's men were rounding the east side briskly. The bald second lieutenant slipped the thin metal disk into his captain's gloved hand.

"Ben, why don't we take the transport, blast 'em from the sky?"

"Damn, Victor, you gormless or something? If they didn't slip underground, we'd all be concentrated in a single vehicle with minimal ablative plating. They'd blow us out of the fucking air. No, this is the only way, trust me. Besides, the wind's kicking up: hard to hit shite with dust screwing up the bloody sensors and gusts shaking us all over the damn place."

They came completely around the hill just as Dmitri's group did. There was no one in sight.

"The fuck?" someone muttered on the cascom.

"Silence on this goddamn channel!"

The field appeared completely empty. Wu activated IR visual. Several smallish heat-exchange signatures were stirring in the moss.

"Down! Get the fuck down!"

A score of camouflaged yaks leapt to their feet as the squad went prone. Blaster fire ripped huge chunks of rock and soil out of the hill, which pelted the horizontal flexsuits ineffectually.

"Mendis: digbot! Dun, unpack the plasma mortar. The rest of you, unsling and let 'em zing!"

As the automated backhoe dug a horseshoe trench five meters from the base of the hill, the squad engaged the mobsters, whose only protection was their superior black-market personal armor. Dun struggled with the mortar, trying to get it set up as quickly as possible: a direct hit from that device would compromise any type of battle suit.

Ben couldn't shake his worry. There were only twenty-odd yaks now: what had happened to the others? He wondered whether they were heading townward at this very moment, these having stayed behind to busy the squad. If so, the soldiers would have to break the line and pursue.

A glance upward through the smoke and flying sand revealed a blackening sky, clouds streaming in upon high winds at the storm's northern edge and filling the light blue void. Suddenly, the troop's smaller transport appeared over the crest of the hill. Ben was about to chew Victor Ketpetch out for calling the ship up when he remembered that his subordinate had given him the control just a couple of minutes before. In a flash he realized where the other yaks had gone and who was piloting the transport. Seizing the control disk in his hand, he signaled its immediate landing. There was no response. After several more attempts, Ben concluded that either the disk had malfunctioned, or the yegsters had a way of bypassing it.

No time to lose.

"Forget the trench: everybody storm the yak ranks! Full out, gunning with everything you got!"

His men hesitated. A missile sped from one of the transport's launch tubes and pulverized the digbot and two of Dmitri's group.

"It's the yaks, you dim bastards!" Ben screamed into the cascom. "They popped out on the other side of the hill and jacked the transport; run toward the other fuckers: no way they're gonna shoot their own mates!"

That got them moving. Ben growled at himself for overlooking this obvious move: the yakuza bunker had an exit on the far side of the hill. His men had fallen into a trap. Sprinting toward Dun, who was finishing the mortar assembly, Ben motioned for the soldier to join his squadmates in throwing themselves against the line of yaks while the captain himself swept the heavy mortar up in his wiry arms and ascended the hill as fast as he could. Screams and moans filled his casque as his men took hit after hit in their attempt to storm the line.

Reaching the top of the hill, Wu jabbed the telescoping base of the mortar into the packed sand and begin sighting the transport on the smart display. The ship was obviously targeting the soldiers, who were just a few meters from the ground-based yegsters. Ultra-heated sprays of sand burst from the field around the advancing squad; their suits struggled not to succumb to the molten silicon that was beginning to coat them.

The transport in his sights, Ben began firing at the places where he knew the ablative plating to be weak. The yaks answered with a pair of missiles that gouged large portions of rock and sand from the hill and sent Ben sprawling as the ground crumbled beneath him. Then, as his men finally engaged the enemy in close quarters, the transport did what he'd counted on its not doing: it opened fire on the yaks to get at the squad.

"Fuck," he muttered as he tried to get a purchase on the mortar and pull himself back to a standing position. The wind pulled the gun this way and that, and the fine coating of dust on his gloves made it difficult to grab. A strong gust knocked him prone again, as woofy curtains of sand and dirt were ripped from the landscape to whelm the clashing forces in wave after wave.

Without warning, a gale-force wind began to blow, and Ben, who'd just gotten a grip on the mortar, was toppled from the hilltop, caroming from outcropping to outcropping down its northern face. As he slammed to a stop at the base, protected from the violence of the fall by his flex suit, Ben was plunged into darkness for a second as the suns were completely blotted out; his casque visual shifted to infrared, revealing a phantasmagoric landscape of destruction.

At that moment, a second transport shot over the top of the hill, rocking wildly in the now spiraling wind, all guns blazing at the hijacked ship. Ben let loose a stream of obscenities into his cascom.

"Frisk, you fucking idiot, I told you to land on the other side!"

The first transport swung around and began speeding toward Frisk and the other squadmen. Frisk, as could have been predicted, continued at full throttle toward the enemy.

"Are you fucking insane?" Ben demanded.

The two transports whined past each other, exchanging plasma rounds and launching rockets that, at such speeds, whizzed harmlessly off into the distance to impact against the landscape. Jak whipped around about 1,000 meters out and began heading toward the hill as the yak-commandeered vehicle, having shot past the hill toward the south, screamed about in a sharp curve and roared directly toward its opponent.

"Jak, pull the fuck up and out, you hear? No playing chicken with these bastards, that's a goddamn order!"

The channel crackled static in reply. *No bloody time.*

The stolen transport was passing right above him, and he was flat on his back. He gripped the enormous gun in both hands, pressed its back end against his shoulder so it wouldn't sink into the loosened sand, and began to fire. His shoulder was immediately dislocated by the recoil, which not even the suit could withstand, but he continued firing, screaming at the top of his lungs as the pain built to a brain-numbing white crescendo.

Suddenly, the plating gave way and the transport exploded. The shock wave knocked the remaining combatants off their feet, easy targets for the rain of ruined metal and fire that began streaming from the sky. Unfortunately, the concussion also sent a massive twisted chunk of plasteel at supersonic speed right into Frisk and the squad, wrenching the vehicle sideways and down. It bobbed and spun as if its pilot were trying to adjust its course, and, despite the speed at which it was traveling, it seemed to Ben that Frisk might pull up in time.

But then, as if some dark god had decreed Ben's complete disgrace, the sky opened up and began to pound them with hail and solid sheets of rain while simultaneously an enormous bolt of lightning seared the air in front of the transport. At this, the vehicle lost all its upward arc and began hurtling toward the few remaining combatants on the ground below.

Ben's attention was occupied by the avalanche of steaming metal that began slamming into the mud around him, some larger chunks boring through to the bunker beneath. He managed to clamber to his feet and dash a few meters, grabbing his dislocated arm by the elbow and pressing it to his body, until an explosion behind him sent him sprawling face first in the thickening mire.

The pain from his shoulder took his breath away more than the fall had, however, and he rolled over to relieve the pressure on it. He lifted his head slightly and was nearly blinded before the casque's visor adjusted its level of sensitivity to the ambient light. The entire plain was on fire: no sign of movement, just flames and steaming metal and cratered dirt.

He again got to his feet and began limping, his back bent under a brutal barrage of hail the size of cricket balls that not even his suit could compensate for. Slowly he made his way through the ruin, looking for the living. Charred corpses he found, scattered limbs he stumbled across, but he soon realized that he was the only survivor.

A glance at the shattered face of the hill confirmed what he'd imagined: Frisk had impacted against it at some ridiculously dangerous speed. *No one lives through something like that.* After a few minutes of searching, he reached the manhole from which the yegsters had earlier emerged. Where there'd previously been a trap door there was now a gaping pit. From the blazing interior of the bunker came sounds of small explosions as stored weapons caught fire and inner walls collapsed.

The storm began to abate as Ben, acting on pure survival instinct and years of training, picked his way across the plain to the rocky wasteland to its west. No sooner had he reached the first looming boulders than a garbled transmission filtered through his cascom. It was Gamma Squad, arriving to provide backup.

"Captain Wu, you're on our screens. Hang loose. Where are the others?"

The hail segued into a simple opaque downpour. Without replying, Ben deactivated his casque, which accordioned back into the collar of the flexsuit. He let the water stream over his head, soaking his queue, flooding his eyes and nose and mouth as he tilted it back in abandon.

The face of each of his men drifted before him as the water stopped his breathing and he fell to his knees. He felt his will to live slacken for a second, a darkness not of the storm edging into his soul.

Then, inexplicably, he smelled his wife's perfume. Orange blossoms and lilac. He knew Qing was with him there at the brink of despair, her presence surrounding him. He could almost hear her voice murmur his name…

Abruptly, he doubled over and vomited, expelling the liquid in a coughing fit. He'd shared as much of their death as he could.

All he was permitted now, it seemed, was to avenge them.

CHAPTER 27

IT WAS THE EVE OF THE FIRST DAY OF CLASSES AT RA-KOREJI.
Brando's stomach kept churning, and not just because of the big launch. The
massacre of Alpha Squad had caused a wave of fear and fury to spread across
the continent. Deputies were about to vote on whether to put Station City and
other major urban centers on lockdown.

Tenshi poured them both a glass of marapu, palm wine from the Ebishi
prefecture now available in Kinguyama's new marketplace. "Any excuse to ruin
the social and economic gains. So predictable, these bastards."

Brando downed the alcohol in a single draught. "I swear, if they shut
the campus down before it even opens—fuck me. Ra-Koreji is more than
just a school. I can see my newly aligned self so clearly now in its structure,
educational philosophy, curricula. Satori feels *so close* right now."

His wife took his stubbly chin in her hand. "It won't fade no matter what
you do. You've put in the work, baby. Sopiya will keep guiding you."

The anchor discussing the vote on the holographic display touched their ear as if getting news from a producer. "Siblings, we go now to the Prefectural Management Complex in Juresh, where Arojin Santo Koroma is about to adress a small crowd."

Tenshi jerked her gaze back toward the projection. "What fresh new hell?"

Santo's sly smile flickered to life before them. "Fellow Jitsujin, citizens and deputies alike. I wanted to speak directly to you concerning our recent troubles. The proposal in the Chamber of Deputies must be—defeated."

Brando's gut roiled even more. "Why is he suddenly on our side?"

"He's got some evil purpose, trust me." Tenshi finished off her drink and poured them another.

"In fact, I humbly accept responsibility for the failures of the ATS. The Oracle and Archon entrusted me with their stewardship, but I have not focused on that role. I've tried to be both prefect and protector. I now see I must choose. As a result, today I'm stepping down from my position with the great district of Mashkanu. I've submitted the name of my proposed replacement to the Archon—Meji Pishan. Their leadership in Kinguyama has proved a worthy example for other towns in the district. They should be in charge of guiding Mashkanu toward reform."

Brando almost spit marapu all over the table. "Wait, Meji-shi? Why would he turn the reins over to a Reporumatu giya?"

"I'm telling you," his wife repeated, "there's a catch."

"Instead of prefect, I will assume the temporary position of Czar of Public Defense. Temporary because it is my intention to work hard to eliminate the need for such a job. We'll be expanding the number squads, broadening their patrols. I promise you—I will make this planet safe again."

"And there you go. He's throwing us a bone, but he's going to have muscle in every prefecture. Something's in the works."

"Doesn't he still have to turn the ATS over to the legislature in two years, after the elections?" Brando asked.

"A lot can happen in two years, love."

Reporting switched back to the Chamber of Deputies, where the proposed lockdown was defeated narrowly.

Though he often felt Tenshi was more paranoid than needed where her uncle was concerned, Brando had to admit that his implied support of reform was suspicious.

What does he have up his sleeve, then?

THE NEXT DAY, RA-KOREJI FLUNG WIDE ITS DOORS and received its first batch of students. Classes were for adults, given three times a week with subjects ranging from basic calculus to construction methods and literature. Tuition could be paid in a variety of ways, from CPCC credits to volunteer work or community vouchers. The latter were Tenshi's idea: she convinced the growing secular economic sector to offer IOUs for services and goods in order to pay the increasing number of Pathwalkers who did work for them, thus circumventing the long-standing Dominatu practice of not earning money for labor. These vouchers, after being used to cover tuition, could in turn be converted to credits for instructors' salaries, or used directly as part of those salaries themselves.

The ultimate goal was to get the government of Jitsu to fund secular education for all its residents. But as the local saying went, *One walks the Path step by gradual step.*

As the first semester drew to a close, Brando had to rethink his plans. No one was a better sounding board than Tenshi, so met with her at Izakiwo headquarters one afternoon.

"The stop-gap system has worked well," he told her. "And we have a huge waiting list. I need to accelerate my schedule."

"Ah, yes. Jitsujin have the right and the means to study now. Of course they're lining up. What are you considering?"

"Expanding to a full five-day week."

Tenshi nodded and stood from her desk, circling around to massage his shoulders. "Sounds good. Wow, you're tense, baby."

Brando sighed, enjoying the feel of her fingers as they kneaded into his muscles.

"We've been going at it for two years straight, Tenshi. How much longer can we keep up this pace?"

She kissed the top of his head. "Can't stop now. Too much momentum. But, then again, I've got my employees and fellow architects. You're going to need more help, too."

"I've got some ideas. But first—let's take a vacation."

She bent her head down to his eye level, blinking. "A what? Really?"

"Yeah. We deserve it. Get one of your friends to watch Tana for a few days? I'll handle the rest."

THE NORTHERN COASTAL PREFECTURE OF EBISHI was known not only for its heady palm wine, but also for its beaches of pink sand. Reformers in Kampun, one of the district's oldest villages, had recently constructed a series of cabins to encourage tourism under the auspices of the new laws.

Brando booked them all for a week. Paid the three local eateries compensation for lost business.

"So that it's only you and me," he explained to Tenshi as they stepped out of their cabin the first afternoon. He laced his fingers through hers and looked deep into her sunburst eyes. "Even if just for a little while, I want no one else around to distract me from loving you."

They walked along the strand, chatting and laughing, watching sea moths dive for floating krill, until the sun began to set. Then they had dinner at one of the restaurants, fresh sea food served over benachin with gourds of the marapu they'd both acquired a taste for.

Walking back with his wife under the bejewelled night sky, Brando felt a need so intense it almost hurt. He stopped her, the waves lapping at their feet, and pressed his mouth to hers. The same fire was rising in her, he could tell. Getting back to the cabin was out of the question. So they pulled each other free of their light cotton clothes and fell together there on the sand, lost in each other as the moon peered over the horizon, its light shimmering first upon the waves and then their entwined bodies.

Brando came to relish the rhythm they fell into over the next few days. Waking to share a light breakfast and hot koro brew, often after making early morning love—without interruptions from a certain curious toddler. Then swimming for a bit before taking a boat out past the breakers so that Tenshi could teach him the fine art of fishing with a net.

Afterwards, they'd cook up their catch and Brando would play guitar for his beloved, singing old songs and new.

"Play the ones your uncle Jean Makomo taught you," Tenshi would invariably ask. "The ones you sing to Tana."

Looking from the porch toward the sea, Brando would strike up "Olele, Moliba Makasi" as she pretending to row their boat against a current. Then, knowing what she really wanted, he'd switch to "Bilanga Na Ngai," and she would start to dance, the brilliant colors of her skirt swirling, her long locs taking on a life of their own.

He'd put down the guitar and dance with her for a while, their steps slowing until they were pressed against each other, eyes locked. Sometimes they'd make love again. Other times they'd go swimming, or climb trees in search of fruit.

But every evening ended the same: the walk along the beach to one of the three restaurants, a hearty meal with lots of palm wine.

A walk back beneath the stars.

Eager sex, on the sand, in the waves, or ocassionally in their bed.

The last night of their vacation, Brando could see a tension in his wife. Not an eagerness to return, but desperation. Almost fear of tarrying any longer.

Rather than one bottle of marapu, they had two. Then a third.

Tenshi kept downing gourd after gourd of palm wine. When it came time for the restaurant to close, she could hardly stand.

"Sorry," she rasped, eyes half-closed. "Nimuyo, newa. I'm drunk."

"It's okay, umpenzi," Brando said. "I'll carry you home."

He swept her up in his arms and began to head back. Even after four years on Jitsu, his high-gravity strength lingered just enough that he managed to cross the half kilometer of sand and reach their cabin without getting too tired.

Tenshi had fallen asleep along the way, so Brando laid her gently on their bed. As he pulled away, she woke up and grabbed his arm.

"Where you going?" she managed to say.

"Nowhere, baby. I'm right here with you. Why'd you drink so much?"

She gestured weakly at the darkness. "Don't wanna go back. Have to."

Brando cupped her cheek with his free hand. "You don't have to do anything you don't want, umpenzi. We can stay a few more days."

"No, not a good idea. So much work. So little time."

Her eyes were closed again. Brando shook his head. "Other people can do the work. There's no hurry."

"Yes," she breathed. "There is. Could end. Any moment."

Brando narrowed his eyes. "What do you mean?"

"Tenshi na tenshi. Newa na tenshi."

"What about your spark?" he asked.

"Told me." Her voice was almost inaudible. "Young. Me. Translated. But dead."

He leaned closer, trying to understand. "Your spark told you what?"

"I'll die young, Brando." Tears squeezed around her eyelids in the gloom. She whispered, her voice fading as she slipped into dreams, "Alone. You and Tana. Don't mourn. Not too much. Don't despair. Translated. I'll watch. From Beyond."

Brando let her sleep. But he couldn't. The idea of losing her had wormed its way into his mind, and it drove all joy away.

He lay by her side in the darkness, trying to unhear her words.

In the morning, he made her groundnut stew, his uncle's cure for hangovers. She was feeling much better by noon, so they took one last walk along the pink strand before getting in her transport and heading back to Kinguyama.

Brando never mentioned the secret she'd revealed.

He was determined to forget it.

AS THE NEW SEMESTER BEGAN, Brando sat down with two of the educators he most respected on Jitsu, Jina Chimari and Modupe Oduyoye. They sipped tea together in the small conference room beside his office.

"Thanks for coming. So, yes, Ra-Koreji has been much more successful than I could've imagined. In fact, our investors—many of them expansionist Consortium businessmen who're pushing for Jitsu to enter the CPCC—are offering additional funding to move the school into phase II earlier than planned."

Modupe patted Brando on the shoulder. "Congrats, mate! What's phase II?"

Before he could answer, Jina set her cup down and guessed. "Elementary schooling, am I right?"

"Exactly. And here's my dilemma. Instructors. With adults, I've had the help of University professors like this old gerrie," Brando jerked his head at Modupe with a smile, "who've signed up to teach part-time. But with little ones, I've got to think of what the Path requires as well."

"Do you mean their religious education?" Modupe asked. "Shouldn't that still be their parents' and the community's responsibility."

Jina tapped the table thoughtfully. "Not necessarily. Ra-Koreji is far enough from surrounding towns that parents who send their children will expect them to be there all day, which makes it hard to attend classes at the teyopan, too. Come to think of it, Brando-shi, there may be parents who want to have their children *board* at Ra-Koreji. Have you given that any thought?"

Brando's mouth went dry. He balked a little. "Oh. No, it hadn't ocurred to me. There's no reason we *couldn't* set up dormitories, I guess, but we'd need satorjin supervisors to live on campus, too. Wow, Jina. I was barely going to ask you for help bringing Pathwalker instructors on board that could teach humanities, sciences and maths as well as provide guidance for meditation and study of the scriptures. But I clearly haven't been thinking this through."

"That," she said, smiling, "is why you have friends and colleagues."

Modupe looked back and forth at the two of them. "Brando, why don't you just ask Arojin Chimari here to head the elementary education initiative? She's the best on the planet."

Searching Jina's eyes for clues to her feelings, Brando asked, "Would you be willing?"

She sipped at her tea, thinking. "Maybe. Give me some time to mull it over, Brando-shi. Invite Meji and me over for dinner in a week or so. I'll have an answer for you by then."

Ten days later, the two couples were sipping palm wine on the veranda after a hearty dinner. Jina let Brando know her decision as she looked out over the desert.

"Okay, Brando-shi. I'm in. But tit for tat. Meji has something they want to propose. To Tenshi, specifically, but it'll impact you."

Tenshi sat up a little straighter. "What is it, Prefect?"

Meji put their hand lightly on hers. "The special election. For the new position as mayor of Kinguyama. I'd like you to stand for it."

Brando looked at his wife. He knew her distaste of politics. She'd repeatedly talked about how much more effective she was as a free agent.

But Brando also knew how much she loved her people. How much their view of her as a leader filled her with joy.

"But," she countered, "there are already two solid candidates. Anshyano Nyota Irujunei served on the council for many years. Djoko Suharto was one of the first to move here from Station City. He's at the forefront of economic expansion. Either would be good."

"I agree," Meji said. "But we need better than good. We need the best. The whole planet, the whole of human space, is looking at our town, Tenshi-shi. At our district. And as the new prefect, I need you to take up this mantle. You're the face of Reporumatudan, like it or not."

IT TOOK A FEW MORE WEEKS, but Tenshi finally made up her mind to do as Meji asked. The other two candidates dropped out immediately. But even running unopposed, Tenshi received thousands of votes, nearly every eligible voter in Kinguyama lining up to show their support for their beloved architect arojin.

Not long after she was installed in her new office, Brando decided to drop by with some lunch.

"Thanks, umpenzi," she said as they sat at the conference table that dominated one end of the room. "I'm up to my eyeballs in data right now. Food is much appreciated."

Brando unpacked the food and served it. "Yeah, I'm running from data myself. I can't believe how this school is exploding, Tenshi. We're barely wrapping up the fourth quarter, but enrollment for next year stands at 700 adults and 321 children."

"Wow," Tenshi said, sipping on the soup he'd poured into her bowl.

"Yup. Studying the stats with Jina and Modupe, I can see those numbers doubling over the course of the next year."

His wife waved her hand at a datapad as she swallowed. "Maybe more. Despite everything we've done to prevent it, a huge wave of folks are migrating to Mashkanu from other, less tolerant prefectures."

Brando's stomach flopped. "Great. So we're concentrating reformers. Doesn't bode well for the general elections in two years. Shit. Ra-Koreji is compounding the problem, isn't it?"

"Since the attacks have slacked off some," Tenshi mused, "we *might* pull this one out. But concentrate more reformers here and in Arusha, and we'd better hope there's no more major tragedies. We'll be looking at a Dominian controlled legislature with Santo pulling the strings otherwise."

Brando picked at his rice and fermented vegetables. "I think I have a way to stave that possibility off. We create satellite campuses in three key prefectures: Shusaku, Kintana and Noparu."

Tenshi wiped at her mouth with a napkin. "The closest majority moderate districts?"

Brando gestured with his fork. "Yeah. They're the ones feeding us migrants. I can put Modupe in charge of the Shusaku campus. And I've got potential deans in mind for the other two. Can your firm build them within a year?"

"Oh, that's the easy part," she said. "But we need legislative approval. Meji can help us push a measure through the chamber. They'll get the prefects to back us so the deputies are more receptive to the idea."

Brando took her hand and kissed it. "Thanks, baby."

Tenshi rubbed her temples slowly. "What a time for this to come up, huh? We've doing so well. But it's a constant battle, no? The war is never won."

He smiled weakly and lifted his hand to gently caress her cheek. "No, not ever. But I'll be by your side throughout the fighting, and you by mine."

Tenshi closed her eyes and leaned her face into his palm with a deep sigh.

"Yes. Thank Sopiya for that."

CHAPTER 28

KONRAU LOOKED AT THE REPTILIAN NEO GNOSTIC'S FACE
AND SMILED diplomatically at the man's request for an update.

"Santo, with Nawabari Platform now under our control—we bought
most of the administration there—we have a better base to launch crews
from. We'll keep hitting the reformer townships, and we've got some new
contacts in Station City."

The arojin's doppelganger nodded at Konrau's news.

"Good. Just don't interfere directly with reformer political campaigns, okay?"

"Got it. That it?"

"Yes. You'll tunnel me if there is a problem, right?"

"Course. Out."

Konrau was pulled from the faux-conference. He blinked calmly at the
brightness of his cavernous office. Security shells stood in the distance along
the curve of the oval wall. The only sound was the slight hissing of the climate

control unit.

So good to be alone.

It seemed only yesterday that he was running with a *klika* on Tenochtitlan, the crowded corridors of the platform his playground and his initiation into the life. There'd always been too many people: his cousins at home, the workers in the eateries, other squinks at the game centers. Most of his childhood, he had hardly been able to breathe. But he'd never let it show. Few had ever learned of this weakness.

He'd told Jeini, though. She hadn't thought less of him for it. He shook his head, trying to rid himself of her visage in his mind. Months had gone by without an apparition. Thinking about her now could only serve to invoke her silent, accusing form again. When he was buried in his plans, making sure Felipe had a major role, all thought of her disappeared.

Konrau took this as a sign. Though he wasn't nearly as devout as Nestor, he imagined the Blessed Child was trying to show him that only through his plan and his devotion to his brother would he absolve himself of his guilt. Perhaps when the Brotherhood was synonymous with human government, Felipe ruling it beside him, Jeini would forgive Konrau, and he would be at peace.

Unbidden, the whole train of images and memories came tumbling out from behind a seal in his mind: his infiltration of the Anhele, meeting Jeini at a party, their many rendezvous. He'd slipped up, then, muddled by emotions he'd never felt before. They'd found him out, told Bruno Andrade.

His hand went to the ghost of a scar at his temple. The pain began to well. His breathing quickened, got shorter.

"Shite." He thumbed a connection to Nestor.

"Yeah, boss?"

"Shunt me the latest stuff Felipe sent on our moves against the Scarlet Chaos Triad on New Beijing. I want to take a look at it, see if we're missing any angles. Need to get those bastards off."

"Course. There it goes. Anything more, Konrau?"

"Nah, that's it."

Hands shaking, the kasike began to manipulate data in the projection field above his desk. Felipe had been quite brutal, but he was getting the job done. Helios was free of the stupid yaks, and soon Tau Ceti would too, despite the heavy AF presence there.

Konrau felt a surge of pride. He'd never had a family before. Not really. His mother didn't count. Jeini—he shuddered with pain. Jeini might have been family, but—no. Now here was Felipe, part of the world Konrau had dedicated his life to, part of the community of brothers that he wanted to see ascend with himself at the head. Konrau's clandestine plan no longer existed as simply a way for him to free himself from others: he had someone to share the power with. He had a greater purpose.

He had an heir for the empire he was going to build.

The pain subsided and his breathing returned to normal. Fidensio approved, it seemed. Konrau sighed, both relieved and agitated. Work had always been the answer. His plan stretched out before him in his mind's eye, beautiful and perfect. The whole Consortium seemed befuddled and afraid. All the moles in the Brotherhood who had been expecting him to "go legit" nice and slow had failed to prepare their true masters for the sudden move against the other syndicates.

First you rip out the competition, then we go legit, he had lied to Nestor.

Disinformation and inexplicable tactics. He had controlled klikas that way as a boy, and he knew he could manipulate governments now. Another two or three years of pushing the yaks farther and farther outward, into the AF's waiting arms, and the Flotilla would find itself at war with the demimundo. Then Konrau would make the Brotherhood go quiescent, focusing only on Jitsu while his enemies destroyed each other.

Then wait. Recuperate.

His strike would come long before anyone expected it. In other decade or so, he and the family heads would have amassed sufficient ships and weapons. And just when all the clever ones expected him to simply take Jitsu, he'd take it all.

The worlds around Nereus would fall quickly, and the battle would be joined. With his brother at his side, he would rumble as his predecessors had only dreamed of doing.

When he thought of this, his head not only quit hurting: it foamed with pleasure.

His com chimed. It was Nestor.

"Konrau, a message from your brother."

"Connect me."

The tattooed visage of Felipe Konrau regarded him with a puzzled look, an expression it seldom held.

"Konrau, you're not gonna believe this. Aztlan Angels just pulled out. Stopped fighting, said nothing, and left. Bunch of AF ships saw the caravan take off, started following it. I contacted some of the other sub-kasikes, and guess what? Scarlet Chaos is retreating, too. Both syndicates are just up and leaving."

Konrau shook his head, unable to believe what he was hearing. "Why the fuck would they do that?"

Felipe shrugged. "Only thing I can think of it is that they've started an alliance or something. Looks like we got a bigger problem than you thought, *ermano*."

As Konrau struggled to understand how this could have happened, the pain in his eye gradually returned, throbbing insanely, the hammer of memory slamming against his skull.

"Right," he gasped. "Okay, uh, tell you what. I'll get back to you."

Konrau slammed the connection shut as pain bored into his skull.

Immediately, the console beeped again.

"What?" he grunted.

"Weird message," Nestor announced. "No source address. Computer says it was generated from within our own system. It's for you; you want I should open it?"

"No, just shunt me the fucking thing."

Konrau's hands fumbled around for a vial of moku, knocking several items onto the floor. The screen darkened and flickered, then the message displayed itself.

> *You don't know nothing, Konrau. Not for reals, anyhow. But that's alright. I still love you, as fucked up as that sounds.*

> *—Jeini*

Clenching his hands against his skull, he strangled a scream and slipped from his seat onto the floor.

"No. I'll fucking kill you, whoever wrote this shit," he panted. "Better not be you, fucking Nestor."

The pain clamped his eyes shut, and, remembering, he heard her voice, sweet and raspy.

> *You don't know who I am.*

So? You're a hot bato, I'm a fem that wants some love. Fuck the rest.

You don't understand, Jeini.

Ah, shite. Nobody understands nothing, not for reals. You act like you understand shite that I don't know, but what do you know, eh? Nada.

Eso kres tu.

Only thing I think is that you need to come over here and do that to me again. Not that, the other thing… yes. Mother Mary, I think I could even love a bato like you.

You don't even know my real name, fem.

You don't know it neither. You don't know nothing.

I know I want you.

For reals?

His eyes unfocused through tears that he strained to repress, Konrau saw her lying again before him, her head a bloody ruin, her legs and arms twisted unnaturally.

"Go away, you fucking bitch," he moaned. "You're just gonna lay there, ain't it? Just gonna torture me with your corpse, you fucking demon whore daughter of a punking Angel."

But her limbs stirred, and horrifyingly she sat up, regarding him with eyes full of blood. Bits of her skull were stuck to her brown hair, dyed nearly black on one side by gore.

That's right. Blame me. Blame my pa. Blame everyone except your own self.

"It wasn't my fault, perra!"

Makes you feel a little better, ain't it. Calling me a bitch. Makes what did you did okay, huh.

"A question of honor. Of brotherhood. Of L'onda," Konrau countered in a babbling tone as he scuttled away from the image, which began creeping forward.

So those crusty old superstitious fucks is what you live for? You sad little piece of shite. You don't even get that all these pendehaaz that you're doing, trying to turn the Brotherhood into an empire, is just you trying to justify this.

Jeini's hand went to her head, pulled away a clump of hair and gray matter with a sickening sucking sound.

You loved me, and you threw that love away for a fucking useless organization that you could give a shite about, in reality. I know what you want for reals. You want to get enough power to erase me from your mind. But that shite ain't gonna work, love. I'm here to stay. No matter how much empty space you put between you and the rest of the people—

"I'm gonna be right here." Her voice rasped like death itself in the silence.

Jeini's specter reached out, and Konrau found he could retreat no farther. Her cold, pale fingers splayed as her hand neared his trembling jaw, and then the room went swirling, faded to black, and her cold touch sent him into oblivion.

KONRAU WOKE UP IN HIS BED. HE IMMEDIATELY CALLED FOR NESTOR. The aging counselor looked even older as he quickly crossed the gravity-tiled floor.

"What happened?" Konrau asked.

"You went through some sort of attack. Doctors don't know what it is. Been about twenty hours."

Konrau nodded, the fog lifting from his head. The vision of Jeini had faded to a dull afterimage, an annoying psychic ghost that he could, at present, ignore. "What's the deal with the syndicates?"

Nestor shrugged. "No one knows for sure, but Yen Bandera tells me that the Angels and Scarlet Chaos, they're in league with each other. Regrouping out in the Chara system. He hears they're gonna make a move against us, just doesn't know when."

"Fuck."

"Konrau, if they come at us together, the two of them, we're punked."

"I know, damnit. Alright. Fuck. We need to pull together. They can't come at us right away, so we've got time to prepare. Let's bring as many ships as we can back here to the nebula. And get Felipe to handle Jitsu for a while. I need you to help me plan a defense, or even better, a preempt."

As Nestor left to start making arrangements, Konrau leaned further back into the pillows. Something was wrong. He felt different. His plans were coming undone, but he felt no intense fear or despair. Just an odd grayness, as if nothing really mattered.

But if nothing matters, then I don't have to worry. I just have to make the old magic happen. I always come back. Hell, I came back from the dead once: this shite ain't nothing.

At the periphery of his vision, Jeini slowly shook her ruined head.

CHAPTER 29

ON HER FOURTH BIRTHDAY, TANA—WHO WAS NOW LEARNING LINGALA—ASKED for a visit with her "mama nkoko Makomo."

Brando was reluctant. He'd only spoken to his mother twice since coming to Jitsu, and he'd terminated both conferences abruptly once she'd started criticizing his choice of a wife and his new faith. Brando had no need to put up with that crap from her, he reflected. Ra-Koreji and Tenshi's mayorship gave him more than enough pressure, thank you very much.

"Brando," Tenshi said as Tana licked icing from her lips. "She's your mother. Tana's grandmother. You can't keep denying them a chance to meet."

"It's precisely because she's my mother that I keep saying no," Brando countered. "I mean, you're not encouraging Tana to hang out with your father, either. And everytime you read Tana the emails that Marie-Thérèse sends, my gut churns with worry. What if she says something cruel or inappropriate."

"I hear you," Tenshi said, hugging him. "But some problems have to be faced head-on. Set up a faux-conference. Supervise the visit yourself. If she gets out of hand, just cut it short, umpenzi."

"Okay, Tana-yi," he announced. "Let me message your mama nkoko, see if she's available."

Despite his secret prayers, his mother answered right away, sending a link to her personal keshiki.

The conference room was pale blue, with comfortable furniture, a plush throw rug, and a coffee table that conveniently separated Brando from his mother. Above her smiling, touched-up doppelganger hung the fertile cross, cruciform within a sphere, the symbol of Wiccan Catholicism.

Tana's doppel rushed over and hugged her grandmother, children being allowed to break faux protocol when under the age of twelve. The two of them chatted like old pals for about fifteen minutes: Tana described her friends at Ra-Koreji, her pet toto—a fuzzy koala-like creature she'd named Fata, short for La Fata Turchina, the Blue Fairy from *Pinocchio*—the books she'd read and so on.

Then Marie-Thérèse sweetly told her granddaughter, "You give me a couple of minutes with your papà? Time's almost up, and I need to tell him something. I'll write you soon, caro mio."

When Tana had disconnected, Marie-Thérèse nodded slightly at Brando. "She has potential. Did her mother teach her that assertiveness?" Implying, of course, that Brando could not have.

"Suppose so."

She clapped her hands delightedly. "That was ironic in such a delicious way, Brandino. No confirmation studies though, right?"

"No. Her parents are Pathwalkers. Our faith works differently."

"I have to admit, this conversion of yours still befuddles me. How quickly you devoted yourself to that whorish clone of the Mother."

Brando tried to stay calm. His old anger was beginning to bubble up. "Marie-Thérèse, whatever your opinion, this religion lets me think for myself, to follow a Way that works best for me. You, on the other hand, always wanted to do my thinking for me."

His mother's smile deepened. "Dear, only because you find it so difficult to think on your own. Your mind was made for the vague profundities of theory. You have trouble with the real world. Look at this Tenshi person you married. Doesn she not control your life? Whose was the idea of starting the school? You? Come, now. You've got a doctor's degree in linguistics. I can't believe you did that just to run a school, Brando."

The worst thing about Marie-Thérèse and those of her ilk, Brando realized, was that they added just enough of the truth to their venom so that you sucked it down and let it poison your soul. *Let her rot in her own self-righteous putrescence.*

"Well, Reverend," he replied icily, "now that you got that off your chest, I've got to go. Nice talking to you."

He stepped out of the transmission beam, and thumbed the pink light off.

A minor municipal emergency required Tenshi's attention, so Brando took Tana to Station City to visit her 'uncle' Modupe, to see a show and have some ice cream. They mounted a slidewalk afterwards, cruising through the shopping district, Tana wondering at the towering spires and asking questions about Earth.

The four-year-old got tired of standing, and Brando carried her in the crook of his arms, the soft soapy smell of her hair bringing tears to his eyes as he held her tightly. They got off at Anakwa Park and sat at a bench near the lake. Ducks, real ones imported from Earth, splashed around inside the faintly glowing force wall that surround the fountain.

"Apa," Tana asked in Baryogo, "Where's my bibinim?"

"Monchu? Inyoni? Baby, you know they're living in Takuba prefecture now. We just visited them like a …"

"No, no." She switched to Standard. "My other grampa. Your papà."

Brando felt a tug at his heart that he hadn't experienced in ages. His life was so full that his past sorrows had faded into the background, the faintest wisp of noxious gas in an otherwise clear blue sky. He slumped slightly and looked at Tana searchingly. Her eyes were wide open in expectation, and her black curls framed her oval face and gray-blue eyes like depths of space cradling a burgeoning world.

"Well, Giacobbe, that's his name, he, uh, he left."

She frowned. "You mean, he died or something?"

Brando decided to simply tell her the truth. He couldn't stomach more lies, and she deserved to understand how people could be. "No, baby. You see, when I was fifteen, my papà left us. He went to another planet, started another family."

Horror filled her eyes. "You mean he left you alone?"

"I had my mamma, and my brother Edoardo."

"But why? Why he left yall?"

Brando put his arm around her. She was genuinely disturbed by what he'd told her.

"I don't know, sweetie. He and Marie-Thérèse didn't get along that well. He was a musician when she wanted him to work in the church. After a while, they just couldn't be around each other. So he left."

Tears brimming in her eyes, she reached out and touched his cheek. "How you felt after, papà? Sad?"

He had to bite his lip not to start sobbing.

"Yeah, Tana-yi. Real sad. But I looked at the sky, you know, all big and blue, and I figured out that my problems were kind of small."

They sat there for a while, staring at the sky themselves, till Tana turned to him again.

"Papà?"

"Yes, Tana?"

"The sky is just a bunch of gas."

"Yeah, I know."

"Promise me, papà." She stood up on the bench and held his face in both her little hands. "Promise you're never gonna do that to us."

This time Brando couldn't keep from crying. All the ominous undercurrents of the last five years threatened to shatter him righ then and there. But he tensed his hands into fists and pressed them against the stone of the bench, letting the pain serve as a tenuous dyke. With every ounce of strength he could muster, he twisted his face into a smile for his daughter.

"No, sweetie. I would never do that to yall. My world would end if yall weren't here with me."

He hugged her tight. She was correct. The sky was just gas. His real shield against the darkness was the love they three shared. He wouldn't ever let anything tear them apart. Anything.

THAT NIGHT, TANA ASKED FOR A BEDTIME STORY, HER FAVORITE: THE marionette Pinocchio. Brando usually avoided the part about the beautiful girl's death, as it had disturbed Tana the first time he'd told her. She hadn't been able to understand why the girl had to die, but Pinocchio got to be converted into a boy. Brando had tried to explain that it wasn't exactly death, only a trial for Pinocchio, a way for him to prove his humanity, but Tana still had insisted he skip the entire scene the next time he told the story.

Tonight, however, she wanted to hear it all. She didn't cry at all, and at the end she muttered 'bella Fatina' and closed her eyes.

After Tana had fallen into the deep sleep that only little children can enter between her parents on their enormous family bed, Tenshi and Brando slipped down the hall to the guest bedroom, as was their custom in recent years, and made love.

Their passion quenched, the couple cleaned up and returned to the family bed. Together they snuggled up against Tana's restful form. The tension Brando had been feeling since Tenshi's drunken revelation dissipated bit by bit as the warmth of his family spread into his heart.

The three of us, together, always.

The darkness was held at bay.

For a time.

THE FOLLOWING WEEK, BRANDO RETURNED FROM WORK TO FIND TANA in tears. It seemed her toto had gotten out of the house and had been mauled by a wild dog at the desert's edge. Tenshi had discovered Fata while out walking, and the two of them had held the dying animal until it finally closed its eyes forever. Then they'd buried it solemnly, Tana holding her tears till after, as she'd been taught to do.

As Tenshi finished explaining this to him, Tana rushed over and clung to his leg. He bent to pick her up and carried her into the garden out back, where the surrounding desert disappeared and it seemed as if the world was young and healthy.

"I want Fata back, papà. I miss her already."

"I know you do, Tana-yi. Maybe you can write a poem for her, draw a picture, make a little shrine."

"But I want *her*!"

Brando ran a finger down the bridge of her nose, wiping away the tears. "She's gone, kiddo. She can't come back anymore."

"Why do things die, Papà? Why? It's not fair!"

"Caro mio, it's part of life. Things are born, they live and then they have to die, to make room for the new things."

"And what happens after?"

Brando rubbed her hair. "If we work really hard and create a soul around our spark, then we get translated. We go to ra-Yindawo and become part of the Ogdoad."

Tana bit her lip, thinking. "What if we don't? What happens to people that don't have enough time to make a soul?"

Brando took a deep breath. *This is going to be hard. But I can't lie to her.*

"Their sparks live on."

Tana balled her little hands in frustation. "But the spark isn't *you*, the teachers say. What happens to, uh, your *self*? Huh? If you die with no soul?"

"Um, first of all, if you aligned it to your spark, the spark gets brighter. Easier for it to help another person make a soul." Seeing her frown deepen, Brando closed his eyes and added. "But the self fades, sweetie. It disappears."

He felt her clutch at his arm. He opened his eyes. She didn't understand, it was clear.

"Why?"

"Tana-yi, people are like Pinnochio." His daughter sat up at the mention of her favorite fairy tale. "We seem real, but we're not. Still, some of us find the Path. We see our spark, which is like the Blue Fairy. She helps us do the hard work of becoming real."

Tears stood out in Tana's eyes as she whispered, "But most people stay wooden, right?"

Brando reached out and hugged her. "Yes, baby. Most do."

"I'm scared," she whispered into his chest. "What if I die before I become real?"

For the first time in several years, Brando's faith wavered.

What am I doing? Is this how my parents felt when they poured dogma into my head?

"Tana, you won't. People live a long time now. Up to 150 years, maybe more. Your umma has enough credits. You don't have to worry"

"But I'll get old, right?" she asked, pulling away from him a little.

"Yes, but they clone your organs, you know, your heart and lungs and stuff."

Tana's brow wrinkled. "What's *clone*?"

"Make a younger copy."

Her face lit up. "They could clone a whole body?"

"Well, yes, but it's illegal. Not allowed, you see."

"And why not?"

"Most folks don't like clones. They don't think that they're real people. They weren't born, but made."

"Papà, you said all people are like Pinocchio."

"But not everyone agrees with me. Not all folks walk the Path."

Tana frowned. "Whatever. I want to clone myself when I get old."

"Baby, it wouldn't have your self inside it. Your self is in here." He tapped her forehead lightly. "The clone would look like you when you were a little kid, but it wouldn't be you, because it wouldn't grow up in the same place, or do the same things, or share the same friends. It would be like if you had a twin, but real young, you see."

"And if I maded a clone and put my brain it in?"

Brando almost laughed. "The brain would get too old. I would get all hard and stop working, and you'd die all the same."

"I'm *not* gonna die! Never!"

Tears running down her face again, Tana slid from his lap and hurried inside, calling for her mother.

Brando stood in the garden alone, watching Higante slip from the sky while Kobito winked cruelly, the red eye of some ancient stellar demon suspended above the desert.

CHAPTER 30

THE DAY BRANDO D'ANGELO SHATTERED AGAIN was also the 501st of Tenshi's mayorship. It was a Saturday; Brando was at a conference in Station City, and Tenshi and Tana were tending the garden when a message came across the outdoor terminal.

"Finish digging up the roots," she told Tana. "Umma's got to check her mail."

At the terminal, she almost shouted an expletive.

It was a faux recording from Isabella Spinelli.

Isabella Spinelli *D'Angelo.*

"Can yall step away?" she told her bodyguards. "It's a private matter."

The men nodded and complied. Looking over her shoulder to make sure Tana wasn't within listening distance, Tenshi played the recording as holographic video.

Isabella was as beautiful as ever, though a little heavier. The additional weight looked good on her, Tenshi noted.

"Tenshi. I've been thinking about contacting you for a while now, but just couldn't find the right moment. And frankly, the way our lives have continued to intertwine has me a little freaked out. But I just read that you've become the mayor of Kinguyama, and I decided to do this today, before any more time goes by."

Isabella took a deep breath. Her breasts rose and fell in a way that made Tenshi ache. There was no shame in the lingering feelings. They simply existed.

"You will have noticed my double last name. It's not happenstance, Ten. Four years after we broke up and I came to Oceania, I married the older man I had been dating. Giacobbe D'Angelo. Yes. Your husband's father. I wonder what would've happened if I had let you know? When Brando arrived there three years later, would you have gotten involved with him, knowing that your former girlfriend—" her voice hitched, "that I was the mother of his half-brother?"

Tenshi leaned toward the terminal. "You've got to be fucking kidding me."

"I can almost imagine your reaction," Isabella said. "But let's choose to think of it like this, Ten: what we had, you and me, it doesn't happen very often. The universe finds ways to keep that connection alive. I have Giacobbe and my little Antonio. Not so little, I guess. He just turned nine. And you have Brando and your sweet little daughter. Saw a picture of her in the story about your swearing in. Adorable."

A tear slipped from Isabella's green eyes. "Anyway. I can never make up for the way I hurt you. And maybe none of this news will be welcome. But for me, at least, the fact that we're related by marriage makes me very happy. All my best, Ten. Keep fighting."

The image flickered and faded.

"Well, Brando, my love," Tenshi muttered quietly. "You have another brother. Wonder if that that'll cure the hate you feel for your apa. Or make it worse."

As she debated whether to tell Brando, trying to gauge what his reaction would likely be, the terminal beeped again. All thoughts of her husband's family were crowded out of her mind as her advisers urgently relayed the news in frightened tones.

"Mayor! Kinguyama's under attack! Looks to be regiments of syndicate soldiers."

"Shit! After nearly a year of nothing. Tana!" she shouted, waving the bodyguards over. The men ushered Tana and Tenshi inside the house, where she connected immediately with Dap Chakrapong, chief of the security detail employed by the township.

"What've we got?" she asked. Adrenaline made her mind sharp and focused, her body tensed and ready.

"About five or six crews, Mayor, more than ever before, and they've got a bunch of shells, you know, them semi-sentient robot thingies..."

"Yes, I know, illegal AI. Tell me, is it too much for yall to handle?"

"Yes, ma'am, I'm afraid so. We've got them stopped in the west and north, but we need help with the south."

Tenshi swallowed dryly. Their house was at the southernmost edge of Kinguyama.

Commander Chakrapong continued. "I've called up the squads. Alpha and Beta are being dispatched to the south and east. I also sent over a couple of my men to back your bodyguards up."

"Shouldn't we go into the city?"

"No, ma'am. Yall are safer where yall're at. The defense missiles will shoot at anything that enters the municipal perimeter, so everything should be okay here. I've signaled the squad that's setting up to the south; they'll be watching you close. Travel right now is a bad idea: there's more fighting over the city itself than there will be here, and no need for yall to expose yourselves to it."

Tenshi nodded. "Keep me informed."

As she began connecting a conference session with the council members, Tana pressed close to her.

"Are we going to be alright, Umma?" she asked, trembling slightly.

"Of course, sweet. We're going to be just fine."

"I wish apa was here."

"Me too," Tenshi assured her.

THE SECOND INCARNATION OF ALPHA SQUAD WAS MUCH
BETTER prepared that the first, reflected Ben Wu as the three troop transports
neared the southern limits of Kinguyama. Along with more veteran squadmen
transferred from other units, Wu had gotten more capable recruits, some
mercenaries and ex-cops trying to catch a little action and perhaps escape
their pasts. He'd trained them extensively: as a squad, in smaller groups and in
pairs. Four years after the disaster his first unit had experienced, Ben felt certain
that Alpha Squad was the best Jitsu had to offer.

He'd gotten over his shock at the lack of consequences for the decimation
of his men. Minister Koroma had chalked the mess up to poor preparation and
Frik's insubordination. Wu'd gotten off with a simple reprimand. But the real
punishment was the memory of charred bodies smoking in the rain, a swirl of
howling black that mocked his skills as a leader.

In his obsession with readying his men in order to exact revenge on the
Brotherhood, everything else had faded, including his responsibilities to his
daughter Ya-Ting, whom he'd not heard from in three years. His in-laws had
tunneled him recently to inform him that the teen was no longer living with
them, but Ben had put off looking her up. He had a score to settle, and all other
considerations were secondary.

Soaring high above the demimundo base camp, where AI shells and
soldiers were being unloaded from several sleek transports, Alpha Squad kept
out of missile range and set down at the edge of the city's defense grid, a couple

of klicks north of the enemy position. Wu was counting on the grid to guard his back, leaving only the south, west and east open to attack. The area was still desert, though, and there were dunes aplenty to deploy behind. He sent a scouting detail (each broadcasting a clearance code to the grid) over the ridge that separated the desert from the town to evacuate any civilians living in the area and to report back on conditions. Wu wanted to have a clear route for falling back, should the need arise.

Gamma Squad, as he understood it, was being recalled from the stations and prepped to back Alpha and Beta in this the largest single assault by syndicate forces in the history of the planet. Nonetheless, he had to plan for the possibility that there would be no support. He didn't want to be caught with his pants down.

His second, Schlomo Frasser, was overseeing the set-up of heavy artillery as Ben approached him.

"They got shells, you saw?"

"Yeah, Schlo," Ben nodded. Once only in his military career had he gone up against the artificially intelligent drones, highly illegal throughout the Consortium. AI was a deceptive name for them, as it implied human intelligence, though they only possessed that of mammals like apes or dolphins, capable only of rudimentary proto-language. Without programming, the shells, as they were commonly called, reverted to a primary goal of preserving homeostasis and were harmless unless attacked. Their programmed secondary goal could be altered or erased with sophisticated equipment that Jitsu predictably lacked. Alpha Squad would have to do this the old-fashioned way.

"How could we counter them, do you think?"

"Bandit's down there with a couple of other guys, burying mines." He gestured at the expanse of sand that stretched before the chain of four dunes that provided them cover. "We got these mortars here, nades, plasma throwers... hell, we could use the transports on remote, too, use their missiles against those fucking robots."

"No." Ben winced. "No. We can't use the transports. I think their codes may be compromised. In fact, we'll need to completely shut them down."

Frasser frowned. "But that means we cut off any air retreat."

"Too bad. That's how they did me in last time. No repeats of that shite."

The squad split into platoons of five pair each, and set up behind the dunes. They'd turned the flat expanse to the south into a booby-trapped minefield. Each dune had a trench dug in front of it and a mortar atop it. Mortar duty would be rotated every fifteen minutes and would be covered by rifle fire from the other squadmen on the dunes.

A crackle in the cascom made Ben turn north. The scouts were back.

"Clear the area?" he asked as they approached.

"Only house belongs to the mayor. She won't budge; says it's safer for her there. Has a couple bodyguards on duty."

Ben nodded. "Let's just keep these bastards far enough away that she doesn't find out how shitty her guards are."

"Cap, shells coming up out of the south."

Ben returned to the dune where he'd left Frasser. In the distance, a dozen metallic figures glided noiseless and quick.

"They'll be here in a couple minutes, mates," Ben announced to his squad. "So fill your dukes, and barrack your brothers. Remember we're a family, here, not just a team. Your brother dies, a piece of you dies with him."

Rifles slapped against gloved palms. Alpha Squad steeled itself for the first exchange.

BRANDO WAS CONFERENCING WITH SCIENCE INSTRUCTORS WHEN his contacts displayed an emergency message in the air before him: *Kinguyama under attack.*

Excusing himself, he hurried to the tarmac. Along the way, his percom filled him in on the situation: battles raging to the west and north seemed contained, but in the south, just a couple of kilometers from his house, the yakuza were using robot sentinels in an attempt to beat a path through Alpha Squad and into the city.

Brando made Tenshi's transport scream as he raced home. Even at top speed, it would take him thirty minutes to travel the distance between Ra-Koreji and Kinguyama. He bit his left hand fiercely, pounding his right against the armrest to distract him from the horrible thoughts that kept leaping into his mind.

Finally, he managed to get through to Tenshi, despite the com drain due to the attacks. Her face seemed pale, but expressionless.

She's stressed.

"Yall're okay?" he asked expectantly.

"Yeah. Couple soldiers came by about twenty minutes or so ago. They said they should be able to keep the yaks away. I've also got my bodyguards and a security detail the city sent me, so we'll be fine."

"Well, I'm on my way right now. Be there in about twenty-five."

"I wish you wouldn't. There might be yak transports nearby that could shoot at you."

He shook his head roughly. "No, no way. I'll be there soon. Not staying away, Tenshi. Don't ask me to."

"Hey, wait. Tana wants to say hi."

His daughter's smiling cherubic face morphed Tenshi's off of the comtable. "Jambo, apa. You coming home?"

"Yeah, I'm gonna be there in a couple of minutes, Tana-yi. You stick close to umma, okay?"

"Course. You bring me something?"

Brando felt his shirt pocket. "Yup. Your favorite candy. I'll give it to you as soon as I get home, okay?"

"Okay, papà. I love you."

"I love you too, baby."

Brando clicked the connection closed and cried silent tears of tension.

NICKER PLATOON WAS BEING DECIMATED. BEN WU ORDERED HALF OF Carpet platoon, on whose dune he'd established himself, to schuss down to the trench and come up behind the shells, which had skimmed over their mine field minutes before, shrugging off plasma blasts like mosquito bites. They seemed bent on bursting through the line, as they'd all headed directly toward a single dune and had begun trying to blast their way over its top. Eight of his men were down, three from Nicker and the five from Bottle he'd commanded to back the embattled platoon up.

"Come on, boys, move your khybers!" he shouted into his cascom. As his men rushed up behind the hulking machines, several explosions came from the minefield. Ben was horrified to see members of Kinguyama's security detail retreating from the south west directly into the booby-trapped plain.

"Goddamn it, who's on sensors? Why didn't you tell me these men were approaching?"

"It was Mphahlele... shells got him and buggered up the punking equipment!"

"Someone get the fucking back-up running then! Rouf platoon, get on it!"

As his men began clambering up Nicker's dune, the shells turned to attack. The men atop the dune popped out from behind the ablative shield they'd set up and pounded the machines with mortar fire.

"Ben, oh, shite…" It was Nehru, the second of Rouf platoon.

"What, damnit? Save the fucking exclamations and bring me up to speed!" He was watching as the security detail tried to organize itself at the edge of the minefield.

"There's a group of twenty-some yaks coming from the west, and our buddies to the south are heading this way too. That's sixty-some-odd bastards and these shells."

"Any word from Gamma?"

"Nah. I keep trying to raise 'em."

Ben switched to the security detail's com frequency.

"Oy, mates. This is Captain Ben Wu of Alpha Squad. What's the sitrep?"

Ben could make out one of the men turning about to face the dunes. "They got air support, sir. Pops in and out like a freaking ghost, strafing us with projectiles and such."

"But they can't go near to the town with that, right? Anti-air missiles would knock them down."

"Sir. But they can pick us off till there's a nice path straight into Kinguyama."

Ben sighed. "Why don't you bring your men down into the trench and up into the dunes with us, so we can combine to keep 'em out? "

He ordered a couple of men down to guide them. The shells were now being pounded by the remaining men of Bottle from the top of their dune, from Nicker, and from the five he'd sent from Carpet. A continuous blaze of weapons fire had superheated the sand and the shells were mired in silicon sludge. Ben smiled.

Then the assault really began. Over the horizon west and south yaks came speeding on sand sleds. The soldiers of Rouf began to sling mortar pulses at them, but their velocity and zigzagging made them difficult targets. As they sclaffed over the mine field, several triggered explosions that sent dead yaks flying, but the sleds kept coming.

"Nehru, tell me Gamma's on its way, mate."

"Aye. ETA fifteen minutes."

Ben shuddered at the odds. He suddenly despaired at his lack of ground experience. He'd been a major in the Consortium Army, but his battalion had been responsible for fighting ship-to-ship battles and occasional platform occupations. No huge open spaces on platforms. Narrow corridors were more his style. He thought of the gorge behind them.

The sleds slammed to a stop at the southern bases of the dunes one by one, yaks spilling from them in a rush to gain the tops. If he had his men stand and fire, they'd be presenting too easy a target, he realized.

"Let 'em come, mates. We got a better chance hand to hand." He noticed his men still blasting away at the now fully mired shells.

"Leave the fucking shells alone, boyos! Yall got yaks sprackling up yall's arses!"

The four surviving soldiers that'd been sent from Carpet turned to confront the terrorists ascending the southern face. Three of them went prone, but Ken Muriyo, a young, cocky AF deserter, began to fire from an erect position. The yaks soon ripped him in half with konk blasts.

Ben didn't see what else befell his soldiers on the farthermost dune, because yegsters began swarming up his own. The first one or two over the top were easiest to dispatch, but soon about a dozen crested at the same time, and before Ben knew it, he was in the midst of a close-up brawl. He variously shot at, elbowed and viciously kicked the Brotherhood sikaritos who neared him. His men whirled about, smashing their armored limbs into the armored bodies of the yaks with varying results.

From above, small missiles began to pound the squadmen, avoiding the enemy as if programmed to lock in on Alpha Squad's com frequency or EM signature or some such detail that should have been absolutely unknown to the Brotherhood. Ben glanced skyward and saw a transport hovering some five meters above him. A door in its belly opened, and more yaks began to leap down onto the dune. It was time to beat a retreat.

"Okay, everybody disengage: fall back to the ridge! Point men watch our sixes!"

In moments, Alpha Squad and their security allies were ensconced on the north side of the troop transport. The approach to the ridge was a narrow defile, and Ben hoped that this would improve their chances of dealing with the large number of yaks. The shattered dunes sloped to a series of low rocky hills on other side. The only way up the escarpment was behind them and slightly to the west where the land sloped upward steeply, but not so much as to impede a climb. Ben had fortunately set the transport down in front of a thick overhanging lip of rock so as to block attacks from above, in the unlikely event that the municipal defense grid went down. It would take many missile attacks to blast through the ten meters of solid rock, he hoped

As they exchanged fire with the yaks who began to pour into the gorge, Ben heard the hum of a transport above them, then the soft hiss of a missile being fired.

So much for the grid. Bloody yaks must be inside the city and shut it down already.

He held his breath: would the over-cropping hold? An explosion rocked the ridge, and stones rained down on his men. It didn't look as if his back-up plan would work: the ridge wasn't as sturdy as he'd imagined. Again he cursed his inexperience with natural landscapes.

"Damn, Ben!" Schlomo muttered. "Couple more of those and that jutting rock's gonna fall and crush us.

Ben regarded the transport. He weighed his fear of the access code's having been compromised with the probability of his men's being ground to nothing beneath tons of rubble. He also considered a retreat up the ridge, but realized how vulnerable that would leave his men to the yak transport.

"Okay. Everyone in the transport, now! Schlomo, bring weapons on line and drive a couple of missiles down their gullet!"

While the men boarded the bulky black vehicle, Ben held back and helped the stragglers with their equipment. As a wounded security was leaning on his shoulder and limping toward the hatch, another explosion came from above and a hail of boulders crashed into them both. Ben was thrown to the ground and held on to bleary consciousness for a few seconds as the yaks converged on his transport and the outcropping of rock began to collapse. Darkness fell before he could see more.

TENSHI HEARD SOUNDS OF STRUGGLE IN THE GARDEN AND PEERED OUT just in time to see a pair of terrorists cut the security detail down, their blood spraying across a pair of rose bushes like exploding buds.

"Jun, Rani!" Her bodyguards came running in. "A couple broke through. They're in the garden. Stop them. I'll take Tana into the great room and call for some help."

The hulking twins nodded wordlessly and drew their sidearms. Tenshi rushed Tana in front of her down a twisting hallway to the eastern end of the house. Gunfire and screams echoed behind them, then an explosion rocked the house. Once in the great room, Tenshi tried to raise Chakrapong on the com, but it had apparently been disabled. The front door wouldn't cycle open, either.

"Umma, I'm scared," Tana whimpered.

Tenshi crouched next to her. "Tana-yi, I want you to hide in the space there behind the sofa, you know, where Fata always used to curl up?" Tana nodded, biting her lip. "Don't you come out for any reason, not till I tell you to. Got it? Okay, go."

As Tana slid into her hiding place, Tenshi slapped her palm against the wall near the door. A panel slid open, and she pulled out a chrome that she had hidden there years ago as a precautionary measure.

Spinning about just as the yaks came barreling into the room, Tenshi squeezed off several blasts that impacted ineffectively against their battle suits before she dove to the side. They pounded great dents into the wall with their konk rifles, but she'd built the house to withstand nearly all hand-held weapons fire, so it resisted.

Tenshi's momentum sent her sliding across the hardwood floor toward a large steel plant stand that occupied a corner of the room. She clambered up as the invaders turned their weapons in her direction. All she wanted was a good shot at a structural weak point in the ceiling, just enough to loosen one of the exposed roughhewn crossbeams and send it swinging toward them…

They blasted the steel structure from beneath her, and she went flying through the air toward them. Eyes fixed on the ceiling despite the nausea in her stomach and flames on her clothes, she extended her arm and fired. Milliseconds later, she crashed into the floor with a bone-crunching thud that sent hammers of pain through every inch of her body, wrenching a scream from some unplumbed depth of her being.

The yaks again turned toward her, oblivious of the falling piece of timber. The shorter of the two was bodily thrown forward as one end of the beam came swinging down. The other end hammered down in an arc and crushed his casque into a bloody mess.

His partner didn't hesitate a second. With five rapid strides he reached Tenshi's side, grabbed her by the throat, and hefted her into the air. The constriction of her throat in his grip was nothing beside the agony flowing from her many shattered bones.

"At least," she gasped, "let me see your face, coward."

With his free hand, the yak tapped his casque back into the collar of the suit. One side of his face was covered with a tattoo, a swirl of unidentifiable hieroglyphics. His hair was raven black, as were his eyes.

"Message from your uncle, bitch. Should've stayed on the southern continent."

There was a click as he unholstered his pistol. She brought up her good arm and tried to punch him, but he head-butted her, and the explosion of pain in her nose wiped all thought from her mind.

"Time to shed the flesh, Tenshi." He brought his gun up slowly.

"No! Not my umma! Don't hurt my umma no more, you ugly man!"

Tana ran out from behind the sofa. Tenshi opened her mouth to scream a warning. The yak whirled about, his gun arm extended.

Darkness was encroaching on the edges of her vision.

But in the swirling black, there was a flicker of blue.

Close your eyes for a moment. You can't stop him, Tenshi.

Her spark. Speaking to her.

There's not much time.

A gunshot. Another.

A dull ache in her gut.

The feel of the concrete as she was dropped.

Look at me, Tenshi.

Though she felt her self ebbing away, she focused on her *soul.*

It was still there, a bright web spinning around her spark.

The spark had her face. Sad. Tears on its cheeks.

It lifted a ball of blue fire.

"Umma," Tana whispered somewhere, gurgling. "Kunabuji. Zio. Uncle."

The blue fire enveloped Tenshi's soul.

Come. I can only save you. Translate you.

"No."

Yes.

"How—"

The ring, Tenshi. Your ring.

BRANDO DIDN'T EVEN BOTHER LANDING ON THE TARMAC WHEN HE SAW the smoke curling from the garden. He just set the transport down in the middle of it all. Two dead security guards were the first things he noticed as he got out, that and a huge hole where the back entrance to his house had been.

Inside, Tenshi's twin bodyguards lay sprawled on the kitchen floor, burned and maimed and dead. A horrible silence filled his ears then, a dark certainty on the periphery of awareness that he tried to ignore. He sprinted down the hall, only partly noting the reddish-brown streaks along its length. A beam partly blocked his way at the end. He clambered over it.

At first, all Brando could distinguish was the blood. Everywhere. Smeared on the walls. In long trails across the floortiles.

Then he saw them. Near the door.

An animal howl bubbled up from inside him as he began to run. He slipped in the blood and slid toward them, then crawled and scrabbled on all fours the rest of the way, sobs wracking his body, the primal scream building. As he slammed into the door and reached for them, he opened his mouth and let out a horrible sound, a flood of bereavement and grief that pierced the failing evening light like a beacon from hell.

Tenshi's lifeless eyes stared at him sadly as he crushed her to him, gibbering incoherently. He pulled her with him as he scooted like a wounded beast toward his daughter's broken form.

Tana's outflung hand rested in a pool of blood in which her little fingers had scribbled what seemed to be the number 7 and the letter U. Groping at her shredded blouse, he pulled her toward him and gave her forehead a trembling kiss.

With both their heads resting against his chest, he began to wail a bereaved, timeless, placeless neume ripped from the innermost depths of his soul. The darkness descended then, thick like prehistoric sludge, filling his nose and mouth and ears and mind, pouring into every crack in his being, drowning him in utter, complete and irrevocable despair.

INTERCHAPTER F

Excerpt from the last will and testament of Tenshi Koroma D'Angelo:

In the event that I die young, as the vision of my spark foretold, these are my wishes.

To my wonderful and loving husband, Brando, I leave our house. Take care of it, because it's the work of our hands and there are few things more precious. Into it I poured my soul, and I want the flesh of my flesh to live there, too. When Tana is old enough, turn the house over to her and teach her this truth: the things we build are holy in a way that few people understand, holier than grass and stone and river, and we must treat them with reverence. Never let the house fall into ruin.

To Tana I leave my shares in Izakiwo, Inc. Brando is to keep track of how my broker handles them and then transfer them to our daughter when she reaches the age of twenty-one. He can instruct the broker to transfer the shares to some other company if Izakiwo were to go under.

I also leave my diary to my daughter, and I am locking it with a time-key that will open on Tana's fifteenth birthday. I stopped writing in it the day I married Brando, because he became my confidant at that moment. But before, starting when I was sent to the clean-up crews, I dictated my thoughts and dreams and troubles into it so that I would never forget what it took me to become the woman I am. These are the experiences and knowledge I hope to share with my daughter while she grows up, but if I die young, my diary must serve as a roadmap to real womanhood. This is not arrogance: it is truth.

To Brando I say this: though I am not leaving you many things in this will, you are receiving the most precious items of all. First off, I leave you my friendship, you who you never left my side, who you gave me the warmth and understanding I had been hungering for all my life. I leave you my love, love that began small and then grew into something so beautiful and immense that if the world could behold it in all its extension and glory, they'd fall to their knees in tears at its majesty.

And I leave you my self, which will always be part of you, always whispered in your dreams, your conscience, your private musings. I am in you, Brando D'Angelo. I am yours, even beyond death, and you are mine. I know that we will be reunited in ra-Yindawo one day. Part of a new whole. Together forever. Inseparable.

Excerpt: XID Interrogation File 89-345A-26//0B9UI2

(The following was elicited after an hour and thirteen minutes of negative neural stimulus in an interrogation session conducted via kewbox by Agent Askar Akayev. SUBJECT is Nicho Arevalo, captain in Jimi Andrade's Meros Matones personal guard.)

SUBJECT: Alright, I'll tell you, just fucking shut that off, you mother-punking puto!

AGENT: There. Now, Nicho, I want you to talk to me about these meetings Jimi keeps having. We already know that Ned Han goes, but who's the other guy?

SUBJECT: Bloke name of Yen Bandera.

AGENT: Yen Bandera? The free agent spy?

SUBJECT: Yeah. That's the fucker. Tall, scars on his cheeks, hair thinning on top, ponytail. Old as shite.

AGENT: And what did they talk about, Nicho?

SUBJECT: The fuck should I know? I ain't in on the meetings, pendeho.

(Seven minutes elapse as more negative neural stimulus is applied.)

AGENT: What? You ready to talk? Come on, Nicho. Course you aren't in the meetings, but rumors fly among yall Meros *Marikões*. What do they discuss in these meetings, far's you know?

SUBJECT: (incomprehensible)

AGENT: Say again?

SUBJECT: How they're gonna gut the Brotherhood. Something about a new drug on some planet yall cunt-sortium putos don't know about yet. Better than moku.

AGENT: What's the planet's name?

SUBJECT: I don't know. It's outside the CPCC, that's all. Some small colony on it, I think.

AGENT: What else, Nicho? I'm gonna pull it from you one way or another, little brother.

SUBJECT: Well, you fucking poet, there's talk of invading Sigma Draconis, too.

AGENT: And whose bright idea is all this crazy-arse shite?

SUBJECT: Bandera, man. Bandera came to Jimi first, couple years back. He's a wicked bad fucker, too. One his men said some smarmy shite to Jimi, Bandera fucking slit his throat, fast as fucking, right there in front of us.

AGENT: And Bandera's the one got them to pull off of CPCC worlds?

SUBJECT: You mean got Ned and Jimi to? Yeah. Took some convincing.

AGENT: So where are yall at now?

SUBJECT: Fuck you. No way. Shite I told you can't hurt them. But I ain't giving my compas up, silver suit. Fucking do what you want to me.

(*No further information could be obtained from subject, who became inaccessible to additional questioning an hour and forty-two minutes later.*)

INTERMEZZO

"There is only one rule: suffer the pain."—Rumi

Two New Worlds Discovered

Ben Traevis

Milan Gazette

5 February, 2690—Two more non-Consortium human colonies were discovered this week, bringing to six the number of independent worlds that we are aware of. Though details are sketchy, the *Gazette* confirmed that these worlds were not settled by sleeper ships like the other four, but by Consortium citizens illegally exiting the bounds of the CPCC, using unregistered fenestration drives. The first world, which Flotilla long-range reconnaissance stumbled across on 30 January, is in the Chara system. Sources in Milint tell the *Gazette* that its inhabitants, some 1,500 humans, are former Mediterranean Blockers, who emigrated from Earth twenty-four years ago, right after fenestration began to reshape human space.

The second world, orbiting Gamma Leporis, was, it seems, settled by various Asian ethnic groups from the Centauri system in 2661. Security is tight on this one, but rumors suggest that yakuza groups have made contact with the colony there.

Debate abounds over whether these worlds should be allowed to remain independent, or whether their colonists' nominal status as citizens of the Conortium impact the status of their new home. The state ministry only comments that they are "in negotiations" with the fledgling governments on both worlds.

Ethnographer Tohti Tunyaz, whose seminal *Amarta: Three Years in the Kingdom of Kunti* was very influential in the formation of the present Ministry of State, cautions against imperialism toward independent planets.

"Anything we that might hint at aggression could be read wrong. These are people who've gone out of their way to escape what they view as oppression by human governments, whether the old USR or the CPCC. We must understand this delicate situation as completely as possible, working to foster strong ties between our peoples."

Syndicate Attack on Sirius Galvanizes Voters

Delta Smith

La Caille Daily

5 April, 2692—After the inexplicable attack on 1 April, during which a dozen yakuza ships pounded the Ministry of Science's heavily guarded research complex on the Sirius end of the military's imrizabu, public opinion has swung decidedly toward the expansionist side. The Affiliation for Human Destiny (AHD) was energized by new poll numbers suggesting that they will hold the majority come elections, just three days away.

The yakuza attack, which ended in the destruction of all twelve syndicate ships and significant damage to the MOS station in Sirius, is still shaking the Consortium. Many people question what the present government might do differently. Prime Minister Jusuf Kumalic continues to be faulted for his weakness on the organized crime crisis. Expansionists clamor for strong military action at Oceania and Jitsu and elsewhere, but Kumalic opposed such moves in consistent vetoes.

If the AHD wins a majority of seats in the CPCC Diet, the next PM is almost guaranteed to be a hard-line pro-military expansionist. High on the list is Jetsun Muntso, the senator from Kush whose father's military prowess is legendary.

Suicide Squad Sends Shockwaves

Staff reporter, *Centauri Free Press Agency*

12 August, 2692—The Consortium was wounded to the quick today as a series of massive explosions ripped through the Flotilla Shipyards in orbit round Sani in the Rigil Kentaurus subsystem of Alpha Centauri 3. Initial reports of the incident detailed the extensive damage done: all seventy-five vessels being built or refitted at the shipyards were destroyed, as were the shipyards themselves, the seven Constabulary patrol ships nearby, and two adjacent platforms that housed over twenty thousand Consortium citizens.

AF special forces that rushed to the scene from Dhara determined within an hour that the explosions were the result of five ships defenestrating right into the heart of the shipyards, perhaps loaded with explosives, though the ships themselves would have been sufficient, opines astrophysicist Eva Kaplan.

"The simple act of exiting hyperspace at .6c in the middle of a more or less dense object would rip a ship to shreds, along with the object into which the ship was defenestrating." Dr. Kaplan went on to add that secondary explosions from the fusion power generators on the ships that were in the last stages of construction would, likely finish the job.

With so many of its vessels deployed elsewhere, like at the Tau Ceti-Sirius Imrizabu and around the various recent Consortium colonies, the Flotilla only has eleven armed ships round and within the Rigil Kentaurus subsystem. However, Flotilla Chief of Staff Admiral Ettore Savelli downplayed the impression that the AF just was not prepared.

"Impossible to protect against insanity, but we are taking every measure to protect key Consortium interests. The Navarch himself is overseeing the deployment of Flotilla forces in conjunction the Army."

Asked whether he considers the attacks a continuation of the underworld activity growing on Jitsu, New Beijing, Podgoritsa and other new worlds, the admiral declined to give a specific answer.

"Only two hours have passed since the attack," Savelli cautioned. "Too early to say."

Kuntian Forces Deep on Dhara

Staff reporter, *Centauri Free Press Agency*

19 August, 2692—La Caille, Dhara's principal city, continues to be assaulted by the forces that were dropped onto Rigil Kentaurus' most populous world just hours after a crippling suicide attack nearly a week ago. The invasion fleet itself, thirty vessels that we now know are from the Sigma Draconis system, is engaged in constant combat with Flotilla ships, more of which defenestrate and enter the system every day. The estimated 50,000 troops that the invaders installed on Dhara right after defenestrating in-system have taken several important cities, including Kadesh, Jericho and Troy. Attempts by the Consortium Army to land additional battalions to support the planetside force continue to be rebuffed by the smaller but more tenacious invading force.

Astrophysicists are still at a loss as to how, in the decade since the CPCC first approved the sale of fenestration drives to the Constitutional Monarchy of Kunti, as the inhabitants of Sigma Draconis style themselves, that independent system was able to master the technique of defenestrating so near to a massive body.

"Given the exit speed and proximity of the planet, the invasion was planned far in advance," suggests Dr. Eva Kaplan, the astrophysicist whose pronouncements are being carried on all the major infotainment sites. "And I would guess with constant, updated intel on astrophysical data from the area around the planet. Reported from someone on Dhara."

Kunti embassies on Earth, Dhara and Oceania are now closed; all Kunti officials and citizens within the Consortium are in 'protective custody,' according to a spokesperson for the Executive Intelligence Division. The XID's central headquarters on Sihtu in the Rigil Kentaurus subsystem remain unattacked, and the division is lending all personnel it can to handling the invasion.

"We should've caught this before it happened," said the spokesperson. "It's our job to make sure it's over quick."

On a difficult side note, Prime Minister Kumalic assured the press that the transition from his government to that of Jetsun Muntso, who was just selected by the now majority AHD Diet, would continue a smooth curve to the December swear-in. "These are times for coming together, not grandstanding," he assured reporters via faux-conferencing. "I intend to afford PM-elect Munsto every bit of help I can."

The Face of the Enemy

Daenyul Maet

Humanity Today

23 August, 2692—One of the most repeated questions in the mouths of Consortium citizens in recent days is predictable: "Who are the Kunti?" In the near four decades since AF scientist Jan Lieske and Travex specialists Wing Ho

and Chan Ling separately invented fenestration drives, space has been opened up for humanity. Beyond the new worlds that we found waiting for us to colonize, we discovered already existing colonies, much to our surprise, founded by humans decades or even centuries ago, people who left the solar system for a variety of reasons. Semanawak and Erin were discovered in 2681, Terego in '83. Gaia and Fusou just two years back. But before those five, Consortium vessels first stumbled across Sigma Draconis.

Sigma Draconis—or as it was renamed, Kunti—is a star system some nineteen light years from Earth. In 2528, during the years of chaos and martial law that followed the dissolution of the United Solar Republics, just twenty-three months before the establishment of the CPCC, an independent, rogue colony ship called the *Bharatayuda* left human space, exchanging one uncertain future for another. Made up of mostly ethnic Javanese and assorted other Hindu people of Indonesian extraction from Amalgamated Kuiper Mining Interests, the one thousand thirty passengers and crew spent seventy-one non-relativistic years traveling through space before arriving at Sigma Draconis. There they landed on the Earth-like planet that they named Bima, and within a century and a half their population exceeded six million souls spread across Bima and other worlds in the system.

When the first CPCCAF scout ship encountered them, the citizens of the Constitutional Monarchy of Kunti were being governed by an elected parliament and an aging king, the Maharaja Tri Leksono. After nearly a decade of talks, the maharaja agreed to a timetable for dismantling the monarchy and creating a Republic of Kunti that would then be inducted into the Consortium. In 2682, in light of the agreements and as a demonstration of good will, the CPCC sold fenestration technology to the Kunti government. Despite public outcry at this sharing of such a powerful technology, then Prime Minister Ginette Lubin continued working close with Leksono, establishing the ministry of state for the most part to smooth the partnership and open the door toward Kunti's eventual acceptance into the CPCC. A timetable had just been set up, the projected date sometime in 2697, when of a sudden the Kunti maharaja died an untimely death.

His son Uki was declared regent at a critical time. Underworld attacks were beginning to blossom all across the CPCC, and Uki secured Consortium permission to purchase heavy planet defense weaponry from a member nation.

In retrospect, it is clear former PM Lubin should have said no.

(The following is an excerpt from "Spinning the Dharma Wheel," an interview with Modupe Oduyoye, former professor of comparative theology and president of Jitsu's progressive Ra-Koreji, published in the *Station City Sentinel* on 24 August, 2692)

Q- So you think we should have known ahead of time?

A- Suspected at least. All the clues were there. The name of their ship, for example, the one they left the USR on…

Q- *The Bharatayuda?*

A- Yes. It's also the name of the third part of the massive epic that undergirds Hinduism: the *Mahabharata*. A great war between two groups of brothers. Each group is the cousin of the other. The *Pandavas*—the five nominally good guys—assume their rightful place as rulers of Kurukshetra, an ancient Indian kingdom. One of the Pandava is named Arjuna; he's also called *Kaunteya*, son of Kunti.

Q- Kaunteya? Isn't that the name Uki Leksono signed his ultimatum with?

A- Exactly. And this is important for the leaders of the CPCC to understand: if Regent Leksono believes his self to be Arjuna reincarnated, then he will not stop. His war effort can't be halted through diplomacy. See, in the midst of the *Bharatayuda*, Arjuna wavers. He doesn't relish the idea of killing his cousins, who he was raised with. But Krishna, the human incarnation of the god Vishnu, convinces him that fighting the war is part of living up to *dharma*.

Q- Dharma?

A- Yes. Cosmic responsibility conforming to one's position in society. It's related in many tight ways to *karma*, destiny-forging action. Uki, I would wager, believes it is his duty and destiny to fight the CPCC, which he undoubtedly sees as the usurpers of the rightful rulers of humanity.

Q- So the attacks won't cease? This won't be the only battle front?

A- I'm afraid not, lad.

Attacks Spread Throughout CPCC and Beyond

Staff reporter, Centauri Free Press Agency

30 August, 2692—As the situation on Dhara grows grimmer, with reports of internment camps and mass executions leaking, the past four days have seen a number of additional strikes, though none so massive and well planned as the first. All three of Achilles' inhabited moons are under siege, many of the bubble-towns being breached. Podgoritsa and New Mecca are also battling Kunti attack vessels (*see home page for further details on Consortium progress and specific death and damage tolls*).

In addition to these attacks, worlds outside of the CPCC are also feeling the bite of Kunti aggression. Flotilla patrols in the comet clouds near both Terego and Semanawak have engaged Kunti ships, and the dozens of almost abandoned platforms orbiting Jitsu, which were once employed to repair ships damaged by imrizabu travel centuries ago, are the target of smaller assault teams of Kunti soldiers.

This reporter was on Rasaro, the principal of these platforms, in recent days and was able to speak with Ben Wu, the former Consortium Army major that now heads up Jitsu's Alpha Squad, main contingent of the anti-terrorism unit.

"We been carrying out sweeps of the platforms," the squad captain, flanked by several of his men, informed. "Several encounters with the Kunti so far. We are hard at work protecting the people of Jitsu from not just the regular yakuza scum we've been engaging on the surface, but with any other hostiles that imagine they can step onto our turf."

When this reporter asked what did the squad members do with Kunti infiltrators, one of Captain Wu's men, a short, massive soldier code-named Kyosu, barked a succinct response:

"We kill the bastards."

Bravery at Lyonesse

Saymun Wigin

Centauri Free Press Agency

5 September, 2692—It is a story of tragedy and of bravery. Of heroes and victims. A story that reflects the character of the Consortium citizenry. For two weeks after the Kunti invasion, Lyonesse, a thriving city on Dhara, tried to handle the foreign forces with diplomacy. But the populace was gradually interred in camps, and the city's mayor, Leyla Soral, led the remains of municipal security in a hopeless but courageous assault against Commander Joko Susilo, the Kunti officer that rules that city with an alien, iron fist.

The inadequate band of CPCC heroes, a recent escapee informs, managed on 3 September to bust in to one of the three concentration camps. As they were freeing Lyonessans from cruel captivity, Susilo's bandits brought their greater might to bear and captured Mayor Soral and her loyal security team.

We can just hope and pray that these incredible women and men hold strong till the CPCCAF in the end forces the foreign vermin from Dhara's face. In any case, they are to be remembered as true citizens and soldiers.

Occupation: Can We Afford Not to?

Outward

Editorial Staff

A little more than a month after the vicious attacks on our Consortium began, we find ourselves on the edge of a dilemma: what do we do when the conflict ends? Our too liberal stance concerning non-Consortium worlds has proved deadly. It's time for a more serious, sovereignty- and unity-preserving position to be embraced. Humanity must be a single whole. Independent worlds should be brought into the fold.

As difficult as this idea may at first seem, there is a single overriding reason to agree: the dangerous nature of fanaticism, especially the religious type. Our present ecumenical enlightenment makes it hard for citizens of the Consortium to comprehend the totalizing nature of the radical religious mindset. The present struggle with a man claiming his gods' support is one example, but dangerous sequels wait in the wings if we do not act soon.

Just three years ago on Jitsu, that symbol of humanity's reach which we have endeavored for years to make join the CPCC, the fanatical Dominian sect almost wrested control of the planet from the more Consortium-friendly Reformer party. Terego, that verdant green sister to Mother Earth, is in the grip of a theocratic government. Will we wait till these worlds decide they too must fight us? We at *Outward* think not.

Our proposal? Occupy these worlds. Take our superior forces and set up provisionary governments to ensure democratic elections and induction into the bosom of humanity. We should not and must not risk further death at the hands of extremists. Once victory is gained against the Draconian Kunti, the next step is clear.

(The following are excerpts from Prime Minister Muntso's inaugural address, given on 1 December, 2692)

In times of crisis, humanity always rises to the challenge. Reflect on Earth's Second and Third World Wars, on the devastation caused by the resurgence of the ice age on that planet, on the Solar War, on the Time of Darkness that preceded the founding of the CPCC—we never give up, we humans. And we will not do so now, either. We will route the Dragon from out our midst and cleave both its whipping, blind tail and its fire-breathing head from its treacherous body. This I swear to each of yall: Sigma Draconis falls within the year.

[....]

Despite the challenges Kunti's irksome progeny present, we must not forget to keep a watchful eye on the underworld, the Demimundo that so many demons are born from. Distracted as we are, we need to be mindful of the opportunity that our crisis affords our other enemies, the enemies of justice and order. Beyond the daily ebb and flow of syndicate attacks, reports indicate, for example, that Gaia, the independent world we have been trying so hard to create ties with, is being infiltrated slowly by members of the Scarlet Chaos Triad, which is interested in the narcotic effects of a plant native to that world. The implications from this example and many similar ones is clear: the Demimundo is becoming more and more aggressive, and with the added temptation of worlds outside the CPCCAF's purview, syndicates are turning toward conquest as a means to expansion. Once Sigma Draconis is dealt with, I plan on exorcising the yaks the same way.

Spinelli Expels Kunti Forces

Scot Jeunz

Oceania Equatorial Information Net

27 January, 2693—There was cheering and celebration in the streets of many cities throughout the Consortium today at the news that the last Kunti ship was driven from the Centauri 3 system by Flotilla forces under the collective command of Commodore Ugo Spinelli. Spinelli, usually head of Flotilla patrols

near Oceania and New Mecca, was transferred to Centauri by Prime Minister Muntso in early December. The commodore made significant inroads, putting troops on Dhara by the end of the year.

When the barrage of syndicate attacks across the CPCC began on 1 January, Spinelli kept his nose elevated, moving forward despite how thin the AF was spread. By 13 January, when things were at their grimmest throughout the Consortium, with dozen yakuza, triad and mafia attacks everday in the most unexpected and unprotected of places, Spinelli broke the Kunti blockade and began freeing cities on Dhara.

A week ago, the syndicate attacks stopped as abruptly as they began, and the Navarch made a large contingent of nearby galleons rendezvous with Spinelli's forces. Under the commodore's command, the superior Flotilla group crushed the Kunti aggressors.

Asked for her reaction, the Prime Minister said the following: "Ugo Spinelli is a great man and a true patriot. Thanks to him we now have the upper hand, and we will take advantage of it."

Pressed further, Muntso would not clarify, though she did promise that "Sigma Draconis will soon feel the wrath of the Consortium."

A Year of Peacekeeping Today

Inocente Ramos

Europa Media Tunnel

2 March, 2694—Today marks the anniversary of Consortium presence in the Sigma Draconis system. Commodore Bernard Dernier spoke briefly to reporters, assuring the public that the timetable for a Kunti constitution is still firm, and that CPCCAF forces are in place just to protect Kunti citizenry and ensure the installation of a government chosen by the people. Today's date is not a source of celebration for the Kunti or CPCC citizens, however: syndicate activity is on the rise throughout the Consortium, and the AF is having to track down remnants of the Kunti military that have ensconced themselves in various sectors. The exoduses from beleaguered worlds, both in the Consortium and outside it, continue, as holing drives permit those unsatisfied with their worlds the hope of finding another.

More significant for today's date is the upswing of mafia movement in Sigma Draconis itsself. Reports leaked by Milint operatives indicate that the Angels of Aztlan, a crime syndicate headed by the infamous Jimi Andrade, has established a foothold in the Kunti system, and rooting them up is a daunting task. Embattled peacekeeping forces await with eagerness the arrival of the first *Cetus*-class galleon to roll off the line at the Dosun Shipyards near Lalande 21185. The massive warship, christened the *Julius Caesar*, is the first of its type, enormous fighting vessels manned by both Flotilla and Army personnel and destined to impose order on regions disturbed by Kunti, rebel or syndicate forces. Anti-expansionist leaders still protest the production of the ships on the grounds that the *Cetus*-class vessels could be used to further expand the boundaries of CPCC territory, which they oppose for philosophical reasons. When pressed for evidence of any such plans on expansionists' part, several inwardists pointed to the names chosen for the next three *Cetus*-class ships: the *Qianlong*, the *Alexander* and the *Moctezuma*.

Teregan Leaders Sign Treaty

Stefan Lönnberg

Crete Courier

23 August 2695—Ending a four-month stand-off between the two political entities, members of Terego's church hierarchy, which at present is the sole governing body on the independent planet, agreed to terms of a treaty that requires them to establish a secular government for the planet within the next two years. The *Ursae Majoris Treaty* is the third of its kind signed in the last year: the planets of Erin and Semanawak both agreed in late 2694 to establish secular, democratic governments.

Consortium insistence on such governments derives from fear of the fanaticism that drove the Kunti invasion and which has delayed the timetable for Jitsu's induction into the CPCC. Anti-expansionists balk at the radical "violations of sovereignty" as they term the requests. Marco Musa, Lunar representative in the Diet, was vehement in his denouncement of the treaties: "We go in there with these behemoth galleons, 'requesting' their cooperation at gunpoint. Any treaty signed under those circumstances, I submit, is invalid, the product of blackmail."

Prime Minister Muntso shrugs off such objections. "We will do what must be done. Human beings everywhere have an innate right to choose their own leaders, and it's our duty to make sure that even on independent worlds those rights are observed."

When asked if the treaties weren't insisted on principally for the protection of the CPCC, Muntso nodded. "Of course that's our main objective. And to those who claim we want to annex these worlds, I'll say the following: it's obvious we want them to join us. But our treaties can't be viewed as coercing them to that end. Inclusion into the larger body of humanity is a decision the people of those worlds must make, and we have given them the means to make the decision."

CPCC Citizens Placed in Ghettos

Herlinda Sánchez

Europa Media Tunnel

27 February, 2697—In a stunning move, Jitsu's recently installed Minister of Immigration, Santo Koroma, has ordered this morning the mandatory relocation of all CPCC citizenry on the planet to government housing centers within Station City, the neutral population center controlled in a joint fashion by both the CPCC and Jitsu's theocratic government.

"The move is just temporary," Minister Koroma assured Consortium citizens in an infotainment-carried address. "Given that our squads show no success in stopping the constant invasion of Jitsu by syndicate and terrorist forces, we need to take more drastic action. This short-lived quarantine will allow us to determine more easily who the incognito syndicate operatives are—they tend to hide among the off-worlder populace— and incarcerate or eliminate them."

The radical measures, which would displace some 13,000 citizens, were approved by Archon Mutemi Rawe, the planet's monarch, and the local diet, which became majority Dominatu in December's elections. The Dominatudan is a radical religious group on Jitsu that disapproves of the planet's entering the Consortium.

Prime Minister Muntso was quick to denounce the ghettoization, deeming it "fascist." "We will not permit the mistreatment of CPCC citizens.

Our Minister of State is at present attempting a diplomatic solution to the crisis,

but Koroma and Rawe need to understand one thing: Jitsu is not Dhara. Never

again will our people be confined to camps that way."

AF informants tell the Tunnel that upon ending their tours in Sigma

Draconis next month, the *Cetus*-class galleons *Agamemnon* and *Ulysses S. Grant*,

along with the patrol ship *Pacifactor II*, will be rerouted to the Eta Cassiopeiae

2 system in case diplomacy fails.

On a related note, Archon Rawe also ordered the closure of Jitsu's Ra-

Koreji, another joint venture between Consortium educators and Jitsuan

reformers. Ra-Koreji, which offered secular education since its founding in

2686, was often the object of Dominatu criticism. The president of Ra-Koreji,

Modupe Oduyoye, gave no comment on its closure.

PART II:
KYOSU AND THE ORACLE

"Dance when you're broken open."—Rumi

CHAPTER 31

IT WAS CHAOS. THE SQUAD POPPED OPEN THE SEAL ON THE HIDEAWAY and hurtled into the dim interior, rotating helmeted heads and shooting several foolish yaks who thought they'd move up the ladder a bit by downing a squad member or two. They fanned out: Taison, Go and Chua to the left, Basan, Endo and Diken to the right. Ben Wu and the rookie, Jing Wong, stood blocking the exit.

The burly, squat Earther they called Kyosu was at point before them, massive legs slightly bent, a taut predator relishing the seconds before its attack. Twelve unwounded *demiman*, caught in the center of this deadly horseshoe, lowered their weapons slightly without seeming unnerved. When the far wall suddenly exploded, they ducked and began to fire. Each squad member dove in a different direction, concentrating on taking out the yak closest to him. For a few seconds, there was no chatter on the squad channel, just measured breathing and staccato grunts. Then Ben Wu began barking orders.

"Kyosu. The breach. Taison, Endo. Cover him."

Kyosu crouched low and bounded two meters into the air. Firing his konk rifle at the floor, he used the weapon's kick to propel himself toward the heavily armed A.I. shells that marionetted out of the dissipating smoke. At the end of the arc he described through the gloom, he kicked off from the shoulders of one of the shells, twisting his body into a spin and pounding the mechanical goons with round after round of concussion blasts. The recoil sped up his spin and drove him upward toward the latticework of girders near the metal laminate roof. He freed a hand and batted at a com cable that coiled down from the central beam. His purchase firm, he hauled himself up onto the catwalk, unslung his pulsegat and, bracing himself against a joist, continued his assault on the shells.

As he punished the robotic soldiers below, ripping off bits and pieces of armor that rained in a spray of sparks onto the concrete floor, he caught glimpses of his fellow squadmen fighting the human members of this mob crew.

The rookie engaged one of the sicarito in hand-to-hand combat. His form was masterful, a brutal yet beautiful Wu Shu that Kyosu envied uselessly, as *his* forte was his lack of fear, not any special fighting skill, though his speed and brute strength were respected by other members of the squad and his Capoeira wasn't half bad.

The low hum of chatter on the cascom kept him abreast of his progress. Four shells had fallen, and eleven more were currently being decommed by the other members of the squad, who'd ploughed through the yaks like a pulse through paper. Kyosu concentrated on the half dozen or so that were jerking through the opening. He ran, twisting and spinning, back and forth along a crossbeam, eluding the targeting beams of the shells and burning three of them before a 'nade ripped the girder out from beneath his feet, sending him and a portion of the roof plummeting toward the floor.

As he fell, his ritual disconnect occurred: sound gone, everything outside his tight focus fading to blue. He hit, pulled into a ball and rolled, avoiding the debris and popping up from a partial handstand into a scissor kick that dented the plating on two shells and toppled them. He'd dropped his pulsegat, so he squeezed some plaz from a container on his belt, slapped a bit on each fallen shell with a five-second cap and rushed toward the breach.

His focus was broken by a far-away reprimand buzzing in his ear.

"Brando, crazy fucking bastard, I've told you a million times not to carry plaztubes on you! Fucking death wish, that's what you've got!"

Ben, concerned father figure. Typical. Brando D'Angelo, the man they called Kyosu because of his former career, couldn't help but smile as he reflected.

The shells were too easy, purely rudimentary intelligence. *A.I. is illegal, but you'd think the Brotherhood would acquire the latest models. Come to think of it, the whole thing is just too bleeding easy.*

A sudden series of explosions behind him cut that line of reasoning off completely.

Sounds like more than just two shells exploding there.

On the other side of the breach was an operations room, 100 meters square and walled with storage bays for the shells and transports. A quarter-sphere of plated steel jutted out from the north wall, high above the bays. Probably a command center of some type. Three demiman positioned on its deck began to open fire on him as soon as he bounded in.

Disconnect. There was nothing to hide behind and he had no gats left, so he just kept on running, accelerating and trying to avoid the blasts. He received two, both at angles that weakened their impact. His suit was able to handle it, though he'd be bruised for weeks. At about ten meters from the wall, having reached a speed of 75 kph, he threw himself into the air and seemed to fly at the command center.

Volare. Niboraru.

The yaks were momentarily stunned, and when they realized what was happening, it was too late. Kyosu smashed into one of them, throwing the mobster against a large console that displayed the chaos in the other room. Simultaneously he heard groans in his cascom, a "who's down" from Ben, "stupid fucking Brando" in three languages and a general hail of billingsgate that pointedly referenced the Earther's mother.

There was no time to wonder what he'd done now. The other two turned, lowering their weapons and then coming at him furiously.

Something behind the console they can't shoot.

One yak, a red-eyed mutant-looking freak, cocked a massive fist and began to swing, ready with a kick if Brando ducked. So he sprang instead, to the height of the yak's head, and thrust an armored boot into his repugnant face, spinning as he descended to face the other gangster, a New Beijing boy if he'd ever seen one, fresher than the rookie.

Weird that he's a little brother.

Brando's back was now to the railing. From this angle, he noticed a lowered pit of some type behind the console. The yak's blaster went up. Kyosu stepped in, eyes locked with the punk's, took the gat away from him with a flurry of movements, and swept his legs out from beneath him while shoving him toward the pit at the same time. Clinging to the yak in a whirlwind spiral, Kyosu kept beating him with the butt of the weapon as they fell toward the metal plating below.

The impact sent the chrome sailing from his grip and scuttling across the floor. The yak had partially pinned Kyosu down with his body, and now grabbed a hold of his free arm in an effort to subdue the squadman. He leaned in close and muttered in poorly accented Kaló, "Po l'ermandá, pendeho."

Kyosu lurched upward and manage to smash the visor of his helmet into the idiot's face. Flinging him off, he yanked his *trucha* free from his belt, thumbed the on plate, and with an upward thrust, inserted the glowing blade into the yak's chest. Rolling the twitching Beijinger off of him, Brando sprang to his feet and spat angrily in Unified Chinese:

"Shuō xīn hàny⊠, gāis⊠ de báichī! Stupid fucking wannabes."

A chuckle made him slowly turn about.

"M'an mandau n'iho de berga, no? You some tough fucker. Short, but, hey, what the fuck, can't get ever thing, ain't it?"

The stringy yak that stared at him was a mademan, no doubt, the **B** burned into the webbed flesh between thumb and forefinger, these two drawn together overlapping to form a circle, the other three digits of his left hand pointing diagonally down toward the right as he displayed the sign above his heart. The Brotherhood, oldest syndicate around. Seven hundred years and going strong. Black hole eyes gleamed with hate and craziness from a scarred visage half-covered in tattoos. Mayan glyphs, the linguist in Brando reflected.

"Giving you a target, *chore*. Ain't you gonna do nothing?"

Kyosu feinted with the blade. Mademan's hand came up, gat popping into his palm as if on cue. Firing. Kyosu, having anticipated this, began to crumple to the floor under the blast, simultaneously driving the trucha through mademan's bodysuit and into the fleshy part of his thigh. Landing face-up, the squadman rolled onto his shoulders, throwing his back, pelvis and legs into the air on a collision course with mademan's gun arm. The gat was ripped from the lieutenant's grasp, and Kyosu, hand-standing for better reach, scissored his legs around the gun arm and snapped it like a broom handle.

"Pinche puto!" exclaimed the mademan, drawing back in a crouch. Kyosu trundled toward him in a side roll, sitting up just in time to avoid a face stamping. To his surprise, the mafioso reached out with his left hand and tapped a peculiar rhythm out on a spot at the base of his neck. The squadman's casque decompressed and slipped into the collar of his suit.

"What the...!"

The tattooed hand smashed into his nose, breaking it and sending drops of blood splattering across the steel floor plates.

"Vas a velo, hosupin," muttered Kyosu in Kaló as everything in the universe save mademan went a frosty blue. His gloved hand shot out and grabbed the mafioso's balls, which he squeezed with cold fury as he hoisted the sorry bastard into the air.

"Name, arsehole. Tu nomme, pero ya!"

Gurgling, face purple: "Felipe, Felipe Beserra." He lifted his good arm, fist clenched for a blow. Kyosu tossed him aside and then suddenly leapt into the air above the sprawling yak, whose eyes went wide. The impact broke several of his ribs. Kyosu grinned through blood as he straddled him.

Beserra. Like the kasike. Ah, fuck it.

"Listen close, you piece of shite. Talk. I want names: your contacts on Jitsu, the captains smuggling yall in. I want coordinates of in-system ships, surface weapons depots and HQ's."

"Chinga tu maje."

"La tuya, kulero. And last," Brando leaned in really close, blood from his smashed nose dripping onto the cap's forehead, "I want to know who killed

Arojin Santo's niece eight years ago."

A slight smile at that.

"Again, fuck your moms. Ain't givin' you shite. You really don't know who you fucking with, ain't it? Sides, you're a squadman. A cop. What you gonna do, kill me?"

In answer, Kyosu began pounding his armored fist against the guy's head. After a couple of seconds, he heard a blood-gargling attempt at speech.

"Got something to say?"

"Mi ermano te vachingar."

"Ooh, your brother. Your pops planning on paying me a visit, too? What about grandma? Little sis? Talk or you die."

Felipe's left hand curled into his syndicate's sign beside his heart. Kyosu activated his trucha.

"Brando! Hold it right there, squadman!"

Ben clambered down a ladder into the pit. After him followed Endo and Wong.

"What've we got, Kyosu?"

"Yak lieutenant doesn't want to spill. My rhetorical abilities didn't impress him much, so I thought I'd do a little selective surgery. Now that Endo's here, I'lltry the box."

Ben looked at Shusaku and nodded. "It's his prisoner. He gets to interrogate."

ENDO UNPACKED THE KEWBOX. IT WAS EQUIPPED WITH AN INTERNAL power supply, but he hooked it up to a nearby console to conserve energy.

"The fuck yall gonna do?"

Ben turned a doleful look on the mobster. "It's like a conference room, just that we control your sensory input, not you. We can pretty much make you tell us what we need to know."

"That's torture. Yall can't do that. Yall are cops."

Endo smiled. "You're not on Mars or some fancy platform, dumb-arse. You sure as shite aren't on Earth, where yall yaks have more rights than yall's victims. This is Jitsu: most arse-backward planet there is. Neogs pretty much let us do what we want, long's we're protecting them from yall scum. Ready, Brando."

He tapped in a command, and a dazzling pink light, made up of thousands of individual beams, began dancing across Felipe's blood-smeared forehead, making thousands of neurons in his neocortex fire in specific sequences.

"He's in."

As Brando prepared a chair to sit in for the interrogation, he felt Ben's hand on his arm.

"Listen, it's obvious you're extra pissed today. That stupid plaz thing back there, which is gonna get you written up, and the way you took these guys on, you alone... don't take this interrogation too far, Brando. I mean it. You just apply the right pressure, and no more. You already messed him up bad here, more than you needed to."

"I know what I'm doing, Ben."

"Damnit, lad, pay attention to what I'm saying. This is fire. I shouldn't even let you be the one asking the kews, but we had a deal, I know. Just... if he doesn't know about Tenshi, don't freak. This guy has to be in one piece for the Major."

"You're trying to say you know who he is?"

The captain glanced away guiltily and then turned an icy gaze on D'Angelo.

"I'm just warning you."

"Ben, what in shite is going on here? He's one of *them*, the bad guys. What, you're telling me I should be nice to him? What do you want me to do, ask him pretty please to give me the information? Give him some sweet biscuits, too?"

"Bastard, just tell me you're gonna use your best judgment and not freak."

"Of course, Ben. I'm a professional."

He gestured impatiently at Endo as he sat down and leaned his head back. Pink light burned away the encroaching blue.

Ben watched his eyes close, the false REM begin.

"Yeah, a professional. But this shouldn't be your line of work."

The interrogation room was dark, except for a single light that shone from nowhere directly into the suspect's face. Typical: it had worked for centuries, so why try to improve on perfection? Felipe was seated on an uncomfortable laminate folding chair with a slight forward incline that kept him from leaning back, unless he wanted to end up on the floor. He was forced to lean forward into the light, toward the wooden table behind which the squadman's doppelganger sat. The tabletop was partially a console as well, and Felipe could only begin to guess at what so many lighted displays implied for him.

"It's simple, Felipe. I won't play any games with you, make you think you might get off easy. You're for certain going south, subterranean clean-up, lowest level, no machines, pure pickaxe, a true nightmare. But first you're going to talk to me, tell me all the things I want to know. Remember, your body's bleeding on the deck of your command center; nobody's doing anything to help you. We get done here, you get help. You take too long, make me drag stuff out of you... well let's just say others die while inside: you wouldn't be the first."

A lie. Boxes had fail-safes that kept such incidents from occurring.

"Tell me, whatever your fuckin' name is, how you can call yourself a cop and do this shite."

"First of all, call me Kyosu. Second, you're a damn criminal. You'd do this shite to innocent people, but I'm doing it to a worthless social parasite. I love the way yaks moan about yall's rights and how they're being violated. Boo-fucking-hoo. The minute you choose to prey on civilians, you execrable bastard, you give up all your rights, far's I'm concerned. The government of Jitsu agrees with me, so stop whining."

Brando tapped the tabletop. Felipe's eyes began to water, and his face went white.

"Slow nausea. No way to throw up, relieve the sick. Now, I can stop this, but you've got to talk. Know that this is just the beginning. From here, everything's downhill."

Felipe bent his arm at the elbow and extended his middle finger. Brando shook his head slowly, incredulously. It was going to be a long session.

ON THE OBSERVATION DECK, ENDO SHUSAKU WATCHED AS JING WONG bent over the New Beijing yak's body and yanked Brando's trucha from his chest. For the briefest of moments, the rookie's face clouded over as if with sadness, but Wong quickly busied himself with checking the body for traps, standard operating procedure in these circumstances. Endo had just turned his head when out of the corner of his eye he caught a metallic flash followed by violent thrashing. The yak had begun to twitch and clutch his chest.

"Guy's alive!" shouted Wong.

Ben clambered down a ladder into the observation pit. "Okay, mates, we got us another prisoner. Jing, take his wretched carcass down to the transports, let the docbots give him the once over. Check on the clean-up progress while you're at it and come report to me in fifteen."

Wong nodded silently and slid one of the three repulsion litters he'd brought with him under the Beijinger, pulling the floating mass after him into the lift located at the back of the pit.

Ben watched the lift jolt into movement and head downward. Turning to

Endo, he indicated the box with his hand.

"How long's it been?"

"Nearly twenty minutes. Incredible. They most times break after five."

His abdomen cramping with the unpleasant possibilities if something went wrong, his every thought evoking Nestor Bos, or rather his doppelganger, glaring stonily at him across the light years, Ben crumpled cross-legged on the plating beside the kewbox.

"I'm going in."

"Kyosu's gonna be pissed."

"Don't give a shite, Endo. Just do it."

A DOOR TO THE LEFT OF THE INTERROGATION TABLE OPENED; BRANDO'S head swiveled angrily. Ben's doppelganger walked inside, regarding the bloody, spittle-covered and sweat-drenched face of Felipe Beserra.

"What've you got?"

"Mothergod, Ben!" He tapped on the console. "Okay, the bastard can't sense us now. I got the location of their present base in Station City, several weapons depots and the ship that it's supplying them."

"Good. Then let's get the fuck out."

"Wait, please. He knows something about it."

"Oh, by Domina's..."

"Damnit, Ben. You owe me this."

"I don't owe you shite, Brando." Brando noticed the slight wince that always accompanied Ben's lies. "You owe *me*. I've got more on the line than you know, mate. Can't afford for you to screw this up."

"Come on, Ben. He says someone high up in the government, some arojin, is involved in all this. Thirteen years of investigation, and you never heard anything like that?"

"Nah, you got him so fried he's trying to tell you whatever you want to hear. Disconnect, Brando. You're wasting time with this crap, and it looks to me like you're about to damage the psyche of a potential witness."

"You don't think it's worth following up, Ben? And right now? The guy says he's Konrau's *brother*. If it's true... what? What's that look for? Wait a minute—you knew who he was already, right? Outside, all that warning stuff... what're you trying to hide?"

Ben turned to the door, his voice muffled by the program buffers as he opened it.

"Disconnect now, or I tell Endo to pull you by force, no matter how much shock it causes you."

Brando kicked at the table angrily, shut off the baffle so Felipe could hear and see him, and cranked everything past threshold. The underboss began to spasm wildly, falling from his chair.

"You tell me, mothergod, who killed Tenshi Koroma? Who gave the order? Why her? It wasn't random, right? ANSWER ME YOU BASTARD!"

Foam flying frenetically from his cracked lips, Felipe groaned, "Came direct from Konrau. Request of his Neog partner. Kill her; kid too. But not you, though. Mistake." He struggled for breath and then spat. "Brando."

"Was it you? Damnit, DID YOU DO IT?"

Somehow, Felipe managed a grin.

"Fuck you. Yeah. Personal treatment, you fucking egghead. Should've known. Couldn't protect yours. No bales berga i lo sabes. You should a heard that little kid of yours whimper as the blood drained outta her."

Brando leapt over the table and began stamping Felipe's doppelganger in the face, screaming like a madman. He hadn't shut off the juice; it would cancel automatically if there were any danger. Suddenly, his foot in mid-beat, he was yanked.

The room swirled into black. The pink lights scintillated strangely, going blinding orange, the color of mad and malicious Sakra, whose grim voice glitched at the edges of Brando's soul.

CHAPTER 32

SANTO LET THE CPCC AMBASSADOR WAIT IN THE VESTIBULE. Since being named Minister of Immigration in January by the new Dominian-controlled Chamber of Deputies, he'd been hassled nearly every day by Leyla Soral or some other CPCC representative. It was unfortunate from a logistical standpoint that he'd been forced to wait seven years to get this quarantine underway, but Tenshi's death hadn't quashed reformer sentiment as well as hoped. Reformers had retained tenuous control of the government until the most recent elections six months ago.

Luckily, their majority had been too slim to push through the inclusion of a deputy from Station City, and the Archon hadn't reacted enthusiastically to the idea of a lower chamber. However, the political impasse they represented had delayed Santo's plans until the public's fear of Brotherhood attacks made them reevaluate their loyalties.

But that had only been part of the problem. Kunti infidels had moved against the Consortium, strengthening expansionist resolve. With the selection of Jetsun Muntso as CPCC prime minister, the military was ensured steady enlargement. The AF had now occupied Sigma Draconis for four years, and a rising tide of popular sentiment throughout the Consortium suggested that, if terrorist attacks and theocracy continued on Jitsu, it would be the next target of CPCC imperialism.

The conflict between the Kunti and the Consortium had also frustrated many of Konrau Beserra's long-term plans, and the mafia boss had begun acting erratically. As the Oracle pointed out, it was only a matter of time before Beserra would betray Jitsu. Santo needed to act, now.

Of course, he hadn't been idle during the last seven years. Once he'd relinquished control of the squads to the Chamber of Deputies, he'd begun a campaign to bring together Dominians and Reformers in 'a spirit of brotherhood,' a slogan whose irony brought a smile to his lips every time he heard it.

Santo's public embracing of his former enemies had gone to the extreme of a well-received speech given at the dedication of a statue erected in his niece's honor within Kinguyama's central plaza. After the Chamber's investigation had turned up absolutely no evidence of a connection between him and the mafia incursions, he'd rapidly become one of the more popular figures in the social sphere of Jitsu, earning the respect of even the most hardened Reformers for his bipartisanship. He was awarded a post as head of the Public Service Department, a non-political offshoot of the cabinet that oversaw the distribution of energy, food, water and other necessities to the population.

Despite this image makeover, Santo continued behind the scenes to direct the flow of events on Jitsu so that they built toward the climax Samanei desire. Through a loyal Major Sosa, he continued to control the squads, sending them on fruitless missions against Nestor's dummy crews, quickly assembled groups of rookies whom the Brotherhood deemed dispensable. Nestor himself, his obvious distaste for Santo notwithstanding, continued to trust Santo's judgment, though the arojin had little doubt about Konrau's true intentions.

Of course, as the Oracle had never planned on keeping to their original plan either, such duplicity was to be expected. Besides, deceit was easily turned against the deceiver.

Santo's connections within the Chamber of Deputies also allowed him to continue to influence the parliamentary motions that reached the floor of the legislature, so that in spite of his feigned withdrawal from elected political life, he had been more involved in the running of Jitsu during the last seven years than ever before.

Now head of the new Ministry of Immigration, Santo had his hands in nearly every crevice of power of Jitsu and had begun confining off-worlders to Station City, much to the indignation of reformers and human-rights activists alike. His justification of the move was the incessant and unchecked infiltration of life on the planet by demimundo activity. As the squads had been unable to quell this invasion, he argued, more drastic measures needed to be taken. So, with considerable support from the Chamber and a surprising thumbs-up from Rawe, Santo had begun transporting off-worlders to government housing complexes within Station City, assuring them that they would be permitted to return to their homes, often in reformer prefectures, as soon as the syndicate threat had been contained.

In the towns where there'd been the most criminal activity, conveniently the most liberal ones, martial law was established to root out Brotherhood operatives.

Needless to say, the CPCC was not at all pleased with the situation. Santo's assurances were dismissed at first, and then countered with ultimatums and posturing. Santo wasn't worried.

Let them stew, let them get angry. Jitsu is not Bima. There will be no occupational force here, the Oracle says. Soon the Brotherhood will be here in force, looking for a fight, looking for revenge.

Santo felt no worry. The Oracle had arranged it all, on her own and through Santo, with the help of the strange Yen Bandera. Military versus syndicate, an all-out clash that would dwarf the insignificant CPCC-Kunti skirmishes.

And his special pawn, D'Angelo, whom he'd so expertly maneuvered into position, would be at the heart of the storm. Santo would soon be free to expunge the infidels from his world, and his people's path to enlightenment would be clear once again, a shining blue ribbon into ra-Yindawo.

His desk com chimed.

"Yes, Ana?"

His secretary hesitated a second. "Ambassador Soral is asking if you're going to see her soon."

Santo smiled. Desperate opponents were always the easiest. "Tell her to come in."

The door irised open, first revealing Leyla Soral's head, her dark hair framing a severe face and piercing green eyes. A moderately tall woman in her early fifties, Soral had been chosen for her present job after the valor and toughness she'd demonstrated during the Kunti invasion of Dhara, where she'd been mayor of an important city. Santo knew the present movement of CPCC citizens was a personal affront to her, as she'd watched her own people, including family members, herded into Kunti internment camps.

As she walked in, Ambassador Soral inclined her head slightly beforing taking a seat without permission. She was an insistent infidel, one worthy of some respect, but Santo was beginning to tire of her. He decided that today was the last day he'd agree to see her. A little surprise was being planned for her that would keep her away permanently.

"Minister Koroma, I am here to make a final offer. Stop this fascist interment of CPCC citizens, and the AF will gladly assist you in ridding your planet of the criminals that plague it." She leaned forward, placing her hands, balled suggestively into fists, on the dull surface of his desk. Santo sat motionless, his own hands folded across his stomach. "This will not be another Dhara, Koroma.

You see, two AF defense ships are fenestrating as we speak. Allowing for decel once they enter normal space, they'll be here in about twelve hours. They can either arrive to help, or they can arrive to blockade you, to revoke this planet's charter and put it under military control until a non-oppressive government is put together by its citizens. You decide, Minister."

Santo continued to regard her coldly for an unnerving space of several minutes. She slowly sat upright, her hands slipping off the desk, her eyes glinting even more angrily than before. Santo reflected that even the typical unctuousness of ambassadors had its limits, and he relished the naked hostility on Soral's face.

"Ambassador," he said calmly, "this is, to be frank, none of the Consortium's concern. An internal matter. I'll remind you that Jitsu isn't a full member in your gang yet, and any interference from you may result in our complete withdrawal and the declaration of our independence. As for your armed forces, you will recall the decades we spent fighting Soltec for control of this planet. We took them on, and we can do the same with you, if that is what you are looking for."

Soral's mouth twisted. "You just guaranteed your own removal from office. Archon Rawe won't be so cavalier in his attitude toward the CPCC, I imagine."

"Rawe is very old, Ambassador. Like most old men, he's getting more and more crotchety. Don't imagine he will care a whit if you threaten him. He'll do as the Oracle instructs him, and she's made it clear that this is her will."

Soral opened her mouth and raised her left hand, but at that moment the door banged open and Deputy Ken Wata rushed breathlessly in.

"Arojin... it's the Archon. He's dead."

Santo surged to his feet. "You're sure?"

"Yes. He was found in the hall outside the audience chamber. Aneurysm."

Santo glanced at Soral. Her eyes were wide. He was also surprised, but pleased beyond words. He hadn't planned on this twist. Samanei had assured him that the Archon would be gone soon, perhaps in the midst of the looming conflict between the AF and the Brotherhood, but she'd given him no hint that it would happen this early. Perhaps it wasn't even her doing. How it had happened, however, was of no consequence. What happened next mattered most.

This unbeliever would be shocked the core of her being.

"Leyla," he said as he turned a reptilian smile on her, "it looks like if this world's about to get it a new leader. Some advice. Were I you, I'd gather my things and take a shuttle off the planet now."

"Is that a threat, *Santo*?" She stood proudly.

He gave a short laugh. "No, dear. In two hours, that monstrous building where y'all infidels house your embassy will become a pile of rubble. I'd hate to imagine those deep green eyes of yours trapped beneath so much concrete." Soral appeared unflustered by this, so Santo went for the jugular. "What's more, I'll remind you that yakuza are not nearly as gentle as Kunti soldiers, Leyla. I understand they forced you to watch them rape your wife during your captivity. I'm sure it was traumatic for both of yall. How unfortunate it would be to see the same repeated, perhaps on yall's son?"

"You mother…" she began, surging from her chair with balled fists. Santo blinked at her sudden rage. She mastered it in seconds, though her hands still trembled and her eyes blazed. Swallowing almost imperceptibly, the ambassador smoothed her jacket down and turned to go. Without looking at him, she intoned, "I'll see you on trial in the Interstellar Court if you do what I think you're planning. It'll be a pleasure to see you squirm, to see you locked up forever."

"Goodbye, Leyla. I enjoyed our tête-à-têtes as much as you. Don't ever change."

She slammed the door as she walked out, leaving Santo and Ken alone.

"Should I call an emergency session? We're on recess, you know."

"Yes, do. We've got much to do, and little time to do it. Get as many members as you need to accept the Oracle's declaration and then initiate a faux-conference with the Jinja ra-Orakuru. Once she makes the announcement, vote right away and broadcast the session to the whole planet. Then get ready for the maelstrom."

When Ken had left, Santo called Ana in.

"Get me a private transport to the Archon's compound. Transfer all my calls to his office, prioritizing any from Major Sosa, Captain Wu, or our young friends from New Beijing. Understood?"

She nodded and hurried out to get started. Santo palmed open a closet, pulled out the blue robe that only an archon could wear, hanging there all these

years, and with indescribable pleasure, began to slip it on.

CHAPTER 33

BRANDO CAME TO HIS SENSES ON THE GROUND OUTSIDE OF THE compound. At his side, Diken and Chua were having shrapnel extracted from their limbs by docbots.

"Guys alright?"

"Fuck you, Kyosu. Why not warn the rest of us next time you decide to blow up a bogful of robots, eh? That way we can, you know, get our arses hid behind some type of shield or something."

Chua nodded his agreement with Diken.

"Yeah, you set off a damn chain reaction, nearly decapitated Go, you crazy, gormless sumbitch. And I hear you killed their fucking cap during your kews. Brilliant. Hey, while you're at it, be sure to shoot a few civilians."

Brando's head snapped up. "That's crossing the line, Chua. They're my wife's people. Mine, too. You know that I do my damnedest to protect them."

"Yeah, well, I wish you could spread some of that Neog concern of yours for your *goddamn squad mates.*"

Brando muttered apologies as he struggled to his feet: "Mengo, mengo."

"Mengo my arse," quipped Diken. Chua just gave him the finger.

Brando shrugged their anger off. He was still groggy and weak from being yanked mid-kew, but the news of the yak's death barely fazed him.

Guess those fail-safes aren't so safe after all.

He was more irritated that he hadn't gotten the name of the arojin working with the Brotherhood.

Fucking Dominians. No matter how hard Santo has tried to get them to compromise, they'd rather step off the Path and ally with truth-blind criminals.

Ben stepped through the door of the compound, accompanied by the rookie, both of them talking quietly. As soon as he saw Brando, his face twisted in anger, and he walked quickly to where the squadman was trying to get his bearings.

"Idiotic wank. This is the last time, you hear? First you endangered the squad, nearly killed us. Then you kill an important source, the brother of Konrau Beserra. Why? Your simple-minded obsession. Year after year. We've got a job to do, arsehole. This ain't no fucking vendetta!"

"I do my job. I keep my planet safe."

"Yeah, you do. But you don't really give a shite about anything—"

Brando clenched his fists. "I've sacrificed everything for my people, you—"

"—except leads on a seven-and-a-half-year-old case you'll never solve."

"Don't say that, damn you."

"Fuckers responsible are long gone, Brando. Couple of yaks that broke past our line and killed your wife and kid, mate. Completely random, no ulterior motive. Why can't you give up?"

"Random? That piece of shite just admitted killing her, and he mentioned a Pathwalker co-conspirator! Don't ask me to give up, Ben. I won't do it, not when I've almost got it solved. It's more than just revenge, don't you get it? I find the arojin responsible, I free this world of its oppressors, too!"

Acid churned in Ben's guts. Even after all these years, the guilt he felt about the death of Brando's family weighed down on his soul like a blood-soaked burial shroud. Betrayal was torture, nearly more than he could bear, but Nestor's rage and all it implied were a thousand times worse. Driven to distraction by helpless desperation he exploded in a frenzy of spittle and vitriol:

"Whatever, you psycho fucking Neog. But stop putting my men at risk!"

Brando's face hardened. "I'll put them at risk if I have to. That's my Path. You knew it when I signed on, you know it now. Since you benefit from my 'obsession,' it should be no problem. It's no longer worth it to you, discharge me. I'll get at the truth without you."

Muttered curses came from the others. Ben shook his head. "So, what you're saying is you don't give a shite about any of us."

"You're hired guns. If I'm with you, it's to make sure you do your fucking jobs."

It was only a half-truth. He did feel a kinship with these men. But those feelings were irrelevant. They could never replace his loves. Nor could his fellow Pathwalkers on Jitsu. He defended them with such zeal because they were also on the Path and because, through Tenshi, he had come to love them. But every battle he fought, he fought as if his wife were watching him from ra-Yindawo. He needed her approval.

"Got a feeling you're dirty, anyway, Ben, so don't lecture me about our mission."

His face betraying nothing, Ben crossed the distance between them in three long strides and, stooping to Brando's height, backhanded him. The blow sent D'Angelo sprawling in the sand, where he lay for a few moments before slowly getting to his feet. He stepped close to his mentor, and Jing seemed surprised to hear him growl softly in Unified Chinese.

"You're my captain and my friend, but if you hit me once more, I'll kill you."

BEN WU SAID NOTHING AS BRANDO SPUN on his heels, hopped into one of the transports, and sped off without asking leave to do so.

"Oh, bloody brilliant." Chua slapped a palm against the sand. "Now we're gonna need to crowd into two transports. Captain, you gotta do something about that sumbitch."

Ben nodded. He would have to act. No more postponing. Too much was at stake. He had to set aside his friendship with Brando, the debt he owed the man. It was time to sacrifice him to save someone much more important.

"Alright, Endo, some fucking answers. What happened to the bloody fail-safes?"

"Well, the diagnostic showed everything was all right, fail-safes running normal. But then I opened the mother up, and… somebody's tampered with it."

"Been out of the cage?"

"Nah, Ben. Stuck it in there last month, and you and me, we're the only ones can authorize it being cycled open."

Except the major. And a certain arojin.

Let it be one of them. Let it be some crazy-arse plan, and not a screw-up on my watch. Images flashed above the display top in his mind: Ya-Ting spinning in her mother's arms, giggling and pure; Ya-Ting hanging on a yak's elbow, guffawing and thoroughly unclean. A shudder to clear his head. His stomach knotted convulsively.

Nestor won't be interested in my theories; he'll want my head for this.

AFTER LOADING THE SQUAD INTO THE TWO ATS TRANSPORTS, BEN AND JING made certain the surviving yaks were secure in the holding cell of the prisoner transport. The New Beijing kid was hooked up to a docbot: his left ventricle had been severed, but he'd probably pull through. Ben stepped up into the cabin. Jing rode shotgun as they headed toward ATS headquarters.

"Ben. That guy yall call Kyosu?"

"Yeah?"

"Well, back there he was talking, what, Kaló to that yak?"

"Uh-huh."

"Then right now he talked to you in Xīnhànyǔ. I mean perfect, too, like my grandpa used to use. How many fuckin' languages does he speak?"

"I don't know. Five? Ten? Used to be a linguist."

"With the AF?"

"Nah, he ain't a soldier, Jing. He was a civ. Taught here at the university. Founded Ra-Koreji. That school they just shut down? That was his baby."

"That crazy bastard was a professor?"

"Yes, fool. That's what *Kyosu* means. Like *Jiàoshòu*. Professor."

"The fuck's he doing in Alpha Squad?"

Wu's fingers whitened on his seat's armrests.

"His family was slaughtered like eight years back. Probably yaks." Ben's stomach clenched bitterly. *Yeah, probably yaks that got past my squad. Fucking Nestor.* "Maybe even this Felipe, if Brando's telling the truth. Messy shite. He got involved in the investigation, but you know how Civil Security is on this fucking glebe. They didn't find shite.

"But he stayed obsessed, came and talked with me and the other vets that were trying to whip the Squads into a decent body of frontier patrols. I'd already lost nearly every man on my squad twice in five years, the second time right before the murder. As if they'd waited for the opening, see?"

Ben didn't mention being taken prisoner. That officially had never happened.

"The shite happened in what used to be a frontier town, Kinguyama. Some mates of Kyosu's got the case moved to ATS. Well, we couldn't figure out shite either, the state we were in. So he asked to join."

"What you tell him?"

"No way in Domina's dank dung hole. Had no combat experience, no weapons training, no hand-to-hand, no nothing."

"And then?"

"He just left all quiet. A year later he came back."

The transport dove into a hole at the base of a dune. Darkness enveloped them. Panel lights brightened in intensity and the vehicle's flood beams illuminated the passageway on all sides. To Ben it seemed the only thing that kept the darkness from crushing him was the speed at which they bored down the tunnel, and the minute they stopped the inevitable would close in on him like a predator, swallowing him as it had sucked his daughter into its maw as well.

He felt impotent, frustrated. How had he allowed someone like Brando to put him in this position? Easily answered: it wasn't Brando who had put him there. Wu's squad, for the second time in three years, had been unprepared. Tenshi and her little girl had died as a result. It was a simple enough equation that not only made him responsible for D'Angelo's loss, but also underscored his feelings of guilt for the death of Qing. Identifying with the professor's plight had merely sealed his doom.

"One year later. You couldn't even tell it was the same man, cept for the sad Earther height, I guess. He was strong, stronger than any of us, and those dirtbunny muscles of his let him do all kind of wild, gravity defying stunts you had to see to believe. His eyes were what convinced me, though. Like craziness focused into a little black beam peering out from his pupil to sear the shite out of you."

"How fucking poetic." There was a strange, ambiguous glint in the rookie's eye.

"Shut up, noob, or I'll reassign your arse to the CPCC building."

"Could he fight?"

"Nah, not really. Probably hadn't raised a fist in his life. But he'd been practicing with battle sims and such. Okay brawler, I guess. Anyways, the major called me in and said to take him. Archon's orders, if you can imagine that. Started training him right away, but a guy's thirty you're gonna experience problems molding him into a fighter. But I pushed his arse, hard. He still doesn't have much skill or flash, even after seven years of practice, but he makes up for it with speed, strength and balls. Guy fights like he doesn't mind dying, that's why he crushes the yaks."

And with him, I never lost more than five men on a mission. He's become the heart of this squad.

"But he's gonna get iced, no? After that shite he pulled today?" Jing seemed almost vehement in his insistence. "He's finished, ain't it?"

The transport autoed to stop in the squad garage. Ben reached out and slowly clicked the door open. The severity of what he was about to do was beginning to sink in. He set his jaw with grim resolution.

"Yeah, poor bastard. He's finished. May the five blessings come to him. And me, too."

Jing peered at him with an odd, thoughtful expression as Ben gruffly exited the transport. When he was sure the captain wasn't looking, the rookie bent over his wrist, muttered something into his percom, and then followed the older soldier into the landing bay.

CHAPTER 34

BRANDO SET THE SAND-PITTED MILITARY TRANSPORT DOWN ON the faded circle of the tarmac beside the sun-bleached narrow length of the now modified Strugar-Rask *Tarhiata* his wife had first given him a ride in, what seemed like eons ago, when he'd thought he could find peace. He still remembered how Tenshi, on her hands and knees, had guided the paintbot through the marks she'd laid out, the phosphorescent paint smelling of childhood to Brando. Getting out slowly, exhausted and emotionally drained, he palmed the lift open and descended into the bowels of Tenshi's leviathan masterpiece. He'd sealed off almost all of its many rooms, leaving only his basement level study, Tana's playroom and Tenshi's workroom. The latter two he'd remodeled years ago, converting them into a huge training area.

Before stepping off the lift, a circular platform that traveled vertically in a cylinder with four arches at each end, he braced himself for the gravity increase. After cashing in Tenshi's shares in Izakiwo, Inc., Brando had installed an expensive and illegal set of gravtiles that allowed him to increase the gees in the basement in a series of concentric circles rippling out from the lift until reaching Earth normal at about fourteen meters out. This was the heavily debated "secret" to his physical prowess: when not on duty, Brando lived and trained at more than twice Jitsu's normal gravity, only leaving his heavy subterranean world to practice Tai-Chi and acrobatics in the overgrown garden.

But he had neither desire nor energy for training today. He trudged to his study and palmed the door open. A massive oak desk sat in its center, a holo projector on the floor beyond it. The walls were taken up by maps, electronic devices and bookshelves full of old medical texts and more modern data storage devices with detailed information on subjects as varied as gene manipulation and transactional physics. The desktop was cluttered with hardcopy, which Brando swept aside to get to the imbedded panel. He thumbed his system on, and the holographic display jumped to life.

"Buon giorno, Brando." Professor Calvino flowed upward out of the projector. A somatoid of him, that is. An artificial persona built upon what Brando remembered of his personality. Calvino himself had died some five years before. His family had sent many messages to D'Angelo, and he'd ignored them all.

"Como stai, professore? Do me a favor, no? Pull the XID file on Konrau Beserra I got from that informant."

"Naturalmente. Konrau Beserra. Head of the Brotherhood, or in Kaló,

L'ermandá. The principal syndicate presently infiltrating Jitsuan business and black-market spheres. Konrau was born to an unmarried miner on Tenochtitlan platform, which has orbited Jupiter in the Sol system for 250 years. Father was Sami Arredondo, a Brotherhood mademan, born at the fringes of an important family. Konrau spent little time with Arredondo, and the brotherhood lieutenant was imprisoned when his son was eight. He died in prison. Despite being forced to live his adolescence without financial support from the Brotherhood, Konrau rose to power as a young man, after eliminating the boss of a rival gang called Anhele d'Atlan, another of the syndicates suspected of presently scrabbling for a stronghold on Jitsu. This boss believed he had killed Konrau years before, having shot him in the eye. Konrau has spent twenty-two years as kasike of the Brotherhood, and his half-brother is…"

"Dead."

"Updating files. Date of death?"

"Today."

"Cause?"

Brando leaned back in his chair.

"Accidental sensory overload during interrogation."

"Very good. Felipe Beserra, it is suspected, was placed in charge of the infiltration about eight years ago after a string of previous underbosses were either eliminated by the ATS's Alpha Squad or by their own men. Felipe Beserra himself was *eliminated* on…"

"Let's go back to Konrau. Why did that boss try to kill him? Did he move against the Angels?"

"Insufficient data to know for certain, though several informants mention the involvement of the boss's daughter. Come Romeo e Giulietta, forse. The most plausible rumor is that he was working as a Brotherhood spy within the Angels' hierarchy on Tenochtitlan when he became enamored of Jeini Andrade. It would appear that either she turned him over or by accident caused his identity to become known."

"I seem to remember intel about some psychosomatic illness of his."

"Yes. You got that information from your interrogation of Paulo Bega. It appears that Beserra imagines he feels pain where he was once wounded. Physiologically mpossible, but psychologically telling, as are his impulse to be alone in wide-open areas and his never getting married."

"Interesting. Shut down, *professore.* I can't think right now."

He stood up and began pacing about. The pressure was building in his head, the darkness swirling just at the periphery of his awareness.

Item: Ben had known he was interrogating Beserra's half-brother.

Item: Major Sosa wanted Beserra brought in to him, alive.

Item: Beserra had ordered Tenshi and Tana's assassination at the behest of an arojin of some standing in the government.

Item: the kewbox's fail-safes had malfunctioned, and Brando suspected foul play.

Item: Felipe had known the squad's casque code, which clinched its being an inside job.

The pieces were finally coming together, after seven years of Brando beating his head against every conceivable brick wall, but he had a sinking feeling that come tomorrow morning, he'd be stripped of his policing powers just when he needed them the most. In fact, there was a good chance that come tomorrow evening he'd be holed up in a detention cell awaiting trial.

Need to get things ready. Might have to move fast once the shite starts to cycle.

He scooted the desk to one side, knelt and keyed a well-camouflaged panel on the floor. Several tiles slid back, revealing a ladder leading into darkness. Down the ladder he went, into a claustrophobic tunnel, southward and gradually down, lights every four meters or so till he reached an airlock. He cycled through, passed alongside consoles, seats and equipment, pausing only to run his hand across two huge transparent cylinders and a refrigeration unit, until he came to a relatively small chamber.

Inside was a large but ancient 'frame and a faux-life interface. He sat in the chair and activated the system, closing his eyes as the pink light played across his forehead and short-cropped hair.

Tenshi's house was restored to its pristine, astonishing original beauty. Brando made his way to the garden out back, where Tenshi was building a play set for Tana, complete with swings and a slide, as their daughter lay on her stomach in the grass, drawing on a datapad. Her head turned toward him as he stepped onto the patio, and her eyes lit up.

"Apa! You're home!"

She jumped up and ran into his arms. He spun her around like a transport at full, both of them laughing. Tenshi set down her hammer and joined them, kissing Brando as he set Tana down.

"Hey, umpenzi. How was work?"

"Good. Better than in a long time."

They sat at the granite table. Tana jumped up, ran inside, and came back with a deck of cards.

"You promised, remember? Quality time with us, playing aguram."

He smiled and nodded. They played a couple of games, engaging in small talk about the weather and Tenshi's progress on the play set.

After thirty minutes, the fail-safes D'Angelo had incorporated into this fantasy world kicked in, as they always did, preventing him from slipping into delusion. He'd had that much foresight, no matter how questionable his visits might be.

Tana set her cards down, folded her hands together, and looked deep into his eyes, an expectant look on her beautiful face.

"You catch them yet, apa?"

"Not yet. But soon, sweetie. Soon. That's why I came so early today. This is the last time I visit you here. Don't be afraid, don't cry. I'll still be with you, just differently."

Tenshi shook her head, smiling.

"Brando, you programmed us to remind you that we aren't your real family. We don't think or feel a thing. We only exist to reinforce their fading echoes. That's what you told us. You also said to stress what was most important. Ona ra-Oni. The Oni Way. Don't forget the jagen, Brando. You have to slay it. If the other stuff doesn't work out, that's life. At least you'll avenge your wife and child. And give Jitsu justice. If you don't despair."

Brando nodded soberly. It would've been easy to slip into psychosis if he hadn't programmed the somatoids to constantly remind him who they were not.

But without these visits, what might have happened? His siblings and teachers on the Path had kept him from suicide. But worse than death was forgetting. Moving on. Acceptance.

For Brando had reached satori, had seen his spark his broken self aglow.

And tangled in that teyo, that illuminated self, were the simran of his wife and child.

DURING THE FIRST FEW MONTHS AFTER THEIR DEATHS, Brando had been devastated, utterly bereaved. He had sunk into a black Charybdis of despair of such depth he'd hardly eaten, much less attended to the pressing affairs that accompany all human passing, funeral arrangements and other rituals that serve to soften the anguish of survivors by forcing them to acknowledge how routinely normal death is.

His mother-in-law had stepped in and taken charge, feeding him when he'd permit it and planning the cremation service. He did not attend. Could not accept what had happened. Was driven deeper and deeper within himself, confronted with his many inadequacies, blamed for the murders by some self-hating part of his being that urged him to join them, the same voice than had urged him to plunge into the icy blue when his father left him years before.

One day Meji Pishan had walked into Brando and Tenshi's home. They had found Brando sitting on the floor of the great room, upon tiles still stained with his loved ones' blood.

"This won't do," the prefect had said. "You won't hear her here. In fact, there's nowhere you can go where her true voice will reach you from ra-Yindawo. But its echo is whispering within you. You walked the Path together, meditated together, explored your selves in the physical world together, building home and school and community. That which made her who she was she entrusted to you. Not her translated soul, no. Her teyo, that swirling mass of glowing self, has left a *simran* in your own. An afterimage that can guide you."

Brando's eyes had looked up at them, the first time he'd acknowledge a person in weeks. "Where can I go to hear it?"

"Lower than this," Meji had said. "To the very bottom. The Well, Brando. Let's go to the Well."

There in that darkness, in the disassociative grip of mohiyo, he had shut out the universe and listened to his heart.

Faint but clear, a voice had rung out. Tenshi's simran. Perhaps his spark

"This is your response to our deaths? What good does it do our memory for you

to surrender like this? To let entropy win? Did you learn nothing from me? Didn't

you say that we were your world? Build, Brando. Build. Your self. Your future. Our

people's future. Find your own personal Way, one that uses our murder as a lever to

thrust this world toward justice."

Indignation had begun to build within Brando, fueling his rise from the darkness. Back at home, he had begun a daily ritual of mohiyo consumption and contemplation of Dreschian kongan during deep meditation. He'd broken himself to pieces again and again and again, discarding all the weakness, all the sweetness, all the fumbling and useless intellect, until all that was left was his raging love, the poignant echoes of Tenshi and Tana, and an overpowering hunger for vengeance. For Justice.

With the backing of the people of Kinguyama, for whom Tenshi and Tana had been converted into martyrs who strengthened the town's pro-reform resolve, he'd taken an active part in the investigation of the murders. And when Civil Security could get no results, the leadership of the town successfully petitioned the Archon to transfer the case to the Anti-terrorism Squads.

Despair had threatened to creep back in when the Squads were unsuccessful. Months of investigation into the private security firm responsible for Kinguyama's defense grid had yielded no answers. The grid had been shut down remotely, and though the ATS and CS assumed control of the town's security, neither could affix blame to Meji Pishan's hired gendarmes alone: many people had had access to the equipment and computers, but the leads took the investigation nowhere.

Brando had become convinced that it was the squads' lack of passion that kept them from unraveling the case, and a roaring orange rage had threatened to consume him.

Kongan 133 had come unbidden to his mind. "You seek to puppet others yet you will not pull the strings of your own limbs."

That was when Brando had finally understood. He would have to act. But he'd held back, afraid, unable to embrace the Way his inner Tenshi had signalled.

The message of his spark kept echoing in his memory.

"There's a reason for the pain. Always remember. Your love matters."

Use my love to endure more pain. Yank myself into action. How can I do it? I am willing to shatter and remake myself once more. But I don't have the skills or the knowledge. Who will take me seriously?

But given the alternative, Brando had shaken off his fear.

I'll make you proud, Tenshi. Your life was not in vain.

Brando had begged for a position on the Squads but was rejected because of his complete lack of experience and physical ineptness. He had found it hard to argue with this truth, and it set his resolve to teetering again. Depression had opened wide its maw.

But then the ramatini had sent him a message. A single word.

Come.

HEKIMA UMCHAWI AND THE OTHER CLERICS of the Shattering Way had attended to him during that second bout of despair. He had followed the same routine as Tenshi there on the Distant Isles—fishing, shaping boats, looking within to contemplate his misshapen self. When asked to be part of baharo hija, he had gladly accepted. The ramatini had placed the kiyish in his hand, and he'd wept to feel the old spark that had often shocked him when his ring had touched Tenshi's.

During the two-month sea pilgrimage, Brando had studied the hidden scriptures: the *Kitabu ra-Chiwaga* or *Book of Bricolage* and *Kiyik juya Shari, Blood upon Sand*. In those arcane texts, he'd found passages that sketched a path to drastic transformation.

He had remembered the fair, his speed and his strength, and had accepted the challenge required of him. Then he'd placed a call to Ambarina Lopes. While at first reluctant despite her own indignation at Tenshi's death, she agreed to supply him with the illegal tools he required.

Brando didn't like to think about the rest of that year: leaving Ra-Koreji, cutting himself off from the town and everything he'd come to love, working every day for eighteen hours, enduring agony, shattering his body as well as his self.

But he had remade himself, had become a man of action, had gone beyond through a disturbing metamorphosis.

A grim satori. But the Path became clearer after that basic enlightenment.

This was his Way. His Matapaye ra-Roho, the projection of his broken soul into the illusory world.

A devastating, dangerous, inhuman machine.

He'd discovered a way to survive the nothingness.

At the end of the year, he had visited Pishan. The prefect had been shocked at the transformation. Brando had cut to the chase.

"Put me on the Squads."

Meji had balked. "Brando-shi, what in the Grey Prison have you done to yourself?"

"I have learned the Wende ra-Kobomaga." The Deadly Blue Dance. Meji's face had confirmed they knew what it entailed. "I will avenge them. I will pull Jitsu from their killer's hands."

A shaken Meji had done all they could, but it had been Santo Koroma who'd become Brando's benefactor. Tenshi's uncle had stepped in and demanded of the Archon that he approve the commission. And he had.

Santo, defying all Brando's preconceptions of him, had helped the former professor enter the ATS.

"Find the men that killed her, Brando-shi. She and I never got along, but she was my niece, and I'll see justice done for her at last."

Arojin Koroma had provided him much information and support

throughout the years. But though Alpha Squad successfully beat back many incursions by the demimundo during his first three years, there were no advances in the case. Absolutely none.

Brando tracked down the survivors of Chago Martin's team, five men with a powerful motive to wipe Tenshi from the face of the globe: revenge for the deaths of their seven fellow yaks. He'd tortured them all, pushed them nearly as hard as he'd pushed Felipe today, and he'd had to conclude they'd had nothing to do with it and knew even less. It was as if Tenshi and Tana had been randomly killed by someone who'd then disappeared from the demimundo completely, leaving no trace or informant to bribe.

Then the Kunti had started trying to infiltrate Jitsu as well, and Alpha Squad had found itself frenetically trying to ward off attacks from sides that drew Brando further and further from his purpose.

Worst of all, Tenshi's voice had fallen silent in his mind. He was becoming tired, and oblivion smiled at him temptingly. So, after he'd blackmailed a tech smuggler who supplied the yaks into 'giving' him a great deal of illegal equipment, including the 'frame that managed this faux-life, he'd been visiting this virtual home twice a week for the last four years.

And he'd never forgotten. Never allowed the image of their bloody bodies to fade in his mind. Never permitted the scrawled, incomprehensible message his daughter had written in her own blood to be erased from his memory. *7U*, she had smeared with her little hand across the hardwood floors as her life bled away.

How many databases had he scoured, how many yaks had he interrogated, trying to unravel the mystery? How many times had he stood before Ben, before the major, before Santo Koroma himself to try to justify his continued....

His heart leapt. The pieces moved tantalizingly within his mind, reassembling themselves around the new bits of data. Stifling an urge to shout, Brando turned to his daughter's somatoid.

"Tana, take apa to the living room, okay?"

She grabbed his hand with a smile and skipped inside, pulling him along. He'd discovered long ago he couldn't face it without her by his side. He trembled like a child, and the darkness spun around him menacingly.

"Query. The blood, please," he muttered as they neared the spacious family area.

His grip on Tana's hand tightened as he was met with the ruddy pools, the streaks and splashes on furniture and walls. And there, near the door—the smeared message his daughter had left for him with the last of her strength.

Across the years, her mute voice screamed at him. He had never been able to hear what she wanted so desperately to tell him. But now, Felipe Beserra's hateful words ringing in ears, his mind finally filled in what his daughter's weak hand had been unable to finish.

Not *7U*.

The letter Z.

The letter O.

ZO.

An Italian word.

Zio.

Uncle.

Brando's fists clenched as if he might grind his own bones to dust.

"Santo," he snarled.

It had been Santo all along.

CHAPTER 35

ONCE HE'D GOTTEN RID OF THE ROOKIE, BEN COLLAPSED TO THE floor of his office and began to weep.

How could you be so stupid, Brando? All these years I managed to protect your crazy, reckless arse, risking me and mine. Why? Just so you can go and pull a fucking stunt like this?

Dead. Konrau's brother was dead, and someone was going to have to pay.

Ton of somebodies, but not me.

Ben clutched at his stomach and rushed to the ban. The light breakfast he'd had that morning spewed in an acidic gout into the jan, whose nearly frictionless surface whisked away the evidence of his weakness. He slowly got to his feet, cleaned up and drudged back to his office to make the calls he'd put off for years now.

He could still visualize their first faux interrogation after he'd been captured on the outskirts of Kinguyama: the konsehero's doppelganger with its unreadable visage, the barrage of images over the table between them: his daughter prostituting herself, drugging herself, killing a civ and uploading credits with an illegal dumppad, stealing transports, fraternizing with yegsters and junk heads and yaks.

"Enough."

Konrau's representative in the virtual meeting had reached out and shut off the stream of filth without moving its gaze from Ben's eyes.

"What. Do. You. Want." The soldier's teeth clenched.

"To help you, Captain. I understand how important family is to you. And your reputation, too, of course."

Ben's job had at first appeared simple: pursue the leads fed to him and stifle any independent investigation of Brotherhood activity. Many of the other squads were simply dummy units, but Alpha Squad had to be impervious to outside probes. It had to actually do its job. Ben's responsibility was to make them look good without actually doing serious damage to the syndicate. He suspected that this was what they wanted all along, but that they'd waited five years for sufficient leverage, assigning lousy recruits to him and destroying his squad twice in the interim to ensure his ineffectiveness.

Nestor had explained his situation very succinctly eight years ago during the captain's brief stint as prisoner of the Brotherhood.

"Your little girl Ya-Ting, as we just saw, has some bad habits. Four years of accumulated vice. She likes the bad life, friend, but she doesn't have the sense to manage herself well, so she's indebted her to us in a real awkward way, if you understand me. Instead of our usual reaction—we most times just gat fools like her—we've decided to be generous and cancel her debt. Well, put it to a side for now, anyways. Of course, she's so into the life now that we got her in our sensors at all times, you understand me. We might change our mind, no? You see what I'm saying?"

Typical, unoriginal, and wholly effective.

Ben Wu loved his daughter as all true men do, more than life itself. During his time in the AF, specifically quelling the Neptune Uprising, he'd been separated from her often. When his wife Qing had finally succumbed, sorrow and grief had compelled Ben to accept a post far from Ya-Ting. As he couldn't have been with her often enough to warrant tearing her from her cousins, aunts and uncles, Wu had entrusted her education to his wife's family, especially his sister-in-law, who'd become a kind of surrogate mother for the eight-year-old.

It was his in-laws that he blamed for her slide into corruption. He had no idea how they'd raised her in his absence, but seeing them as responsible for her criminality eased his own sense of guilt at preferring a solitary life to one with a constant reminder of how he couldn't keep his wife alive. Now that he knew the extent of Ya-Ting's ruin, he had no choice but to own up to his part in it and to pay the price.

Ben Wu had sold his soul, just as she had, to the only devils he believed existed. He and all the other squad leaders were either former JLA officers puppeted by Sosa, or utterly compromised, with Damocles' swords of incredible reach and sharpness dangling above their necks. He suspected that Santo Koroma was the author of the anonymous orders that arrived after the Major's. There was nothing to connect the arojin to the Brotherhood, however.

For a time he had hoped that Brando, despite the goose chases that Ben himself engaged the ex-professor in and despite the intermittent distraction of Kunti remnants, would have discovered something, but Kyosu had dropped his wife's suspicions of the Neog leader years ago, after the arojin had distanced himself from the squads, turning them over to the increasingly Dominian-dominated Chamber of Deputies.

Besides, hadn't Santo gotten him on the squads? Hadn't Ben and others worked hard to make Brando trust the old arojin?

Now someone had tampered with the kewbox, and the brother of the most powerful man outside of Solar space was dead. A nagging doubt surfaced in Ben's thoughts, and he called the barracks.

"Put Endo on."

A few seconds of silence.

"What's on, Ben?"

"You get that box out alone, or did you send someone else?"

"You and me, we're the only ones…"

"Yeah, yeah, but you could thumb a keypad for someone else to open it for you, no? That's what it is you did, right?"

"You won't be pissed?"

"Endo, by Domina…"

"Okay, jake. I sent the rookie. I was busy stowing gear, and he'd been sticking to me like a bleeding condom, asking all these questions about Brando and you. Real annoying arselick stuff, you know, so I…"

"How long did he take?"

"Don't know. Had to go to the ban: the squirts, you know how I get. Was there when I came out. Hey, you don't think…"

"Thumbing off, Endo."

Ben tugged on his queue of gray-rimed hair thoughtfully, running the scenario through his mind as he placed another call.

Sosa assigns me the rookie, tells me to hit the yasa the next day. I ask him if Koroma approves because I know Felipe's holed up there. He says yes, sends me in anyways. Jing has the box for a good long while, more than enough to mess with it. Brando's out-the-lock kew techniques are famous planet-wide. Set up. Must be.

His encrypted call to the major suddenly went through, and Ben shook off his thoughts to concentrate on the moment.

"Report." Major Sosa's aged voice still commanded respect and no small measure of fear, especially from those who understood what he was capable of.

"I'll cut straight to it. D'Angelo kewed Beserra's brother, found out something about their connection to the government and his wife's death. He killed the man during the kew session."

"He what?" The ancient warrior appeared on the verge of apoplexy.

"Apparent tampering with the kewbox shut down the fail-safes. What I do, Major?"

"Shiperaro zo! Wait!" Major Sosa's purpled face abruptly disappeared.

Not in the know! More twists.

Ben waited. Sweat pooled in the small of his back, prickled his armpits. Two minutes. Five.

I'm right? Find out soon.

Sosa's face jutted up from the comtable again.

"Listen to me close. Take every man you got. Converge on his house. Eliminate him."

"Huh? How can I? How will you justify that to Archon Rawe?"

"Archon Rawe died three hours ago, Captain. They're swearing Koroma in right now. The Oracle attested to his quantum enlightenment. Time to close this mother up, got it?"

Ben nodded. "You realize it's gonna take me a good thirty minutes to round the boyos up and equip them. Most of them are already headed home. Brando lives near Kinguyama, about an hour away."

"I suggest that you get moving, then, Captain. He's not there, you converge with Beta, Gamma and Delta outside Station City. Bastard has to go there. That's where his contacts are. That's where the Brotherhood's based. You go in and get him, if you ain't finished him off before that. Then you start the evacuation of every non-Jitsujin in that city to the platforms with military transports."

Shite. Brando, you unlucky sumbitch. Santo's cycling you out the lock. Looks like he gots his own game now. Still a way to save me and mine, though.

"One more thing." Ben blinked in confusion. The major hadn't thumbed off. "I want you to send over Jing Wong with that New Beijing yak your report says Brando stuck a knife in."

"Well, fine, but you want me to wait for the kid, or..."

"No, you leave now, no delay. I can tell Wong to rendezvous with yall at the city. Thumbing off."

Clarity. Wong was a plant; so was the yak. Ben was willing to bet a sizeable portion of his measly salary that Santo was going to use them to strike at the heart of the Brotherhood. Suddenly, Ben's hand was strengthened.

Show them my loyalty, feed them this info, I might make it out in one piece, with Ya-Ting still alive. Then I'll leave this fucking glebe and get her back.

Quickly, he began coding a message for Nestor. Once he'd sent it tunneling into subspace, he called the barracks again and ordered all hands to the transports, geared and ready to clash.

INTERCHAPTER G

From: hark@chinwag.pub.nbj

To: nb1@tunnelizer.pub.ort

Subject: update

Date: May 5, 2697 10:03:19 (SST)

Decrypted 10:12:57 via FAE

The old man said I should tunnel you a message to this address if anything happens. Well, the ATS raided our desert HQ. Your boss's brother's dead. That one that they call Kyosu killed him during interrogation. The Archon's dead, and Santo just took over. He started evacuating people, so you best call your boyos out. I was wounded and I'm in custody, but I got my connections (that's why you're reading this message). I'm gonna get out fast and get up to Nawabari. Full report then.

Wong Hark

From: <u>wuben@ats.gov.jit</u>

To: <u>nb1@tunnelizer.pub.ort</u>

Subject: Caution

Date: May 5, 2697 11:53:49 (SST)

Decrypted 17:25:38 via FAE

Nestor, we got big problems.

Koroma arrowed us against Felipe. That arse-rooter Jing tampered with the kew-box, it seems, and Brando pushed Felipe too hard in the interrogation. Fail-safes never kicked in, so Felipe died. Beware: Jing and this New Beijing lad on Felipe's squad are working for Santo, who's now taken over as archon because Rawe's dead. Don't trust them. I think Santo is planning for them to strike against you.

As for Brando, Sosa is sending us after him. I hope we can catch him in time, because he pretty much figured ever thing out, and he'll be gunning for yall. Tell your boyos to keep their eyes wide.

I'll report to this address any new stuff that comes up.

Ben

CHAPTER 36

IT WAS NESTOR'S SEVENTIETH BIRTHDAY, BUT HE ALMOST FORGOT.

Men like Konrau and me don't celebrate birthdays. Every day might be our last.

The aging advisor regarded his leader with a bittersweet mixture of fatherly affection and genuine disgust. Konrau was like the son he'd never had, had never *dared* to have. The Bos men were destined for horrible deaths: Nestor's father, Omero, had been beaten to death by cops on Mars; his grandfather, Baldemar, had similarly died at the hands of prefecture police; and his great-grandfather, Mateo, the first of the Bos clan to turn his back on the CPCC and join the Brotherhood, had fallen prey to the Pope-worshipping Aztlan Angels.

No more, Nestor had often thought. *I'm the last Bos.*

But while the gangly yegster had chosen not to bring a young squink into the universe to carry the Bos name, he did look at Konrau with fatherly affection.

Theirs was a nearly familial bond: after Ria had died, Konrau had insisted that Marisela Bos, Nestor's mother, stay with the kasike's own mother and cousins in the enormous house he'd built for them on Oceania, near the Arrambide fortress. There she'd lived the last two decades of her life, dying peacefully only a few months before, her funeral a glorious homage planned by the kasike himself.

Yes, Nestor owed Konrau much, and his life had been dedicated to repaying this debt of gratitude. For twenty-two years he'd served as Beserra's counselor, his advice molding the present and future of the syndicate as a long line of konseheros' words had done before him. He was also a reluctant but hopeful partner in Beserra's plan to wrest control over humanity from governments and other syndicates, to rule human space as dictator.

The difficulty had always lain in the need to keep the families of the Brotherhood in line, as they viewed Konrau as their hired protector: boss of bosses, but not their monarch. And the Kunti-CPCC war had set them against Konrau's aggressive policies, his machinations on Jitsu and elsewhere.

The war had strengthened the AF and swung voters toward military expansionists. Jetsun Muntso's ascension to the post of prime minister had sent Konrau into a screaming, frothing fit after which he'd been in a coma for an entire week. The kabesitas' qualms were not calmed even when other syndicates ceased criminal activity within the Consortium. They wanted a change in Konrau's policies, immediately.

So Konrau had punked each of them.

Cleverly, quietly and quickly, the kasike had abducted the children or grandchildren of many of the heads, holding them as "guests" at the Arrambide family fortress. Using Nestor's considerable insider information, he'd been able to blackmail the rest, so that soon every family was essentially in Konrau's thrall.

Afterward, despite the increasing power of the Flotilla and the Army, Beserra had continued with his steady move toward greater power, though Nestor sensed that there was a hidden element to the kasike's plan that he'd not been able to ferret out, despite even Yen Bandera's far-seeing eye on his side. Nestor's personal opinion was that the syndicate was now too unwieldy, what with the steady creation of new demimundo infrastructure on a dozen or more new worlds, but Konrau gloried in its expansiveness.

Jitsu was the thorn in his side. Nestor'd always told him so. Over the past thirteen years, it had served as a testing ground for their later, more refined techniques of conquest on other worlds, but the multitude of gaffs, tragedies and foot-dragging on the part of their associates on the ugly planet made the syndicate's meager profit from the enterprise, most of which was still uncollected, utterly insufficient.

Yes, conquering Jitsu and the entire Eta Cassiopeiae system would be a symbolic gesture: the once center of the AF's stranglehold on commercial and personal travel through space would now be the cornerstone of a new *aetherocracy*, as Konrau fancied such control over the void. Santo's ridiculous plan was taking too damn long, though, risking their exposure to the CPCC and costing too many lives.

The worst of it was that Beserra had sent his little brother to take charge of the Jitsu operation eight years ago, once again ignoring the advice Nestor'd given him, though the counselor had recently installed a pair of New Beijinger eyes, kindly dredged up by Yen Bandera, to keep watch over Felipe.

Konrau had been so impressed with his half-brother's successful assassination of Kinguyama's mayor that he had slowly given him more and more autonomy in running the infiltration, heedless of his personality flaws. Felipe was too unstable, not a well proven enough leader to handle the responsibility, too prone to jump into the fray rather than to simply shout orders from the camp. And Jitsu was a dangerous world: fifty-nine true brothers dead so far, most at the hands of Alpha Squad, despite Nestor's control of its captain.

Bandera had recruited a large number of more expendable decoy sikaritos for Nestor, but it still galled him for useful men to be wasted. Konrau, on the other hand, had always viewed these losses as acceptable and necessary for making the inhabitants of that planet believe the Brotherhood was actually being combated. The fact that he was planning a double cross of the planet's government made the deaths almost sweet: they served to keep both the public and the politicians who conspired against them complacent.

Now his plan was backfiring. Minutes ago the news had come.

Felipe was dead. The archon was dead. The planet was in turmoil.

Except for Felipe's death, these events had been planned. But not for this year. Ten more cycles of forty days were supposed to go by before the final evacuation of non-Neogs from the planet and the transfer of the CPCC-leased worlds around Kobito to syndicate control—*after* another prime minister had been sworn in and the change of government had the pinche Consortium slightly off-balance.

Nestor struggled to get his mind around the new developments: those on the Jitsu end of the conspiracy knew Konrau well enough to understand that his brother's death would bring swift action.

Tremors of understanding.

They want to preempt us. Make us do something sudden, draw the AF onto our arses. While we're bashing at each other, Santo takes the whole system. Hoputa!

"Tell them to prep the ship."

Nestor's head jerked back around toward his boss. "What, the *Echos Maje*?"

"Yes. We're gonna go to Jitsu. Tell them to get Ernesto to serve as swain. Only him."

"But," Nestor balked, "shite, Konrau, it'd take us days to get there."

Konrau looked at him oddly, his gaze distant, then motioned for Nestor to follow as he set off toward the sled that shuttled them around inside the planetoid that served as Brotherhood HQ. The kasike had remained calm ever since receiving the news, quickly giving orders in a measured voice that betrayed no bereavement at his half-brother's death, and now his movements were precise and nearly mechanical.

Nestor shuddered at the thought of the rage that boiled beneath that flat expression, knowing full well that when it was released it would obliterate all in its path. It would be better not to let Konrau discover the mole, especially since the punk had failed to keep Felipe alive and had been captured by Alpha Squad.

Damn Bandera, anyways. How come I keep trusting him?

Of course, he'd had to tell Konrau that the news of Felipe's death had come from Wu and not the New Beijingers. He wondered what was keeping the older soldier's message—was there betrayal coming from that front, too?

They climbed inside the sled, and Konrau ordered it to the docking berths while Nestor swallowed his impatience at his boss's not being very forthcoming about the details of their upcoming trip. As the two of them hurtled along corridors that twisted madly in many directions, Konrau spoke, his voice flat and dead.

"We have an imrizabu right at the edge of the system, Nestor. I never told you about it. Just me and the heads know, plus Ernesto Mendosa and the rest of the crew of the ship that discovered it."

The news twisted like a knife in his gut. "A hyperspace vein? Like the one the AF found between Tau-Ceti and Sirius? Shite, Konrau! What does it open onto?"

So that's the secret. That's the hidden thing I been sensing. He felt betrayed. Punked in the arse by his bezzy mate a second time. *You can't never trust them. Power goes to their fucking heads.*

"Onto the Nereus system."

"Sweet Fidensio! You could fucking spill ships right into the heart of the Consortium without warning. And you *sat on this*?"

Konrau reached over and grabbed his konsehero's black jacket in a fluid, violent motion, yanking him close. "Don't you fucking act shocked, Nestor. I put the Brotherhood before your feelings and your ideas of how shite should be. I've got my reasons, and the heads are with me on it. Komprennite?"

"Si, komprenni." Nestor's heart was beating like it hadn't in years. In a devastating moment of clarity, he realized that Konrau had probably been right to hide this from him.

I nearly compromised it all, fucking trusting Bandera. Fuck me.

There was silence between them as they reached the berthed junk and boarded her through a narthex. Konrau saw Ernesto, an aging sikaryo with a pinched face, in the principal corridor and waved him over.

"Nestor, go prep our pods. I'll be right there."

As the older man walked away, he heard his boss begin to explain. "We're going down the vein, then fenestrating like a madhatter into Jitsu's system. How long do you think…"

Their voices faded as he rounded a corner and took a lift to the executive quarters. Nestor berated himself in a low, rough voice. "Stupid fucking old man. When did he start doubting you, eh? Was he reading your messages all this time? Does he know about your little sneaky shite? Fuck."

He muttered curses at himself throughout the prepping of the hypostasis pods, beginning to see himself as the one to blame for Konrau's distrust, promising himself he'd regain the kasike's confidence, somehow.

After about fifteen minutes, Konrau walked into the room, his eyes dull with a thirst for vengeance. He briefly sketched what the trip entailed, and then he motioned brusquely at the pods.

Nestor stripped his clothes off and stowed them in a locker as Konrau looked their suspension pods over, making certain the suspensor gel had filled them sufficiently and was of the proper density. Everyone onboard the syndicate's fastest junk, *Echos Maje*, would have to spend the entire seven-hour trip in hypostasis, controlling the ship through a virtual bridge as the swain and the computer performed an incredible feat, one that still had Nestor's mind reeling.

A trip through an imrizabu, followed by a series of highly dangerous extended fenestrations that violated the Consortium's regulations on the duration and spacing of holing events. The suspensor gel Konrau was examining had been specially designed to cushion travelers' bodies against the wrenching gravity of accel and decel, and it was especially necessary on an urgent and potentially deadly trip like the one the kasike, his counselor and twenty of their most trusted foot soldiers were about to embark on.

Konrau straightened, turned to face his counselor, and began to undress. "Tell me more about this D'Angelo."

Nestor snapped out of his reverie, eager to be useful. "Before joining

Alpha Squad, he was a professor. Guy that we had his wife and kid killed, remember? About eight years back, at Santo's request."

Konrau swallowed as if in pain. "Of course. The job Felipe volunteered for so it would get done right. So this is about revenge. This Brando's wife: architect killed Chago's men, ain't it?"

"Right. Anyways, he's still alive because Santo always said he's too popular to eliminate, and most times he was off on nowhere tangents I feeded to Wu. Killed a bunch of the suicide crews we sent in. Busted up some of our legit guys, too. Nailed Tripó Lameda's group all the way: Chore Yakima's still in a coma; don't know if you remember, but we pulled the other brothers off the southern continent quick."

"He ripped us off, too, ain't it?"

"Yeah. Had a little smuggler of ours in his pocket for a while, scraped up some medical equipment plus a fast little sub-light ranfla. Seems he was retrofitting it for holing, because he acquired a first-generation Lieske fenestration drive, too. Wu never found out where any of it was."

"What he was doing interrogating Felipe? No one told that wankstain Wu not to let the egghead near him? Matter of fact, what was Alpha Squad doing at the warehouse anyways? You didn't tell Wu to stay away, or what?"

"Of course I did. Minute they told me Felipe was going to be on the surface, I sent specific orders to the arojin that the squad shouldn't—oh, bendita maje Mariya."

Layer upon bleeding layer. Arse-punking upon arse-punking.

Nestor's sagging flesh prickled and his stomach flopped. His boss slammed shut the locker he'd just dumped his clothes into and punched it as it cycled and locked.

"Santo set it up," the kasike growled. "Bastard! Thinks he'll elbow us off Jitsu."

Illuminating aftershocks continued to shake understanding into Nestor's mind: why Brando hadn't been assassinated, why he'd been allowed to live and thrive in the squads.

"Worse than that. We're gonna walk into a trap. Santo's manipulated everything to send that crazy dirt bunny against us, and on top of that…"

Konrau interrupted with a forced snort. "Whatever. The *Matō* and the *Maliyas* will rendezvous with us at the platforms. Couple shuttles coming up from Jitsu with several crews. Lot of men, Nestor. The fuck can one guy do against couple hundred little brothers? Santo has shite for brains. We'll grab the platforms, kap this D'Angelo fucker and ram his cold corpse right up Archon Koroma's arse."

Nestor continued his previous point. "What about the AF? There's a couple of ships in route right now to try to get Santo to stop quarantining off-worlders. We really want to butt heads with them right now? Don't you think drawing us into the open is part of Santo's ploy?"

"Screw the AF. About time we showed those bastards who is boss. They fuck with us, I'll make them eat a couple antimatter rockets. Besides, we'll exit the vein close enough to Jitsu to arrive in about six, seven hours: quick accel, hole five quick times, decel like a hoputa, and we're there. We got the highest tolerance gel, fastest drives, let's put them to use. Preempt everybody's arse, be the ones running the show. I got a thousand ships, Nestor, waiting for crews that they have already been trained."

Nestor's lips moved silently. A thousand ships

"All this blackmail and so fucking forth? It's been about that. Getting the kabesas to live up to their end of a bargain you weren't aware of. Creating an army to conquer Nereus. So, Konsehero, let's just throw the fucking gauntlet down, what say?"

Wonder fluttering in his chest, Nestor nodded and quickly turned to a console to transmit encoded messages to the other two ships. He had urged such balls-out measures many times over the years.

Still, as he eased his gaunt form into the suspension pod, as the pink beams began to dance across his face, connecting him to the virtual bridge, he couldn't help but wonder whether this time Konrau's vengeful brashness might be both their undoing. The time just didn't seem right. Their enemies were too strong. Openly attacking the Consortium's armed forces could put the kasike's long years of clandestine work at risk.

The old mafioso said a silent prayer to the Blessed Child before being whisked onto the virtual bridge.

Give us strength and wisdom, Fidensito, and victory. Over all, give us honor.

CHAPTER 37

HOW COULD I HAVE BEEN SO BLIND? AFTER ALL HE DID TO TENSHI AND SAMANEI—I still fell for his lies. Why?

The answer was easy. He'd needed to get on the squads, and his dead wife's uncle had made it happen. Santo had also turned over all his files to Brando when he gave up control of the squads. The arojin had even supported Brando's investigations, both financially and morally, when others in the government had begun to question his methods and obsession.

"Stop at nothing," Santo had urged. "Catch the scum who killed her. Eliminate them. I will deal with the fallout."

The doubts Brando still harbored began to fade as Santo had dialogued with reformers, showing repentance for his previous hard-line stance. When the Chamber of Deputies absolved the arojin of complicity in the Brotherhood attacks, the new squadman had instead focused his energy on finding the yaks who'd survived the attack on Kinguyama.

Santo and he had gotten along well enough afterward, discussing whatever leads that Brando felt the older Pathwalker might have insight into. A grudging respect had begun to grow between them, at least until Santo's appointment as Minister of Immigration and his ghettoization order. There'd been a nasty argument at that, and Brando had stomped out of Santo's new office, punching holes in the walls as Santo called off the security officers with a sly smile. The doubts had resurfaced then, though at the very edge of his consciousness.

Why? Because it was easy. He played me like a master does a guitar, plucking at my gut strings, his fingers tight around my neck. Mothergod, I was so naïve. What would Tenshi say? Fuck it. No time for regrets. Just for revenge.

Brando knew what she would say. Her simran was already murmuring in his mind.

You weren't willing to accept it. Deep down, you knew he was the responsible one, but killing him with no evidence would've meant making him a martyr. He would've won that way, and you would've been made an example of. Better to keep your doubts deep within you and pretend not to believe what you did believe.

"Time for pretending is over," he muttered as he stamped through the house. Stripped to his jock, Brando packed. Four konk rifles. A variable projectile chrome. A pair of lazgats. Twenty-five tubes of plaz. A highly illegal light fusion canon. A dozen grenades.

The comtable chimed.

Turning, he thumbed it on. Santo Koroma's head and shoulders oozed upward from the glass projection screen.

"Soburi."

Still has the gall to call me nephew. Brando wasted no time.

"I know about it."

"What is this *it*, Brando-shi?"

"Everthing. You. Beserra. Tenshi. Tana."

No expression. Guilty.

"I don't know what you think you know, but let me tell you, it's probably not as close to the truth as you may want to think."

"I know you're responsible for their deaths, and that means I'll be responsible for yours."

"That's ironic, considering I called to warn you."

"Warn me about what? I'll be sure to do the opposite, you treacherous, naffing…"

"Captain Wu and your friends are on their way right now to your dwelling, with orders to eliminate you. I know this because I gave the order. You can ignore me, if you prefer, or you can get as far away from there as you can, now. Your choice, soburi."

"Oh, I'll leave, alright. And you'll see me soon, no matter if you try and hide in the deepest cave of the southern continent. I'm coming for you, Santo. I'm coming to exact payment for the evil you've done. I'm coming to be sure you scream until the very last, and I'll blow your fucking head to little bits of nothing so won't be translated, not that you ever would, you twisted piece of darkness."

He slammed his hand against the *terminate* square.

No time to unravel this particular mystery. Stick to what I know: Beserra and Koroma, coconspirators. Murderers of wife and daughter. Deserving of death. Details be damned.

As he crossed the room to his wardrobe, he caught a glimpse of himself in a cracked mirror: corded, knotty, hairy bulk, veins interlaced with myriad scars, rib cage mottled with bruises. Heavy lidded eyes. Salt and pepper stubble covering head and jaw. Drawn, macabre features from multiple head blows, extreme diet and little sleep.

Monstrous, that's what he had become. Twice his original mass. Three times the typical girth of a space-born human or Jitsujin. Children shied from him on the rare occasions that he ventured out in public.

He didn't care. He wanted one thing, and he was going to get it at long last.

The wardrobe irised open, and he yanked out a uniform, sliding into its semi-stiff flexibility. Without the suit, he felt wrong; when he pulled it on, it was as if the Blue itself had curled around him, cushioning and protecting him from the black that lay scant centimeters away at every breath. He strapped on his belt and holster, scooped up the bag he'd packed and headed for the rooftop tarmac, where he activated the com system on Tenshi's transport, just in case he needed its deadly modifications, and boarded the boxy black hulk he'd borrowed from the ATS.

As he sped away, he passed a convoy of military transports presumably heading toward his house. For a few seconds they continued on their way, but suddenly one of them whipped around and gave chase. The others took longer to react, but in seconds all seven vehicles were bearing down on him like a pack of oni after a wounded jagen. The image made him give an ironic laugh.

"I'm not the jagen, mates. I follow the Oni Way."

He called up his personal comcode on the transport's system.

"Wake Tenshi."

Feeding in the frequency of the ATS vehicle he'd borrowed so he could be tracked, he yanked the manual piloting system down from its ceiling compartment, activated the pulsing pink interface, and took the controls into his hands. His perspective shifted completely: he was now flashing over the barren rubble at the desert's edge, his vision not limited by physical restraints.

"Rear."

The convoy was whistling toward him at several hundred klicks per hour.

"Fore."

Beginning to jut above the horizon before him was a series of auxiliary water tanks, heavily armored to ensure their integrity in times of severe drought.

"Connect to captain's transport."

A soft gurgle.

"Brando?"

"It's me, Ben. What yall boys are doing, tell?"

"Come on, Brando. Should be obvious. We've got to take you in."

"Just take me in, huh. Not eliminate me, say, on Koroma's orders?"

"Well, Koroma's the archon now, mate. Not a damn lot anybody can do about that. But the answer's no. Just have to bring you before the major, is all."

Archon? Oh, mothergod. He didn't just play me for a fool. He fucked us all.

"Then why the seven transports? Everyone came to get me? I'm that dangerous?"

"We just had a feeling you might not be, uh, amenable to the idea. You've got a reputation, and we know it's been watered down. Figured you'd be kind of hard-headed about things."

"You're not wrong."

"Listen, mate. You figured right. I'm compromised. But I promise you, you turn yourself in, I'll do everything I can to make sure you'll be okay."

"You'll forgive me if I don't believe a damn word you say. Anybody'd betray everything they're supposed to stand for doesn't deserve my respect and confidence. So, tell you what, yall fuck off to the chinga, and I'll be on my way."

The tanks were looming just a dozen klicks away now: monstrous relics of Soltec's dominance of the world.

"Brando. Don't do this, please."

"Damn. Never heard you beg before. Must be some big thing they got on you, make you endure such humiliation. What say we chat about it, mate? You, me, the squad: we can work it out, whatever it is."

"Nah. I'm too compromised for that. You want to help me, you need to turn yourself over to us."

"Well, I guess that's a mutual *fuck you*, no? Come and get me, if yall can, lousy fucking john-hops!"

He shut off the com channel. A sense of uneasiness and doubt welled up from deep within him. He'd worked with these men for years, after all. They were, if not his friends, at least deserving of his respect. Shaking off horror at what he was about to do, he shoved those thoughts back into the darkness of his mind. All that mattered was survival. And vengeance.

"Accel to four hundred klicks."

The tanks rushed at him. Warning bells went off, messages flashed at the periphery of his sight. He ignored them. Trying to imagine his squad's reaction, he risked a glance back. They'd begun fanning out: only two were directly on his tail; the others had begun to chart a path around three sides of the tanks, anticipating what they imagined to be his strategy: turn off at the last minute and send them careening into the tanks.

He had never been predictable, however.

Disappointing that they so easily underestimated me.

One of the transports behind him and the one above began to strafe him with a volley of blast fire, which his plating sent stramming off in weakened waves. He had to roll twice as the transports that had pulled ahead of him sent a pair of small fission rockets racing backwards in his direction. Any compunction he might still have felt about destroying them to protect himself evaporated as his vehicle shuddered and groaned under the sustained attack. Another minute and a half more of this and the hull would be breached.

By Sopiya's sparks, let her arrive soon.

A spinning icon blocked his view of the tanks momentarily: Tenshi's vehicle was nearly in range. A sudden, thunderous sonic boom: his cue.

Manually braking to a fourth his speed at a klick away, Brando spun the car ninety degrees and headed toward the desert.

"Antimatter bomb in 3-2-1."

The heavily modified transport that had been his late wife's pride and joy screamed maniacally as it plunged on autopilot from the clouds at stomach-wrenching speeds and scaled a black and silver oval at the tanks just as the seven transports swerved to continue their pursuit.

"Accel to supersonic."

Brando was slammed backward against the seat as the transport blew gouts of sand hundreds of feet into the air in its dizzying rush into the desert. The bomb was triggered almost at the same time, creating a short-lived ball of chaos that managed to take out the tanks, five of the transports, Tenshi's vehicle, and a huge crater of earth as the blast surged outward spherically. The shockwave followed close on D'Angelo's tail as he sped a mere ten meters off the desert floor. When he was certain he'd avoided it, he whipped the transport around, nearly being ripped from his seat by the gees the maneuver generated, only his suit protecting him from the bodily damage of such stress.

Wheeling toward him from the clouds came the last two transports. He throttled down to a stop and hovered patiently, targeting first one, then the other. They were counting on his not being able to deal with both of them at once.

"Lock on farther target. Go to automatic. Fire salvo of missiles and blasts in ten seconds."

As he released the controls, his awareness was yanked back into the cabin. Quickly unsealing his bag and withdrawing the fusion canon, Brando popped the ceiling exit and hauled himself up onto the scalding roof of the transport. Hefting the canon to his shoulder, he took aim at the closer vehicle and fired.

The combination of his lack of leverage, the transport's release of the ordered barrage and the other squadmen's strafing of his vehicle sent him flipping backward through the air some half dozen meters. Rolling as he landed, he came up into a crouch and fired again at the general direction of the attacking squad. Both transports went hurtling toward the sand and ploughed into it with a force that knocked D'Angelo prone.

He pushed himself to his feet and sprinted to the nearest wreck. Its mangled form suggested no survivors. The other was more intact, and indeed he heard scrabbling from within. He had just strapped the canon to his back and palmed a chrome when a section of the bulkhead exploded outward and Ben

Wu leapt out, lazgats in both hands, firing like a maniac as Brando bounded into the air to avoid being hit.

Ben smashed into the sand and trundled over, blasting at the sky where he expected Brando to be, but the ex-professor, anticipating this move, had twisted as he jumped in order to land at Ben's left side. As he did, he kicked one of the pistols from his captain's hands and collapsed to one knee beside him, chrome's barrel butting up against the older soldier's temple.

"Don't think about it, mate. You managed to save your scranky arse thus far, but we know who's better hand-to-hand. You got the fancy moves, but I'd nail you so fast you wouldn't even be able to use Domina's name in vain."

Ben seemed to weigh his options; then he let the gat fall to the sand. D'Angelo didn't bother to reach across him to grab it: a stupid rookie move, that.

"Get up."

Once on his feet, Ben regarded his protégé with watery eyes.

"What have you done, Brando? Thirty-nine men, your mates, like that. And with an antimatter bomb… that's a capital offense."

For a moment, the faces of the men on the squad flashed before him: Endo, Diken, Chua and the others. Hard men, yes, even amoral, but his fellows nonetheless. The enormity of what he'd just done twisted his gut with icy stabs of black, like some virulent strain of bacteria gnawing at his innards.

It's an illusion, he told himself. *Wooden men. Sparkless.*

The mantra didn't help much.

"I did what you forced me to do. You know what's at stake and who the players are. I couldn't let you capture me, and I've got stuff to do before I die." Gesturing tiredly at the transport, he added, "Besides, they're not all dead. I'm sure some of the boyos in your ride survived."

Ben rubbed his left eye.

"Guess you weren't shitting when you said you'd put anybody at risk, Kyosu. What will you do with me and the others on board?"

"Just leave yall here. Start walking now, yall should arrive at Station City just in time to clean up the bodies."

He motioned Ben to step back as he bent to collect the other pistol.

"What's your plan? I'm not saying shite, swear. We were mates once."

Brando looked away for a second, the slightest twinge of regret flashing in his guts.

"Yeah, we were. I'm going to eliminate them."

"Who?"

"All of them. You know who."

Ben looked almost hopeful.

"Do me a favor? Take out Nestor Bos. It's her only hope."

"Whose?"

"My daughter. She's in their sensors, you know what I mean."

"Damn, Ben. That's how they got you, right?"

"Yeah, and I feel like shite, but... she means everything to me, Brando. You can understand that, how everything else just kind of fades to naught. A father has no choice, right?"

The squad leader gestured expansively at the wreckage around them. A sudden flash: the image of Tana and Tenshi's smiling faces nearly made D'Angelo double over in pain. He grimaced instead.

"No. Guess he doesn't. Still leaving you here. For that exact reason. Good luck, Ben. I doubt we'll ever see each other again."

Brando vaulted onto the roof of his still-hovering vehicle and dropped inside.

As he sped away, he watched Ben limp toward the crashed transport, growing smaller and fading from sight as both men moved toward uncertain destinies.

CHAPTER 38

SANTO'S FIRST ACTION AS ARCHON WAS TO RELEASE SAMANEI from the cryogenic hypostasis Rawe had placed her in fourteen years ago. Santo recalled their exchange at the end of that first virtual meeting, when she'd revealed her reasons for cutting herself off from him physically.

"And you'll stand by my side," Santo had whispered, "when I evacuate the off-worlders?"

"Of course, Santo. That is the only way anyone will ever permit it."

Four hours ago, he'd watched as omedeyo attendants pulled her meager form from the blue gel of the cryogenic hypostasis chamber, wiping the gunk that clung to her flesh with abject reverence: the Close had not touched the skin of theophany in many years. Perhaps they suffered a hunger similar to his own.

Work had tempered his needs. His machinations within the theocracy, his crafting of a decoy personality for himself, his careful creation of crises.

Older and wiser, he had met with the Oracle less frequently over the years.

She had spent most of her time connected to the interstellar net, coordinating her plans with Yen Bandera and their other contacts, forcing Konrau Beserra's back against the wall so the syndicate cacique would have no choice but to engage the CPCCAF.

During the intervening time, Santo had noticed a change in her dealings with him. Rather than berate him, she spoke softly and listened to their plan's progress, as if quietly biding her time. He recognized that he would need her, now and perhaps for several years more. But as the attendants had cleaned her emaciated body, a terrible desire to rid himself of her had seized him, as if some kernel of his being rejected her divinity.

Now, recalling how she'd foreseen today's events, the archon begged the Eight to forgive him for *ever* doubting the theophany.

Before arriving at the jinja to witness the Close's ritualized ministrations, he'd installed himself in the archon's suites. He had just begun reorganizing the staff and adding his own people when he'd received a com from the Major: Brando, doing just as the Oracle had said he would.

Santo had acted as appalled as his joy permitted him, ordering the capture of his dead niece's widower. Then he'd called the ex-professor to warn him. As Samanei had predicted, Felipe Beserra, that unbalanced braggart of a man, had obviously revealed the conspiracy and the details surrounding Tenshi's death.

Perfect. Once Brando is captured, he'll be shipped on an auto-piloted transport full of weapons to the Brotherhood's local orbital base.

Santo hoped he'd wreak as much havoc there as he had on the surface. If for some reason he couldn't be captured, however, Samanei had a back-up plan: the brothers from New Beijing.

Not long after these coms, the Chamber of Deputies had convened and via faux-conference had received and approved the Oracle's selection of Santo Koroma as the new archon. His first order was the evacuation of all off-worlders to the Rasaro platform, and the demolition of the CPCC embassy, which he cited as a hotbed of terrorist conspirators. The chamber, despite a public outcry against the extreme measures, had backed the archon's decision.

Now that the Close had fed and dressed Samanei in her deceased sister's clothing— only lightly sketching the four double rhombuses of the Marummo on her forehead, cheeks and chin—the attendants brought her to Santo's auxiliary office in the jinja complex.

On their heels came Warden Hoya Okubiri, head of the Karibudan guild.

Samanei addressed Archon and Warden both, her voice rough, her gestures weak.

"I need the Close to leave this place," the Oracle. "Half of my attendants should travel to Kinguyama to prepare my new residence in the teyopan. The other half need to head to the Southern Continent. I want them to purge Jinja ra-Shamanga. Round up the apostates."

"Orakuru-zin," Okubiri put in, their face full of shock and concern, "you will be left defenseless."

"No one will attack this place," Samanei assured her, "and the Archon's squads can always intervene. If it makes you less anxious, Warden, stay behind with a handful of your best guards."

The Warden bowed their head and hurried off to comply.

"My aids have just finished setting up the emergency transmitter," Santo told Samanei. "It can override the feeds of local infotainment providers."

With muscles only barely saved from atrophy by years of monthly nanodoc injections, Samanei jerked her head in his direction and spoke in Dresch's voice.

"So it's time, is it?"

"Yes, Founder. It is."

"What about the surgery? You promised to return this girl's body to a semblance of normality."

"Of course. But first I need you to address Jitsu, as you promised you would."

"Yes, fine. After that, though, the rest is up to you."

The desk's com chimed. It was Colonel Sumura of Civil Security.

"Archon-zin. There's been a massive explosion in Mashkanu, near the desert's edge. While investigating, we discovered that Alpha Squad has been destroyed, all men dead except for seven, including the captain. We've detained him for questioning."

"Keep Wu in a cell and the others under observation in the infirmary. I'll get back to you later on what to do."

Santo turned toward the Oracle. "Something you didn't quite foresee."

"True, but it proves he's determined to do what we need him to, and it helps us paint a dark picture of the situation. He may even go against Konrau on his own. In any event, Jing and Hark are heading to Nawabari soon, and they can always do the job alone. Come. Let's get started right away. Time's running out."

Santo activated the transmitter as Samanei rounded the table to stand beside him. She smelled faintly of soap and rot. When the connection with all info terminals on Jitsu was made, she suddenly leaned forward upon fingers splayed widely on the tabletop, an eerily Tenshi-like movement.

As she spoke, Santo's stomach went sour: the friendly but firm intonation, the word choice, the tossing of her shaved skull—every movement the Oracle made and every word she spoke seemed to come directly from her twin. For the first time in many years, doubt pricked at him.

Is this Tenshi, talking from beyond? Could she have been translated? I can't stand the idea. Must be Samanei, pretending to be her. But if Samanei can so expertly dissemble, she might be able to—no, impossible. Some things she could not know. Anyway, who's to say the Ogdoad can't evoke the incipient soul of any being? Maybe I'm being tested.

"First message," Samanei smiled Tenshi's easy smile, "is for my people. Fellow Jitsujin, your Oracle addresses you as a sister, as a loving, translated sister who seeks to guide you to enlightenment. We are faced with a crisis: the criminal off-worlder presence on this planet has wounded us with another tragedy. Alpha Squad has been obliterated, every member murdered." An interesting lie. "Our shield against terrorism and the mob has been irreparably compromised. We must act now, decisively. The other three squads at this moment are converging on Station City to begin the evacuation of all non-Jitsujin to the orbital platforms until the demimundan elements can be eradicated. Those willing to wait out what could be a lengthy process will be welcomed back to Jitsu. I urge all brothers and sisters to support their Archon and Oracle in this critical time. Our goal is not to close our doors to the outside world, but to make our world safe for those who would make it their home."

Samanei switched to Standard and cocked her head a bit. "To our non-Pathwalker friends, I say forgive us. Yall won't like the process of evacuation we must force on yall, but please understand that it's for yall's protection and ours. More than fourteen years now, the Demimundo has been jabbing at us, ripping away everything we love, shredding our social fabric. We must act. We must move yall to the platforms till we find them and stamp out the plague they represent. They've destroyed our strongest defense, Alpha Squad. Either we do this now, or we hand the planet to them, docile and conquered. We won't give in. We beg yall: help us. Don't resist. As soon as this ordeal's over, yall can come back, and we'll live together without fear, like we once did.

"The Oracle thanks yall. Be enlightened."

Santo spoke then, explaining the evacuation procedure and informing the population of Station City of the various pick-up locations. With a final exhortation for the support of all, he terminated the transmission.

Samanei immediately slumped, enervated and impatient, against the table.

"The surgery?"

"Come, Orakuru-zin. I'll escort you there."

Santo led her down several levels into the bowels of the shrine to a state-of-the-art operating room. At Samanei's command, Santo had brought the chirurgic to the depths of the jinja where no one else would disturb it. Now it whirred to life as omedeyo attendants disrobed the Oracle and helped her onto a padded table.

"How long will it take?" Samanei asked.

"Twelve hours. At the most. Orakuru-zin, if—when the operation is successful, will you give me a hand again, should things get out of control? I still feel D'Angelo is a possible threat. Once he kills Beserra, he may get away and come here."

Samanei smiled enigmatically. "If that happens, come get me. I'll definitely help you."

Then the chirurgic put her under, and Santo slipped out. There was much to attend to: Jitsu was about to become a single teyopan, and he its giya.

CHAPTER 39

AS SOON AS HE CROSSED INTO THE MUNICIPAL GRID, Brando found himself being pursued by two smaller squad patrol vehicles, used instead of armored transports within Station City. But he knew the city better than they did. He led them on a circuitous chase throughout various sections until he shook them at last where the gold zone met the business district.

Knowing they'd find him again any minute, Brando glanced at the navigation map.

He was just a block from the building that housed Izakiwo, the architectual firm that Tenshi had founded. Slapping his hands on the steering yoke, he burned his way toward it, pointing the transport at the light glow of the forcefield that marked the entrance to the employee parking area on the 22nd floor.

Flicking the vehicle's coms back on, he punched in the his wife's old executive docking code, praying that it had been purged from the system.

The glow stopped. He braked as he entered, setting the scorched transport down in the first gap he found.

The com system kept dinging alerts. Brando ignored them, instead putting in a call to Meji Pixan, who had been appointed Minister of Education just three years ago.

"Brando?" the omedeyo arojin said as their face shimmered in the holographic display. "Where are you? The new archon is trying to track you down. He told the cabinet that you slaughtered the rest of Alpha Squad."

"Acharya-zin," Brando said with impatient respect, "I don't have much time to explain. I found out that Santo's behind Tenshi and Tana's murder. Carried out by Felipe Beserra at his brother's command. I have one chance to avenge them. To stop what Santo's trying to do. To save Jitsu. But I need intel. What's going on right now? Tell me anything you can."

Meji's eyes were still wide at the revelations, but they nodded and ploughed ahead. "The other squads are overseeing the forced evacuation. But they're encountering serious resistance from the CPCC police force within Station City. Also from armed residents who refuse to be sent to the platforms. But Pathwalkers and offworlders in Reformer towns have been complying, especially after the Oracle's transmission."

"Wait, what?"

Meji scratched at their silver locs. "You haven't seen it? You need to."

"In a minute. Are the terrorists ... I mean, the Brotherhood up to anything that you know about?"

"Reports keep coming in. They're trying to leave Jitsu. Commandeering shuttles to get up to some of the platforms. Lots of tension right now at the spaceport, skirmishes between them and the squads that are escorting folks offworld."

"Okay," Brando said. "Thanks. I'll reach out again soon."

"Hold on," Meji said, lifting a hand as if they could stop Brando. "What are you planning?"

"I've found the jagen, Meji-shi. Time for the Wende ra-Kobomaga. I've studied Domina's words closely."

"The Oracle never intended—" the minster began.

"No?" Brando countered. "Then why did she write about the Oni Way? Why did the Dominatudan try to hide those teachings? She killed them all, Acharya-zin, everyone who had tortured and raped her. The oni showed her the way, and she did the dance. Her uncle fell before her. Santo and the others will fall before me."

Without waiting for a response, Brando ended the call. Then he looked through the alerts on the transport's terminal, One was a loop of the original message by the Archon and Oracle that had disrupted all transmissions an hour ago.

As Samanei leaned forward toward her audience, Brando surged to his feet.

Tenshi! Every neuron in his brain sang out. An emaciated, bald Tenshi, but her nonetheless. Gestures, tone, diction: all hers. And she looked to be no older than twenty-five or thirty.

"What in Sopiya's name are you planning, Santo? Have you been feeding her faux-recordings of Tenshi, training her for this charade? Think you'll get them to follow you like meek frigging sheep? Think you'll whip me into a frenzy?"

His blood pounding like pistons in his head, he snatched up the satchel and slammed his palm against the exit pad. Jumping out, he darted toward the entrance to the suite of offices.

Interns, secretaries and other employees were frantically packing. They looked up as he barged in, wearing his ATS battle suit, and backed away, hands raised.

"Give us just another five minutes," a woman pleaded. "We're almost—"

Brando gestured her to silence. "Where's Luisa Canales?"

"I-in her office."

Stamping down a hall toward the room his wife had used for years before her death, before the firm was taken over by her protégé, Brando felt rage and sadness bubbling up within him, ready to burst at any moment.

Soon, he told himself. *Soon.*

Luisa looked up as he slid the door open. "Brando? What are you—"

"Give me the access code to your transport," he growled. "I need something fast and less conspicuous."

After a second's pause, she closed her eyes recited an alphanumeric string, voice trembling.

"Thanks, Luisa." He turned to go, but then looked back. "Tell your employees not to bother. Yall aren't going anywhere. I'm going to stop this fucking travesty myself."

BRANDO BROUGHT THE SPORTY TRANSPORT TO A STOP right outside the spaceport. He used his government override codes to gain entrance to a maintenance shack and descend into the web of access tunnels that ran under the landing areas.

He was looking for Raghib al-Masih, a Martian mechanic that he'd made his fizgig four years ago in exchange for turning a blind eye to the man's small smuggling operation.

When Raghib caught sight of Brando bounding down the access tunnel that linked landing area seven to areas twelve and seventeen, Raghib almost bolted in panic. But wisdom or experience appeared to get the better of the mechanic, and he just stopped and waited for the squadman.

A sigh was his only welcome.

"Raghib." Brando refused to call him "Rag" like many of his shady associates did.

"Kyosu. Heard you died, long with the rest of your mates. Brotherhood doesn't want to admit they did it, but everyone's talking."

"What's been going on?"

"Between the Brotherhood and the ATS, the port's been a fucking mess.

Secrets and confrontations, uneasy truces and much credit exchange. Mainly shite-loads of protesting citizens and helmeted squadmen. They've all run my arse back and forth along the twenty-seven landing areas. I've checked so many transports they've begun to blur into a single shuttle. Wish I could hop on board and get the fuck of this glebe, too."

"The yegsters are leaving, right? Where to?"

"Half the crews have flown up to Nawabari Platform."

"Why?"

Raghib shrugged. "I keep hearing them mutter about the kasike, like he's gonna be up there. Seems a little hard to believe, no? I mean, so they're chucking everybody who isn't a Neog. The fuck does the kasike care? Besides, his brother can't take care of this?"

"No. I killed him."

The mechanic blanched.

"Oh, you are so fucked, bloke."

"Shut up." Inwardly, Brando's heart leapt. A chance to get Konrau, too. Then come back and take out Santo. Yes. "Any more shuttles heading up to Nawabari?"

"Well, yeah, in bout ten minutes Wero Guzman's crew is blasting from area seventeen. Just checked them over when you came throttling toward me."

"I want on it."

"You want me to smuggle a squadman onboard a Brotherhood

shuttle? Think I'm looking to die, something? You like to act like some tough fucker with no limits or compassion. But you're a fuzzy little toto compared to Konrau Beserra."

Brando's eyes flashed and his hands balled into menacing fists. He started to growl something unintelligible.

"Wait, goddamnit, let me finish." Raghib crossed his arms over his stained jumpsuit. "I kind of like you. You're a gormless cop, but it'd be sad if you went up against this guy and got killed. Think I don't know? Everything you do is because you want justice, for your dead woman and child, for all the fucking addled Neogs on this planet. You're just fucking brimming with love and righteous anger. But Beserra? The father of the girl he was shagging shot him in the eye, so he came back from the dead and killed them both. You can't go up against somebody like that, Kyosu. He'll fucking eviscerate you before you can snarl some snide comment."

"You finished?" Brando's right arm shot out and grabbed Raghib's jumpsuit roughly, dragging the taller man's face down close to his own. "Bastard ordered my wife killed. You think I give a fuck how cold-blooded he is? Now, get me on that shuttle, damn you!"

"Alright, shite, come on."

They sprinted back up the tunnel and took the lift, emerging at the underbelly of the ship. The cargo door was open, though the ramp had been retracted.

"Up to you, now," Raghib muttered. "By the way, the CPCC's local constabulary force has put in a call to the AF about the forced evacuation. Couple galleons and a patrol ship was already headed out here to quell this fascist Dominian shite, and now they've got even more reason. Yep, grunts gonna be showing up soon, make things *real* interesting. Good luck."

As Brando stepped off the lift, Raghib thumbed it back down.

Doesn't want to be seen helping me, Brando thought. *Doesn't think I can stop this. Wants to be on the victors' good side.*

Looking up into the cargo hold, Brando heard the mechanic muttering far below, his voice faint but clear.

"Yeah, good luck. Hope they kill you, bastard."

CHAPTER 40

FROM THE SHADOW OF THE SHUTTLE'S UNDERBELLY, BRANDO could make out masses of people being herded by squadmen into the squat military gloom of the ATS low orbit transit ships. A tumult of insults, crying and shouted orders drifted across the distance. Occasionally the armed escorts would fire a blast above the off-worlders' heads to keep them moving. Since no one other than CS, the ATS and CPCC's constabulary forces was allowed to possess a weapon, there was little actual conflict here, just the odd fistfight between soldiers and civilians.

Brando lept into the darkness of the cargo hold, his satchel of weapons cradled in both arms close against his body to soften the impact. The interior was cramped, with wall-to-wall crates and luggage secured by netting from floating around in zero g. Brando eased into a corner and hunkered down, running scenarios through his mind as he awaited take-off. After a few minutes, he heard whispered voices and felt the bulkhead vibrate: two people had entered the hold. As they crept around the boxes and moved closer to his position, he began to make out snatches of their conversation, which was in Unified Chinese.

"And how the fuck are we supposed to leave the station? Magic?"

"I told you, Hark: Yen will pull us out once the situation has calmed down. All we have to do is sit tight in that room I was telling you about for a couple of days, and he'll show up for us."

"I've never trusted that old bastard, Jing. You know that. But what you don't know is what the yakuza will do to us if they find out what's really going on."

Jing. The rookie. The other one, Hark, has to be the yak whose arse I kicked. Stowaways like me. Double agents? Yen? Could be Yen Bandera, that free-lancer.

"Don't worry, little brother. Yen has assured me that in two days there won't be any more of these mafia types on the station. It's all been arranged, seriously."

"Well…"

"Shhh!"

A dozen pair of boots could be heard tramping around outside, and the cargo door suddenly cycled shut, cutting off the only illumination in the hold. Brando held his breath and tapped his casque into place. It made a soft whooshing sound.

Fuck.

"Did you hear that?"

"Yeah. Someone's in here. Put on those IR goggles."

Brando also switched to infrared. The shuttle roared to life. He reached into his bag, his hands coming up full of firepower as he surged to his feet. A jolt forced him to lean against the bulkhead at the very back of the ship. He made out two heat signatures at about four meters, standing and moving side to side as if searching for something.

Come on, yaks; take off already! Don't want to fight them in normal gravity.

"I see him! At the back!"

The ship lurched violently, causing the New Beijingers to stumble into each other. Brando could feel the increasing speed under his boots. He felt heavier.

Any minute now. No guns, if it can be helped. That would just call attention, maybe punch a hole in this can.

The two figures climbed up onto the boxes and began moving toward him quickly. He aimed.

Suddenly all gravity disappeared, for only a microsecond, but one that seemed frozen in time as the blobs of red, yellow and green threw themselves into the air at him. Then the thrusters kicked in: four gees of force hurled the brothers against the bulkhead and pinned them there as the floor tilted up crazily. Brando's arms were thrown up and back, slamming with a painful crack onto the wall he was leaning against.

Only a few seconds; move.

The nearest of the New Beijing boys was groaning a meter above him as the gees continued to smash him flat. Brando rolled in agony toward him, then atop him; straining with the effort, he managed to straddle the young spy.

"Get the fuck off me!" It was Jing.

"Hey, Jing," he replied in Unified Chinese. "Fancy seeing you here."

Grunting, Brando supported himself with one hand as he pushed his torso away from the rookie, lifted his arm, and let the gees smash his gloved right fist into the punk's pretty face.

"Hey, bastard!" shouted Hark from a couple of meters away. "Leave my brother alone or I'll fucking kill you!"

Brando lifted his fist again and again as Jing made increasingly weakened attempts to lift his arms and ward off the blows. In seconds, his face was a bloody mush.

Then there was another shudder, and gravity disappeared permanently. Brando quickly pushed off the wall, flipping over backwards and snagging the netting that secured a crate nearby. Hark bounced toward his brother; as he embraced him, the two of them went into a spinning trajectory that would in seconds fly them over Brando's outstretched legs.

"Jing, you alright? Fuck!"

Unbending his arms, Brando propelled his legs toward Hark just as the punk let his brother go to unholster a weapon. The squadman wrapped his legs tight around Hark's waist and pulled him down, freeing one hand from the netting to knock the gun from the spy's grip.

"It's you, ain't it, Kyofu or whatever the fuck they call you. Well, this time I'm gonna finish what I started down on Jitsu."

A trucha activated in his hand, its sudden light disturbing the balance on the IR of Brando's casque. The squadman released Hark from the scissored grip of his legs and kicked solidly in the middle of the spy's chest, disarming him and sending him caroming off another bulkhead and into his brother's inert form. The force of the kick propelled Brando backward swiftly; he tumbled and straightened in the air so that his legs jutted out behind him to absorb the impact.

Bending his knees as he smacked jarringly into the bulkhead, he pushed himself forward at a disarming speed in Hark's direction. The criminal managed to grab onto something dangling from the ceiling, a hook, Brando saw as he approached, set in a grooved track and probably used to hoist and position crates. Hark pulled up on the hook and swung his legs around in pair of vicious kicks to Brando's head, deflecting the cop at an angle downward.

Rolling into a ball, D'Angelo smashed into a large crate and rebounded with a curse. He'd probably fractured his arm, he reflected as he reached it out, wincing in pain, to grab Hark's foot and lever himself upward with legs toward the ceiling behind the spy. He clamped his thighs around the punk's neck and started to squeeze. Hark pedaled his legs back repeatedly, sending several nasty kicks against Brando's casque, which thankfully absorbed most of the force. Soon Hark stopped struggling and released his grip on the hook, floating off slowly as Brando untangled himself.

"Turn around, fucker."

Brando yanked his head about. The reddish-yellow blob in front of him with a chunk of blue in its outstretched hand had to be Jing, his feet inserted cleverly into the mesh to keep him still.

Shite.

A slight jostling sound from outside told Brando the transport was preparing to dock. There'd be a bit of gravity any minute now, once they'd osculated and the ship was in the platform's gravity sink. A good amount of gravity, in fact, as they'd be at the very edge of the field.

"Jing, you can't fire that thing in here. It'll make too much goddamn noise. You don't want those bastards to find you in here."

"Got a silence module attached."

"You might punch a hole through the bulkhead, compromise air pressure."

"Not if I hit you. Besides, you're standing in front of the wall between the rest of the ship and the hold."

Brando glanced around, getting his bearings. Jing was right, and that meant his satchel was on the other side of the hold. He thought he heard the starboard thrusters fire. They'd be osculating with Nawabari Platform any second.

Keep talking.

"Yeah, well, if you miss me, they'll notice real quick the big-arse hole in the bulkhead, don't you think?"

"How could I miss? You're just floating there: nothing to grab hold of, nothing to push off of, no weapons. Face it. This is the end for you, Professor D'Angelo."

A spot of red blossomed in the blue of Jing's gat. Brando slammed his left hand onto his own shoulder, emergency-decompressing his casque and sending it folding rapidly into his suit's collar. The change in air pressure drove him a meter down as the energy beam singed his hair and ripped through the bulkhead behind him.

At the same moment, the transport started docking with the station and gravity returned, sending Brando sprawling onto the floor below as it toppled Jing with a crunching sound. Brando exploded into action, spidering over the tops of the crates to the corner where he'd left his satchel. Before he could reach it, an orange ghost popped up in front of him and punched him full in the face. He recovered quickly and grabbed Jing by the throat, hoisting him into the air and flinging him over his shoulder. He clambered over the remaining cargo to his original hiding place to the sound of a torch ripping through the bulkhead that Jing had just compromised.

The satchel wasn't there.

"Looking for this, you sumbitch?" Jing called from behind him. "Before you throw somebody round the place, you ought to check what they might have on them."

The lights went on then, and a crew of brothers poured in. Blinded by the illumination, Brando was unable to resist, and, after he'd broken a couple of bones here and there, he was bludgeoned to unconsciousness.

HE CAME TO IN A DOCKING BAY, ON HIS KNEES WITH A COUPLE DOZEN yakuza soldiers in a circle around him, gats and rifles pointed in his direction. His hands were tightly cuffed at his back, and his legs were numb. From the stiffness in his joints, he calculated that he'd been unconscious somewhere between fifteen and thirty minutes. Behind him, someone grunted.

"Awake yet, Doctor D'Angelo? We just arrived, and we find you already here. How punctual! Nice of you to pay us a visit. Always nice to meet a victim's surviving family members, believe me."

Out of the corner of his eye, Brando began to make out a tall, emaciated skeleton of a man with a shiny pate and heavily wrinkled skin. His honey-colored eyes glittered with laughter as he walked around to stand in front of Brando.

"Santo was real stupid thinking that you would be able to touch us. You couldn't even handle a couple of ex-triad putos that don't possess the loyalty of a rabid dog."

Brando laughed. This had to be Nestor Bos. He suddenly remembered his promise to Ben.

Play this right. Give him the New Beijingers, buy some time.

"What do you think is funny? The fact that you're gonna die squealing like a little girl?"

The squadman pushed back the image of Tana's broken body.

"No, just that you're so naffing stupid you couldn't figure out what's going on with Jing and Hark. Hell, you probably don't even know who Jing is, right? I mean, Yen passed you Hark for the crew, but his brother—that little bonus was behind your back."

That information broke through Nestor's smug exterior. He ordered the men to retreat to the edges of the bay. When they were too far away to hear, Nestor grabbed him by his hair and hauled him to his feet with a wiry strength that the old man's weak-seeming exterior cleverly masked.

"The fuck you know about Yen?"

"Don't you get it? He's playing you, Nestor. Has his own agenda. You thought you had him, exclusive? I'd wager the two of them, him and Santo, have spent years working together to punk your trusting arse. That old ronin passed Jing to Santo and had him rig my kewbox so that your boss's little bro would die. Him and Hark, they were planning on hiding out on the station till the Brotherhood was wiped out; then Yen was gonna come and pick them up."

Veins stood out on Nestor's head as he struggled to keep his composure.

"Torture them, you want to confirm it. But I don't think you need to. Why was it so easy for me to snag that psycho Felipe, eh? Hark was who I had to get through. How was it he got out of the brig so quickly, eh? Come on, Nestor.

Yen fucked yall. Whatever plan yall had with Santo, it's gone to shite now. Hell, Yen might be working with the AF, which is on its way, you know."

Nestor let go of Brando's hair with a brutal shove. The squadman collapsed on his hands, twisting his wrist painfully. He noticed they'd stripped him of his suit, leaving him with just the one-piece undergarment. He was utterly vulnerable now: the black edged closer; he could feel its cold nails on his nascent soul.

Let me take Konrau out before you devour me. I beg you.

There came a low beep.

"Yeah, Nestor here."

Into his percom?

"There's a message for you, tunneled to the nebula first, then bounced back over here. Kind of a big delay, sorry. It's from Wu."

"Patch it through to the bay office."

Brando closed his eyes and waited.

INTERCHAPTER H

From: Soralm@cpcc.gov.sol

To: muntsoj@cpcc.gov.sol

Subject: Archon Koroma

Date: May 5, 2697 15:37:24 (SST)

Prime Minister Muntso:

I'm reporting to you again as promised to update you on the situation here on the surface. About two hours ago, the Oracle and the Archon made official the fatuous process that has been going on since this morning. He seems bent on impatronizing to Jitsu all CPCC-controlled territory without regard to any treaty stipulations. Speaking in specific terms, he has transplanted some four thousand citizens of Station City to the Rasaro and Tod platforms. Commander Ly, head of our constabulary force here planetside, continues to shine in admirably; however, his gendarmes are spread thin, some of them keeping the demolition crews at bay near our office complex, others engaging both the planetary security forces and anti-terrorism squads. They are at the very ends of their abilities and resources: without immediate backup, they may not be effective for much longer.

CPCC citizens are being treated roughly. I personally spoke to a few that complained about brutality and disregard for the rights of individuals. ATS captains, confronted with their troops' behavior, have pointed to how many citizens are taking up white arms, knives and such, against the soldiers. I imagine this is an ostensible explanation for the violence. We've got personnel taking depositions from complainants whose cases warrant future investigation.

There are continued reports of significant underworld movement. I received word that several dozen transports of the sort L'ermandá uses were seen shuttling between an orbital platform and the spaceport. No independent evidence of this claim. I remain firm in my assertion that Archon Koroma is working in cahoots with elements of the underworld to engineer the crisis that permits him to immure him and his people behind walls of isolationist religious fervor.

You and I both believe how important it is that all independent worlds join the Consortium, true umbrella of humanity. When I accepted this position, moving my family to a dangerous world even after the tragedy and pain we went through, it was because of your vehement resolve not to let what it happened on

Dhara ever repeat its self.

I remind you of your words to me concerning Jitsu: *we can't afford to permit the precedent of its socio-political solipsism, and we will not allow it to become another Dhara.*

I truly hope you intend to back those words up. Soon.

Meygin Soral

CPCC Ambassador to Jitsu

Ministry of State

CHAPTER 41

KONRAU STOOD BEFORE A BANK OF MONITORS IN THE PLATFORM'S control center, watching events on the station unfold: Nestor and D'Angelo talking, Nestor going to the shuttle bay office to read and answer a com from Wu, Nestor having the two New Beijingers shot, Nestor and a pair of guards dragging the ex-professor toward the control center.

Beserra knew something needed to be ferreted out here, something crucial to the Brotherhood's survival, but he was unable to focus. Events seemed distant and unconnected to him. His plan continued to unravel before his eyes in a spiral that had begun with the Kunti, whose attacks had galvanized the CPCC just when Konrau had hoped to weaken it. Yes, his tenuous plan, held together with threats and bribes, was spinning apart, but Beserra no longer cared.

Eight hours of distance between his initial dispassionate response to his brother's death and his present blinding anger had taught him that all he wanted was D'Angelo before him, on his knees, begging and broken. He shrugged off attempts to massage his shoulders made by a pair of sluts that Nestor had brought into the control center and sank deeper into himself.

Nearly twenty-seven years had passed since his hit on Bruno Andrade, and Konrau hadn't felt quite as alive since. It was as though he'd lost his only real possession, and not even years of amassing those of others could replace it. Those two years of planning, savoring the revenge that he'd exact, basking in the glow of hate and anticipation, an eagerness to win her back and make her father pay—there'd been purpose in his life, a reason to fight through the day.

Preparing to bring the CPCC to its kneew had eased the psychic pain caused by her loss, but it had been a dead joy, a lifeless pleasure unconnected to anyone that mattered, a masturbatory exercise in isolation on a grander scale than had ever before been attempted.

Until he'd focused on Felipe. The closest that he'd come to recapturing that vital feeling was in his efforts here, on Jitsu, watching his brother thrive, the young man's talents no longer squandered as someone's soldier but taken to their maximum extreme as a leader of men. Nestor's whining about Felipe's methods had been meaningless to Konrau.

His brother had potential to be a greater kasike than he. Nestor had no inkling that this move to convert the Brotherhood into the most powerful organization in human space was meant for the younger Beserra, not the elder.

But this Brando fellow, just like Bruno—their names were even similar, he mused—had stripped Konrau of what was his, and now he would pay. Once the cop was taken care of, then Konrau could turn his attention to Nestor and those triad punks, one of whom had been part of Felipe's vanguard, and the other of whom had been serving with Brando.

There was something there, no doubt about it, the very sort of treachery he'd always suspected, the feared holes in his organization that had kept him from revealing the imrizabu's existence to any but a select few, that had pushed him to grip each family head in a vise of blackmail and leverage.

But he would take one thing at a time.

The door cycled open, and in the reflection from the monitors, Konrau saw how two of his men, one hilariously taller than the other, deposited D'Angelo in the middle of the room. Nestor strode up to his side and announced, "Here he is. I had to ice the triad putos. They were being, you know, uncooperative."

Konrau nodded. "Fine. We'll discuss that later. For now—"

He turned and regarded Brando. Though short, a bit like old Toni Benemerito, he was massive, reminding Konrau of the gorillas in the primate protectorate on Ganymede. His knotted muscles were barely contained by a ripped and blood-specked one-piece undergarment, standard issue for use with battle suits.

As Konrau examined him, memorizing the form of his enemy, Brando jerked his head up, his brown eyes murderous beneath the inverted *V*s of his eyebrows.

"Konrau Beserra. Funny, I was expecting more. I don't know; you sure don't look like an evil gangster overlord to me. More like a street punk, flexing his muscles for the rest of his sib."

Konrau looked at the guard to Brando's right, who had pulled his rifle up, and nodded. The butt of the rifle slammed into the squadman's mouth; a spray of blood sketched a half-circle at Beserra's feet.

"That's right, D'Angelo. Keep it up. Get it all out of your system. We've got a long way to go before we're done, and you might as well do the bravado thing now, since later— well, later you just won't want to, let's leave it at that."

Unable to wipe the blood and spittle running down his chin, Brando simply lifted his eyes and, his demeanor completely altered, though not cowed, directed what seemed the most compassionate gaze a human is capable of at the triumphant cacique.

The sketchy smile on Beserra's face melted away. He hadn't expected such a look. No one had looked upon him with pity since he was a child, and Konrau had sliced that look right off its owner's face.

"What?" he spat. "What the fuck are you trying to say with that naffing expression, dead man?"

"Just trying to imagine what's it like, being so empty inside, so uncomfortable with yourself, that you have to surround you with tons of yesmen and assorted panocha, fawning over you and licking your arse, making you feel somebody when you're not shite. Back off, hosupin." The shorter gunsel had drawn his rifle back for another blow. Konrau motioned for him to hold. "Ever been alone, Konrau? Just you and you and you and the blue-spangled blue?"

"Fuck you talking about, pendeho?"

This was not what he'd been expecting at all. Rage, yes. Threats, shouting, silence even. Konrau had been prepared to deal with all of it. But this piercing consciousness boring into him—it was maddening, maddening that with one look the ex-professor should understand so much.

"The nothing that is everything. Sparks in the void. Drifting in the swirling black. Just your ego and the universe. Didn't like it, right? Made you feel small, nothing. Couldn't handle it, true? Got to play pretend now, blaze up with the orange heat of false godhood."

Just behind Brando, the ghostly outline of Jeini's ruined head threatened to resolve itself into being. Konrau felt his face flush, his hands tremble in anger and trepidation.

Got to get him out of here now, before I lose it in front of them all.

In a measured voice, struggling against the pain that began to pound mercilessly in his skull, Konrau directed, "Yebesen esta myerda d'aki."

Konrau's counselor motioned at the guards to follow him. Each of them took hold of an arm. Brando remained limp, not trying to struggle, resigned and almost happy, judging by the smile he wore. As they dragged him away, he raised his voice.

"I've been there, my criminal friend. Eight mothergod years, Konrau. Learned to spin in the abyss, like oni dancing beneath the belly of a jagen, ready to slice. Now I'm going to rip the life out of you as sure as if you'd never been born!"

The threat was uttered without a hint of anger, just with plenty of volume, as if Brando were making a decree before an assembly of subjects. As echoes died, Beserra saw her out of the corner of his eye.

You sent him, ain't it, bitch? He closed his eyes, chilled to the core. Her blood-specked smile hung in the dark of his own mind. *You sent your brother years back, but that hoto left off fighting soon as the Kunti moved in. So now you've brought this fucking loko against me. Well, fuck you. Send all your fucking ghouls, bitch. I ain't backing down.*

Really? Jeini's smile grew wider and more cadaverous. *What about* him?

Felipe's tattooed visage floated into view beside hers, and Konrau opened his eyes with a start, stifling a scream.

Standing abruptly, Konrau muttered in hoarse whisper, "What do yall want?"

Revenge. Their voices in unison declaimed, and the implication was not lost on the mafia boss.

CHAPTER 42

SEVERAL CORRIDORS. LIFTS LOWERING HIM INTO THE ANCIENT platorm's depths. He struggled to pay attention, memorize the route. Nestor caught on pretty soon, had a guard smack him across the forehead, long gash from which blinding blood began to trickle.

"Not the first tough guy I've had to deal with, dekaman."

The submerged linguist in Brando flipped through a mental file: dekaman. Solpat. *Cop.* They passed another yegster, just standing there, trying to act like he was supposed to be guarding something, when in all reality he was probably loafing. Nestor snapped at him.

"Tu, deha d'aserte pendeho; be me trais gaz i alkol d'infirmari."

The yak straightened as if slapped. "On kea?"

"Lebol seis. Purale, baboso."

Infirmary, level six. Information, though who knew whether it'd ever be of use.

SOON THEY REACHED A GAOL BLOCK, THE TYPICAL SET UP ON SMALLER platforms: ten cells in five groups of two, each group with its own guard station, a dull metal control console with an uncomfortable swivel chair meant to discourage sleeping on the job. Not that it would help the prisoners any for the guard to take a nap: the cells consisted three walls of solid, seamless plascrete and a ceiling and entrance of high frequency energy mesh, powerful enough to keep even the most pain-resistant captive snugly inside.

The yak from the corridor rushed in, the alcohol and gauze in hand.

No medskin for me; oh, well, another scar.

Nestor motioned at Brando's forehead, and the yegster splashed the cold, stinging fluid directly onto the gash, dabbing at it with a wicked smile. The powerful smell and the sharp bite in the wounds on his face brought Brando back to full attention, forced him to focus on any opportunities.

The ugliest of the gunsels stepped behind the console and shut off the energy mesh at the entrance of one of the cells. Brando was immediately booted inside, his head banging against the metal slab that jutted from the back wall as he fell. Blood began to flow again over his left eye.

He lurched to his feet and spun about as the mesh hummed back to life. Lunging toward the mesh as if to run right through it, he saw Nestor shake his head with sarcastic disappointment.

"I was you, wouldn't even try it." Konrau's counselor glanced around, grabbed a metal stool from behind the console. "This energy mesh is a bit different than you're used to. Has a real nasty effect on things."

He thrust the seat through the entrance, releasing his grip on it with a grimace as the sparking heat was conducted up the three legs. The stool's forward momentum sent it completely through the mesh; it collapsed in a molten pool at Brando's feet.

"Imagine what it would do to your flesh, dekaman."

Brando said nothing as he stared at the cooling mess before him, then tilted his head back to regard the series of horizontal and vertical energy bars a meter above his head.

Not getting out of here, am I?

As Brando pondered his situation, the mobsters all left, except for the shorter yak, who stayed behind to guard him.

AN HOUR LATER, DRENCHED IN SWEAT, bitterness rising within, Brando concluded that there was indeed no way out. Dark despair settled upon him, and he slumped onto the metal slab, his cuffed hands pulled taut behind him. Impotent fury boiled beneath the despair; black waves threatened to drown him in madness.

So close. So damn close.

Closing his eyes, Brando began to breathe in deep, ragged gulps, forcing his heart rate down and clearing his mind. He focused on Kongan 71.

The cosmos is a mirror. I looked into it. There was nothing looking back.

The myriad flashing images and voices vying for attention in his brain faded as he envisioned a sea of blue blotting everything around him completely out. Despair was his enemy. The orange flame of hate was his enemy. He himself was his own enemy.

He'd learned this lesson well in the months following his wife and daughter's deaths. Powerless, raging in wounded solitude, he'd nearly given in to the inverse of the Blue. That ancient fire taunted him, beckoned him, promised cessation of pain, offered surcease of sorrow through immolation of self.

His Pathwalker teachers and Tenshi's simran had pulled him back from the blind embers, but they'd not given him the key to his survival.

The Oracles had.

A month into the sea pilgrimage, Brando's cohort had reached a remote set of coordinates near the equator, in the nearly landless western hemisphere of Jitsu. The shard from the Urim had been passed up from the hold, hand to hand, until everyone had touched it except Brando, standing by the gunwale, contemplating the green-gray sea. He had reached for it, but as his wedding ring had touched the rough black rock, he'd been knocked onto his back on the deck.

A vision. Like after the fairground massacre.

Tenshi's bloody body in his arms.

Her eyes flitting open, utterly black, sparks swirling in their depths.

The voice. Not her simran. Not his spark. Tenshi.

"Read deep the hidden words. Take one away. Bring two back. Prepare them."

A pause, and then more gentle, less cryptic.

"I will come back to you. I swear it."

Brando had jerked awake from the vision to find the others kneeling around him. They had helped him to his feet, and he had thrown the spike into the sea, watching it sink into the depths. One more point on an inscrutable grid.

Read deep.

Shutting himself up in his cabin, he had spent the return trip scouring the two sacred books he'd first seen with his wife years ago on the Distant Isles.

First was *Kitabu ra-Chiwaga,* the *Book of Bricolage.*

He had read the text before, twice. Not trusting his own brain—which filled in gaps and skipped over words—he now ran searches.

Tenshi. Five occurences. Once passage resonated most.

"There are two fires we face. The Roaring Orange comes not from without, but within. It roils inside us all, for we are facets of the Grey Prison, the smoke that rises from that raging blaze. Some never need face it. Community and family give us sufficient support. It has no opportunity to rise, to engulf the selves we attempt to align. But others must fight off their personal auto-da-fe. Even learned professors huddle at dusk, on a 'darkling plain,' lighting not torches but kindling at their own feet.

"A few of those assaulted by Sakra's bleak nihilism discover the Path.

They see their spark, burning impossibly bright and blue at the heart of the swirling black. Breaking their illusory selves, rebuilding bricolage replacements that lead to ensoulment, they follow a new flame, one that must be protected and nurtured. They may linger for years in the dusk, right on the edge of that precipice. But the Path is better than the abyss that looms on either side, orange streams of magma flowing ever-hungry in its depths."

That phrase. Ukwazi kyosu. Learned professor/s.

Another search. *Kyosu.*

His heart thudding in his chest.

Impossible.

"And here the transcriber must interject. Beloved, broken Kyosu, hear me across the years. The self is a delicate thing. Learn to build a fortress around it, Seer. Learn to fight the dark, as Domina once did. Learn to fight."

Hekima Umchawi had written those words more than six decades ago.

But Brando knew they were meant for him.

Learn to fight.

Domina once did.

A difficult book, *Kiyik juya Shari*. Though it ended victoriously—the blood spilled upon Jitsu's sand freeing Domina at last to create her soul and escape Sakra's grasp—the lost volume of the Oracle's journals laid human depravity out in stark relief.

Brando's suffering paled in comparison.

No hidden, paradoxical messages.

Instead, a Way out of despair into triumph.

Domina's voice, surging from the page.

"Ship's library intact. These bastards never read. Me neither, truth be told. But Asiri does. Believing I'm an Oracle, they show me what the previous ones have written about revenge. I'm learning, oh, yes. Lao Tse helps me to empty myself, and to take heart in the fact that the weak can destroy the strong. The *Bhagavad-Gita* shows me how to remain resolute and disciplined, unchanged in defeat or success, calm in my vengeance, not prone to dark inertia or all-consuming fire.

"But who am I, really? Bolormaa Munkhbat? Domina Ditis? No, that girl and that woman are gone. Broken. Most of the pieces of them discarded. Still, something remains. The *Bardo Thodol* discusses the *gotra*, that pearly blue drop that lies at the heart of a person. That's the tenshi, the spark, priceless and enduring. I've seen my own. Am shaping a new identity that echoes its power and endurance, shard of Sopiya that it is. I remember my teacher, back on Titan. She made us trace our fingers along the nested diamonds of the Marummo, repeating the names of the four umbini and the colors that went with each:

"Areteya-Notsu, green-red. Zowe-Rogosh, purple-yellow. Henosi-Akeratosh, white-black. And Sopiya-Sakra, once Ennoya-Bitosh before the Secession. Blue and orange. A cruel sun in a ever-arching sky.

"Ubiquitous blue. Tibetan Buddhism connects that color with

Akshobhya, one of the five archetypal mild Buddhas, responsible for the transmutation of delusion's poison. The Grey Prison is Maya. The blue light of my tenshi effaces illusion.

"Of every Oracle down the long millennia, however, none touches me the way Jelaluddin Rumi does.

The sky is blue,

and the world's a blind child

who toddles near the Path.

But I who see your emptiness

see beyond the blue and the blind.

I am a realm where souls finally live.

Stare into this deepening blue,

while the stars whisper a secret to you.

"But the lines that most move me, the words that spell out my purpose and destiny clearer than anything else I've ever come upon, describe opening the door through the *turn*, the feverish dervish of physical extremes, the mad rush that permits the union of human and divine. It's like the *wende*.

Dance when you're broke open.

Dance once you've torn the bandage off.

Dance in the middle of battle.

Dance though you're smeared with blood.

Dance as if you're totally free."

Toward the end of the volume, the strands weave together:

"I've found my Way at last. This morning, the oni came to me again, bringing more mohiyo leaves. The female that leads them—I can't pronounce her name, so I just call her Sajan—gestured at me. 'Come,' she said. I was delighted she's learned a few words. I told Asiri to stay with Arehanja. The rest of the oni band was gathered together near a mountain. They stank. Had smeared themselves with jagen shite. Shite. Shite. Scream. Shudder. Take handful, cackling. Once again. Own volition? Don't know. Hard to hold on. Precarious. Old ways reassert. Can't process. Filter. Need blue. Can't.

"Up mountain. Little hands on my waist, legs, pushing. Jagen senses movement. Eyes bad. Nostrils wide. Just shite. Nothing more. Encircling it. Two dozen, leaping. Hands on knobby spine, pulling it over, exposing belly.

"Sajan beside me. Putting shard in my hand. Black. Volcanic. Sharp. Jagen's legs scrabbling, swinging through air, deadly claws. Sajan runs forward. No! What? Stop!

"Dancing. Oni is fucking dancing. Amid the flailing limbs she dances her way close. Soft underbelly. Twitching limb knocks her flat. Running forward. The blue of the sky. Everywhere around me. The blue of Sajan's blood. She struggles to stand.

"You won't die today. Because Domina can dance. And she does. She twists and spins, somersaults and dives, pulling Sajan to her feet, slamming against the pliant belly of the beast. Together, the human woman and her alien friend will sink their blades into that flesh and rip it open. The viscera will spill forth, fetid and foul, bathing our erstwhile heroine in black viscera. Unhinged, knowing nothing but the need to destroy the monster before it slays her or her diminutive allies, Domina Ditis will plunge her arms into those squirming guts and cut the beast's fucking heart out, screaming in triumph as the oni ululate wildly.

"*This* is Ona ra-Oni. The Oni Way. It ends in the Wende ra-Kobomaga, the Killing Dance. And woe unto you, Uncle Zamilan. Because you're next, motherfucker."

Brando had set the texts aside, his eyes full of tears. He had taken a square of the High Sacrament and gone wordlessly down into the ship's hold, to the darkest and dampest corner.

A fortress around the self. Learn to fight. Dance in the middle of battle. Cut the beast's fucking heart out. The Oni Way.

The voices had echoed louder and louder in the inky black of the hold until the reverberations had cracked open the world itself, and the blue light of his spark had floated before him, illuminating the glittering seams of his kintsukuroi soul.

Brando D'Angelo, fully revealed.

Satori.

"Now," his spark had whispered, "you can reforge that self and the body it inhabits."

Now, in the gaol cell, he recalled the hormones, the nanobots, the brutal twenty-hour days, training his body and mind, learning to use weapons he'd never imagined touching before, pushing his flesh to bend to the force of his will and determination.

More than just a physical transmutation, Brando's was a psychological sea change. When he had addressed himself to Santo and other members of the government, the men had noticed this startling metamorphosis. No more smiling, self-deprecating banter. He had been all business, forceful and blunt.

That control helped him now. He was focused, ready. His head hanging limply, his breathing shallow, he appeared beaten, but that was just superficial. His moment would come, he knew. Someone would make a mistake. An opportunity would present itself.

He would be ready.

CHAPTER 43

BEN WU EASED HIMSELF INTO A SEAT ON THE TRANSPORT, breathing a sigh of relief that his disguise and fake documents had fooled the security personnel. Getting out of the cell back at headquarters hadn't been too hard. Though he'd been stripped and searched, his queue had been left alone by the rookie squadmen in charge of him while more experienced officers handled the evacuation.

Unfortunately for their futures in law enforcement, the thong that tied his hair off was actually a field disrupter coil that he'd taken to wearing after his capture eight years ago. Once the novices had left him alone, it was a simple task to shut down the doorfield and slip out. A bit of sneaking around and theft had gotten him to an abandoned mine shaft where, not long after being compromised by the Brotherhood, he'd hidden all he needed to assume a new identity in the event that he ever got free of his Faustian agreement.

The worst thing had been the loss of his queue, but he figured he hadn't deserved the honor represented by that cultural badge for years. Slight

adjustments to his skin color, nose, ears and lips created an overall effect that

might trigger a sensation of recognition in casual acquaintances, but that kept

them from pegging who he was. Ben was still careful, because anyone who'd

spent a lot of time with him would see through the façade within minutes. Ben

was no actor, and disguising his gestures, mannerisms and way of speaking was

beyond his ability.

His nervousness was heightened by the bizarre message he'd gotten from

Nestor Bos. The com, which he'd accessed from a public terminal in Station

City, had simply read *K and me are here. Hang on for more instructions.*

He'd checked the transmit addie: Nawabari platform. Wondering

whether Brando had discovered how close his enemies were, Ben had clicked

off the terminal and taken a deep breath. Nestor had arrived, mere kilometers

above him. The corrupter of his daughter. The man who'd wrenched what

little honor Ben had had away from him. And there was nothing he could, or

dared, do about it.

An old off-worlder bent his knees painfully and lowered himself into the

seat beside Ben. His tight gray curls and orange-brown eyes were very familiar:

Ben soon recognized him as the president of the recently shut down Ra-Koreji,

Modupe something or the other. Brando's friend.

The old man had tried to get a hold of the crazy ex-professor many times,

but Ben had had to turn him away at Brando's request. Modupe, a recent convert to Neo Gnosticism, had been living in Kinguyama, as far as Ben knew, which meant that Santo's cultural cleansing had reached out into the farthest crevices of Jitsu's social structure.

Ben felt the old man's eyes on him, but he continued to occupy himself with adjusting his seat and ceiling lighting. As the two of them had only spoken a few times, Ben hoped he wouldn't be recognized. In a few moments the shuttle's swain soon announced their departure, and the hum of the ancient engines masked the low voices of the other passengers.

"Thank you."

Ben glanced at the old man. Modupe had obviously uttered the phrase, yet his eyes were glued ahead as if he were focused on the information scrolling across a display at the front of the cabin.

"Excuse me?" Ben wanted to just ignore the man, but couldn't. He'd been Brando's best friend, and so had Ben. They were connected, and a warrior could not ignore those invisible threads of responsibility.

"Don't worry; I won't reveal who you are. They're looking for you, of course, Captain. It's not your disguise that it gives you away: I studied you a lot when Brando joined the squads, and I got a sense of the kind of man that you are."

Ben nodded, looking ahead like the old professor. "Why did you thank me?"

"For being his friend when I couldn't. When he wouldn't let me. For teaching him to be a better fighter."

"If you knew what I really am, you wouldn't be so thankful."

"Oh, I've got no illusions about you, Captain. I understand, though, that you wanted to help him. For whatever reason, you couldn't. Not the way he needed. I don't think that there was a choice for you, though. At least, you imagined there wasn't."

"Well, he's got his chance now. I hope he's a better man than me. I don't think I could do it."

Modupe turned and looked at him with watery eyes that nonetheless bespoke an unusual strength. "No, maybe not. But maybe you can help him now, no? Maybe there are things you know that could alter the outcome."

Looking away, Ben stared at the infoscroll for the longest time, his guilt building. After a moment, his eyes focused on the words.

A ship had just braked madly into the system.

The station looming above the shuttle had been declared CPCCAF jurisdiction.

Ben straightened. While the AF ship was probably suffering structural damage from the way it had defenestrated and braked, it was loaded with soldiers and weapons and a fighting chance. A chance to right some wrongs. A chance to rip Ya-Ting from those naffing bastards' hands. For the first time in years, hope surged in Ben's chest like a storm-swollen river.

"Yeah. Yeah, I think I can do something, Professor."

In silence he began to prepare himself for the task ahead.

AFTER THE SHUTTLE DOCKED, BEN TOOK HIS LEAVE OF MODUPE AND, exiting the directed flow of refugees, approached a CPCCAF soldier, who immediately pointed his rifle at Ben's midsection.

"Get back in line, sir."

"Listen," said Ben, squinting at the man's uniform, "Corporal Wehbe, my name is Captain Ben Wu, head of Jitsu's Alpha Squad, former officer of the army branch of the AF, serial number AR5-9083-67BM. I got some real important info for your commanding officer that might affect the outcome of this little squabble."

"Hang on." The lance corporal used his percom to report on the situation up the chain of command.

Ben stood motionless for the three minutes it took for a reply to come. He felt confident he'd be allowed to see the captain, especially once they'd run his name through the system.

"Okay, Captain Wu. Follow me."

Wehbe and another soldier led Ben though several levels of identically paneled halls and lifts to the command section of the station, where intelligence personnel were still setting up equipment, tapping into the station's systems, and monitoring the com and shuttle traffic around Jitsu. Treading confidently around the room was an imposing man in a captain's uniform. He paused from time to time to point out errors or to lend a hand, his low frequency voice sending rumbling tremors through the air and floor. His circuit soon brought him to where Wu stood flanked by the two soldiers, who saluted crisply upon the captain's approach.

"Ben Wu." The captain regarded him intensely for a few seconds. "My brother-in-law headed a company in your battalion during the Neptune uprising. Krishna Farishta?"

"Ah, yeah," Ben chuckled, momentarily transported. "Krish Farish. True officer and friend. Nice to meet you, Captain."

"Same here. All right. Make it quick. I got a nutty bastard down on Jitsu who's trying to demolish the CPCC consulate and take over Station City. Got to take care of him."

"You got a bigger problem than that, Captain."

Mukerji's right eyebrow lifted high into the mottled mahogany expanse of his forehead.

"For real? What, exactly, is that?"

Here comes the test. "One thing."

"Ah, the man wants to barter."

Ben swallowed a sudden flash of anger. "My daughter is in a lot of trouble… her life's in danger. I need yall to help me get her out. If what I tell you pans out and yall come out on top, I want you to help me."

The captain looked Ben squarely in the eyes, seeing the determination and despair within them. Krish had been right about this man: he was, at heart, an honorable warrior.

"Of course, Captain Wu. That's our job, anyway, isn't it? Seeing to it that justice is done? Now, let's hear what you've got for us."

Ben calmly released the breath he'd been holding.

"Santo Koroma is working in secret with the Brotherhood to take over Jitsu. The massacres, all the posturing, the squads—it was all fabricated." Conversation on the control deck hushed immediately. "Not only that. Konrau Beserra is about 500 kilometers away from us right now, on Nawabari Platform, with a contingent of Brotherhood soldiers." Ben had done some thinking. "I imagine they got a ship or two hidden on the day side of the planet."

The captain's eyes were wide, but apart from that, he showed no emotion. "Prove it."

"Give me access to a com terminal."

Mukerji motioned a shipman off of a stool and gestured at it. Ben rapidly encoded a message and beamed it at Nawabari Platform: *contact me now urgent info about cpccaf.*

The wait was agonizing. If Nestor had decided Ben was too much a risk, he might not answer. Perhaps Brando could take the Brotherhood on by himself, but Ben wasn't going to risk Ya-Ting's life on that possibility. He'd already risked her enough.

A real-time com chimed on. Ben motioned everyone out beyond the visual perimeter of his own end of the broadcast and answered.

"Nestor."

"Make it quick, Wu."

"Brando…"

"Already got him. You were right. The Neog bastard Santo is trying to shag our arse."

"More problems. CPCCAF…"

"Yes, yes. They're here. There, even. Where you're transmitting from. You see anything?"

"They're concentrating on the planet. Don't seem to know yall are in-system. Ship is damaged. Look, I need out. I need you to get me out."

Nestor smiled with nosferatu aplomb. "Sure thing, kwate. You just hang in there. When the *Maliyas* comes up over the curve in a few hours, we'll take care of the CPCCAF, then I'll take care of you. Don't worry: you and Ya-Ting're will have your teary-eyed reunion soon enough."

Ben nodded.

"Nestor out."

A second of silence, then the intelligence operatives burst into activity. Mukerji had his people well trained: they immediately turned their attention to the Brotherhood-controlled platform while attempting to bounce a scan off of a more distant station to verify the position of the enemy ship.

"Okay, soldiers, you know what I want," rumbled the captain. "Get it to me as fast as you can." He turned to face Ben, who stood from the stool. "You stay here. I might need you. You think Santo will communicate anymore with

Beserra?"

"No. Konrau would never believe anything he says anyway."

"All right, then. Shan, put a com through to Archon Koroma, on the main terminal."

After the com had been routed through various offices, secretaries and ministers, Santo Koroma's head oozed up from the surface of the large central terminal.

"Yes?"

"Bud Mukerji here, captain of the *Pacifactor II*. I'll get right to the point: call off the demolition crews from the CPCC building and put an immediate end to the forced evacuation of CPCC citizens from Station City, named by a treaty between your world and the Consortium as governed by CPCC law. Do this now, and there can be a diplomatic end to this situation. If you don't comply, I'll send troops to occupy Station City and the CPCC building. I'll order them to open fire on any hostile Jitsuan armed security force attempting to stop them from carrying that directive out."

Santo's lips pursed slightly, and rather than answering, he directed his gaze at Ben, who was standing just to the left and a little behind the captain.

"Captain Wu. No queue? Heh. I see you escaped and are spreading the lies you and your mafia friends concocted. Very good." His eyes closed momentarily and then refocused on Mukerji. "There are syndicate ships in orbit above my planet. They've got control of one of my stations. And you, *Bud*, expect me to trust off-worlders who, for all I know, may in reality be Brotherhood agents? Will not happen. Do what you think you need to, *Bud*. You'll just reinforce what I have always told my people: the CPCC can't be trusted. Koroma out."

The archon's image slithered back into the darkness of the com terminal's top. Some indistinct voice on the far side of the center muttered, "Bastard."

"Okay, boys and girls, this is it. Send a message to the *Agamemnon* and the *Santa Anna*. Let them know what they've got waiting for them here in-system. The shuttles loaded up?"

"Affirmative," came the reply.

"Well, then, let's go wipe that stupid grin off the Archon's face. Send three shuttles to the surface to provide back-up to the constabulary forces there. I need to talk to the squadron leaders on the other five. They got some yaks to roast."

Bud turned to Ben, a smile unexpectedly crinkling the mottled shades of dark brown in his complexion. "This might turn out to be fun. We're worn out from observing heretic Kunti, but a soldier's never too tired to fry yegster, what."

CHAPTER 44

NESTOR BOS STOOD BEFORE KONRAU, AND THE KASIKE WAS struck by how old his counselor looked, despite only being seventy.

Brothers age faster.

In Nestor, the age was compounded by emaciated thinness and an almost delicate pallor of illness, though the man was healthy and strong.

The discovery of Nestor's collusion made him livid with rage, but Konrau realized he didn't want to kill the old man. Nestor was no father figure, but he had become, though the kasike would never admit this to anyone, a surrogate mother. Like an spinster aunt who is annoying but tolerated.

Nestor had devised a plan, and it had backfired. However, he'd not intended Felipe's death, so Konrau decided that punishment would be sufficient. The deaths of the people actually *behind* Felipe's murder would be carried out soon enough.

"Never," he muttered low, leaning his head close to that of the counselor, "ever do shite behind my back again. I decide to wait to tell you something, that's my decision. You and me make a plan and it don't work, that's tough shite for us both. But you go around hiring fuckers with other agendas and put them on a crew of mine, you give the enemy all the ammunition they need. I'm not going just forget this, vieho. You betrayed my confidence, and Santo fucked me."

Nestor's eyes dropped. He was visibly shaking.

Fear? Or anger? After all, I was lying to his ancient arse, too. But it was the honorable thing. Had to protect the Brotherhood. And I was right to. He was a leak. My right hand was the weak spot in my organization.

"I ain't gonna kill you, Nestor. I'm just—fuck—I'm just in shock that you would go sneaking around—huh?" Nestor had muttered something. "What?"

"I was trying to protect you," Nestor said, and Konrau noticed a hint of liquid in his yellowing eyes.

Oh, shite. This I don't want to see. If he goes all fem on me, I'll gat his wrinkled arse and fuck L'onda.

"Protect me? I don't need protection. You never believed in me, ain't it? Couldn't trust me this time, eh? Was no problem back when you wanted Toni taken out, though, right? No, don't say shite. Go pack, Nestor. I need you to get back to the nebula, you hear me? Contact my uncle, tell him the plan's a go. We need a courier. Our tunnelers are bollixed from the imrizabu. Beides, I need you away from me right now, because I'm bloody pissed and once this shite gets started, I don't know if I might change my mind. Felipe's dead and it'll take a lot of blood to pay that debt. Get back to Beta Pictoris, and run things till I'm done, got it?"

Nestor nodded numbly. "Thank you."

"Don't bleeding thank me: *bete a la chingaa!*"

Clearly relieved to be alive, Nestor ducked out of Konrau's temporary office in the rec room. Konrau waited a few minutes, then summoned a couple of little brothers to accompany him to the gaol block.

Once there, he had his men shut off the energy mesh. Brando was sitting on the floor, hands pulled tightly behind his back by the cuffs, head drooping upon his chest.

Overcome by rage, Konrau yanked a lazgat from the holster of a nearby soldier, dialed it to its lowest setting, and began shooting the squadman. Brando's body twitched with every jolt of energy, falling sideways and flopping on the floor like a fish even after he'd lost consciousness.

"Water," Konrau said as he eased his finger off the trigger mechanism.

"Huh?" A little brother stared at him, uncomprehendingly.

"A bucket of water, now."

The man rushed out to the ban down the hall. In a moment he was back with a cubic container filled with cold water.

"Throw it on that bastard."

The water hit D'Angelo, reviving him at the same instant that Konrau burst into the cell, clenching both hands around the ex-professor's bull neck and yanking him onto the slab.

"Strong yak, aren't you?" Brando muttered weakly. Beserra smashed his fist into the squadman's face, once, twice.

"You fucking dared, cop, to walk onto my station and bleeding threaten me? You're just now figuring out how strong I am? Who the fuck you do think you are?"

"I'm the man whose family you and Santo sent that maniac Felipe to kill! What's with this fake outrage of yours? Shouldn't you be angry with yourself for getting your little brother involved in this shite?"

Again Konrau felt himself paralyzed by Brando's uncanny insight. The squadman lay before him, bloodied, muscles still spasming from the shocks he'd been given, yet from between split lips he was able to rasp words that did more damage to Beserra than any blow.

Guilt for the deaths of those he'd loved settled heavily upon his mind, and his eye began to throb.

"What are you doing here, anyway, Beserra? What's the point of all this death? Why expand your power if it means losing your kin? Explain it to me, because it seems real frigging stupid."

Konrau spat in his face.

"Fuck you. It's to preserve the group, not that you'd ever understand that, coming from Earth like you do, everyone separated out, no sense of community, faux this, faux that, no real jobs, no real community, uplinked half the day, no responsibility except the contracts you watermark. The Brotherhood, it's a family. You don't like what do we do, but who are you to judge? We take care of our own, give them a life, but the Brotherhood must come first. Anybody fucks with it, even one our own, we eliminate them. If that means stretching our arms out and crushing the CPCC, the AF, and their bloody aetherocracy, that's what we'll do. Neogs here on Jitsu are the same way: it's a community, and it has to be preserved at all costs. That means rounding up offworlders, then that's what the true Jitsu guys will do. Means killing some pilgrims, that's what'll happen. Means knocking off Reformer cunts like you who ain't looking out for the good of the community, then they got to go."

"But who decides what's good for the community, you bastard?" Brando spat. "The guys in control? And why we should believe them when they say it's good? Because they tell us to? Bollocks, Beserra. Just a couple of frigging dictators sapping yall's people dry, that's all you and Santo are. Want to justify the shite yall do with words like honor and brotherhood and community, go ahead. Lie to yourself. Want to explain away killing my wife by invoking the common good, that's your own mental masturbation. But don't expect me to nod my head in agreement, you piece of shite. You're a fucking murderous corridor rat, and like I said before, I'm going put you down."

Konrau reached out, grabbed Brando's right ear and slammed his head repeatedly against the back wall of the cell. "*How*, motherfucker? HOW?"

Brando jerked free of Konrau's grip, rolled back on his shoulders and pounded the soles of his manacled feet into the kasike's chest. As Konrau went sprawling toward the entrance to the cell, Brando gained his feet and crouched to spring. The three soldiers outside the cell rushed in and began pummeling him with their fists and the butts of their rifles. Several blows to his face knocked out his top front teeth, which he spit at the guards as they beat him to the ground. Crunching sounds told of ribs breaking, and Konrau reacted at last.

"Stop! *Parelen!*"

The guards backed out of the cell, and Brando regarded the kasike through blood-curtained eyes, his body already mottled purple, black and red from the blows.

"Why?" Konrau asked, suddenly calm despite the immense pain in his chest. "You're suicidal, or what? I mean, I know your family's dead, but why this? Why look for death like this?"

"Because," Brando managed to growl, "my system, the system of real human beings, requires that justice be done. You're like a foreign object that must be expelled."

"So it ain't revenge, eh? Then you're just fighting to preserve the same social system that created me, cop."

"Bollocks. You created yourself, Konrau. You made the decisions, did the acts, talked the talk. Don't fucking try to pin that responsibility on anyone else. You betrayed the best in you." He paused a moment. "You did it when you killed Jeini."

Konrau's face hardened and twisted. "Iho de tu puta maje… Say that again so I can kill you right now."

"One good thing in your life, and you destroyed her. How sad, for real. No wonder my wife's life meant shite to you."

Thinking *how he can know all this,* Konrau dialed the lazgat's setting to maximum and extended his shooting arm toward the battered figure. "Your life means shite, too."

Strident claxons went off, and Konrau whirled to face his men.

"Ke karaho?"

He strode over to the control console and flicked a com channel open.

"Nestor? What the hell is going on?"

A slightly fuzzy voice responded. "This is Chuy, boss. Nestor just left the main hangar, heading out like you ordered. We got CPCCAF shuttles approaching, three of them. They're broadcasting a demand: they want you to surrender."

"Nestor said that they—ah. Shite. I'll be right up."

Never trust that fucking hoto again, Baby Fidensio damn him forever.

Any guilt he'd felt at keeping information from Nestor was obliterated by waves of cold anger. Turning to assess the situation, Konrau decided on a course of action.

"I need yall two," he pointed at the men who'd accompanied him, "to head to shuttle hangars A and B in a minute. I'll send down a couple guys to escort this myerda. When they get here, yall get moving."

With a final hateful glance at Brando, he strode from the room to begin a war that had lost all purpose except release.

BRANDO WATCHED THE YAK BOSS LEAVE THROUGH A HAZE OF AGONY. One of the guards entered the cell again, booted D'Angelo a few more times in his cracked and broken ribs, and then hoisted him back onto the slab, face-down. Brando concentrated on pushing his consciousness away from the pain and focusing on his plans.

The arrival of the CPCCAF was good news. It would keep the yaks occupied and leave the halls of the platform clear of most surveillance. Of course, there was the little problem of the cuffs and the manacles, which even now were being squeezed further together so he'd only be allowed slow, shuffling steps.

A hum penetrated the dark of his closed eyes: the energy mesh had been reactivated. He drifted in and out of consciousness and a strange fugue state. He was aware of a churning mass of discordant inner voices, regarding and discarding alternatives in a frenzied attempt to find a way to escape and kill the two men he needed to get past.

Soon he heard voices outside his head, and understood that the two yaks were leaving, their replacements having arrived. Brando hoped they were less competent. He needed every edge. Slowly he opened his eyes.

He still lay on his stomach upon the plascrete slab, hands pulled upwards behind his back in the most uncomfortable position due to the cuffs. Every centimeter of his body throbbed and ached, at least those parts that hadn't gone nearly numb from the torture and beatings. He knew the moment was upon him when through the energy bars of his cell he watched the two new yaks, chromes holstered at their sides, rifles in hand, stride into the room. They mumbled something, and the guard who'd been in charge of Brando until now ambled over to the console that stood at the right of Brando's cell, and, leaning over its back, his face toward the wall, shut off the bars.

What an idiot. Brando imperceptibly shook his head. *Turn his back on me like that.* Then he realized: he represented no threat to these three at all.

"*Lebantate kulero.*"

"Help me up, then. I can't do it alone."

"Fuck you. Up, now, or it's over right here."

Brando managed to roll off the slab, not looking the least bit menacing on his knees in the middle of the cell. Separating his legs as far as the manacles would allow and thrusting his knees against each other, he surged upwards to a standing position.

"*Sal pa hwera.*"

He stepped out as ordered, but slowly. If there was any chance, it had to be this instant. But nothing occurred to him. Darkness swirling. No music. The guard turned as Brando cleared the cell's entry, leaned over the back of the console, and reactivated the energy mesh.

The molten stool leapt into Brando's mind. The yak's gat in full view. His back turned. The other gunsels unconcerned. One scratching his balls.

No. Fucking. Way. I can't.

Sure you can, Tenshi's simran reassured him. *You've endured worse.*

Then he heard the children of Kinguyama, chanting years ago, when he'd first stood before the old teyopan at Tenshi's side.

Amo inyani, iruju tani.

It isn't reality, it's just a mirage.

And his spark's voice echoed in his memory as well.

There's a reason for the pain. Always remember. Your love matters.

Taking a deep breath, Brando stepped back.

A shower of sparks erupted as the mesh split the left cuff and reduced Brando's left hand to a bloody stump.

A wave of horrible agony began to crest, but he didn't wait for it to hit. Four hops forward, swinging his free and only hand around, seizing the guard's lazgat, lifting to fire once, twice, thrice, three yaks on the floor with bubbling brains in less than five seconds, a little laugh, then the wave hit.

Brando fell to his knees, vomiting on top of the sizzling gray matter as blood continued to spurt almost comically from his stump. Lowering the chrome's setting amid the swirling darkness, he aimed carefully as possible and cauterized the artery.

A tube, a tube, my left ball for a tube of moku.

He began giggling, which set him to retching. Leaning on the console, he slowly stood. When the darkness sought to shut his eyes, he popped his temple with the butt of the chrome. Reset and a single shot freed his feet. The anklets actually looked fashionable, he reflected morbidly before the pain wrenched his nervous system.

Let the blue fall, he begged. *Let it fall.*

The infirmary, Brando. Level six, remember?

Grimacing, he thought of the probable yaks in the hall, perhaps drawn to the gaol block by the muffled blasts. A glance at the monitor in the corner across from the console confirmed it: a half-dozen men made their stealthy way down the hall.

I got no armor. Defenseless. These yaks just got jumpsuits.

He hobbled around the control console and examined the storage compartment beneath it. There were odds and ends, wires and wrappings, and a small molecular bonder for sealing and splicing. He took it up in his one hand and regarded the yaks on the floor. He yanked a belt off of one, buckled it around his waist and holstered the weapon and the bonder. Grunting softly, he dragged one of the yaks on top of another and used the bonder to meld their arms together, creating a gruesome sort of fleshly armor.

Planning to stick your nose in those brains?

"No way."

He drew the lazgat and seared their heads off, leaving only a cauterized gap upon their shoulders. The effort of concentrating helped keep the pain at bay, but he needed to get to the infirmary fast, or the black would overtake him

"This is going to suck."

But against the well-prepared yak soldiers, his only chance was surprise. Insanity. Becoming a dervish.

He awkwardly hefted the flesh-armor into the air and over his head, thankful for the station's low gravity. Trying not to think too much about the cold, dirty skin pressing against his, he palmed one of the pulse rifles and slammed its butt against the door release.

As he lurched into the hall, he realized the dead yaks' legs were too long, or his too short: stumbling, he began to fire at the four men approaching from the outer end of the corridor. They returned fire, and he was spun around in midair as the blasts impacted the corpses he'd draped about him. He hit the floor facing the inner end and the three yaks running toward him soon fell beneath his fire. Concussion bursts slammed into the dead gunsel at his back, forcing splinters of bone from the corpse into his own skin.

"Fuck this," he muttered, rolling over with great effort and nailing the nearest yak, who was thrown backward toward his fellow soldiers.

Brando wriggled out of his armor and sprinted toward the three dead little brothers, piling one atop another as a sort of barricade behind which he positioned himself prone. The other yaks ducked into rooms along the corridor.

Shite, they're going to come around behind me!

He leapt to his feet, slung the rifle over his back, yanked a knife from the belt of one of the dead soldiers and began running toward the inner end of the corridor, where a lift could take him to level six. He skidded to a stop in front of it, just as the door chimed and hissed open. Two soldiers stood inside, one holding a pair of boots, the other with an EVA suit draped over his arm. They both opened their eyes in shock and reached for their weapons.

Brando was on them like a raging oni at the same second, the knife in his hand ripping across their throats and through their hearts with deadly speed. Behind him came a shout, and a lazgat burst slammed into his right buttock, ripping off a good chunk of flesh and making him forget the other pains he felt. He fell back against the right side of the lift, punched the button for level six, and unslung his rifle, leaning forward to shoot at the yak who was about to barrel in. Then the door shut and the lift began to move up.

The EVA suit was combat ready, which meant that it would absorb most lazgat and chrome fire, though not konk rifle blasts or nades. His one-handedness making the process unwieldy, he pulled on the suit and the gravity boots, tucking the excess legging into them and sealing them tight. He felt blood trickling rapidly from his semi-cauterized butt wound.

I'd better get to the damn infirmary now.

He looked around, but there was no helmet.

Why the fuck did they want an EVA suit without a helmet?

As the lift began to slow, he activated the boots and walked up the side of the lift, grabbing at the lighting fixtures so as not to bend too far backwards. Soon he was crouching on the ceiling of the metal-surfaced lift, the fingers of his only hand being burned by the heat from the ceiling light.

Won't be able to see me.

The lift stopped. The door slid open, and a barrage of weapons fire ripped the two corpses and the back wall to shreds. When the brief but furious hail of energy blasts had stopped, Brando let go the ceiling with his hand and yanked his lazgat from its holster in a single motion, firing at the control panel as his body swung down, his boots still firmly stuck to the ceiling. The blood rush nearly made him pass out, but he stomped along the ceiling, out the stuck doors, and along the corridor, firing upside down at five sikaritos whose battle lust was hampered by Brando's bizarre tactics.

They recovered their wits after two of their number had fallen under Brando's fire, and two of them opened fire on him with gats while the third remaining yak pulled a konk rifle from one of his dead comrades.

Brando's body swung back and forth in painful little hyperboles as the energy blasts were absorbed by the suit. His gat went dry and he tossed it, taking up the rifle instead and ripping one soldier's legs out from under him, then decapitating another. A blow from the third yak's rifle slammed into his left arm, sending him arcing backwards, knees bending as his back banged against the ceiling. A sharp pain followed by a numbing sensation warned him that his arm had been yanked from its socket and most likely broken in several places. The yak was really close, nearly beneath him now, and Brando slapped his rifle against the sensor that activated or deactivated his boots.

In a twisting tumble, he fell down and outward, knocking the remaining soldier to the ground. They landed with Brando's knees around the yak's head, and in a violent, satisfying jerk of his hips, the ex-professor broke the man's neck.

For a moment, Brando just knelt in the hall, panting wildly, oblivious to everything in the universe but the hammering of his own adrenaline in his veins. Then his conscious mind became aware of the pain: everywhere, and extreme. Waves of darkness rolled over him and he retched, coughing up pinkish acid.

Okay, now really need to get to the infirmary. Struggling to his feet, he stumbled down the corridor, which began to vibrate crazily under his feet. *Platform's under attack. Good, keep them busy, boyos.*

He soon came to the door of the medical station. It didn't open upon his approach, so he blasted at the control panel with his rifle. It still wouldn't open, so he blasted at the door itself till he'd ripped a sizable hole in it. Peering inside, he saw two civilian medical staffers huddling in a corner. No yaks in sight.

"Yall want to open this door? I'm a squadman, and I need some medical assistance right fucking now."

CHAPTER 45

THIRTY MINUTES AFTER THE ATTACK BEGAN, KONRAU FOUND himself nearly alone in the conference room, only a couple of people manning communications stations and keeping him up to date. The *Maliyas* was coming around the divide and would hopefully draw off the *Pacifactor II*, which, despite the lie that Nestor had been fed by that bastard Ben Wu, was in good enough condition to engage the Brotherhood battle transports while smaller CPCCAF shuttles pounded the platform. The station's weapons, added gradually over the last decade, managed to keep the shuttles far enough away to do little damage.

"Message from the *Matō,* boss," Chuy announced. "They just unholed and are at maximum decel."

"Let them know how things stand."

The large holographic display above the main terminal in the center of the room altered slightly to show the *Matō*'s position relative to the conflict. Though the ship had defenestrated in-system thanks to the extensive data its frame had received on second-to-second changes in gravitational and magnetic fields, three hours would pass before it would be in range to have an effect on the battle.

That was okay. Konrau was ravenous for destruction—he wanted the AF to keep pounding him, wanted the chance to blast them into oblivion. As long as the concussions rocked the platform, as long as his mind was ringing with the claxons of alarum, Konrau wouldn't be able to see Jeini and Felipe, wouldn't hear their muted voices in his mind telling him it was all for nothing, that he'd thrown their love away for meaningless, empty power.

"You get through to my uncle yet?"

Chuy shook his head. "Nah, boss. I'll keep trying. Our tunnelers are still shot to shite, and this ancient wreck ain't got much new tech to speak of. I might be able get the *Maliyas* to relay the signal through their own equipment."

Konrau nodded. *So soon like I raise him, I'm striking now. Tell him to load up and ride the tunnel. Fuck it if the AF is stronger than our ships. The fuck I been blackmailing the heads and hording ships if I ain't gonna use them? Even if we fail, give them a fucking fight. Rip Nereus and Jitsu to pieces, that's what I'm gonna do. Ain't never gonna forget me, fuckers.*

The kasike looked around him, searching. The last half hour had gone by in such a flurry of activity that he'd forgotten about his prisoner.

"Chuy, chingaa maje, where are Bisko and Danyel? I sent those pendehoz to bring D'Angelo more than thirty minutes ago."

"I can't raise them. Their percoms show they're still in the hall outside the gaol block. Shite. I told Nestor to set up in the security station, boss, but he said you was gonna want a bigger space. Hang—let me patch into the surveillance cameras on that hall."

The image of Jitsu's star system winked out and was replaced by a grainy view of several bloody cadavers.

"What? You mean nobody saw this?"

"Boss, most of the boys are at the shuttle hangars and defensive stations."

"And the weapons discharge sensors?"

Chuy simply shrugged. Konrau balled his hands into tight fists. *Too much shite happening all at once, and my counselor compromised and returning home.*

"Where's Brando?"

Chuy keyed in the id code of the cuffs. "Says he's in the infirmary."

"Send some little brothers down, armed heavy and ready to kap him if need be."

"I send some of the guys from out there? You got like two dozen watching this door."

"Yeah. Buzz them, let half go. I want that dekaman bastard, and I want him *now*."

Konrau heard movement outside the door as twelve soldiers tramped off toward the lifts.

"Try calling the infirmary. Put an image up."

A low beep. The display switched to the infirmary. A young man's face filled much of the image. It was a Neog nurse, one of several station staff that Santo had provided. On a table behind him lay an indistinct male figure, covered with a sheet.

"Uh, medical assistant Sararegi here."

"Yall got a wounded man there?"

"Uh, no. A dead one."

"Walk over to him and uncover his face. Chuy, pull in close."

As the man nervously approached the shrouded cadaver, the sound of concussion fire came from out in the hall. Konrau grabbed a nearby railing to steady himself. The image centered on the dead man's face: a little brother named Luis Sainz.

"Where's D'Angelo, you Neog fuck?" Konrau screamed at the medical assistant. The weapons fire continued beyond the door.

Quivering, the young man managed to gasp, "On his way to pay you and Koroma back for these atrocities, you damn yak."

"Yak? I look like I'm from Saturn, hoputa? Fuck! I should've killed all yall freaking Neogs the minute I stepped onto this platform! Chuy, call those soldiers back! Tell them that fucking cop, he disguised him as one of us!"

With an ear-shattering boom, the door exploded inward and a little brother stepped in, a short one, heavily armed. Konrau's eyes focused through the drifting haze of soot, dust and smoke: it was Brando, dressed in Brotherhood garb.

"I told you I would put you down, Konrau."

Chuy and the other three brothers in the room leapt to their feet and palmed their weapons. At the same moment, there was a flash from the display, bright enough to blind everyone for a moment. As Konrau rubbed his eyes, he could have sworn he heard Jeini's voice, whispering something he couldn't make out.

BRANDO SHOT FROM THE HIP, DOWNING CHUY AND BIG BOY, AND THEN leapt high into the air to land beside Paulino. The redheaded yak immediately let loose a barrage of kicks and blows, most of which Brando countered. Being one-handed and doped to the gills, not to mention pumped full of nanodocs that were in a constant struggle to maintain his vitals, interfered with D'Angelo's abilities.

He leapt free of Paulino, twisting to avoid the sizzling bulls that Mando, the other yak in the conference room, sent whizzing from the barrel of his chrome. One of the projectiles ripped through his thigh, but Brando was so hyped on painkillers and stimulants that he barely noticed.

By Sopiya, I was lucky to find a Pathwalker nurse. Or Santo was stupid for leaving them here. Or he did it on purpose. Shite. Who cares?

He jumped and bounced off one of the consoles that rimmed the circular room, firing as he spun through the air in the direction of the long-haired yak named Mando. By the time he impacted with his enemy, the man was already dead.

Rolling, he leapt to his feet.

"Boss!" yelled Paulino. "Boss, move! What's wrong?"

Konrau was standing still in the midst of the carnage. Brando turned to see just what had frozen the kasike to his place.

KONRAU COULDN'T MOVE. HE COULDN'T TAKE HIS EYES OFF OF WHAT HE was seeing on the display, over and over: him, as a young man, gun pointed at Bruno, who held Jeini. Him, firing a shot that wrenched the life from his only love. In a loop. Over and over.

"No," he whispered, stumbling backward and slumping to the floor against a console. "No."

The image froze, and Jeini turned her eyes on him. Her face filled the projection field, blood dribbling down the bridge of her nose. Her eyes teared up, and her lips formed a soundless word: *why?*

Konrau, who hadn't shed a tear since he was eighteen months old, could not stop the flood of heaving, gasping sobs that surged from the darkness in his heart to wrack his body much in the way the station itself was being pummeled by CPCCAF fire.

"I'm SORRY!" he cried, a great, wrenching cry of despair and humiliation. He understood everything at once. All that he should have done and never had. The love he had squandered. The lives he'd destroyed. It was too much: his heart and mind began to crack.

BRANDO FALTERED AS THE KASIKE COLLAPSED TO THE DECK, SOBBING like a bereft parent. The face of Jeini Andrade turned to the squadman and spoke with Tenshi's voice.

"Kill him now, Brando. No hesitating."

D'Angelo lifted his konk rifle, hypnotized by the voice, yearning for what he'd lost, what'd been ripped from him.

Paulino started to raise his own weapon, but the scan console beside him suddenly exploded, sending bits of shrapnel ripping through his flesh.

"Now, Brando."

For a second, Konrau's eyes met Brando's, clear hazel reflecting sudden utter comprehension. Amazingly, he gave the slightest nod, as if granting D'Angelo permission, as if accepting that history would forever view him as a strange *felo-de-se*.

Then Brando blew his head off.

"Yes. Good."

Brando turned to face the image, now morphing into Tenshi's hauntingly beautiful features.

"Now, come, my love. Come to me."

"Fuck you, Santo. I don't know how you're doing this, but you can take your mind games and shove them up your arse."

Tenshi's image laughed softly. "You don't understand anything, Brando. But that's okay. You want Santo? Come get him. He's yours."

"Sick old man," Brando muttered, turning the muzzle of the rifle on the terminal and blasting the image into showers of sparking phosphors. He stepped closer to Konrau's cadaver, now slumped sideways, the spurting blood at its neck slowing to a trickle.

Brando tried to feel something, relief, release, nausea, anger, anything.

But there was nothing. Just—nothing.

Hurrying out of the conference room, he was confronted by twelve soldiers dashing his way.

When the enemy outnumbers you, Kyosu, become the enemy. He's never gonna suspect that shite.

Those had been the words of Bily Kim, a vicious fighting man who'd served on Alpha Squad for six months a few years back before moving on. Brando had taken the advice to heart in the infirmary, as the one nurse he hadn't shot had set and fused his arm, sealed his wounds and injected him with drugs and nanodocs. He'd quickly gotten up, pulled the dead out of the hall, and donned the clothes of a brother. This had allowed him to walk right up into the midst of the soldiers guarding the control center and kill them all before they could react.

Now their confreres were back, and he was shite out of luck.

As they slowed to take in the carnage, he darted into one of the circular corridors that ringed the central axis of the platform. He'd been on the stations several times on missions, and knew several short cuts to the shuttle hangars. Shots whizzed by him as the yaks gave pursuit: he luckily was able to run much faster than they. The floor shook under a renewed and heavy attack by the CPCCAF.

Keep at it, boyos.

He turned outward at the access corridor, a wide hall specially designed for moving large, recently off-loaded crates into a series of storage rooms that lined it. At the end of the hall stood a good number of guards, and between them the shimmering glow of the force-field-protected entrance to the hangar.

Just as they began firing, he twisted sideways into one of the storage rooms, hurtling up a stairway to its second level. From there he shot a ventilation grill to shrapnel and threw himself into the airshaft that led straight to the hangar. He slalomed along its slippery metal interior, propelled by momentum mainly, and slammed to a stop where the duct made a turn. To his right was a ventilation grill that, if he had calculated correctly, hung a couple of meters above the catwalk that traced a squarish *U* above the main hangar. He figured they'd be expecting him, and for a moment he thought of trying one of the auxiliary hangars above and below this one.

No. I got to get off this platform now.

Santo knew he was coming: Brando had lost the element of surprise.

Taking a deep breath, he kicked the grating free and slid out into thin air. His eyes scanned the bay as several weapons fired at him. Crouching low and moving inward along the catwalk, he was dumbfounded: fifty-plus guards surrounding a large ship, a holing-capable Brotherhood junk.

Konrau's very own.

Drawing himself erect and running, he took out the three guards up on the railing with him.

Gravity seems weaker: my imagination?

Shouts below, and heavy fire was aimed in his direction. No place to hide, fifty yaks shooting. Against twelve men, with an element of surprise, he could usually handle himself. But these odds were ridiculous. Time seemed to slow: a bull ripped through his shoulder, another grazed his cheek, and blasts ripped the metal walkway to unnavigable strips behind and before him.

Nowhere to go. Then he heard music, and he saw the blue, falling like a funeral shroud across his eyes. The world receded.

Nowhere but toward the jagen's belly.

Time for the Wende ra-Kobomaga.

Time to dance, motherfuckers.

Clambering atop the railing, Brando hurled himself toward the guards below, firing not at them, but at the hydrogen drive section of the junk, lazgat fire sending him into a spiral, projectiles slamming into his right foot and left arm.

Flying into the blue-spangled blue.

He was oblivious to all, caught in a whirling fever of concentration as he fell: the drive, the hydrogen cells, concussion after concussion.

The engine exploded, flinging him up and back like a rag doll, sending large chunks of metal in all directions to smash the horrified yaks into bloody smears. The explosion breached the floor beneath the ship, and the passenger section tilted back and collapsed into the auxiliary hangar below. The wall he'd just leapt from was now racing toward him: he fired the last three concussion rounds at it, and the recoil pushed him back toward the smoldering chaos below.

He had no way to cushion his impact.

Death imminent, the blue lightened, and Brando in a diaphanous moment knew he'd survive: objects were beginning to float, which meant that somehow the platform's gravity had been nullified. Perhaps the g-sink had been damaged in the space battle. Brando's momentum carried him into a patch of still-solid floor, but he was prepared and rolled off in another direction, suffering only a few more fractures on ribs and arm and some severely pulled muscles.

He angled off the wall opposite where he'd first entered, heading toward the ceiling at a much slower pace. Grabbing a hold of cabling that ran along its length, he kicked off toward the fiery hole in the bulkhead below.

Drifting in the midst of burning debris and smashed body parts, Brando reached auxiliary hangar A, where several of the small troop transports had been damaged by the explosion and collapse of the ceiling.

Near the hangar doors, however, sat two battle shuttles, clinging to the floor with magnetized landing struts. There were a couple of demimundo soldiers floating around, trying to make sense of the hellish situation, but none of them noticed Brando as he pushed off and dodged and worked his way toward the transports.

Reaching the closest one, he cycled through the cabin airlock and gained the interior. In seconds he had started the pre-flight sequences, demagnetizing the struts and using steering thrusters to turn around and face the doors.

They won't just open them so I can fly out.

He barked a short, almost crazed laugh, primed the short-range missiles, and blew the hangar doors to scrap metal, allowing the sudden pull of the vacuum to draw him out into space along with the debris and the screaming yaks.

INTERCHAPTER 1

From: mukerjib@pacifactor2.gov.af

To: muntsoj@cpcc.gov.sol

Subject: Mission update

Date: May 5, 2697 21:45:43 (SST)

Prime Minister:

We defenstrated the *Pacifactor II* at the edge of the system at 13:13 Solar Standard Time, 11:50 local. We put off braking until the last possible moment because I decided to push the ship to its structural limits. Military grade suspensor gel is rated at even higher gees, but the *Pacifactor II* is no state-of-the-art galleon. It's a fifty-year-old ship coming off a six-month stint at Sigma Draconis, without even the benefit of modern tech, despite its multiple retrofits and despite being the namesake of the ship that it pulled humanity's collective khyber out of the hell that was the Centauri Rift. But that's another complaint, for another time, Madam Prime Minister.

We docked at Rasaro platform at 18:38 SST. Right away I began to assess the situation, preparing eight teams of soldiers to disperse to Station City and the CPCC building. At 19:30, I received word that Captain Ben Wu of Jitsu's Anti-Terrorism Squads wanted to share intel with me. Based on a pair of communications he engaged in (annexed to this message), I became convinced that a large force of Brotherhood troops were on Nawabari platform, their transport ship on the dayside of the planet.

As a result, at 20:00 I sent just three of my shuttles to the surface, ordering the other five to engage the orbital station. We soon discovered that its defenses had been improved over the years. However, because of the skill of our swains and weapons people plus a strange lull in enemy activity, by 21:15 we had disabled most of Nawabari's external defenses. About five minutes later, there was a massive gravity failure on the platform, which allowed our people to board with complete body armor and gravity boots to begin to clean up the mess that they discovered inside. Perhaps an internal conflict, some schism or squabble, resulted in scores of Brotherhood members dead.

This cleanup was "helped" when the doors of one of the auxiliary shuttle hangars exploded and its contents sucked out into space. We're being forced to be careful navigating the debris field, which contains entire ships wrecked by the internal explosive event. With luck, most of this will be drawn into the atmosphere to burn up or fall into the ocean.

While these events were going on, the *Pacifactor II* engaged and defeated a Brotherhood attack cruiser. At about 20:21 the ship, which we'd already detected, came into sensor range. With Captain Wu's help, we had created the illusion that our ship was crippled by our entrance into the system, so we sat as if unable to move, firing shots misaimed on purpose to draw the enemy closer. At 20:30 they had approached to well within our weapons' range. I had my weapons officer target their hangar bays and fire the minute they opened. Despite the advanced tech of these demimundo ships, they have no experience fighting AF firepower or defenses, preferring to prey on merchant vessels or other private ships. I point this out to explain the most probable reason we able to completely disable that ship in fifteen minutes. With their small ranfla fighters eliminated in their hangars, the syndicate commanders of the ship were at a loss. And that's the way it always is with them: so dependent on their expendable soldiers that they can't manage without them. Volleys of plasma missiles to their drive, weapons and communications system, and we soon had them under grapple. At this moment, I've got several teams preparing a boarding party. While I am sure it'll be a bloody conflict, I feel confident that my men, better trained and loyal, will take control of the enemy ship soon enough. Prisoners will be held awaiting military tribunal, like you indicated.

On the surface, our men are still trying to get CPCC territory back under our control. We've retaken the area around the Consortium's building in Jitsuan territory, but we still have real problems in Station City. In order to get that situation in hand, I'm sending another two shuttles with teams for back up. That is, course, if the *Agamemnon* can catch this new Brotherhood frigate that is headed our way. We fed them the data they need to defenestrate in-system like the Brotherhood did. If they can't, I might need to recall my troops and get ready for another little naumachia up here. At the very least, it won't be a happy gam. I realize that any backup you've called for us must be a day away at the best, so we'll handle it on our own. I won't let you down. None of us will.

Bud Mukerji

Captain, *Pacifactor II*

CHAPTER 46

SANTO WATCHED THE REPORTS POUR IN WITH A MIXTURE OF pleasure and apprehension. The CPCCAF patrol ship the *Pacifactor II* had crippled a Brotherhood frigate, and it was at the moment handling the Nawabari Platform. Contingents of CPCCAF soldiers had taken up position within Station City and around the CPCC building and were supporting the Consortium's local constabulary troops in fighting off attacks from Jitsu security forces and the ATS. However, another Brotherhood vessel was approaching Jitsu, and Santo knew that the forces plaguing him would soon have other problems to deal with.

It was uncanny how well she had foreseen this moment, the AF and the Brotherhood drawn together in a conflict that, she had assured him for years, would leave him free to rule Jitsu unhindered by either group.

He wanted to buzz the Oracle, but she'd left strict instructions not to be disturbed. The operation returning her to normal physical function had been a success in half the time anticipated thanks to the chirurgic's years of planning, and she'd been put in a recuperation room.

Samanei had demanded a faux-connection to the interstellar net. She had been locked in for hours without communicating with Santo at all. Inconvenient, given the fact that Jetsun Muntso, Prime Minister of the CPCC, was insisting on an immediate faux-conference with the new archon.

Santo knew that his interchange with the Consortium commander-in-chief had to be handled perfectly to strike the right balance so that the Brotherhood became her only target. He needed the Oracle's counsel.

Annoyed, he checked his com queue to find out if the messages he'd sent her had been answered. He discovered a brief note from Samanei: *meet with her. You'll know what to say.*

The faux-conference room he uplinked to had been designed to resemble the Prime Minister's actual office in Milan, a high-ceiling room known popularly as the *Chapel*, and a huge wooden desk separated her avatar and his, underscoring the distance between them and her own self-image of superiority. Her plaited hair was pulled back severely, and her amber eyes bored into him without mercy.

"Archon Koroma," she said smoothly, "listen carefully. For months we attempted to dissuade you from this course. As head of Jitsu's immigration ministry, you managed to befuddle the Minister of Colonization to the point that he believed the goodness of your will. The Minister of State herself was reluctant to believe you capable of Kunti-like betrayal, despite your ghettoization campaign and your refusal of AF assistance in clearing up your supposed terrorism problem. Ambassador Soral, more aware of your duplicity, managed only recently to make you show your true intentions."

"And what, dear Minister, are they? Please enlighten me, more than I already am."

"You unctuous smiles and backhanded insults will do you no good, Archon. You want, it is clear, to break all the treaties signed between your world and the CPCC, despite the fact that they provide yall's main economic support. Without the royalties that we pay to mine yall's Oort cloud and the leases you gave different corporations to use the planets around Kobito, how do you plan to continue providing 300,000 people food, shelter, energy? Through tourism? Please. But that's not all: you want to displace seven and a half thousand CPCC citizens, behaving like the very *late* Regent Leksono in confiscating Consortium and private property without cause."

"Oh, I have plenty of cause. We spent the last decade and a half being increasingly attacked by underworld groups. Where were yall then, eh?"

The Prime Minister gave a scoffing laugh. "Ah, yes, the Brotherhood incursions. We suspected all along that you were behind those, just like some of your own fellow citizens did. Of course, there was never any hard evidence, or any witnesses at all. Or rather, the few people who volunteered information met with some rather unfortunate accidents. And need I remind you, *Archon*, that we constantly offered our help, but your predecessor refused it."

Santo grew impatient. "Then, if yall have no evidence and know what I'll reply to all this silly political pressure, why are you and I talking?"

"Hmm. Understand, neither Milint, the AF's investigative branch, nor the XID, the executive's own agency, possessed any conclusive evidence before, but some new, very recent breaks came up today. Our special investigator for Jitsu—perhaps you know him, used to be mayor of Station City—Seni Chunhawan?"

Santo cursed the man inwardly. Annoyingly impudent off-worlder.

Should've killed him when he was here.

"He now has two crucial elements for his case against you, Archon. First is Captain Ben Wu—"

"A liar and coconspirator with the killer Brando D'Angelo," Koroma fired off angrily.

"—and second is a fascinating compilation of encoded messages between Jitsu and the Brotherhood, bounced off of an illegal tunneling post in orbit around the fifth planet of this system, which, by the way, we confiscated moments ago. The *Cetus*-class galleon *Agamemnon* slowed its braking speed just enough to scoop it up on its way to Jitsu. The anonymous person who provided us with this valuable information also forwarded us a key, one that even our best decryptors would've been troubled by. Guess who the correspondents are? You, dear Archon, and the infamous Konrau Beserra. Conspiring to commit murder. Fraud. Coup d'etat. The list goes on."

Santo said nothing. He could not think. Had Nestor sold both him and Konrau out? Because this evidence would not only have repercussions for Koroma: it would give the CPCC the authority it had been looking for to step in and clean house in the demimundo, which of course was Santo's goal, his smokescreen, but hardly a desirable outcome for the Brotherhood.

No. The strange old spy. Bandera. But why didn't the Oracle foresee his betrayal?

"So I am talking to you to make an offer: stop this insanity now. Turn your government over to the interim regent we're sending on the *Agamemnon*. In exchange for your cooperation in shutting down the Brotherhood, we're willing to give you prosecutorial immunity. You won't be able to reside on Jitsu anymore, but perhaps one of the Neo Gnostic monasteries on Mars could become a refuge for you."

For the briefest of moments, despair building within him, Santo almost acquiesced. The Oracle's plan seemed to be unraveling before his very eyes. Then he re-ran the Prime Minister's words through his mind, and an idea began to coalesce.

The Oracle was right to trust me with this. I know just what to do.

"I see. Well, Minister Muntso, I appreciate the thought, but as I have no idea what you're talking about, I will close this link and ask you to reconsider any planned action against the people of Jitsu. We might not be many, but we have enlightenment on our side."

Muntso stood up suddenly and with obvious anger.

"Fine, Koroma. We'll play it your way, then."

She stepped out of the faux-beam, her avatar winking into nothingness. Santo disconnected and called a technician in to help him edit a section of the conversation. Soon he began broadcasting to all of Jitsu.

"My children, we have a dilemma. The Consortium just decided to force its off-worlder, infidel ways on us." He motioned for the recording to be played. The Prime Minister's avatar could be seen and heard pronouncing damning words: "So I am talking to you to make an offer: stop this insanity now. Turn your government over to the interim regent that we're sending on the *Agamemnon*. You won't be able to reside on Jitsu anymore, but perhaps one of the Neo Gnostic monasteries on Mars could become a refuge for you."

Santo's image once again filled the terminals across the northern continent. "They want me to abandon yall, but I won't do it, my children. I'll fight by yall's side, to the death. Quantum enlightenment for everyone that dies for Jitsu. Remember Mother Domina! She gave her life so that this world would be kept free from the Demiurge. Resist at all costs!"

There, he thought as he terminated the transmission. *Let's see if the AF is prepared to shoot unarmed civilians. If did so, the Ogdoad forbid it, member planets and colonies would balk and perhaps play into my hands. Even independent worlds like Terego could enter into the equation, seeing how the CPCC once again forces itself on a planet. They are already jittery over the occupation of Kunti.*

His secretary chimed him. A message was being sent, coded, from Nawabari

Platform. He took it immediately. The man on the other end was Simon Sato, a technician loyal to Dominatudan and planted by Santo on the station.

"Archon, blessed be your name, enlighten me. Holy One, the situation here is chaotic. We've got no gravity. The station is still being hit pretty hard and being boarded by AF troops. The major news is that Konrau Beserra is dead, and one of his lieutenants, a guy named Eri Sanchez, took over. He plans to negotiate with the CPCC because of the two battleships approaching."

Santo experienced an odd mixture of relief and fear.

"At the hands of what person Beserra died?"

"Everyone's saying that it was Brando D'Angelo. He apparently escaped and killed lots of men, then the kasike. But they can't find him: he was going into the main hangar when there were two major explosions that compromised the bulkheads. Force fields can't be shut off in the main hangar or the lower auxiliary one, but most of what was in there got sucked out into space. Unless he managed to get out in time and is hiding somewhere on the station, D'Angelo probably got expelled with all the other stuff."

Santo rolled this around in his mind. D'Angelo was resourceful, a survivor. The odds were against his ever returning to Jitsu, but Santo was still nervous.

Got to hide myself and the Oracle away.

"Holiness, the other faithful like me, we don't want to be here anymore. So we're going to slip onto a shuttle in the remaining hangar and escape. Please, could you tell the AF that we're Jitsujin so they won't fire on us?"

Konrau nodded solemnly. "Of course, my son. Come on home, and be enlightened."

No such call would be made. There were things more important that those men to preserve. He hurried to the room where the Oracle rested and barged in. She was standing, a white cotton robe draped over her, hiding the wrappings that, along with nanodocs, were speeding her recovery. She slowly shuffled toward him. He bowed his head.

"Oracle, someone has just betrayed us and the Brotherhood both. The Prime Minister has hard evidence of collusion, and Wu went over. I think it was Yen Bandera who betrayed us."

An indecipherable smile pulled at Samanei's lips.

"Yes. Don't worry, Santo. Everything is happening for a reason. It will all turn out just as I planned, I promise. Now, let's go. To the heart of the honden, the inner sanctum. Let's go and wait, Santo, and see what happens."

CHAPTER 47

MEJI PISHAN SAT AT THEIR DESK IN THE GOVERNMENT COMPLEX, contemplating an ancient kleinball, handed down through the generations of the Pishan family, all of whom had become arojin and all of whom presented for Meji a model of spirituality that they had endeavored his entire life to live up to. They turned the kleinball around and around in their expert hands, tracing its twisting, ostensibly one-dimensional surface, searching for wisdom. For guidance.

The great ramatini of Ona ra-Shamanga had taught Meji that the self was not bounded by the flesh, but extended into the exterior world. In Tenshi Koroma, they had found the perfect partner for the reformation of Jitsu. For a time, the vision of the second Oracle teetered on the brink of realization.

Tenshi's uncle, however, had proven a ruthless and cunnng opponent, a champion of Dominatudan's severe conservatism. Now Brando had discovered just how far the fundamentalists were willing to go. Santo Koroma was a murderer, many times over. A traitor.

And Meji was wholly unprepared to fight that sort of inhuman blaze.

The Oracle herself had chosen Santo Koroma as the ratowanin, and part of the Path was the acceptance of the leaders the Ogdoad permitted to rule. Meji wanted to believe that despite the atrocities that the archon was perpetuating, Samanei's hand was moving every element of the situation, guided by the Eight. For a time, they retained hope that enlightenment would yet come of the apparent evil.

But now word had come over the infotainment feeds—Samanei had sent the Close against Jinja ra-Shamanga. Were it not for an unexpected alliance of clerics from the Distant Isles and young Reformers on the clean-up crews, the guild would have already dislodged the ramatini.

She foresaw this. Or the second Oracle did.

Samanei, however—what possible motive could she have for hurting Hekima Umchawi?

A low beeping from his terminal notified Meji that there was an incoming message, government priority level seven, encoded with an old and secret Reformer encryption algorithm.

Brando.

Apprehensive, they reached out and thumbed the connection open.

Brando D'Angelo's face surged from the terminal surface as if rushing to push his entire body through as well. Before their exchange earlier today, it had been several years since the two had spoken, though Meji, since his appointment as Minister of Education eighteen months ago, had seen the ex-professor on occasion around the complex of boxy government offices in the capital.

Brando avoided meeting with his old friends: Modupe Oduyoye, who'd taken over as head of Ra-Koreji when Brando had resigned, had speculated on several occasions, when he and Meji had lunched together, that continuing old relationships didn't pain the ex-professor. Instead, those friendships threatened to *ease* Brando's pain, an eventuality that the man couldn't accept, at least not until he'd seen justice done.

Brando's face bore the scars of his Killing Dance. A huge gash across his forehead leaked droplets of blood, his nose was obviously broken, mottled bruises and burn marks seemed to form a pattern, as if he'd painted himself for battle. On one side of his head, his short-cropped hair had been singed to the skin, where a nasty-looking furrow led like a road from his ear to the back of his skull.

"Brando! Are you okay, child?"

Brando smiled, the first time Meji had heard of such a reaction from him in years. "I took care of our demimundo problem, Acharya-zin. One of the ones responsible for their deaths has been brought to justice."

Meji winced but nodded.

"Be enlightened: this is good news. But I pray your dance is done."

"Don't worry, Minister. The CPCC will be handling things on the syndicate front from now on. I am out of that field permanently."

"You're where right now?"

"In a shuttle, crossing the dateline into night. In about thirty minutes I'm gonna be setting down near the jinja, and that's what I want to talk to you about."

The jinja? What does he want there?

"Brando, that's an unusual destination. In fact, if you aren't an arojin, it's off-limits."

Brando nodded. "That's why I need you to get on a transport and meet me there."

Meji stiffened. "Why?"

"I need to speak to the Oracle. It's urgent. I'll probably be arrested soon, so I need to see Her before that happens."

"But you still haven't told me why. Seeing the Oracle is not something permitted to just anyone."

Brando's face began to betray desperation and impatience. Meji began to worry. What if, the Ogdoad forbid it, Brando's Killing Dance was *not* done? If the wende was spinning him toward more death?

"It's a private matter, Minister, but suffice it to say I need the absolution only She can provide." After a pause, he added, "Santo is with her, isn't he? That's what you're afraid of."

"He is, yes. I know you want revenge on him as well, but you can't kill him, child."

Brando sighed. "I don't want to. I want to turn him over to the CPCCAF before he does anymore harm. I won't have any weapons on me."

Meji arched their right eyebrow. "Given your strength, I'm betting you could kill him with your bare hands."

Brando lifted his left arm. It ended in a scarred stump. "Hand. Singular. I'm in no condition to fight. Help me bring him to justice, Arojin-zin."

"Okay, Brando-shi. I will. But your interest in the Oracle still concerns me. Is it because she spoke with Tenshi's voice?" Meji asked. "Is that it? Are you hoping to speak to your translated wife, Brando-shi?"

Brando said nothing for a moment. Then he swallowed heavily.

"You know what Tenshi wanted for her sister, Meji-shi. I can't do it without you."

Meji closed their eyes for a moment, thinking of the Close attacking the ramatini.

"Right. From internal government memoranda, the Oracle and the Archon are secluded away somewhere in the honden, the innermost part of the jinja. I have been only once. It may be difficult. But Samanei has sent most of the guild that protects her away. We should be able to gain access." They stood, nodding. "See you at the gate."

Twenty minutes later a government transport dropped Minister Pishan off at the small tarmac adjacent the jinja. Leaning against a transformer box through which the sanctuary's energy was supplied, Brando raised his gloved right hand in a greeting. The squadman was a disaster: he wore a Brotherhood jumpsuit and heavy boots, but the suit was ripped and scorched in places and the boots had been taped up with emergency compression tape, the sort used on ships for quick engineering repairs. His left arm hung uselessly at his side. Tourniquets were cinched tightly about the arm and Brando's legs, and his left shoulder had been wrapped in compression tape.

"By the Eight," the arojin said as he approached, "you look horrible!"

"Yes. Heavy doses of drugs and the nanodocs dancing in my tissues right now are managing to block the pain pretty well, but I know I'm messed up. You just see the outside. I imagine my organs are in worse shape. It will probably take months for me to get back to normal, whatever that is."

At the gate they had surprisingly little trouble. The omedeyo guard looked at Brando, checked something on the data pad they were holding, and waved them through without a word.

"Okay." Brando shook his head. "That was weird, and too easy."

And so it was at nearly every stop along the way from the outer circles of the sanctuary toward the honden at its center. Brando asked one of the attendants why they were being permitted to pass without question.

"The Oracle told us you would come. We've been expecting you."

This made Brando more nervous than a firefight would have. What nefarious trap did Santo have waiting for him? What sort of death awaited him in the depths of this supposedly holy place? Brando discovered he suddenly didn't care. He had a purpose, a central purpose, for being here. If he could accomplish that task, it did not matter so much that his hopes, the other future he'd planned, might not be fulfilled. He'd given up all claim to happiness long ago: revenge, justice… that was his reason for existing now. Were he to survive, so much the better. He would love the chance to be able to try it all again and do it right this time. But if that dream could not be realized, he would be satisfied with seeing Santo's corpse before his own death.

They were stopped by another omedeyo guard of the Close in front of a metal, airlock-type entranceway.

"The Oracle ordered me," they grunted, "to tell you that you have a choice: you can go through the ritual ablution or you can go on like you are. She recommended you to take the first option. She told me, and I'm quoting, 'Tell him it is better to be clean when one does the work of the Eight.'"

Meji glanced at Brando. "I'll help you, child. Let's get you washed up."

The procedure was long. Painful for Brando. Heartbreaking for Meji.

At last the archon draped white linen robes on his student's thick and scarred limbs, his wounds having been washed and medskin applied them all.

Meji led him through the brief mantra:

Ante ra-Eidan, tani tenshi to roho. Yonke iruju nikdeharu.

Before the Eight, only spark and soul. I leave every illusion behind.

While reciting the words, Meji's eyes fell on the bandaged stub at the end of Brando's left arm. As much as they longed to be rid of the flesh, they could not imagine losing a hand. This realization struck them as significant, and for years to come they would ponder its implications for their own quantum enlightenment.

Revealing that the Oracle was neither in the Black Room or the White, the guard indicated that they should follow a large, spidery-limbed chirurgic that was to check the Oracle's physical recovery from her surgery.

"Surgery?" Meji wondered aloud. "What kind of surgery would the Oracle need, and who would order it done to her?"

Brando clenched his one hand into a fist. "We're about to find out."

As they stepped through the irising entrance to the honden, where the bones of Domina Ditis still lay in the precise spot Dedalo Mostrenco had buried them nearly two centuries earlier, Meji almost wished Brando had decided to bring a gun.

CHAPTER 48

THE SOFT WHIRRING AND CLANKING OF THE chirurgic's progress through a series of twisting passages and large, empty chambers set Brando's mind to working. What was Santo's plan? Why and how the image of Jeini Andrade on the station? The exploding panel? The sudden loss of gravity? Words spoken by one of the Beijing brothers drifted back into his consciousness: *Yen assured me that in two days there won't be any more of these mafia types on the station. It's all been arranged, seriously.*

Was Santo working with Yen Bandera to double-cross the Brotherhood? What could the archon possibly pay that ancient ronin to make him risk his life against the most powerful organization of the demimundo?

A chill passed over him, and he realized that the chirurgic kept stealing glances at him, odd behavior for an only partly sentient medical robot. Like a boy caught eyeing the girl of his dreams, the AI swiveled its head to face the direction they were headed.

"What?" Brando demanded gruffly. He wasn't particularly fond of AIs, having fought many of the illegal hunks of metal over the last seven years.

Before the chirurgic could attempt to answer, they came to a shimmering force field. The robot motioned at them in a oddly human fashion and stepped through the curtain. Brando and Meji followed.

The inner sanctum of the honden was simply a round, high-ceilinged chamber. At the far end a rectangular aperture was cut into the floor, with steps leading down, perhaps to the remains of Domina Ditis. In the middle of the cavernous room was a raised dais on the steps of which sat the Oracle.

Brando's heart ached suddenly: She was *so* much like Tenshi, so identical physically to the woman who had made him a man. He checked an urge to run to her and embrace her.

On the dais itself, in a throne-like chair, with a portable terminal on his lap, sat Santo Koroma. He looked up in utter shock as the other two men stepped out from behind the towering chirurgic.

"But—" he began. Words simply would not come to him. His eyes watered and flashed, as if he were trying to fight off a mix of emotions and comprehend what it was he saw before him.

Samanei stood and spoke.

"Koweke. Thank Domina you came."

It took Brando a second to realize she was addressing him. *Brother-in-law.*

"This monster," she gestured at Santo without looking back at him, "has had me in his claws for so many years that I'd lost hope that anybody would ever come and take me away from him. But that's what you're going to do, no? Tell me you're here to save me."

Brando couldn't speak. He nodded.

"You'll have to kill him. It won't be hard: he's old and has no weapons. The fighting he knows is long distance, via pawns. That's how he killed my sister: he had her assassinated and then gloated about it in front of me."

Santo's eyes continued to flash and leak, but they also began to narrow in anger. He seemed to be understanding something, as if a reality he'd never been aware of had been revealed, the artificial guises ripped off the world in a single, painful jerk.

"Brando," he groaned, his voice squeezed out of a throat constricted by terror and rage, his breath coming in ragged gasps, "I did terrible things to you. I won't deny them, nor tell you that I'm sorry, because I find you to be execrable and beneath me. But listen to me carefully: do not trust this thing before you. I don't know what to call it, but it spent the last twenty-five years lying to me, manipulating me. Only now do I understand the enormity of what it has done, what it is doing."

Samanei laughed a tired, sad laugh.

"Yes, that's right, Uncle, try to escape justice one more time. Use that voice of yours to convince Brando that *I* am somehow behind all the sick things that you have done. I already know you're not a real man, anyway. Why you should start acting like one today?"

Santo set the portable terminal on the dais beside him and leaned forward.

"I depended on her for guidance, Brando. She was my Oracle, my spiritual leader. I always put her commands first, above all I thought was good or bad. She's the person that ordered Tenshi's death."

The archon stood.

"I agreed with it, I won't lie, but don't imagine that all this was just me, Soburinim. This insane creature was there all the time, pushing me to do what you would consider terrible acts. She's brilliant, I grant," he spat, looking over at Meji, who appeared dazed and ready to faint, "but she's no innocent victim here. She even did what I would never have dared: she killed Archon Rawe. She spent years connected to the interstellar net. Domina knows who she met out there in that faux version of this false reality."

Brando felt dizzied by the situation. Santo was admitting his misdeeds in front of Meji Pishan, a good sign, as there'd be a witness. Samanei's role in this, however, he had never considered, and his mind began spinning multiple scenarios at blinding speeds. Santo couldn't have gotten Yen Bandera to help him. Yen Bandera only cared about intel and money. Santo had none to speak of, at least not enough to be worth the wrath of the Brotherhood.

The fighting he knows is long distance, via pawns. That's how he killed my sister.

Samanei's words reverberated in his head.

What if she's talking about herself?

Samanei stifled a frustrated scream.

"I can't believe we have to stand here and listen to a man we *all* know is a sociopath hungry for power blame the woman that *he* kidnapped when she was all of thirteen, the woman that *he* ordered locked away, that he mutilated, that he played out his fantasies on."

Meji looked as if they might collapse at any moment, like a person whose entire existence is rendered meaningless in a second.

Like me after their deaths.

Santo descended a step in Samanei's direction. Brando quickly moved to the base of the dais, linen robes swirling lightly.

"I don't know who's telling the truth here, Santo, but let me make something clear. You stand right there without moving, or I'll break your neck. We're going to hear what the Oracle has to say."

"Thank you, Koweke. I'm sure you know already about how Santo 'discovered' that I was the Oracle. Tenshi no doubt explained it all to you very clearly," there was a strange tone in her voice when saying this, "though I don't know if she got it all right. But there are some things that nobody knows except me and Santo here. Things that he doesn't want anybody to know."

"You filthy animal! Soulless creature!" Santo looked petrified.

"Shut up, Santo, or I'll crush your windpipe so you can't make a sound." Brando balled his one fist up and placed a sandaled foot on the first step leading to the dais to show the seriousness of his threat.

"I was about ten at the time. Different from Tenshi, I loved the teyopan school and wanted to learn more and more. I wanted to be enlightened. My uncle here, he knew a lot about the Prophet and Domina, so I was always looking for an excuse to be where he was there. One day I noticed him going into my grandma's house, so I slipped around back and peeked in the window, hoping that I would hear him talk more about enlightenment."

A hoarse, choking sound came from Santo. He was visibly shaking, his hands clenching and unclenching wildly. Brando ascended another step toward the dais.

"What I saw I didn't quite understand. My grandma was sitting up in bed with her robe down around her waist. Uncle Santo's head was cradled in her arms, and his mouth was to her breast like a baby."

Santo made as if to spring at her, and Brando crossed the remaining distance between them, passing close to Samanei, who gently ran her fingers along his left arm as he went by.

Standing on the dais a step above Santo to equalize their heights, Brando seized one of the older man's arms and twisted it behind his back. As Santo gasped in pain, the ex-professor felt a surge of adrenaline, but not the pleasure he'd always imagined. He had the old bastard, the man responsible for his family's destruction, in his power, yet he felt no better.

Santo had placed a doubt in his mind. He was a villain, no doubt.

But he might also have been a pawn.

"Go on, Samanei."

The Oracle had turned sideways and was looking back and forth between Meji below her and Brando above. She smiled when he said her name.

"I like the way that sounds. Just Samanei. There was Santo, suckling at his mother's wrinkled old breast, and she was stroking his hair and telling him stuff: 'You're the best. You'll lead them all to gnosis. Do whatever you must. Morality is irrelevant. Just enlightenment matters.' More stuff, too. About how he was born to this mission, some kind of reincarnation of the prophet. And him just sucking away, eyes squeezed tight. Then something weird happened. I was looking at them, and of a sudden I could see through them, at the pieces of their selves, all black and full of holes, and the whole world opened up and I could see it all at once, all the small and big things, every detail people most times overlook, it all came streaming in like blue rain and I couldn't stop it, I couldn't understand it all and in the middle of it came the voices, all the voices, above all His—Dresch spoke to me. He spoke and I fell away from the window and curled up inside of my own being and He told me I didn't need Santo anymore, not as a teacher. I didn't need anyone because He was gonna teach me all the things I needed to know."

Meji had fallen to his knees. Brando stood, dumbstruck and fascinated at the change that was coming over Samanei. She hunkered down on herself, making herself smaller, and her voice got quieter and more child-like.

"Then the neighbors, they came, and they found me all dirty in a little ball, and, and they knocked on the door, and uncle, he comes out of the house with my bibi, and they pick me up and carry me back inside and Bibi, she takes my clothes off and gives me a bath and checks my little part and asks me if I bleed yet and I say no not yet, Umma says maybe next year. Then uncle, he comes in and gives me some clothes to wear and asks me what was I doing on the ground in the back yard, and I feel Him take over my mouth and He says with my voice that I was just playing in the dirt and the hot sun made me faint. But He tells me in my mind to look close at uncle and I see uncle don't believe me, though he gots doubts. Bibi takes him aside and I can hear her tell him to keep an eye on me because I could help or hurt."

She straightened up and looked Brando straight in the eye.

"And you know what happened next. When I was thirteen, he found me with the stigmata, he took me from my family, none of them trying to stop him, and he sealed me up in this horrible place. He made me play the role of Bibi, Brando. He suckled at my breast like a baby. And I stroked his hair the way he wanted me too. He's a bad man, Brando. He's hurt people long enough. He had Tenshi killed. And Tana, too, so young and innocent. He made them slaughter her like a pig. Remember her poor little broken body. Kill him, Brando. Kill him now."

Anguish and rage descended like night, and before he knew what he was doing, Brando released Santo's arm, put his own around the old man's neck, and twisted sharply.

With a sickening pop Santo's spine was severed, and he collapsed dead on the steps, sliding a bit before twisting sideways and stopping.

"Good. Now, let's go. We can't stop here. There are many deputies and government officials whose inertia and complicity allowed this evil to happen. You're still in the midst of the Killing Dance, your nascent soul caught up in that grime wende. In no time at all we'll eliminate them, slay the jagen once and for all. Then you can help me rule this world for real."

Brando shook his head. He looked at Santo's lifeless body, then at Meji, who was weeping.

Samanei's presence altered. Her hands hung loosely at her side, and she tossed her head with a carefree motion. Then she spoke with Tenshi's voice. "Come, Brando, umpenzi, it's not too late for us. We got used badly by everybody, but it's our time now. We can remake a family. That's what you really want, no? Another family? Well, this body's back to normal. *Look at me!* The same as when that bastard killed me. Come closer, love. Put your arms around me. You waited so long. Me too. Why should we suffer anymore?"

His heart was hammering in his chest.

How can she do this? I don't understand. But no, it isn't Tenshi. I can't let this thirst be slaked by her lies.

"No."

"No?"

"No. I'm not going to kill anyone for you. I won't be your pawn. As for family, you're not Tenshi. And I don't just want another family, damn you. I want my own *back!*"

Samanei clicked her tongue.

"Look at Santo, Brando, dead there at your feet. Don't feel any better, eh? Thought you would, but it's not enough, never enough. They die, your enemies, but you go on. Maybe when you pull everything they ever did down in piles of rubble and gore, maybe *then* you'll find peace. But you'll never get your family back. They're dead and gone and sapped into the black of nothingness, never to return."

Brando surged toward her in fury, and Meji finally found his voice.

"NO! Brando, don't kill Her! Stop the killing now!"

"Oh, he's not going to kill me, child. I remind him of his wife. Besides," she muttered, patting her abdomen, "he needs me."

Regaining their feet, the arojin asked, "What do you mean?"

"Ah, of course you couldn't know." Her voice was a chuckle. "He's going to clone them."

Brando's head snapped about. He glared at Samanei uneasily.

How could she know? His stomach twisted nauseously. *What the fuck is she?*

"Clone who?"

"Tenshi and Tana. He's gotten his revenge, now he's going to remake his family. Kind of sick, no? He'd be better off with me."

Meji stepped closer to where Brando and Samanei stood only feet apart. Their eyes were bleary with disillusionment. Behind them, the chirurgic began ticking one of its limbs against the floor, as if nervous.

"Tell me this isn't true."

Head whirling, Brando swallowed heavily. "No. She is insane. That wouldn't bring them back. Why I would do it?"

Samanei eyed him with amusement.

"So dei campioni di sangue. So che hai comprato l'apparecchi."

Taken aback by her use of Italian, Brando reflected in panic. It was possible that someone might know he'd swiped the blood samples from the evidence room, or at least guess it had been him. Perhaps she could have learned of the purchase of so much illegal medical equipment, too.

On the net for more than a decade. Every minute of every day.

Unexpectedly, the chirurgic whirred its way forward and spoke.

"Brando D'Angelo. I have a message for you. Playing in three, two, one."

As if awaiting apocalypse, the three humans stood frozen and dumb, the silence looming like some dark beast. A weak but compelling voice, old and full of gravel, began to speak from the robot's innards.

"D'Angelo, this is Archon Rawe. I'm recording this message on Santo Koroma's docbot. I'm pretty sure what it's meant for, the complicated operations that the Oracle will require to be made a regular woman again. I have no idea how all this will play out, and I fear the worst, but I know her, and she will try to get you here, somehow. I hope this chirurgic can get a message to you in time.

"Don't trust her. Whatever you do. She isn't what it is she seems to be. When she first came to the jinja, I was full of selfish hope. I'll admit that openly. She knew in an instant where I was weak. When I wasn't expecting it, when my eyes were closed in meditation in the White Room, she—oh, by the Ogdoad, she lifted my robes and pleasured me. Then she spoke to me with my dead husband's voice and I was so eager to believe I could be with sweet Aroha again that—"

The message broke off into a sob for a second. When Rawe continued, he was more subdued.

"The details aren't important, but she began to play Santo and me off each other. She encouraged me to embrace reform while, I discovered later, berating me in front of Santo and urging him to oppose me. She insisted I cooperate more and more with the CPCC, and she got Santo involved with the Brotherhood.

"Though I had suspected this for years, some events made me relax. Samanei putting her in permanent hypostasis was one, Santo's apparent rejection of the hard line was another. My doubts came back when Santo started his move to quarantine off-worlders, and she told me to play along. Didn't seem right, so I got an off-world tech to bug her connection. Everything was heavily coded and impossible to read, but we traced destinations: she was communicating with every major demimundo organization in and around

CPCC space, as well as religious and mercantile organizations on every major human settlement. Her motives and goals are inscrutable. But she manufactured this situation, D'Angelo. Jitsu would already be part of the CPCC now if she hadn't interfered. Several hundred inhabitants of this world would still be alive, including your wife and daughter.

"Now we come to what is truly dangerous. In a fit of anger as a teen, Samanei once revealed to me her hate of her twin. In the Oracle—in *Samanei's* mind, Tenshi did nothing to help her because she wanted Santo to take her twin away, lock her up and remove her womanhood. She swore she'd see Tenshi and all she loved destroyed.

"You see? All this—mess we're in the middle of, it's just a sick little girl striking out at the sister who was powerless to protect her. That seed of hate, I suspect, opened her up to Sakra's voice. I don't think she's connected to the Ogdoad at all: it's the Demiurge she communes with.

"She discovered my tap on her line, I'm sure. I think she's capable of anything to cover her tracks. I don't have much time, and no one will believe me if I tell them what I fear. But I can warn you, yes. Don't trust her. Don't pity her. And for the sake of us all, don't let her leave in this place. Disconnect her and lock her away. She's evil and twisted inside, capable of destroying us all."

The chirurgic's message ended. The silence felt even heavier than before. Black, inky silence smothering them slowly.

Then Samanei laughed.

It was a horrid, cackling, maniac laugh, the sort of stereotypical laughter of a villain on some infotainment drama.

Brando heard an undercurrent of sarcastic commentary in that laugh, but beneath that a deeper level of true madness and evil that made him tremble involuntarily.

"Ah, yes, horrible evil sick sick sick Samanei. I know yall, the 'normal' ones, quote quote, think I'm sick. Yall imagine that the way that yall see the world, the way yall think inside yall's limited brains, that that's the right way. What if yall're wrong, eh? I pity yall; never hearing all the voices burbling blue there in yall's subconscious," she looked at Brando pointedly, "or just hearing them a bit, thinking it's yall came up with those ideas. Heh. I hear them all, I see it all in crashing waves of blue, all the things that would make yall quiver in fear like the animals yall truly are. And I can let yall hear those voices, let yall peer into the majestic blue light of absolute wisdom, complete and panoramic seeing."

Stretching her limbs and cocking her head to the side, Samanei underwent a mesmerizing transformation. She walked up toward the dais, brushing brusquely past Brando, striding the way a man would, her shoulders and arms held in a completely new way. Turning to face the two men and the robot, she eased into Santo's old chair and began to speak in a man's voice using a very old dialect of Standard:

"Imagine, if you will, a young girl, barely thirteen, whose life is shattered not only by her mental illness, but by the machinations of her wily if Oedipuscomplex-driven uncle. He steals her away while her family stands idly by, even her twin sister, whose much-vaunted aggressive nature and non-conformity completely and quite conveniently fail her in this instance. The young girl is thrust into a situation in which she is compelled to make important religious and political decisions by a group of older men who, despite having sworn off the pleasures of the flesh, are sexually attracted to the teen, to such a degree that they have her surgically altered so as to prevent themselves from giving in and molesting her. Of course, they justify this to themselves by arguing that she will not be bothered with either the temptations or the excretions of the flesh, but deep within them they know, as men throughout the ages have known, that her sex is a weapon that they will impale themselves upon if permitted.

"What is this girl to do? Meekly give in to the oppression? Or turn it against the men, against their culture, against the government that permits such a culture, against the species that permits such a government? Why should she pay a price and not they? In the end, all she wants is to be set free. Returned to womanhood and released from her prison."

Samanei leaned toward them, a look of exhaustion pulling at her features. "I just want to get out of here, do you understand me? Let me go. Please."

Brando felt his carefully welded heart break within his chest.

"You," he rasped, "foolish girl. Don't *you* understand? *She was trying to set you free!* Every reform she pushed through, every step she took along the Path—oh, Samanei, it was because she *loved* you enough to risk everything else!

Reform would lead to an Archon from Ona ra-Shamanga, who would have torn down the jinja and let you be the leader you were meant to be. But you didn't trust her. You had the means to reach out to her. But you preferred to marinade in your pain, letting it rot you to your core. Oracle? You're no oracle. You haven't even had the vision. Couldn't have."

Samanei spat at him, growling.

Meji, whose head had dropped at the sound of the Founder's voice, lifted their eyes and asked that which could not be answered.

"Freedom. You're sure that's all you want, Founder? I sense a larger agenda here, forgive me my impudence. You spoke of ruling this world, of turning against our species. This is just wanting freedom?"

While Meji asked their pointed questions, Brando made his decision. He was tired of the speeches, of wondering whom to blame. Perhaps there would never be an end to the assigning of culpability: perhaps the chain of responsibility was so long and interconnected that there was no honest way of singling out a villain. He suddenly felt weary to his very heart, a sapping weariness that could never be erased because it required the kind of rest only a family could provide: that sense of belonging, that peaceful fulfillment that would never come to him again, he feared. It was time to act.

Rushing up the steps as Samanei rose to perhaps flay Meji with words and prophecies, Brando struck his sister-in-law at the base of the skull with the edge of his open hand, and she collapsed in his arms. He hurried down again, slinging Samanei's unconscious form over his right shoulder. She was as light as a child.

Meji inhaled air sharply.

"What are you going to do, Brando-shi?"

"Take this crazy fem off this planet to a place where she can't hurt anyone, first off. Then I'm going lose myself out there, somewhere. Alone like I'm meant to be." He hefted Samanei's emaciated form, threw her over his shoulder, and walked over to the chirurgic. "Come with me, understand? Show me the fastest way out of this place. One that avoids the guards of the Close."

"Yes, Mr. D'Angelo. Follow, please."

Leaving Meji standing amid shattered illusions, Brando followed.

CHAPTER 49

HALFWAY TO HIS HOME, BRANDO NOTICED that Samanei had woken up and was gently trying to pull free from the compression tape he'd used to strap her into one of the passenger seats. She looked over and saw him staring at her. Across her face spread an ironic smile.

"Guess this means you don't trust me, right? And after all I did for you: hacking into Nawabari's central frame, impersonating Jeini Andrade, doing the research to create a believable recreation of her tragic demise, monitoring the station, making sure years in advance that there'd be a couple of helpful souls on the platform—"

"Yeah, yeah, shutting down the gravity, the list goes on and on. Weighed against the murder of my wife and child, plus all the other deaths you caused, it's bloody insignificant, Sam."

"Ah, from Oracle to Samanei to Sam. What's next: Sa? Sssss? Yessssss I like Sssss."

"You would."

Samanei laughed outright and with apparent glee. "I'm so glad that your sense of humor wasn't pounded out of you. It'll make life with you so much easier."

"Don't get too comfortable."

Samanei craned her neck around the back of her seat. She laughed again, a girlish giggle.

"What now?"

"You brought the chirurgic along. Not confident in your own abilities, eh?" She looked forward at the display and became very serious. "Thank you. I was trapped in there twenty-five years. It's nice to be out, even taped to a seat."

Brando decided not to reply. *Let her babble.*

But she fell silent, and he was left with his thoughts. Once things calmed down, there would be a tribunal. Despite the good he had done, Brando had engaged in multiple illicit activities, highest among them the killing of thirty-odd squad members with a very illegal weapon. Perhaps he would get a civilian trial and avoid military execution, but he would certainly be put away forever. That would be justice, but he had lost faith in justice, or at least in its power to heal. He'd killed three of the people responsible for his wife and daughter's deaths and had the fourth in his hands, but he felt no relief. Instead, the other collateral deaths were already weighing on his mind.

Listening to Samanei's babble, he'd also begun to understand that Ona ra-Oni was not the Way that Tenshi would have wanted him to follow. Its overwhelming power blotted out all else but the task at hand, keeping him from tracing a route into the future. He didn't want to be the dervish anymore. He wanted to be a father, a husband, a planner and a thinker. He wanted quiet warmth, snuggling softness, crinkly paper between his fingers. Gentle, thoughtful habits repeated every day in simple wonder.

Brando had to bite his tongue not to cry in front of his sister-in-law. Perhaps none of that could be his. Perhaps he deserved nothing. The crimes and brutality he had committed demanded payment, not rewards. It was possible that he had never deserved happiness. But he would try to be happy, try to recreate a family, despite all the facts and laws in existence.

His plan had been to do start over in some remote corner of the Southern Continent. Foolish. Impossible.

As the borrowed transport hurtled across barren terrain, a new destination occurred to him, one he had learned of years ago, during those first few days on Jitsu.

They drew up to the house that still echoed Tenshi's soul. A transmission hummed throughout the shuttle.

"Brando D'Angelo, this is Sergeant Yanuar Hurek of the CPCCAF. Please set down the shuttle away from the house and await more instructions."

Brando quickly checked the display panel. Two AF shuttles would be on him in six minutes. Without a word, he quickly banged the shuttle down on the tarmac, grabbed the hypo he'd prepared, and shot Samanei full of drugs.

"Oh, great. Another man doing what he wants with me," she managed to get out before slipping into unconsciousness. Brando used a trucha to quickly free her arms.

"You, chirurgic. Come carry this woman and follow me."

"Yes, Mr. D'Angelo."

They hurried into the lift, the robot compressing its near three-meter height in order to clear the arches. As they hit the basement level, D'Angelo hurried out. The change in gravity strength as he approached the office pounded home the damage his last little adventure had wreaked upon his body. By the time he cycled open the door and leaned against the desk, he was drenched in sweat and the pain was affecting his concentration.

"Mr. D'Angelo," the chirurgic said in its calm, oddly human voice, "I feel very heavy."

"Yeah, well, get used to it. This is how it'll be where we're headed. Now, push this desk out of the way."

The robot did so while still holding Samanei in two of its four upper limbs. His knees popping agonizingly, the linen robes he still wore spreading in a halo of white, Brando knelt and keyed open the trapdoor. He looked up at the chirurgic: it would probably fit, but not carrying Samanei.

"Ah, shite. Here, put the woman on my back when I'm standing on the ladder." The robot complied. He gripped her with his remaining hand while his left arm hugged a rung. "Now grab that shirt over there, no, higher—damnit, on the next shelf, you useless—yeah. Okay. Bind her hands around my neck with it. Good. Now, follow me down."

Samanei wasn't very heavy, but Brando was exhausted. Still, he made it to the bottom in about forty-five seconds and quickly closed the trapdoor from the access panel in the tunnel. The AF would be inside his house any second, and he didn't want them following him, at least not yet.

"Are we returning to the jinja?" the chirurgic asked as it reached Brando's side. It was odd, a docbot's asking questions.

"No. We're going to a ship. Now shut up, take the woman, and follow."

"Yes, Mr. D'Angelo."

They traveled the southbound tunnel for about a kilometer, heading deeper into the earth. It had taken Brando a year to finish the digging with the help of advanced tunneling tractors. Almost the entire house was filled with the dirt from the excavations, except for the basement. The AF troops wouldn't have to search far. They'd no doubt found the panel on the floor and were trying to bypass the codes. Not much time.

Soon Brando and his companions had reached the airlock. Opening it, he motioned the robot inside. "Take her all the way to the back of the ship, to the hypostasis chamber." Then he shut down the far entrance to the tunnel remotely and activated the timer. Ten minutes.

In the physical navigation alcove, Brando initiated the pre-flight sequence. He then dashed to the hypostasis chamber himself. The chirurgic was already inserting Samanei into the suspensor gel of her capsule, even though it hadn't been instructed to. Brando stripped and eased into his own, finding the gel slightly warmer than room temperature. The life-support devices snaked their way to his body, and the pink light of a faux-connection danced over his head. He linked to the faux bridge: immediately he found himself in a vivid virtual room much larger than the simple alcove that actually existed. He walked to the captain's station and sat down. The automated systems were all represented by somatoids of Brando's college friends from Earth, a programming choice that, though whimsical, pleased him every time he thought about it.

"Giuseppe, let me address the passengers on board," he instructed, meaning the chirurgic. The somatoid nodded and opened the ship-wide channel.

"Robot, wherever you are, check the seals on the d-sleep chambers and get to the dormitory. Lay down on the bunk and strap the net across you. We'll be experiencing heavy gravity in a moment. Giuseppe, flip to AF frequency number four. Open? Sergeant Hurek, this is Brando D'Angelo."

"Where are you? We told you to set down outside your house and wait. You're just causing more problems for everybody. We found your trap door, and we're about to open it up, so get ready to come out calmly."

"Listen to me, Sergeant. You've got exactly four minutes and ten seconds to get your men out of my home, into yall's shuttles, and far away. I planted explosives throughout the house. Small transuranic bombs, in fact. I'm surprised your scans didn't detect them. You did scan the property, right?"

There was just silence.

Brando nodded to himself. "Close channel. Piero, prepare to blow the cliff face."

The defense subsystem somatoid nodded. The tunnel ended in a hangar that was smack up against a cliff overlooking the desert to the south. Once the wall was blown, the autopilot would take them out and up, and the accel would begin. In about eighteen hours, once the ship reached .6c just beyond the Oort cloud, fenestration would begin, and Brando's refitted ship would plow through hyperspace to emerge at the edge of explored space, untraceable. Of course, he was counting on the battle above to keep the AF largely off his tail, but he knew he might be pursued all the way to his holing spot. As long as he could keep far enough ahead until then, however, he'd be in the clear.

The chronometer ticked off the seconds to the house's destruction. Brando felt a pang, but he'd be *damned* if anyone would ever live in it, or on the land that lay beneath it.

Ten seconds before detonation, he ordered Piero to blow the wall. The ship lurched out into the open air and nosed upward, just as the huge, beautiful home a kilometer or so away exploded in a deafening hail of concrete, steel, sand and rock, ballooning upward and out. Brando called for the max accel the hypostasis tubes could protect him from, and the ship went screaming through the atmosphere and into the swirling blackness of space.

As he regarded the rapidly receding sphere that was Jitsu, his father's voice unexpectedly rang in his ears: *mentre il mondo pian-piano spariva lontano laggiù.*

"While the world slowly vanishes into the distance below," he crooned to the specters of his loved ones, all of them lost to him, even the living, and he a doppelganger of a man, shuffling through and past them, down the Path, into the limbo of the future.

CHAPTER 50

TWO MONTHS LATER, ORBITING A DEAD WORLD IN AN UNCHARTED system, Brando prepared to rid himself of Samanei forever. As the chirurgic had predicted, the gene therapy they'd put her through to eliminate the physical source of her mental illnesses could do nothing to right the trauma that now drove her. She'd nearly caused him to crash into the planet twice, he'd caught her on the verge of tunneling a message to Sopiya-knew-who several times, and it had become obvious that she couldn't be connected to the faux-life of the ship because she knew how to hack into the virtual bridge. He'd had to keep her strapped down, locked up or drugged while the chirurgic extracted what they needed from her body.

Now here they were, twenty million kilometers from a barely earthlike world, sister of the one they presently orbited, and Kyr—as he'd begun to call the chirurgic—reported the embryos were fine and should develop perfectly.

Brando was relieved. He'd soon be free of his sister-in-law.

He had loaded the escape pod with a couple of weapons, plenty of charge cartridges, knives, a foldable plexisteel domicile, rations, extra clothes, a small portable library, and a host of other supplies she'd need to survive, including a medpack and a scanner for detecting poisons in native food as well as a small protein recombination unit that would help her subsist if she couldn't find edible plants and animals.

From time to time as he packed her things, Brando felt a twinge of guilt, but then he reminded himself of all she'd done and all she was capable of doing. She no doubt deserved to die, but he couldn't bring himself to kill her, couldn't risk turning her over to the authorities. He himself was a wanted man now. Leaving her here was the best option: let fate decide whether she lived or died.

Their escape from the Eta Cassiopeia 2 system had been relatively anti-climactic: the battle raging in space above the other side of Jitsu had kept him free of pursuers except for the one AF shuttle from the surface that hadn't been blinded by the explosion, and even it hadn't been able to keep up with the intense burn Brando's heavily modified *ranfla* was capable of. The shuttle had fired on him several times, damaging a few minor systems, but it had eventually turned back, leaving Brando to clear the system and hole his way into oblivion.

His scans of the unexplored area he'd unexpectedly defenestrated into after a bizarre computer malfunction had at first seemed fruitless. But just when he'd been about to leave in search of another, more promising slice of space, Kyr had pointed out vaguely promising readings that had led him to this frightening system that the star charts called *Castor 6*. As his ranfla had approached, Brando had discovered a sextuple star system made of three binaries, two of the pairs bright visual stars, the other pair dim red flare stars, brighter in X-ray wavelengths than the first four. Around one of the red twins he'd come upon a series of icy and stony worlds, one of which was marginally habitable.

Once the ship was locked into a parking orbit around a dead planet, the chirurgic had begun to help Brando extract ova from Samanei (locked in her claustrophobic cabin, she only allowed the chirurgic to approach her), and they had used recovered DNA from the blood samples of Brando's wife and daughter to clone the two.

They'd failed on several occasions, despite the advanced tools they had at their disposal. Neither of them, despite their understanding of the cloning process, had ever done this before. It was a highly illegal procedure punishable by death, looked upon since for the past two hundred years ago as evil and immoral. Their job was further complicated by the genome masking that Brando insisted on doing, a process that would keep his loved ones' true genetic identity from being discovered except through the most rigorous of scans.

The chirurgic had never balked at the job, though it surely had been programmed with the knowledge of the prohibitions against it. Brando found himself talking more and more to the machine in the absence of any sane human company. It was childlike and had a one-track mind, but its unexpected intelligence and, difficult though it was to believe, apparent compassion for Brando filled the ex-professor with gratitude. He'd even given it a name.

Of course, as the robot was now to be his only companion, it was good that they got along so well; otherwise, the strain of so many repeated failures might have warped Brando's mind. Six weeks ago, they'd succeeded, and the embryos were still maturing and healthy. Samanei was no longer needed, and Brando didn't want to give her the chance to finish the task she'd started: destroying Tenshi and all that she'd loved.

Palming the intercom on the wall open, he gave the order: "Okay, Kyr, bring her down."

Soon the robot floated down the ladderway to the lower corridor where Brando waited at the escape pod's hatch. In his arms, bound and gagged, was Samanei. As Kyr used its other appendages to push down the corridor, Brando hooked himself onto the wall and regarded his sister-in-law. She'd filled out well, and she painfully reminded him of Tenshi more and more every day. He couldn't get her to do anything about her shock of hair, however. She'd never had to care about her appearance, and he wondered if she ever would.

As he took her from Kyr and eased her into the g-netting, she aimed a viscious kick at him. But her muscles were too weak. Brando was glad that the world they were sending her to had such low gravity, as years in hypostasis and months in space had seriously deteriorated her muscular and skeletal systems.

For a moment, he almost changed his mind about sending her into such terrible exile: he realized there was a very good chance she wouldn't survive. But then he hardened himself and removed her gag.

"Well, Samanei, this is it. Time to say goodbye."

"You can't do this, Brando. Leave me alone on some world light years away from anybody else. That's evil."

"No, it's the one alternative to killing you I've got. You'll be fine. All those resourceful neurons working overtime, you're going to blossom down there. And just think: a whole planet, all to yourself. No ambitious people trying to use you. I would think you would be thrilled."

"What about my babies?"

"Those are *not* your babies."

"You used my little eggs. They're mine." She strained against the mesh.

"Okay, this conversation is over."

"You know, you're just as crazy as me, Dr. D'Angelo. I hacked into that little faux-life of yours, saw those avatars of Tenshi and Tana. How much time you spent in there, Koweke? You ever, you know, relive the romantic moments with my sis? Little 'dock the rocket' with the old doppelganger?"

Brando shook his head. He couldn't even feel rage at this thing before him. All he wanted was to be free of it forever. He slipped back out the hatch, prepared to close it.

"You're nuts, Brando. What normal man would clone his dead wife and raise her as if she was his daughter? Stark, raving mad. Don't think you can run from that, or your past either. It's all going catch up with you, Koweke. It'll sneak up when least you expect it. And me too. You'll never be free of me, not if you send me into a black hole, even. Just wait. You've got no idea, Brando, who I am or what I see. You think your fleeting vision of some faint blue spark gives your existence meaning? You fool."

She stretched her face toward him, and he recoiled at what he saw in her eyes.

"I have been down to the deepest depths of *Gumun Gereza*, to the greyest of cells of this vast prison, and I saw Him, roaring orange in all his glory. Not Dresch, Doctor, but HIM. Domina's son. Sakra made flesh. He wants to meet you, Brando."

Shuddering, Brando remembered Sakra's voice, bleak and spiteful.

You seek shattering? I will break you.

Samanei smiled at his hesitation. "Ah, that's right. You've heard Him speak. He's not done breaking you, Koweke. He's waiting there in the growing grey, just for—"

With a grimace of disgust, Brando cycled shut the hatch and cut her off mid-rant. He sighed, then punched the launch button.

The hull reverberated with the thrust of Samanei's departure for a couple of seconds, and then there was silence.

"She called you *Dr.* D'Angelo. You want me to call you *Dr.* D'Angelo?" Kyr floated to Brando's right, two arms close to his wasp waist, the other two held out for balance.

"No. Call me Nando Miranda. That's my new name."

"Okay, Nando Miranda. I like your new name."

Brando had to laugh. "Let's go check on the girls, Kyr."

Up in the medical alcove, Brando and Kyr verified the embryos' progress. Already in their sixth week, the lumps of cells were starting to take form. Beside them in the lab floated Brando's nearly grown replacement hand, which they'd cloned several weeks ago and forced to age more rapidly in a specially charged nutrient bath. After the surgery the following week, it would be time to prepare the injections that D'Angelo would be taking over the next eight months. Gene therapy, designed to return his body to its previous adaptive state, one that could handle a thicker, Earth-like atmosphere and gravity, came first, and then the genome masking. His physical appearance would also have to be changed, permanently.

It would be a grueling, painful time, but nothing compared to the past eight years. He had a new language to learn, as well, and a new religion to adapt to. His choice seemed to fly in the face of the Path, but he could continue to create a soul for himself in any environment. Nando Miranda was just a extension of his self into the physical world, a construct like Tenshi's house or Samaneino Teyopan. A tool for enlightenment.

"Take one away," Tenshi had said to him in the vision. "Bring two back. Prepare them."

Brando had sworn to obey. He had taken Samanei from Jitsu. He was bringing back Tenshi and Tana. He would prepare them. If he didn't, she had warned him in that first dream in the hospital, the end would come.

But she had also made a promise.

"I will come back to you."

And he believed. Just as he believed in the Path, in the Ogdoad, in his own nascent soul, he believed that somehow, somehow, Tenshi would return.

Hope. Love. Faith. Gifts that Jitsu had given him.

He thought of his father's guitar, sealed in a case in the cargo compartment. He hadn't touched it in eight years, and he couldn't bring himself to yet. Perhaps, with time, he'd be able to play those old songs again.

After all, it no longer hurt to think of his father. There was no anger left in Brando's heart for him.

Once he found a new Way, perhaps all those old pains would fade.

As Kyr clicked and clattered away, performing some maintenance task or another, Brando strapped himself onto a stool and sipped some coffee from a flask. Eight months to get ready, then the babies would be removed from the tank and placed in the hypostasis tube. They'd accel to .6c and fenestrate to their new home. This time he'd do it right. This time he wouldn't leave their side. This time they would survive, because he'd teach them what they needed to survive. It was his penance; it was his joy.

He stared for the longest time at the tiny embryos suspended in blue-green fluid within the tank. His hand went to his and Tenshi's wedding rings, hanging from a chain around his thick neck, and he wondered.

How similar would they be to the real Tenshi and Tana? Would he be able to keep the truth a secret from them forever? What would happen if they discovered the truth, read Tenshi's journal, scanned Brando's files? Would they consider him a monster?

Would they consider themselves monsters?

In the end, he decided, these last questions didn't really matter. They were all monsters, all three of them. So was everyone else, when you came right down to it.

That's how the demiurge forged us.

His grim, grey smoke billows within us all.

But at its center, Brando thought with trembling joy, glows a holy spark.

A tenshi.

A bit of the divine.

EPILOGUE

From: <u>MejiPishan@jitsu.gov.jit</u>

To: <u>modupe@oduyoye.per.nng</u>

Subject: Going-ons

Date: September 16, 2697 20:15:29 (SST)

Professor Oduyoye:

Good to hear that you're doing well. The condition of you sister brings me great sorrow. She'll be in my mind during meditation.

Tomorrow Regent Alwan turns control of Jitsu back over to the restructured government, though a small peace-keeping force will stay behind to ensure that the resettled inhabitants of Station City—which they'll be renaming, did you hear—are safe and unmolested. I'll be sworn in as interim prime minister at noon in a ceremony that most people in the capital will likely attend. As head of Jitsu's first secular government, I'll have a lot of work on my hands, but that's fine. I love this world, and I want to see it grow. I wish you would reconsider my offer. We're definitely going to reopen Ra-Koreji, and there's nobody better than you to run it. But I'll respect your decision.

The past four months were a whirlwind, what with the CPCC investigation and military trials. Major Sosa's conviction and public execution hit the Dominatudan hard, but I think they're too ashamed of what he did to make waves. The deaths of the squad leaders and the dozen or so functionaries that were involved has squelched any debate.

Which brings me to Ben Wu. You asked me to find out the outcome of his case, so I snooped around and learned that yes, he did recover his daughter, with the help of the AF. For turning state's evidence, they charged him with a lesser crime, and it looks like they'll commute his sentence. I hope he and his daughter find peace and enlightenment.

The AF, I understand, is still battling the remaining Brotherhood forces, which have now broken into warring factions. The AF ran them out of the Beta Pictoris system at last, though at a huge cost. All those men and women lost when Brotherhood HQ exploded—may their families find comfort. But it wasn't in vain. They discovered a massive plan to take over the CPCC. A thorough one, but thank the Founder it failed. Have you heard whether they figured out who ordered the heads killed? The AF found a cache of ships and weapons in the lifeless Gamma Doradus system, I saw. The Brotherhood was already trying to move the materiel out, but the AF was able to compound about five hundred vessels. Five hundred. Just imagine what might've happened. It's a good thing Jitsu became the stumbling block.

In truth, our mutual friend did, no? I often think about him. The CPCCAF wants him for questioning, though it seems Wu testified that Brando did nothing he wasn't forced to do by the circumstances. They can't find him, though. He went somewhere he can't be traced, and the Oracle, or rather, Samanei, is no doubt keeping him busy. I hope that, far away from the traumas that opened her nascent soul to Sakra's spite, she's begun to heal.

Wherever they are, I wish them both peace and life. Theirs was taken away by force. I can't, for some reason, be angry at them. Even though they did terrible acts, I keep asking myself what I would've done in their place. It's not my duty to judge. That's what our faith teaches us, and no matter how much these events have made me waver, my faith is sure.

At the same time, I suppose it *is* my duty. As prime minister, it *will* be. So I guess, if they were brought before me, I would need to apply the full force of the law against them.

Let's hope they stay forever lost, no?

The Ogdoad enlighten you.

Meji Pishan

APPENDICES

APPENDIX A: GLOSSARY

The origin of words not common in Standard is indicated by an abbreviation: B for Baryogo, K for Kaló, Sp for Spanish.

Al-Muzzaml—private intelligence network run by Yen Bandera

Anca L'ermandá—(K, lit. "House [of] the Brotherhood") area in the Cimmeria Region of Mars where most of the ruling families of the Brotherhood reside.

Anshyano—(B) a *satorijin* who doesn't work within the government or as a giya.

Aransa—(B) midwife

Archon—Standard translation of the Baryogo word *ratowanin*: ruler of Jitsu's theocratic government and of the Neo Gnostic religion on that world.

Arojin—(lit. "other-born") one who has achieved *gnosis*.

Baryogo—a Belter creole spoken on Jitsu.

Grey Prison, the- Neo Gnostic term for the physical universe.

Blue, the—see *Wende*

Bouncecom—an illegal communications device that circumvents normal channels

Chirurgic—a now illegal AI medical robot (also *docbot*)

Chrome—projectile handgun whose nearly frictionless barrels and laser targeting give its bullets deadly supersonic speed and accuracy.

Civil Security—Jitsu's policing force and army

Close, the—see *Karibudan.*

Conduit, the—discovered in 2523 by Dédalo Mostrenco near Alpha Centauri, the Conduit was a path through hyperspace which allowed Soltec and the military to dominate human expansion into space for close to a century, until Mostrenco killed himself in an explosion within the Conduit that closed it forever in 2619.

CPCC—the Consortium of Planets, Corporations and Colonies; the unified government of nearly all human habitats, founded in 2530 as a replacement for the dissolved United Solar Republics.

D-sleep—the practical cessation of bodily function for the duration of a space flight to allow a body's encasement in suspensor gel. When accompanied by participation in a faux-life, d-sleep is referred to as hypostasis.

Defenestration—exiting higher dimensional space

Demiman—(K) a criminal (term originated on Mars)

Demimundo—(K) the underworld; the criminal underbelly of the CPCC

Diet—legislature of the CPCC, made up of three houses: the chamber of deputies, the citizens' assembly and the senate.

Dominatudan—ultraconservative group of Neo Gnostics on Jitsu that want to cut the planet off from the rest of humanity. Also known as Dominians or Strict Dominians.

Eight, the—(also called the *Ogdoad*) the eight-sided being, a quantum singularity believed by Pathwalkers to exist separately from our universe; two separated from the Eight, providing the basis for our universe. Every time a human reaches quantum enlightenment, a piece of the two is returned to the Eight.

Enlightenment—1) in Pathwalker theology, the gradual process of reaching *ra-Yindawo*, i.e., becoming a higher dimensional being (*quantum enlightenment*) 2) in underworld lingo, an assassination in which the body is left to be found, usually as a message.

Faux-com—technology that allows users to "exist" in virtual environments by means of direct neural stimulus.

Faux-confererencing—use of virtual environments for communication.

Faux-life—a fantasy world generated by frames. During space flight, travelers typically log into a faux-life and mentally 'live' there in virtual bodies (*doppelgangers*), interacting with *somatoids*, virtual personas that appear completely real, and surrounded by *keshiki*, interactive environments.

Fenestration—(also known as "holing") travel through higher dimensional space; a ship must accelerate to .6c in order to fenestrate, and upon defenestration, must travel a considerable distance from the defenestration point before holing again.

Fidensio—(affectionately "Fidensito") the legendary healer and prophet revered by Fidensistas, followers of a syncretic religion blending Catholicism with Mesoamerican shamanism.

Gimmal—rotating chamber that creates gravity. Older ships without gravity sinks or gravity tiles have an outer hull around an inner gimmal that *purls*, or spins to create centrifugal gravity.

Giya—(B) the guide to enlightenment in charge of a teyopan

Gnosis—the third and penultimate stage of enlightenment: complete self-knowledge

Gunsel—criminal

Hesukrito—(K) Jesus Christ

Hypostasis—the combined system of d-sleep and connection to faux-com or existence in a faux-life.

Iho/a d'angel- (K, lit. "son/daughter of [an] Angel) member of one of the Aztlan Angels' ruling families

Imrizabu—a tunnel through higher dimensional space

Interstellar Net, the—information, communication, entertainment, education all depend upon this massive, Consortium-wide network that uses tunneled transmission beams to maintain its connections.

Jagen—(B) enormous, fifteen-meter long reptilian monsters, which roamed Jitsu's vast wastelands for a million years, but which are now confined to the southern continent.

Jinja—(B) the Oracle's shrine, built on the site of Domina Ditis' grave.

Jitsu—(B, corruption of "Ditis") originally called Ares, Jitsu is the second planet of the binary star system Eta Cassiopeiae 2; claimed officially by Soltec in 2533, it was actually discovered by Domina Ditis twelve years previously when she was sucked through a spatial rift and stranded there with the abusive crew of her uncle's ship.

Jitsujin—(B) inhabitant of Jitsu

Juresh—(B) capital city of Jitsu

Kaló—offshoot of Latin-American Spanish spoken in the Cimmeria Region of Mars, some orbital platforms around Jupiter, and in other areas controlled by the Brotherhood and the Aztlan Angels.

Kantō—(B) home, house

Karada ra-Kusini—the southern continent of Jitsu

Karibudan—(B) The Close, a guild of omedeyo that provide security and care to the Oracle.

Kasike—(K) syndicate boss

Kasikeria—(K) the rule of a kasike (both his authority and the physical reach of his power)

Kedarumsha—(B) someone who has reached quantum enlightenment while still alive

Kehatsu—(B) awareness, the first stage of enlightenment for Neogs.

Keshiki—virtual interactive environments

Kewbox—a portable faux-life connection with a basic *keshiki* that is used for interrogations.

Kinguyama—city in the *Mashkanu* prefecture on Jitsu; birthplace of both Tenshi and Samanei Koroma; first municipality on Jitsu to adopt a non-religious governmental structure

Kiyish—(B) a spike from the Urim carried on pilgrimages; dropped into the sea at particular coordinates dictated by the ramatini

Kleinballs—tools used in meditation; contemplation of them is supposed to turn the mind inward on itself and help push one toward gnosis.

Klika—(K) gang

Konk rifle—slang for *concussion rifle;* this weapon fires com energy waves and is typically used against large targets

Konsehero—(K) counselor

Koweke—(B) brother-in-law

Kude Kisiwa—(B) a chain of islands between the Northern Continent and Southern Continent, also The Distant Isles

Kwate—(K) friend

Kyosu—(B) university professor

L'ermandá—(K) see *Brotherhood, the*

L'onda—(K) Brotherhood code of honor

Lazgat—small energy pistol

Matakite—(B) seer, a person who accepts the Pathwalker faith after having a vision

Materia—(K) spiritual medium

Mitawa—(B) title for Pathwalker ascetics

Moku—(B) mild hallucinogen and depressant used in meditation, derived from the mohiyo plant

Mothergod—a slightly offensive expletive, used commonly by Wiccan Catholics and natives of Earth

Muher—(K) wife

Mushri—(B) leader of a religious order

Muwanani samadan—(B) the unenlightened: derogatory term for non-Pathwalkers.

Nako—(B) a term used to describe activities or objects that hamper enlightenment

Narthex—airlock between sensitive systems on a ship; tubular interface between vessels.

Navarch—commander-in-chief of the Consortium Flotilla

Neo Gnosticism—*see* Path, the

Neog—(slightly derogative) Neo Gnostic, an adherent of Neo Gnosticism or pertaining to that religion. Preferred term: *Pathwalker*

Nosisu—(B) see *Gnosis*

Nuova Rinacenza—the New Roman Renaissance, a cultural movement that spawned the Nuova Pace Romana, a Wiccan Catholic Empire that lasted from 2305-2419. It was defeated in the Solar War (2410-2420) that gave birth to the USR.

Ogdoad—(see Eight, the)

Ohete—(K) jerk; unnecessarily mean individual

Omedeyo—(B) a non-binary, intersex, two-spirit, or genderfluid person

Oni—(B) feathery haired, upright, meter-high monkey analogs

Oracle, the—Pathwalkers' direct connection to the Ogdoad. A sort of prophet, an Oracle appears once every century or so and is the only living being in constant communion not only with the Ogdoad, but also with the created souls that have been rejoined to it.

Orakuru—(B) see *Oracle, the*

Osculate—to dock using a narthex

Path, the—religion begun by Alejandro Dresch on Earth in 21st century: very popular on Mars, Jitsu, the asteroid belt and some corporate platforms. Called Neo Gnosticism by many non-believers. Teaches the creation of souls through enlightenment.

Pocho—(K) born into the Brotherhood but raised without knowledge of its ways.

Portbot—semi-sentient robot used for menial tasks.

Purl—(n) the spin of a gimmal; (v) to engage the gimmal

Quantum enlightenment—the final stage of enlightenment; the joining of the created soul to the Ogdoad.

Ramatini—Sage, an ancient title usually designating the closest companion of an Oracle.

Ra-Koreji—(B) school founded by Brando D'Angelo and Tenshi Koroma

Ra-Yindawo—(B) the nirvana-like plane that contains the Ogdoad

Rasaro Platform—principal orbital transport hub for Jitsu

Ratowanin—(B) see *archon*

Reporumatudan—faction of Pathwalkers that want Jitsu to embrace off-worlders. Also Reformers.

Samadan—(B) new members of a teyopan (children born into the community became new members at seven): unenlightened seekers of enlightenment.

Sancha—(K) mistress

Satori—basic enlightenment, the second stage on the Path to ra-Yindawo.

Satorijin—(B) any Pathwalker who has reached *satori*.

Seudo-novelas—(Sp) faux-lifes broadcast daily that are similar to present-day soap operas.

Shangazi—(B) omedeyo sibling of one's parent (like aunt/uncle, but nonbinary)

Shimanga—(B) Shattering, a denomination of Neo Gnosticism.

Shell—illegal artificially intelligent mercenary robot

Sikarito—(K/B) lowest level in syndicate 'army'

Slidewalk—common form of public transport for pedestrians.

Soburinim—(B) my niece/nephew

Solpat—patois of Japanese, English, Spanish and other languages (similar to Baryogo)

Somatoids—computer generated pandemoniac personas within a faux-life. Can adapt and alter in personality, just as though they were actual people.

Sonari—the name of the clan Tenshi's family belongs to

Squink—youngster (Martian slang, derived from K *eskuinkle*)

Standard—(also *Solar Standard*) derivative of English used as the lingua franca of the CPCC

Station City—a neutral area of Jitsu jointly controlled by the CPCC and the government of that world.

Sub-kasike—(K) underboss in syndicate

Suspension pods—used for g-intensive spaceflight. One's body is cushioned and suspended in suspensor gel, simulating more normal gravity. As bodily functions must be slowed down to d-sleep for the duration of the trip, the pods are generally equipped with links to the Interstellar Net and a faux-life generating 'frame, allowing passengers to keep mentally active and crew to pilot the ship from a pseudo-bridge.

Suspensor gel—a high-impact colloid which cushions the body against the stresses of gravity-intensive space flight. Used in conjunction with suspension pods.

Takiwajan—(B) district head, prefect

Tanim—(B) my daughter

Texas—area of a space craft that contains the crew's quarters

Teyopan—(B) Pathwalker place of meditation and learning.

Teyopanjin—(B) full members of a teyopan, those who've attained kehatsu. Most people within a prefecture stay at this level their entire lives, cut off from the rest of humanity by a series of dogmatic restrictions that limit them to a non-material existence.

Trucha—(K) laser blade.

Umbini—(B) a dyad or dual being (normally used to describe any of four entities that make up the Ogdoad)

Umma—(B) mother

Unified Chinese—(Xīn Hànyⵗ) unification of various dialects of Mandarin that was imposed on Unified China in the 23rd century.

Urim—a strange meteorite on the Southern Contient.

Welkin—Solar slang for all space beyond the Solar System

Wende—(B) (also *awomi*) a psychological state in Pathwalker meditation, achieved typically through rapid, unthinking action. According to Dominian doctrine, *wende* occurs when the reconstructed self reaches out to the Ogdoad, yearning to become a soul and reunite with the source. Called the *Blue* in the original English version of the *Revised Bible*.

Wey—(K) guy, man

White Doom, the—the environmental and economic collapse brought about by mismanagement of Earth's resources by white hegemonic capitalism, leading to the present ice age.

Wiccan Catholicism—the faction of Catholicism that in 2305 joined forces with extreme leftist groups to exile the pope and dominate Earth, imposing brutal, Roman order on the deadly anarchy and destruction that had broken out after the beginning of the ice age. Through its Nuova Pace Romana, Wiccan Catholicism ruled Earth and parts of the Solar System for more than a century, till the Solar War broke up the empire and the United Solar Republics were founded.

Yaks—short for (J) *yakuza*: common term applied to underworld criminals

Yegster—criminal

Yorukaki—(B) communication with an individual soul within the Ogdoad

Zazen—(B) meditation with drugs, virtual mandala, kleinballs, etc.; *samadan* must undergo seven years of this before achieving *kehatsu* and becoming *teyopanjin*

APPENDIX B: PHRASES IN BARYOGO AND KALÓ

Phrases in Baryogo with translation, in the order they appear in this book:

• *Wapi tubo taru ka, chupeka?* Where are the tubes, bitch?

• *Open shikasero zo!* Open it!

• *Amo okanjuwa.* Not ambition.

• *Jambo.* Hello.

• *Muwema michana.* Good afternoon

• *Amo Jitsujin.* Not inhabitants of Jitsu.

• *Manta raha.* Pleasure to meet you (literally "much pleasure")

• *Raha na newa, soro.* The pleasure is mine, rather.

• *En kurin shigotuta.* She worked in cleaning (i.e., the cleaning crews")

• *Tiksaberu ka.* You know, right.

• *Sajana!* Hey, boss!

• *Bishaberu.* Greetings.

• *Meiru yegachu.* Mail has arrived.

• *Baryogo shikaburaro wa, aburonim.* Let's speak Baryogo, Uncle.

• *Nan? Shikihiro zo!* What? Say it!

• *Shiperaro wa.* Wait, please.

• *Niboraru, nikantaru en paransek awomi rai pin.* I fly, I sing in a blue-hued Blue without end.

• *Kanshon mishgutachu ka?* Did you like the song?

- *Kesekki.* Asshole.

- *Omenim.* My twin.

- *Mishonari.* Missionary.

- *Ummano toto.* Mama's baby.

- *Shinechayudaro. Dai naseru.* Help me. I'm dying.

- *Yoyote mikkereru.* Whatever you want.

- *Amo inyani, iruju tani.* It isn't reality, it's just a mirage.

- *Newano okanim.* My dearest heart.

- *Umpenzi.* Beloved.

- *Quena.* Yes.

- *Shamanichu yewano biye, tenshi zikwepachu.* Their body burst, it became sparks of truth.

- *Umonim.* My mother-in-law.

- *Annidaru nidaru nizikwepachu.* I don't exist, I exist, I have become myself.

- *Zumbinaro soro!* Be truly one from two!

- *Shemejinim.* My son-in-law.

- *Aponim.* My father-in-law.

- *Nimuyo, newa.* I'm drunk.

- *Newa na tenshi.* My spark of truth.

- *Bibinim.* My grandparent.

- *Mengo, mengo.* Sorry!

Phrases in Kaló with translation, in the order they appear in this book:

- *Puras pendehaaz.* A bunch of nonsense.

- *Bendita Mariya.* Blessed Mary.

- *Pura Ermandá.* The Brotherhood rules.

- *Kalmau, ese.* Calm down, man.

- *Grasias por benir.* Thanks for coming.

- *Si ya sabe uté.* Please: you already know.

- *Maje de syelo.* Mother of Heaven.

- *Pa ser franko.* To be honest.

- *Kó to respeto.* With all due respect.

- *Solo eres omme, kompa.* You're just a man, buddy.

- *Soy kasike de L'ermandá.* I'm the head of the Brotherhood.

- *Yo tammen.* Me too.

- *I yo.* And me.

- *Weno, toy dencho.* Okay, I'm in.

- *Chingos.* A shit-ton.

- *Ohetes.* Assholes.

- *Weno. Lo ke tu keras.* Fine. Whatever you want.

- *Ó vá tar las apareishons de L'ermandá?* Where are Brotherhood operations going to be?

- *Pendeho.* Dumb-ass.

- *A poko?* Really? You don't say.

- *I naa.* And nothing.

- *Bato.* Dude.

- *Puto hosupin.* Fucking bastard.

- *Kalmate, ermano.* Calm down, brother.

- *Kwestate.* Lie down.

- *Pa naa.* Not at all, no way.

- *Kiubole?* What's up?

- *Chinganno la maje.* Annoying the fuck [out of someone]

- *Mi kasike grandote.* My great big boss.

- *K'onda, hefa?* What's up, mom?

- *A ber.* Let's see.

- *Komprennes?* Do you understand?

- *Karnaliyo.* Little brother.

- *Kabrō.* Fucker.

- *La puta maje ke t'iso nacer.* The bitch that gave you birth.

- *Pos, a mover el kulo.* Then, get your ass moving.

- *Entendites?* Did you grasp that?

- *I chinga tu maje tammen.* And fuck your mother, too.

- *L'ermandá pa sempre.* The Brotherhood forever.

- *Eso kres tu.* That's what *you* think.

- *Perra.* Bitch.

- *Po L'ermandá, pendeho.* For the Brotherhood, dumbass.

- *M'an mandau n'iho de berga, no?* They've sent me a tough fucker, huh?

- *Pinche puto.* Stupid fuck.

- *Vas a velo, hosupin.* Just wait, bastard.

- *Tu nomme, pero ya.* Your name, *now.*

- *Chinga tu maje.* Fuck your mother.

- *La tuya, kulero.* Yours, asshole.

- *Mi ermano te vachingar.* My brother's going to fuck you up.

- *No bales berga i lo sabes.* You're not worth shit and you know it.

- *Komprennites?* Did you understand?

- *Si, komprenní.* Yes, I understood.

- *Yebesen esta myerda d'aki.* Get this piece of shit out of here.

- *Tu, deha d'aserte pendeho; be me trais gaz i alkol d'infirmari.* You, stop acting like a dumbass; go get me gauze and alchohol from the infirmary.

- *Lebol seis. Purale, baboso.* Level Six. Hurry up, numbnuts.

- *Parelen.* Stop.

- *Ke karaho?* What the hell?

- *Lebantate, kulero.* Get up, asshole.

- *Sal pa hwera.* Get out.

- *Chingaa maje.* Goddamnit.

APPENDIX C: CHARACTERS

Andrade, Jimi—head of the Aztlan Angels sindicate

Bandera, Yen—an ancient free-lance spy; head of the Al-Muzzaml network

Bek, Inho—personal secretary to Archon Rawe.

Benemerito, Toni—kasike supremo of the Brotherhood before Konrau

Beserra, Felipe—Konrau Beserra's younger half-brother

Beserra, Karmen—mother of Konrau and Felipe Beserra

Beserra, Konrau—kasike supremo or leader of the Brotherhood crime syndicate

Bos, Nestor—counselor to Konrau Beserra

Canales, Luisa—architect, protégé of Tenshi Koroma who runs the firm Izakiwo

Chimari, Jina—spouse of Meji Pishan, Reformer teacher in Kinguyama

Chono, Zamilan—abusive uncle of Domina Ditis

Chunhawan, Seni—mayor of Station City

D'Angelo di Koroma, Tana—Brando and Tenshi's daughter

D'Angelo di Makomo, Brando—professor of linguistics from Earth

D'Angelo di Makomo, Edoardo—Brando's older brother

D'Angelo, Giacobbe—Brando's father, left family to start over on the world of Oceania.

Ditis, Domina—a previous Oracle of the Path; founder of the Dominian sect

Dresch, Alejandro—author of *The Revised Bible*; founder of the Path

Gizensha, Ana—former giya of Samaneino Teyopan in Kinguyama

Harakore, Miko—mother of Monchu and Santo

Kikwete, Wan—Speaker of the Jitsuan Chamber of Deputies

Kino, Maryam—wife of Santo Koroma

Koroma, Monchu—Pathwalker missionary; Tenshi and Samanei's father; older
brother of Santo Koroma.

Koroma, Samanei—the third and present Oracle of Dominian Neo Gnosticism;
twin of Tenshi Koroma

Koroma, Santo—important religious and political leader on Jitsu; uncle of
Tenshi and Samanei Koroma

Koroma, Tenshi—architect and reformer leader, sister of the Oracle

Lameda, Tripō—footsoldier for the Brotherhood

Leksono, Tri—*maharaja* or ruler of Kunti (Sigma Draconis)

Lopes, Ambarina—captain of the *Velvet*, Tenshi's former lover.

Lubin, Ginette—prime minister of the CPCC from 2680 to 2686

Makomo-D'Angelo, Marie-Thérèse—Brando's mother; cleric in the Wiccan
Catholic Church.

Martin, Chago—captain of a Brotherhood crew sent to Jitsu.

Mostrenco, Dédalo—former CEO of Soltec and founder of the Consortium

Mukerji, Buddhadev—captain of the *Pacifactor II*

Muntso, Jetsu—prime minister of the CPCC from 2692 to 2698

Oduyoye, Modupe—professor of comparative religion, friend of Brando
D'Angelo.

Onamata, Inyoni—mother of both Tenshi and Samanei.

Pishan, Meji—a respected arojin who supports reform

Rawe, Mutemi—*ratowanin* or archon of Jitsu when Brando arrives.

Sanaustin, Arehanja—disciple of Domina Ditis and lover of Dédalo Mostrenco. Jitsu's moon is named for her.

Soral, Leyla—mayor of the city of Lyonesse on the planet Dhara; later CPCC ambassador to Jitsu

Sosa, Michiyu—former major in the Jitsu Liberation Army; heads Anti-Terrorism Squads.

Spinelli, Isabella—a biologist; former lover of Tenshi Koroma

Tayibo, Nosowa—head of the Modern Languages Department at the University of Jitsu

Trinh, Nikki—owner of Trincon, the biggest supplier of construction materials on Jitsu, friend of Tenshi Koroma

Umchawi, Hekima—priestess at Jinja ra-Shamanga, the Shrine of Shattering. Considered a ramatini or sage of the Path.

Wu, Ben—military officer, retired from the Consortium military and hired to lead an anti-terrorism squad on Jitsu

Yesuro, Areshan—prefect of Inkungu and close friend of Tenshi Koroma

APPENDIX D: PLANETS

The following star systems are referenced in *The Blue-Spangled Blue*. Planets' distance from their stars are given in astronomical units (AU).

CPCC MEMBERS

ALPHA CENTAURI 3

Alpha Centauri A (Rigil Kentaurus)—located 4.4 light years from Earth.

- *Sihtu* (.5 AU)—Tidally locked world close to star. XID (the CPCC's Executive Intelligence Division) established its HQ on the dark side of Sihtu, in honeycombed caves beneath the surface, in 2530.

- *Sukra* (.95 AU)—Rocky, hot world encircled by platforms and stations, heavily mined starting in 2540.

- *Dhara*—Settled in 2522 when it was marginally habitable. Terraformed completely by 2556. Home of CPCCAFHQ. Year is 1.34 Earth years. Two moons: Chandra and Marama. Principal city: La Caille.

- *Sani* (3 AU)—Gas giant with many moons and platforms.

Alpha Centauri B (Utu)—located 4.4 light years from Earth.

- *Ninsianna* (.75 AU)—Terraformed over a century, from 2530 to 2661. Owned by Centauri Terraforming Group (formerly Soltec).

- *Simuud* (1.2 AU)—Cold hunk of rock; mining center, mainly.

- *Fetutea* (2.5 AU)—Smallish gas planet (a little smaller than Uranus) with ten moons, five inhabited (enclosed cities): New Nigeria, Kush, Nubia, Mali and Kerma.

Alpha Centauri C (Proxima)—located 4.2 light years from Earth.

- Site of one of the gates for the Centauri-Eta Cassiopeiae Imrizabu, dubbed The Conduit, destroyed in 2619.

- *scher Wynde*—heavy comet shield/Oort cloud surrounding the triple system.

ETA CASSIOPEIAE 2

Higante—located 19.4 light years from Earth. One settled planet, three others:

- *Waro* (.69 AU)—Originally named Archird.

- *Jitsu* (1.13 AU)—Found in December 2521, then rediscovered by Dédalo Mostrenco in January 2524, who named it Ares. Settled by Soltec starting in 2533. Independence won in 2621, under the name Jitsu. Year is 1.1 Earth years, or 401.4 Standard days (ten forty-day months plus an extra week every five years). Days are 23.8 Standard hours long.

- *Kurishto* (4.1 AU)—small gas planet with four moons (Maryam, Makdarena, Pejo, Sanchago)

- *Banken* (8 AU)—icy and barren

Kobito—located 19.4 light years from Earth.

- *M imune* (.2 AU)

- *Chiye* (1.3)

- *Anjeliku* (3.2)—Originally named Tod.

Sol—by 2422, the Solar System reached political equilibrium, and a series of roughly democratic republics was established.

- *Earth*

- *Luna*

- *Mars*

- *Union of Belter Concerns (UBC)*

- *United Jovian Habitats (UJH)*

- *Republic of Saturn: Tuxing Gòng Hé*

- *Confederate Imamates of Uranus (CIU)*

- *Nation of Neptune*

- *Amalgamated Kuiper Mining Interests (AMKI)*

- *Associated Trans-Neptunian Objects (ATNO)*

Lalande 21185—located 8.3 light years from Sol. Owned by Transcom. No inhabited worlds, just mining platforms.

Ross 154—located 9.7 light years from Sol. Owned by BelCorp. No inhabited worlds, just mining platforms.

p Eridani 3—Controlled by Strugar-Rask since 2663. No inhabited worlds, just mining platforms.

BD+56 2966 (Nereus)—4.9 light years from Jitsu, 21.3 from Earth. Site of four corporate worlds, both subject to major radiation problems because of massive flares from their sun.

- *Thetis*- capital Ligyron (controlled by Jindalco)

- *Peleus*- Major cities Neoptolemus, Hermione (Kozancorp)

- *The Myrmidons*- largish planetoids and asteroids in a belt (Berger-Liu Energy)

- *Achilles*- three moons: Briseis, Pyrrhus and Patroclus (owned by Bing Yushu corporation)

Zeta Tucanae—28 light years from Earth

- *Atlantis* (at 1.14 AU)- settled in 2660 by Transcom (first new world settled since closing of Conduit). Year 1.25 Standard. Small island chains on mostly water-covered world. Avalon, Horaisan, Hy Breasail, Mag Mor, the Symplegades, Frisland,

BD+63 238 (Helios)—32.5 light years from Earth. Two settled planets:

- *Oceania* (at .69 AU)- Discovered in 2650. Settled in 2673. Surface completely covered by water. Year: 212 Standard days.

- *New Mecca* (at .55 AU)- Found in 2652. Settled in 2680. Barely habitable and quite hot.

Tau-Ceti—11.9 light years from Earth. Connected to Sirius 2 via an imrizabu.

- *New Beijing* (at .67 AU)- Settled in 2666. Year 225.6 Standard days.

• Lieske Scientific Complex- Established in 2680 on a planetoid at the

fringes, near the imrizabu's exit point. Heavily guarded by the AF.

Sirius 2 (Dog and Pup)—8.6 light years from Earth. Restricted

area dedicated to CPCC Ministry of Science and AF military

science work. Scanned and mapped. Heavily guarded because of

milizamu between the system and both Tau-Ceti and HR 453 AB

Epsilon Eridani—10.5 light years from Earth. Controlled by BelCorp.

• *Podgoritsa* (at 0.51 AU)—Settled in 2665. Year 150 Standard days.

Very few native organisms: bacteria and other single-celled creatures

in the oceans.

Chara—light years 27.3 ly from Earth.

• *Gaia* (at 1.1 AU)—olonized by Mediterranean escapees from Earth

in 2666; discovered by CPCC in 2690.

Gamma Leporis—29.25 light years from Earth.

• *Fusou*—Habitable world founded in 2661; controlled by Scarlet

Chaos Triad.

INDEPENDENT

Sigma Draconis (Kunti)—18.8 light years from Earth.

• *Bima* (.62 AU)—In 2589, the colony ship Bhatarayuda reaches

Sigma Draconis, renaming the star Kunti and settling a world

the colonists name Bima, which sits inside the orbital distance of

Venus in the Solar System. It has an orbital period of only about 199 days, or over half an Earth year. One moon called Gatotkaca. Bima is the seat of the Kunti system's government. From 2589 to 2692, the system was a constitutional monarchy. In 2692, the last Maharajah sent an invasion force against Dhara in Rigil Kentaurus. From 2692 to 2695, the system was in chaos, caught between invading syndicates and CPCCAF peacekeeping forces.

- The Kunti system also contains five other planetary bodies: Karna, Harjuna, Yudistira, and the twin gas planets, Nakula and Sadewa.

47 Ursae Majoris (Suno)—45.9 light years from Earth.

- *Moroni* (at .75 AU)—rocky, barren world.

- *Terego*—Settled January 2656 (Day one of 1st month of Teregan year 1).

  o Teregan day: 28 hours 12 minutes (divides into 7 hour sleep period, 7 hour work and study period, 7 hour family period) 1692 minutes

  o Two moons: Luneto and Hyrum

  o Teregan year: 420.14 Teregan days (14 months of 30 days, every seven years there's an extra day) 710,786.88 minutes (about 493 Earth days, about a third more, so multiply/divide by 1.3)

  o Diameter: 4,470 km. Six continents: Zarahemla, Novameriko, Kanaano, Tevantepeko, Utaho, Misurio.

- *Enoš* (at 2.1 AU)—Massive gas planet that orbits once every three years. Very close to Terego. Many moons, including Nefi.

- *Elija* (at 3.73 AU)—Massive gas giant with orbital period of nearly seven years.

- *Eter* (at 10 AU)—Gas giant whose orbit lasts 38 years and whose mass is 1.7 times that of Jupiter

82 Eridani—located 19.8 light years from Earth

- *Semanawak* (at .8 AU)—Settled in 2605 by the natives of the generation ship Ilwikamina, which left Earth in 2218. Discovered by CPCC in 2698. Year 275 Earth days.

Beta Pictoris (El Webo)—62.9 light years from Earth. Surrounded by a circumstellar disk of dust and gas some 1,100 AUs wide, around 10 times the size of the known Solar System and much more massive than the disk that the Solar System formed out of. Oddly enough, the outer disk has elliptical rings, and one side of the disk is 20 percent longer and thinner than the other. This disk is commonly called the Uraká Nebula, and was first discovered in December 2521 by demimundan ships thrown there by entering the Centauri Rift. In June 2682, a Brotherhood schooner (*El Pesau*), preparing to fenestrate away from the 'nebula' after dropping supplies off to those readying Konrau Beserra's new HQ in a planetoid of that system, discovered an imrizabu which leads directly to the edges of the Nereus system.

APPENDIX E: THE PATH

Jitsu's official religion, the Path (*Oturi* in Baryogo) is often called Neo Gnosticism by non-believers. Adherents of the faith simply call themselves Seers (B. *matakite*) or Pathwalkers (B. *Oturitu*). The members of specific branches of Neo Gnosticism have additional labels for themselves (such as the Baryogo terms *Dominatu* for Dominians and *Shimangatu* for followers of Kosiya Yemo's expunged teachings).

Origins

Towards the middle of the 21st century, Alejandro Dresch Sifuentes, a philosophy student at the University of Texas, was arrested and put on trial for a strange string of alleged crimes including murder and terrorism.

Dresch claimed that he had been visited by the biblical Lazarus, alive two millennia after being revived by Christ. Lazarus, Dresch alleged, had revealed to him the true nature of the Godhead. Such affirmations captured the attention of a viewing public addicted to scandal and yellow journalism. Tabloid sites and webnews alike streamed every word he said during his trial for all to hear. He was convicted and sentenced to life in prison. For the first fifteen years, Dresch posted to the net a new set of scriptures called *The Revised Bible*. A populace hungry for something momentous and reality-shattering couldn't help itself: his every word was read with a morbid curiosity. When he was killed by an overzealous guard, what had been just a fad became something more.

Belief

Alejandro Dresch sketched out in *The Revised Bible* the following cosmogony.

The Ogdoad

In the early moments of the life of the universe, eight beings (joined in complementary pairs called *umbini*) evolved into a quantum singularity of great power called the **Ogdoad**, the **Eight** or **The Collective** (B. *ra-Wanane*). Over time discord arose concerning both the purpose of the universe and the role of the syzygies. One umbini, Ennoya-Bitosh or Idea-Depth, was convinced that the reason for its existence was to evolve sentient beings capable of reaching gnosis. Ennoya-Bitosh also clung to its individuality, refusing to lose its identity in The Collective. Rejecting the indifference and introspection of the Ogdoad, the umbini separated from the Eight, naming itself Neweru and abandoning *ra-Yindawo*, the plane of existence in which The Collective dwells. But the separation was traumatic, and one half of the umbini went mad, believing itself the only being in existence.

The Grey Prison

This mad half, the Demiurge (B. *Umenzi*) blindly seized his complement, who now named herself *Sopiya*. Believing he must destroy in order to create, Umenzi tried to reshape her. Sopiya was violated and reduced, but she fought the Demiurge with every bit of her being. Their struggle set off the waves that generate everything around us, the physical universe, what Dresch calls the Grey Prison (B. *Hayiro Gereza*), a very small and insignificant part of what truly exists. Convinced that his mangling of Sopiya was the origin of all, the Demiurge arrogantly declared, "I am God, and there is no other God beside me," for he was ignorant of his strength, the singularity from which he had come. For that reason he is called *Samayeru* (the blind god) and *Sakra* (the foolish one). Those who rebel against him, despite all odds, are said to be Unblind (B. *Samanei*).

Sopiya's First Sacrifice

Unlike Sakra, Sopiya remembered her true nature and understood the danger that her insane complement now represented for the universe. However, she saw even deeper truth; her separation from the Ogdoad and Sakra's madness were necessary means to a necessary end: the strengthening and broadening of the Ogdoad itself. She saw in a flash of wisdom the Path, and she understood her role in the self-actualization of the very universe, a process known as *Aburakusa*.

Ceasing her struggle, she put herself in Sakla's power and allowed herself to be shattered. This first sacrifice is termed *Shamanga*. The innumerable pieces of her being (B. *tenshi* or "sparks") drifted throughout the Grey Prison, merging with the illusory physical universe of which Sakra believed himself creator.

As sentient life arose, Sakra in his madness again believed himself the cause, and he from time to time intruded on their minds, warping their perception and causing them to worship his cruel and childish ways. But every sentient being contains a small spark, a bit of Sopiya's broken being, and over the ages some fought against Sakra's tyranny in any way they could. Every once in a great while, in fact, one of these sentient beings would, through recognizing and cultivating that spark within (tenshi), create a soul for themself that could survive beyond death. These souls eventually made their way to the Ogdoad, and over millennia a small fraction of Sopiya was restored to The Collective.

The Rise of the Oracles

Finally, Sophia had reconstituted herself enough to commune with the Ogdoad and share her vision of the path to Abraxas. Through her connection with the Grey Prison, the Ogdoad caused guides to arise: the Oracles, who encourage sentient beings to turn their attention inward and seek self-knowledge. To follow the Path.

The Path

The grand purpose of the physical universe, Neo Gnosticism declares, is *Marejesho ra-Sopiya*, the Restoration of Sophia. In order for this goal to be reached, as many sentient beings as possible need to achieve *kedarum* (quantum enlightenment) at death. For those who do, their souls survive beyond the flesh and enter *ra-Yindawo*, the nirvana-like plane that contains the Ogdoad. The Path to haskalah entails a variety of activities that are collectively referred to as *Uchimbaji ra-Tenshi*, (the Extraction of the Sparks).

Awareness

For an individual to be initiated into the *teyopan* (local Pathwalker congregation, part of the larger community, B. *hapori*), they must affirm the Three Tenets of the Path:

1. Humans are born without souls.

2. The universe is a fractured piece of the Ogdoad.

3. Humans' fate is to create souls for themselves through self-knowledge and in that way help to restore the Ogdoad.

A new convert (B. *tahuringa*) is still considered *sama* or unenlightened (lit. "blind") until they have performed daily *zazen* (meditation with drugs, virtual mandala, kleinballs, etc.) for typically seven years, especially in the case of children. Adult converts may move through this stage more quickly.

By the end of the seventh year, the ivver should have the *kyunsun* or vision of their own blind self (B. *aham*), their divine spark (*tenshi*) and the Ogdoad. When they have peered beyond the Grey Prison, they are declared a *matakite* (lit. "seer") for having reached *keihatsu* (awareness). Then comes the rite of *upanayana*: their giya or some other anshyano will witness their affirmation of the Three Tenets and will place the *intambo* or Pathwalker cord around their chest (over left shoulder, under right arm). This cord—woven from eight strands, each a different shade of blue—signals they are a *teyopanjin,* a full member of the congregation. Children born into the community typically become teyopanjin at seven years of age.

Basic Enlightenment

Further zazen and ritual reflexion (varying from sect to sect) in all areas of the self, from the most wretched to the most sublime, elevate matakite to *satori* (lit. "secret knowledge") or basic enlightenment. Matakite who attain this level are called *satorijin*. They are said to have lit up their selves with their spark (such an illuminated self is known as a *teyo*). The most respected satorijin in a community are refered to as *anshyano*.

Full Self-Knowledge

The next step is *nosisu*), gnosis or complete self-knowledge that leads to *Hanga ra-Roho,* the creation of a soul. Rejecting the world, satorijin begin the process of shattering and bricolage (B. *shamanchiwaga*), by which the kludged self (B. *marecho teyo*) is broken and rebuilt around the spark, giving birth to a soul. Pathwalkers who have created a soul and seen it in the second vision (B. *umbono*) are called *arojin* (lit. "other-born"). Many arojin become *giya,* guides to enlightenment for sama, matakite and satorijin in their congregation.

Quantum Enlightenment

The last rung on the ladder to escaping the Grey Prison, *kedarum,* occurs when the created soul escapes the flesh to be reunited with the Eight. Certain individuals, called *kedarumsha,* achieve kedarum while yet alive. Kedarumsha spend much time in the state of *ukaribu,* their created selves in constant communion with the Ogdoad, though not with the individual souls rejoined to the Eight, a privilege known as *yorukaki* in Baryogo, reserved only for the Oracles.

Dominian Oracles of Jitsu

1—*Domina Ditis*. Born Bolormaa Munkhbat in the floating city Kunming on the moon Titan in 2492. Parents are indentured by the Republic of Saturn to the company Naftek after criminal convictions. When Naftek adopts Wiccan Catholicism as its company religion, her parents rename her Domina Ditis (adopting the out-of-date fashion of using Latin names when converting to that faith). Naftek is acquired by Soltec when Domina is six years old, and she attends a corporate school for several years, where she is taught the Path before being kidnapped by her maternal uncle Zamilan Chono. In 2521, her uncle's ship crashes on the world that will later be named Jitsu. Domina dies in 2524, leaving behind new scripture in the form of her journals that becomes the basis for the Dominian Path.

2—*Kosiya Yemo*. Born in Jitsu's Misitu Prefecture in 2590. Revealed to be the Second Oracle in 2604. In 2619, the Conduit is shut down, and an object expelled from it impacts against the Southern Continent while the Oracle is meeting with religious leaders there. She orders the Shrine of Shattering to be built. By 2622, the theocratic government of Jitsu decides that the Oracle's teachings undercut their power, so they build a shrine to contain her, declaring portions of her scripture distorted by Sakra. She eventually dies in 2631.

3—*Samanei Koroma*. Born in Jitsu's Mashkanu Prefecture in 2658. She's revealed to be the new Oracle in 2671 and is immediately confined to the Jinja ra-Orakuru (Shrine of the Oracle). Despite being cut-off, she begins to manipulate global politics, ordering the creation of a legislature with Chamber of Deputies in 2675 and establishing free elections for deputies by 2682. In 2697, she is taken from Jitsu by her brother-in-law.

If you liked *The Blue-Spangled Blue*, you might also enjoy reading the following titles available on Amazon from Castle Bridge Media:

Austinites *By In Churl Yo*

Castle Of Horror Anthology Volume 1
Castle of Horror Anthology Volume 2: Holiday Horrors
Castle of Horror Anthology Volume 3: Scary Summer Stories
Castle of Horror Anthology Volume 4: Women Running from Houses
Edited By Jason Henderson

FuturePast Anthology Volume 1
Edited by In Churl Yo

Isonation *By In Churl Yo*

Surf Mystic: Night of the Book Man *By Peyton Douglas*

Nightwalkers: Gothic Horror Movies *By Bruce Lanier Wright*

Please remember to leave us your reviews
on Amazon and Goodreads!

CASTLE BRIDGE MEDIA
DENVER, COLORADO, USA

**THANK YOU FOR SUPPORTING INDEPENDENT PUBLISHERS
AND AUTHORS!**

castlebridgemedia.com

www.ingramcontent.com/pod-product-compliance
Lightning Source LLC
Chambersburg PA
CBHW050118030726
47505CB00007B/1923